THAT FIRST *Flight*

JENN MCMAHON

BOOK THREE OF THE

Firsts in the City

SERIES

Cover Design: Emily Wittig

Copy Editing: Caroline Palmier

Developmental and Line Editing: Kelsey Muller, Salma R.

Proofreading, Formatting: Cathryn Carter

To all the single moms who thought they would never find their happy ending and put their own dreams and aspirations aside for their kids. It's never too late to chase them. Having your kids watch you chase your dreams and reach them is the greatest feeling I've ever experienced.

You got this, mama.

To my husband, who loved and accepted not just me, but my son. For being my rock through the hard times, being a light in the darkness and constantly making me laugh whenever I want to cry. I love you more than any word I could possibly write.

A NOTE FROM MACEY

Thank you for being here and taking a chance on my story. I wanted to forewarn you that my past is pretty heavy and might trigger some people. I got pregnant with my daughter when I was sixteen years old. I've also dealt with anxiety and depression which is brought up a few times through my story as well as dealing with narcissistic and controlling parents.

While it's a lot to unpack, it's also what has made me who I am today. I hope you stick around for it, and if you don't, I understand too!

Xo, Macey

CHAPTER ONE

Oliver

You know what I hate more than anything in the world? Snow.

This is the first time I've seen my brother's cabin since he purchased it at the end of the summer. I've been itching to check it out but couldn't find time. Now, due to an impending snow storm, I'm the one up here making sure everything survives the fluffy white stuff with no damage.

This town is where my brother, Marc, realized he was head over heels in love with Avery.

I don't understand it myself. How people can just fall in love like that.

The idea of it makes me queasy.

"Your destination is on the right," the GPS says through the truck speakers.

I let out an audible groan as I maneuver the truck down the first entrance of the horseshoe shaped driveway while simultaneously thanking Mother Nature for keeping the snow to a flurry so I can make it here in one piece.

His idea for buying such a giant property with a mansion-like cabin on it, was for the entire family to use it as a get away from city life whenever we needed a change of scenery. Except I'm only partially here for that, thanks to this storm.

They are calling it the winter storm of the century which leaves Marc uneasy about this place while he whisks his now real fiancée, Avery, off to Paris for a surprise New Year's trip.

My first reaction when he asked me to do him a solid was, '*Why don't you ask Thomas?*' But my oldest brother is living happily ever after in the honeymoon bliss stage of life. Again, how people fall in love like those two saps did is beyond me.

As much as I love living in the city and being close to my two brothers and little sister, I'm not cut out for city life and the billionaire lifestyle my bank account tells me I should be living.

I've learned that I'm more of a small-town guy from all the little towns I've traveled to. I drive a pickup truck when I'm in the city and live in dark wash jeans and tees. I stick out like a sore thumb.

It's one of the biggest reasons I started traveling the world and blogging it on my social media accounts.

When dad died, we all received an inheritance. Thomas used his share to invest in dad's business. He took over in his early twenties and has been wildly successful. Marc used his share to buy his dream sports car and whatever else he decided to spend it on. Who the hell knows because he was already successful in his real estate career. His boss just handed him the keys to the entire company a few months ago and his life is more than he's ever dreamed of now that he's got the business and the girl.

Emiline, our baby sister, is working her way through nursing school. She didn't receive her inheritance until she turned 18 years old, but when she did, she used it to buy her own apartment in the city so she can start her independent living.

I'm not a fan of it, if I'm being honest. I'm protective as hell over her and hate the thought of her living alone. We all are. I don't care that she's 22 years old now, she'll always be our baby sister.

As for me, I used my share to buy myself the best camera money could buy and started traveling. My first trip was a small one to Charleston, South Carolina. My plan was to build up a few small blog posts to grow a following before spending money on bigger trips.

Well… that one took off like a rocket.

People from all over the world were enamored by the little bed and breakfast I stayed at for the weekend. The post was packed with pictures of the food I enjoyed at the restaurants, the coffee shop downtown, and a few shots of me at the beach.

My best friend, Logan, swears up and down that it went as viral as it did because the I was shirtless in the beach pictures. I take care of myself, so I can see why he thinks that. But I'll never know if that was really the reason or not. I certainly haven't stopped sharing random candid photos of me in my posts though.

My phone vibrates in my pocket. When I pull it out to see the name on the screen, I click accept right away. Because, speak of the devil… Logan.

"Hey."

"Hey, yourself." Logan laughs. "What are you up to tonight? Want to head out for the night?"

"Unless you're planning to come to Roxbury and hit the corner gas stop that doubles as a bar, I don't think I'm making it."

"Shit. I forgot you're house sitting for Marc."

"House sitting. Working. Solitude for a week. All the same shit." I laugh.

He scoffs. "This isn't work. This is you getting away. Work is when companies *pay you* to go away."

Ever since that first blog post, about ninety percent of my trips have been fully sponsored by companies wanting me to promote their products, or businesses wanting me to visit and share my experience.

The other ten percent are me taking advantage of just having the luxury to travel the way I do. I'm not tied down by a wife and kids. Not to mention the fact that I *love* the variety of women I've found everywhere I go.

"You gonna find a local lady to whisk away to your bed tonight?"

"Not tonight, man."

He sucks in an exaggerated gasp. "You should find the nearest hospital up there when you're sightseeing. Because you need to be checked."

I usually *really* enjoy the different women I get to meet at each place I go to. I just haven't been feeling it on my last couple of trips. I can't pinpoint when, but I know it was sometime over the summer, that I just stopped giving a shit about making that my priority.

My brothers tell me all the time that someday I'll grow up and find that special someone. I beg to differ. As a people person —and wildly charming, might I add—I love chatting with locals everywhere I go. I've met plenty of people on my journey who live this single life until they are old and gray, and I've never seen them happier.

"Har har," I mock. "Very funny. Listen. Service blows up here. I'm heading inside the cabin now to get settled. Don't get in too much trouble tonight."

"Me? Never."

"And stay away from my sister," I add.

"Relaxxxxx," he draws out. "If you wanted me to stay away that badly, you should have taken me up there with you."

"One, I don't *ever* travel with people. You know this. And two, we're gonna murder you, ya know?"

"Enjoy your trip," Logan says in his most smug tone before he hangs up.

Sometimes I can't tell if he's joking about my sister or if he's serious. Either way, he's been warned for years that she's off limits. I know Logan's history with women, and he's the last guy I want to see Emiline end up with.

I shake my head as I put the key into the front door of the cabin.

Once inside, I take in the insane entryway of this place. For most people, this would be a dream home. Definitely not a second house to come visit here and there.

Marc has lost his ever loving mind.

As I tour the place, a sense of happiness engulfs me. There's something about traveling alone that just fuels my soul. In a way that brings me peace and solitude. It's why I never travel with friends or family unless it's for an event or some family function.

I prefer it when it's just me, my camera, and my trusty tripod to take all the pictures I need.

"A week of just you and me, hot stuff." I slap my hand on the giant kitchen counter overlooking the mountains, talking to the house as if it's going to talk back.

The sun is setting over the mountain peaks while snow flurries dance across the sky and it's the most gorgeous sight I've ever seen in New York. Listen, I can hate the snow with a burning passion and still think it's the most beautiful thing Mother Nature creates.

I grab my bag that I dropped by the front door to pull out my camera. I make my way to the back deck and snap a few photos.

I'm in complete awe of nature's beauty.

It's so raw. Unfiltered. Stunning.

I'm killing two birds with one stone on this trip. Not only will I be helping my brother but I'm also planning a blog post about this town. My home state. The only mountains I haven't visited in my posts.

Scenic images are some of my most viral photos. I refuse to put a filter on anything and love to show the world the beauty that's out there in hopes it sparks inspiration for people to get out there, start traveling and just *live*.

Avery and Marc have already filled me in on a little bar and grill downtown from their first visit here. It's *actually* called 'Bar and Grill.' Talk about lazy marketing, but I digress. They said it's good and I should hit it up immediately to mingle with some locals for more recommendations for the rest of the week.

My stomach growling reminds me that I should probably

head there sooner than later because I'm worse than a starved bear in the woods right now.

Which is half true, since I'm already in the woods.

Within thirty minutes, I'm pulling my truck into the parking lot. When my eyes land on the restaurant, I can't believe this is the place Marc recommended. It looks like it's about one hundred years old. The brown siding on the outside looks worn down from the weather.

When I step foot inside though, it feels like a totally new place. There's a jukebox off to the side, and it's lit up with a soft glow from the beer signs and dim lighting. Off to the other side is a door that leads to the back. It's open so I can see it's an outdoor patio with heaters spaced all over the place.

I take back what I said, this place is cozy, maybe even… decent?

I assume this is their busy season, noticing that almost every table is full and there's only a couple of chairs open at the bar. Which makes sense since there's a ski resort half a mile up the road and they've gotten fresh snow this week. Not to mention tomorrow is New Year's Eve.

I take a seat on the stool at the far end of the bar. Just as I open the menu to see my choices, a nervous energy engulfs me. The hairs on the back of my neck rise while chills run down my spine. It's something I've never felt before.

Everything shifts and I feel on edge like something big is about to happen.

What the fuck is that all about?

CHAPTER TWO

Macey

"Flora, are you good if I step out for a second to call Mackenzie?" I ask my boss.

"Of course, sweets. You know you don't have to ask me to check in on her," she says.

I laugh and roll my eyes at her. "But I do. You know it's a busy Saturday night. I can't just step out from behind the bar without asking."

"We have everything handled here. Go." She shoos me with a bar rag, backing me up until I'm close to the kitchen doors. "You forget I've been running this bar since before you were even a thought in this world."

I return a smile and nod before stepping back into the kitchen.

Flora and Samuel have been true angels on earth since I showed up in this small town of Roxbury. I came here five months ago with nothing but my daughter and two suitcases to get as far away from the shitty life we were living. I didn't know this was where I would end up, but I got a taxi from the airport and told the guy to take me as far as every dollar in my pocket would take me.

When we pulled up to this bar, I wasn't sure how to

approach things. The first order of business was to get a job before I put a hotel on a nearly maxed out credit card.

Flora's husband, Samuel, was working the bar that day and there wasn't a soul in the place since it was the hottest day of the summer in a ski resort town. He greeted me with an enthusiastic hello and the first words out of my mouth were, "*Do you have any job openings?*"

Looking back, I'm almost positive I made the worst first impression.

I remember Samuel scanning me up and down, his eyes traveling along my exposed tattooed skin, to my luggage and then to my eight-year-old daughter standing next to me. He somehow hired me on the spot. Turns out, he and his wife have been working alone for the last few months and needed another set of hands before the busy season started come winter.

Flora showed up at the bar about an hour later to meet the new bartender working for them. When she asked me where I was staying, I didn't have an answer for her. I was about to lie but the look on her face told me that she knew I had nowhere to go.

Something shifted in her features as she took in my tear-soaked cheeks while a heavy silence hung in the air between us.

It was that exact moment that these two took Mackenzie and I under their wings. They immediately got us set up in a small cottage on their property down the road later that night.

It surprised me more than anything. In my experience, particularly with the older generation, when people see someone with tattoos, they tend to think the worst possible things about them. That they are taking part in shady business or are completely unprofessional. These two saw me for who I am within seconds of meeting me.

And I spilled my entire story to Flora that night only making them want to help me more.

The small cottage on their property works for us. It only has one bed and exactly one small nook for someone to eat dinner.

The kitchen consists of a small counter spot and only the necessary appliances.

Flora invites us over to dinner more often than not, and Mackenzie likes to stay at the main house with them to watch television or play on her tablet. When it's time for bed, I sleep on the couch and let Mackenzie have the bed because she deserves her own space.

My daughter deserves the world.

I can sacrifice a comfortable bed for a little while if it means a step towards a better future for us. One day I'm going to give her everything she deserves.

All of the hurt. All the brokenness. It will be worth it one day.

"Hello?" Mackenzie says as she answers the phone.

Yeah, my 8 year old has a phone. I bought it for her with my first paycheck here because I wanted a way to get in touch with her on the days or nights I'm working behind the bar even though she's never really alone. Samuel and Flora take turns with her. One is always with her, while the other is always here with me helping to make sure this bar runs smoothly.

More often than not, it's Flora at the bar with me.

Samuel has a soft spot for Mackenzie since she reminds him so much of his two granddaughters. Unfortunately, they only see them about once a year because they live in California. He's the happiest person in any room when Mackenzie is around.

"Hi, babe. I wanted to call and check in."

"Mom," she huffs. "I'm fine, for the ninth time tonight."

I swear, she's eight going on eighteen. Her sass drives me wild, but it just shows me how strong she is. Stronger than I'll ever be.

I swallow the lump in my throat. "What are you up to?"

"Uncle Sam is teaching me to use a bow and arrow. Our target is the deer grazing in the backyard. Then we're gonna bring it to the shed and chop it up for dinner tomorrow."

"He is not!"

She laughs. "Relax, Mom. We're just watching a movie."

I smile despite the fact that she can't see me through the phone. "Okay."

"It's starting now. I'm going to go."

"Okay, babe. I'll see you in the morning. Make sure you go to bed when he tells you to."

"Okay. Love you," she says.

"Love you most," I say back before I hang up.

I lean against the deep freezer door in the kitchen, and breathe out a sigh.

This wasn't the life I dreamed of for us.

Then again, my life plans didn't involve having a child at sixteen years old and trying to figure it out on my own. I didn't want to do it alone, but I *had* to figure it out on my own.

Mackenzie's father has never been in the picture.

I was naive to believe that Brad, my high school sweetheart, was my soulmate. He was a year older than me, and I truly believed that he loved me at the time.

It wasn't until the day those two pink lines showed up one morning and I told him that he was going to be a dad, that he confessed I was nothing but a decent lay for him. He wanted nothing to do with me or our daughter after that.

Once Mackenzie was born, I learned what true love felt like. Alone in the hospital, giving birth to the most perfect baby girl, I made a silent vow to myself that I would be the best damn mom I could be. One that she deserves. One that is nothing like my own.

My friends dropped me from their lives when I got pregnant and I'm betting my mom and dad wish they could too.

Needless to say, I've struggled a lot since she was born. I've hit rock bottom more times than I care to admit, and have thought things I'm scared to ever admit out loud. I lived with my parents through everything despite the hell they gave me for getting knocked up. They are the true definition of kicking you while you're down.

The sound of a plate falling to the ground pulls me out of my bubble. I give myself the time to take three deep breaths, fix my apron and head out of the kitchen.

"I'm back," I announce to Flora. "Thank you for that minute."

"Anytime, sweets."

"Is everyone served? Where have you left off?"

"That blonde hottie at the end of the bar just sat down." She winks. "That's all you."

"Stop that! You're married!"

"I'm also older than dirt," she scoffs. "But my eyes still work just fine to notice from afar the looks on that man down there."

"You're craz—" My words are cut short and my steps falter at the same time my stomach bottoms out. I'm pretty sure my jaw falls to the floor when they land on the man reading the menu.

Because I know this man.

A heartbeat passes before I'm transported back to when I met him.

It was when I was running away from my life to start a new one.

On my flight from Montana to New York.

CHAPTER THREE

Macey

Five Months Ago

"You don't have any two seats next to each other on the plane?"

"I'm sorry, ma'am. The flight is booked solid," the gate attendant says. "If you want to wait, I can get you set up on the next flight to New York."

"When is that?" I ask, full of hope.

"Not for another nine hours."

"Dammit," I groan. "Fine. I'll take these two."

I grab my tickets off the counter as Mackenzie and I make our way to the seats designated for all the passengers boarding the next flight out of Montana. I'm not waiting another nine hours to get out of this hellhole.

My decision to book a one-way ticket to New York without telling a soul where I was going was initially just a plan to piss off my parents. Living with them is overbearing and miserable. They treat Mackenzie like she's theirs and make me feel like I'm incapable of being her mom. I constantly feel like I'm never even given the chance to be the mom I know I can be with them hanging every mistake over my head.

I know grandparents are amazing. As they should be. But I could never get past how much they have tried to take control over her. For the last few years, they have been trying to mold her into who *they* want her to be and not who *she* wants to be.

Mackenzie is *my* daughter, not theirs.

Every waking moment is a chance for them to judge me on how I decide to parent her, whether it's what I feed her for dinner, or how I let her stay up until nine instead of eight. And they never once miss the opportunity to throw my 'fuck up' of getting pregnant at sixteen in my face. They constantly play on my weakness—my daughter. And I can't have her thinking that's normal. That's not what love is.

I reached my breaking point late last night after yet *another* argument with them over what she had for dinner. She had pasta with meatballs, but it wasn't gluten free and it's *'too heavy for a dinner before bed.'* The argument might seem minor, but it was the straw that broke the camel's back.

I immediately packed two suitcases. And as soon as they left for work this morning, I took a taxi to the airport and knew I wanted to get us out of here as fast as I could.

This trip has turned into me taking the first steps towards building the future I've always wanted, despite the guilt eating me alive over finally doing something for me. But when you spend eight years caring for someone else and locked under the metaphorical chains of your parents who don't give a damn about your own goals, you realize that it's finally time for you to do something for yourself.

I want to show my daughter that it's never too late to chase your dreams.

To add to this train wreck of a morning, Mackenzie is not happy about this decision. I don't blame her, I'm pulling her from her school and all the friends she's made over the years. Small town living means you're in the same school, with the same group of kids from kindergarten until high school. She's old enough to understand why we're doing it, but that doesn't make me feel less guilty for uprooting her entire life.

A middle-aged man takes a seat next to me. He looks alone.

"Hi, sir? Are you boarding this flight solo?"

"I am," he grunts in annoyance.

"Any chance you're sitting by row 9 or row 23?"

"I'm in row 9, actually. Why do you ask?"

"You see—" I start, but stop myself because I'm a known blabbermouth. I'll spill my entire life to a stranger out of pure nerves. "My daughter and I got separated with tickets and I was wondering if you would be able to switch seats with me so I can sit next to her?"

"Where are you sitting?"

"Row 23," I say.

"Sorry. No can do," he says matter-of-factly while shaking his head. "Too far in the back for me. I want to get off the flight as fast as I can when we land."

"I understand." My head falls in defeat.

We haven't even left the state and I already feel like I'm failing my daughter. A twinge of panic sets in, causing me to falter and wonder if we really should be doing this.

"Mom, it's fine." Mackenzie nudges me with her elbow. "Once we're up in the air, the doors are locked and I can't go anywhere."

"I know, but I can't stand you being that far away from me."

"I'm not a baby," she says with full conviction. "I'm almost a teenager. I can handle a flight. I have a book to read anyway."

"You're not *almost* a teenager," I snap back. "You still have a few more years to go before you are."

She rolls her eyes, crossing her arms over her chest before she sinks into the seat.

"But you're right," I admit, offering her a smile. "I know you can handle the flight. It's my job to worry about you though. You have to understand that."

"I get it, Mom."

"How about this… when we land in New York, don't leave your seat until I get up to you. Okay?"

"I can do that."

"They let people off the plane row by row. So since I'm pretty far in the back, just wait in your seat."

"Got it."

Nervous energy dances through my stomach over the next half hour we sit and wait to board the plane.

Who would have thought that the first flight I ever take in my life, is to chase my dreams and give my girl a better life. I don't have a clue on how I'm going to do it and make it work, but I'll be damned if I don't try.

Once we're finally on the plane, I make sure Mackenzie is situated in her seat. Thankfully, she's seated next to another parent with a daughter who looks to be about the same age as Mackenzie.

Thank you, universe.

"Excuse me," I say to get the woman's attention. She smiles up at me. "I'm Macey and this is Mackenzie. Our seats are separated on the flight. Would it be too much to ask to keep an eye on her for the flight?"

"Oh my gosh, of course!" the woman says with her hand to her chest. "I brought some coloring books for the flight and a few extra snacks."

My chest tightens at the kindness of this total stranger. "Thank you." I'm barely able to get the words out.

"Us moms have to stick together," she says with a wink.

"I appreciate that so much," I say to the woman before I look back at Mackenzie. "I'm right in the back if you need anything, babe. I love you."

"Love you too, Mom." She smiles up at me.

I make my way to the back of the plane, and notice I have a middle seat. I groan internally at how annoying the middle seat seems. It looks like I'm about to be sandwiched between two strangers.

I send up a silent prayer that they are plane sleepers and just leave me be.

I look to my left and the elderly woman next to me is already sound asleep. I glance up and over the seat in front of me and notice the entire flight has boarded, and the aisle seat to my right is still empty.

I should have Mackenzie just come back here.

Just as the thought crosses my mind, a man comes rushing onto the plane with a rolling carry-on, sunglasses and a baseball cap that reads '*You had me at bacon*.' Once he reaches my row at the back of the plane, I realize this is the man that's going to occupy the vacant seat next to me.

The flight attendant stops him as he approaches our row. "Sir, this flight is completely booked. There is no room in the overhead bins for your suitcase."

"Shit," he mumbles under his breath. "I don't want to have this checked."

She eyes him up and down at the same time a flirty grin reaches her lips. She's clearly checking him out.

"No worries, sir," she purrs. "I'll store it in the back here for you until you get off."

With a wink, she grabs his carry-on suitcase from him and wheels it to the back of the cabin. I don't miss how he watches her backside as she walks away.

Bringing his focus back to his ticket, he removes his sunglasses to read it and I think my jaw drops. His ocean blue eyes move from the ticket to the numbers above the seat before they land on me. A wicked grin fills his face and my stomach bottoms out.

"Hey there, seat wife. Looks like I'm the happy owner of this spot next to you."

I don't have a chance to respond before he's plopping down, and stuffing the backpack he has around his shoulder under his seat. He turns to face me again, letting his eyes scan my body up and down the same way he did the flight attendant. I feel every part of my body light up from just the way he looks at me.

I want to look anywhere else but at this gorgeous specimen of a man sitting next to me, but I just can't find it in me to stop staring. It should seriously be illegal to look as good as he does.

"Where're you headed?"

The corner of my lip tips up. "Well, this is a flight to New York, no?"

"Oh, she's a ball buster." He laughs, nodding his head. "I like you."

"You don't know me," I deadpan.

"Lucky for me, we have four hours and some minutes together so I can get to know you." Then he shoots me winks before he settles into his seat, resting his head back on the headrest.

I should not be affected by the way this man just winked at me, but my body betrays me.

He is... gorgeous.

I mean, blonde hair, blue eyes, and a razor sharp jawline is a deadly combination when it comes to a man that looks the way he does. There's no doubt in my mind that when he was a child, his parents knew he would be a heartbreaker. Just his presence and a glimpse of the personality he's given me, tell me he breaks any heart that crosses his path.

Not to mention he's built like a true outdoorsman. He's dressed in dark wash, distressed jeans and a plain black t-shirt that complements his tanned skin perfectly. He takes up most of the seat, and I can tell he's probably double my size. Then again, everyone is double my size. I'm a solid four-foot-eleven on a good day. And damn, his arms... his muscular forearms tell me that he's probably really good with his hands.

Stop.

I didn't even realize we've taken off already and are cruising midair until the same flight attendant interrupts my dirty thoughts of the stranger sitting next to me.

"Can I get you anything to drink?"

"I'll take a whiskey on the rocks," he says before looking over at me. "What's your poison?"

"I'll take a Diet Coke. Please."

"With vodka," he adds, looking at the flight attendant. "She hasn't picked up on the fact that it's always five o'clock when you're traveling in the sky."

She lets out a chuckle and I see her cheeks heat up at the way he speaks to her. So carefree and easy going.

He probably doesn't even realize he's about to crush another heart in his path.

But my brain quickly stops itself, remembering what he just asked for. *Vodka.*

"Oh, no." I wave my hand in the air, catching her attention before she walks away. "No vodka for me." I avert my gaze away from the Adonis sitting next to me so I don't see his reaction to my next words. "Thank you, but I don't drink."

The flight attendant simply nods as she retreats to the back of the plane to make our drinks.

I nervously look down at my hands as I clasp them together in my lap. People look at you differently when you don't drink alcohol, let alone tell someone you've never had a sip of alcohol in your life. But I've never had the desire to drink it.

I watched people around me in my hometown fall into addiction, thinking they need it to have a good time. My priority for years has always just been Mackenzie and I never wanted to give anything the power over me to take the place of that.

Every time I say I don't drink to someone new, there's always a series of questions. For some reason *'I don't like it'* or *'I don't want to'* aren't good enough reasons for them. Which leads to an uncomfortable game of twenty-one questions. Like *'Are you in recovery?' 'Are you pregnant?' 'You know one drink won't hurt right?'*

Saying that I'm sick of having to explain myself to people is an understatement.

"I respect that." His words break my trance.

My head snaps in his direction and I see a grin plastered on his face. There isn't an *ounce* of judgment in his tone.

I offer him a feeble smile back.

I'm not entirely sure of this man's intentions. Is he just being nice because he's stuck next to me for the next few hours?

My question is answered for me when the flight attendant returns with our drinks, leaning down over dramatically to showcase her tits for him to see. There's no doubt that she spent a couple grand on those.

"Thank you, but can I change my mind?" he asks her as he hands the cup back to her. "I'll just take an orange soda."

"No problem, sir."

I can't help it when my hand covers my mouth and my shoulders shake with a quiet chuckle. This grown ass man just ordered an orange soda on a flight.

Now who's judging who, here?

"Don't you laugh at me." He starts laughing with me. "Orange soda is superior."

"That's just…" I shake my head, unable to wipe the grin off my face. "The most random thing someone can order on a flight. I expect something like a Coke or a Sprite. Definitely not an orange soda."

"But it made you laugh."

My laughter dies down at his statement as I nod my head, forcing my smile to stay put. Unable to really say anything back because this stranger is right. I can't remember the last time something other than my daughter made me laugh or feel carefree about anything.

When you struggle with demons, it's hard to find joy in everyday life. It makes you tired all the fucking time. Exhausted to the point that laughing is a struggle. I put on a good mask in front of Mackenzie, because I refuse to let her think her mom is broken, even though sometimes I worry I am.

"And I'm willing to bet from the little time I've already spent with you, that you don't do that very often."

My smile completely falls and I drop my gaze back to my hands. Shaking my head to silently tell him that I don't. How on earth did we go from laughing about orange soda to a deep conversation about how I don't laugh enough?

This man is very intuitive.

"Well." He claps his hands together, rubbing them back and forth as if he's in the freezing cold tundra trying to warm them up. "I'm a goal setter. It's part of the job. And I think I just unlocked my goal for the next"—he glances down at what looks like a *very* expensive watch—"three hours and change. And it's to make you laugh more."

"Is that so?" I shoot him a side eye glare.

"Yup."

"What exactly is your job, funny guy?"

That earns me a chuckle from him. "My number one job is to make people laugh. I love to see it. So I'll take that nickname because I hold that title with honors. But my real job is that I'm a blogger."

I tip my head to the side, giving him a questioning glare.

"Doesn't sound like a real job right?"

"I wasn't going to say it." I hold up my hands in defense.

"You're not the first person to think that," he says as he nudges me with his elbow, shooting me another deadly wink. "But it's what makes me the happiest and that's a motto that I *live* by. I travel, visit places and blog about it. Mostly, it's restaurants or showcasing products of companies that sponsor me."

"That actually sounds incredible. So… are you heading to blog something now? Or are you leaving a place you just blogged about?"

"Wouldn't you like to know…" The word lingers on his tongue as he urges me to share my name.

"Macey."

"Macey." He says my name with a broad smile.

And it's a contagious one that forces my lips to curve up and match his, making me feel the lightest I've felt in years. I finally relax into my seat as his presence seems to calm every one of my fears.

This stranger sitting right next to me has successfully turned any bit of nerves I felt just hours ago into hopeful anticipation for this fresh start for me and my daughter.

CHAPTER FOUR
Oliver

Five Months Ago

I'm captivated by the stranger sitting to my left.

And it's more than what's on the outside that has me drawn to her, because yeah, she's breathtaking. Her black hair is pulled into a messy bun and perched on the top of her head. She looks like she rolled out of bed without a stitch of makeup on and rushed to catch this flight.

Which is the same thing I did, so I get it.

But it's not the jade green eyes staring back at me behind long, thick lashes that have me enthralled by her. And it's definitely not how perfectly her body is wearing a pair of ripped jeans and a graphic tee that exposes the tattoos trailing down her arm. It's what people don't see that I pick up on.

The way the littlest thing I've said in such a short amount of time has made her laugh.

The way her eyes tell me she's downright exhausted.

This woman carries some heavy weight on her shoulders.

I've learned to see it in people from witnessing my mom deal with depression after my dad died.

"If you must know, *Macey*." I shoot her a wink and a light

nudge with my elbow in hopes to see that smile light up her face again. "I'm heading home from a blogging trip."

She nods but remains silent.

"There's just something about the mountains," I continue, resting my head on the headrest of the seat. "I could live and breathe them every day of my life and be a happy guy. As long as there's no snow."

"You sure it's not bacon that makes you a happy guy?"

My head jerks in her direction, the corner of my lip tipping up just the slightest.

"Did you just make a joke about my favorite food on earth?"

She giggles in her seat. "Your hat kind of gave you away."

I pull my baseball cap off my head, running my fingers through messy hair as I bring it down to assess what she's talking about, completely forgetting that *this* was the hat of choice for today.

"Dammit," I joke. "I do love me some bacon. Please tell me you do too. Because I couldn't live with myself if you don't."

"That's dramatic." She rolls her eyes, but laughs anyway.

I've made a lot of people in my life laugh, but hearing the sweet song of Macey's laughter is something else.

"You caught me."

"I did, didn't I?" She smirks. "Tell me about this blogging thing you do since we have some time to kill."

"I've always wanted to travel the world. See the beauty of it all through my own eyes instead of on the internet. I also love being people's go-to guy for recommendations on places to eat, places to visit and things to do. I figured what the hell and decided to combine two things I love into one, which was how this all started. Plus, I had zero desire to join my family's business. Being an investor was not on my life bingo card." I laugh.

"Wow, a family of investors."

"Well, just my dad." I shrug. "He was a big wig investor in the city. My brother took over that business after he passed."

"I'm so sorry." Her smile falls and she directs her gaze to her hands in her lap.

I watch as an uncomfortable feeling washes over her.

"Hey, none of that. No need to be sorry." My left hand touches her exposed forearm and listen… I don't cook, nor do I know the first thing about it. But I'm pretty certain that's what it feels like to put your hand on a burning hot stove top.

Touching her skin burns me right to the core.

She must feel it too because her eyes land on our connected skin and they widen in shock.

"No need to be sorry," I repeat, pulling my hand away as I try to ignore what the heck that was all about. "We're all okay."

"Okay," she says, barely above a whisper.

Her right hand lifts to rub her left arm where my skin touched hers and my eyes are drawn to the beautiful ink covering it. I can tell by the way it disappears under her shirt that it's a full sleeve, but what sticks out the most is the large dragonfly covering the majority of her forearm.

"That dragonfly tattoo is beautiful."

I lean forward, invading her space. The intoxicating aroma of vanilla engulfs my senses, pulling me closer toward her as I clasp her hand in mine to get a better look. The same burning feeling from before is back in full swing, but she doesn't make a move to pull away. My eyes stay glued to the tattoo.

There's two types of people who get tattoos. The ones who get random ones when they are drunk and decide to ink their body with whatever they want and the ones who get tattoos that hold meaning. From this short encounter with Macey… I'm going with the latter.

"Tell me about this one," I ask her, finding myself interested in knowing more about her.

"It's just a tattoo," she says with hesitation.

"Mmhmm." I grin at her in understanding that she doesn't want to tell a stranger. "I like it. I've been wanting to get a tattoo forever now."

"You don't have any?" she asks.

"Nope." I shake my head. "Another fun fact about me is that I'm absolute chicken shit. I'm afraid of needles and being near them. I'll pass out at the sight of one."

Her unease evaporates at my admission. "And yet, you want a tattoo?"

"My sister-in-law jokes that I need to get an olive tree tattooed on me somewhere."

"That's oddly specific and weird." She tips her head in question. "Is there a reason for that?"

"My name."

"Which you have yet to tell me, seatmate."

The smile that hits my face as I continue watching Macey transform in this short time to being more open to conversation, laughing and joking is just something I can't control.

"First of all, it's seat hubby," I joke back with her. "And my name is Oliver."

"Oliver," she repeats, as if her brain is trying to process it and store it for later use. "The name fits you."

"How so?"

"The name Oliver is derived from the Latin word *olivarius*. Which means *Olive Tree Planter*."

I interrupt her, bringing my finger up to stop her thoughts. "Do you hang out with my brother on the side?"

"No?"

"Interesting." I nod my head. "Him and his son jokingly call me a gardener. Not sure why, but continue."

"Anyway, the name Oliver stands as a symbol for peace and friendship."

"Okay, so what I'm hearing is that you want to be my friend, Macey?"

She giggles in the seat next to me.

"I'm taking that as a yes. But if we're going to be friends there's something I have to tell you."

"What's that?"

"If you ever meet my other brother, don't tell him that I called his fake fiancée my sister-in-law. They aren't married. It's a long story that I don't want to waste on our short time together, but he'd kill me. Come to think of it"—I huff out a quick breath as if I'm blowing out a candle—"Avery would kill me and the last thing I want to be is on the bad side of Avery Woods."

She covers her mouth with her hands again because she can't hold back the laughter before she says, "Noted."

For the next two hours, we talk about the most random things, but nothing about her life, where she's going or what she's doing on this flight. Don't get me wrong, my curiosity wanted to know, but I wasn't going to push it.

There's a ding over the speakers in the cabin before an announcement is made to prepare for landing.

"We made it." I nudge her shoulder with mine.

Her smile falls, and I notice that her anxiousness is back in full force. It happens so quick that it's like someone flicked the light switch off and she's back to who she was when she boarded the plane. She lifts her head slightly to assess the front of the plane as if she's looking for something, or someone.

I follow her movements, as if I'm looking for what she's looking for.

"Are we looking for something?"

"Uhh…" she pauses. "Yes. No. I mean… Can I ask you a favor?"

I raise a brow. "Are we about to commit a felony?"

She releases a breath she was holding. "Nothing like that. Listen, I'm meeting someone at the front of the plane. Would it be okay if I scoot out past you when we land so I don't lose her. You know, the back of the plane equals last out of the plane problems."

Out of every word she just said, Macey telling me she didn't want to lose *her* is the only thing I heard. It's an odd feeling of relief that washes over me. Why? I have no clue. I'll never see this woman again in my life, I'm sure. But knowing that she isn't meeting another man makes me relax in my seat.

"Of course."

She hesitates before a soft smile touches her lips. "Thank you."

"That's what friends are for." I wink.

As the next few minutes pass, disappointment engulfs every part of me when I realize that I'll never see this woman again. It's not in the sense of wanting to date her because that life isn't for me, but just being in her presence feels like an honor. I want more of it.

"Hey, you never told me if you're coming home or leaving it?"

She rests her head on the back of the chair, keeping her gaze locked to the seat in front of her as if she's trying to process my question. Her eyes flutter closed, and she smiles. She simply smiles in bliss. She looks like she just had a major epiphany with my question.

"I'm coming home," she finally says.

"Well since, New York happens to be both of our homes…"

The flight attendant announcing that we may now depart the plane cuts off my sentence. Macey shoots out of her seat, eager to meet her friend in the front of the plane.

"Maybe I can get your number and we can meet up for dinner sometime," I continue, as she rushes to gather her things before the aisle clogs up.

"Can I give it to you outside of the plane? I have to meet her right now," she says in a hurried tone.

"Yeah, of course." I wave my hand out towards the aisle. "Go catch your friend and I'll meet you out there."

Without a passing glance, she's rushing down the aisle towards the front of the plane. Saying "excuse me" left and right to people in her attempt to meet her friend. I watch intuitively as she stops in her tracks and leans down to greet the person she's meeting. At the same time, the flight attendant interrupts me.

"Mr. Ford, I have the suitcase that we stored back here for you."

I turn around to find the same flirty girl from earlier that took our drink order, her tits even more on display as she hands me my luggage with a wink. I immediately dismiss her because I'm not trying to lose my line of sight of where Macey went.

I'm determined to get her number, but I'm even more eager to learn more about her and why she captivated me so much.

Except, she's gone.

Of course, being in the back of the plane didn't help matters either. I end up getting stuck behind an elderly gentleman who is clearly having trouble getting his bag out of the overhead compartment. Not a single person lifts a hand to help him. They are the worst type of people in my opinion because we could all be off this flight a hell of a lot faster if someone took three seconds of time to help the man get the bag out of the bin.

Finally, I cut through them and help the man grab the bag.

He thanks me endlessly as if I just handed him two solid blocks of rare gold.

Once we exit the plane, my eyes scan the area in hopes of catching a glimpse of the jet black hair I've thought of running my hands through during our entire flight.

Macey is nowhere to be found.

CHAPTER FIVE

Oliver

My mouth is salivating reading the menu of this little hole in the wall bar. The double bacon cheeseburger with a side of French fries is screaming my name. A drink also sounds really good right about now.

"How did you find me?"

A voice cuts through my thoughts of food.

Not just any voice… *her* voice.

The voice that I haven't stopped thinking about since this summer when I met her on a flight from Montana to New York.

It forces me to drop my menu and snap my head to the green-eyed beauty staring at me from across the bar.

Her black hair cascades across her shoulders and is long enough to cover her chest. Her olive skin looks sun-kissed despite it being the dead of winter. She's still just as beautiful as I can remember.

"What are you doing here?" I ask skeptically.

"I asked a question first."

Damn, that sass. Hot.

"But to answer your question, I thought the apron would give it away." She smirks. "Most people who stand on this side of the bar and wear an apron are here to work."

I bark out a laugh. "Ooh, she's got jokes."

A smile touches her lips and it dawns on me that I never really got a good look at her on the flight. I mean I know it's not the easiest thing to do when you're sitting shoulder to shoulder with someone for a few hours.

I thought Macey was beautiful then. Hell, I was even enamored by her and wanted to know more about her. However, now, sitting across from her while she stands behind the bar… it's a whole new level.

Something was off on our flight. The more I thought about it after we got off the plane, the more I assumed it was just jitters from flying. But I still couldn't stop thinking about it.

I never stopped thinking about her.

She adjusts her apron, the smile never leaving her face.

My eyes narrow at her. "Don't you think this is kind of a far drive for work?"

"It's not that bad." She glides around the bar with ease as if she's been here forever. "What can I get you to drink?"

I sit back on the chair, cross my arms over my chest as my eyes scan her from head to toe. I can feel an involuntary smirk form on my lips and I can't help it. "Here I thought we were friends."

"Ahhh, that's right." She nods, raising her pointer finger in the air and pulling a drinking glass from below the bar. Macey's green eyes flicker to me, her smiling growing as she fills the cup with ice before using the soda gun to fill it. "Orange soda."

My eyes catch a glimpse of the same dragonfly tattoo on her forearm. Her shirt isn't as oversized as the last one she was wearing, which exposes more of her sleeve and I notice pieces of a cherry blossom peeking out of her t-shirt sleeve.

"I knew you didn't forget about me, dragonfly."

She shakes her head. The grin on her face hasn't left since I saw her. "I didn't."

Something about her admission sends a shiver shooting through every part of my body. I didn't forget about her. I thought about her more than I care to admit. Which is totally unlike me because I don't think about women this much. I was annoyed as shit that I couldn't even get her number and I thought she was just… gone when I finally got off the plane.

And now she's here.

Standing across the bar from me.

Working in this small town where my brother bought a cabin.

"Can I get you anything to eat? Or are you only here for our stellar orange soda?"

"Food. Yes." I pick up the menu and try to remember what I was planning to order before she walked back into my life. "I think I was planning to go with the cheeseburger."

"Are we adding bacon tonight?"

I groan as my head tips back. "You're killing me."

Why does it turn me on so much to know that she remembers all these little things about me? We talked about the most mundane things, but she remembers everything I said I loved the most.

"Of course, I'll take the bacon," I say with certainty.

"If you didn't, I would question your love for it. You can't own a baseball cap that says, *'You had me at bacon'* without ordering a cheeseburger loaded with it."

"A girl after my own heart."

With my comment, something in Macey shifts.

It's almost like she caught herself before she took it too far. As if she allowed herself to get lost in our conversation for one sentence longer than she wanted too. But before I could say anything more, she moves to the other side of the bar to tap in my order on the screen and then helps out some other customers by getting their drink orders.

My eyes never once leave her.

I can't help but be mesmerized by her.

God, what the hell is wrong with me.

There's just something about the way she moves, the way she

smiles, the way her green eyes sparkle in this dimly lit bar. I want to know more about her.

To stop my racing mind, I decide to fire off a text to the boys.

I FOUND HER!!!!

Less than a minute passes before my phone chimes in with multiple messages.

LOGAN

Who did we find?

TOMMY

Oh Christ.

The girl from my flight home from Montana.

TOMMY

Here we go.

LOGAN

Wow.

First Tommy and now you? Fate is working overtime for you Ford brothers.

Except I'm not obsessed with her like Tommy was with Peyton. That was some next level shit.

My oldest brother, Thomas, met a girl at a charity gala one night a few years back and he became obsessed with her. The story I heard involved a fire that started in the kitchen of the Edison Ballroom which forced a massive evacuation of the place. The two of them lost each other during the process only for her to show up in the city five years later looking for a job as a nanny.

My sister, Emiline, had found an ad and met up with her to interview her for the position to watch my nephew, James. That was the day their paths crossed again and Tommy has been head over heels with her since.

Now the two of them are living happily ever after bliss as husband and wife.

LOGAN

Ok. You got a point.

TOMMY

I was not obsessed.

MARC

Stop lying. Yes you were.

TOMMY

You're one to talk...

Another point made. Marc fell head over heels for his fake fiancée over the summer who just so happened to be Peyton's best friend, Avery. She's a wrecking ball and we all love her for who she is.

Can we get back to the topic at hand?? I FOUND HER.

MARC

What do you want us to do with this information?

LOGAN

I think we're supposed to be happy for him?

But I feel mixed things.

You all suck.

"Are you ready for something stronger?" Macey interrupts.

I place my phone face down on the bar top, leaning on it as I clasp my hands together. I don't answer back and just shoot her an award winning, cheesy smile. Anything to put a smile back on that pretty face of hers.

It works, because she lets out a small chuckle and I don't miss the pink that forms on her cheeks.

"That's better."

"You're something else, Oliver."

I like hearing my name come out of her mouth. But I won't say it out loud.

"I'm good," I say. "The pretty bartender in front of me doesn't drink so I'm perfectly happy sticking with soda tonight."

"You know that doesn't bother me right?" She laughs, bringing her hands out as she looks around her. "Clearly, I work in this industry and I'm used to it."

"Well, it's not good for my liver anyway." I point a finger at her in a very matter of fact way. "And not to change the subject, but I thought you lived in the city? What are you doing working all the way up here?"

She scoffs. "I wish."

Her response catches me off guard. I don't know who in their ever loving mind would *want* to live in the concrete jungle and deal with that mess on a regular basis.

"Wish?"

"That's the end goal. To make it to the city." She rests her hands on the bar top, leaning in as she lowers her voice. Her close proximity pulls me towards her like a magnet to hear what she has to say. "This place is just a stepping stone for me."

"You're killing me," I whisper back to her. "Do you realize talking about goals is equivalent to dirty talk for someone like me?"

"I pegged you for food talk being your weakness."

I grin. "That too."

"Speaking of the city"—she pulls back from being close to me—"what are you doing up here? I thought *you* lived in the city."

"I do. I'm cabin sitting for my brother. But I decided to kill two birds with one stone and do a blog post about the Catskill mountains too while I'm up here."

"Oh yeah, the blog." She nods.

"Yeah, that little thing." I smirk. "I'm going to shoot some photos of the mountains and probably share some food I've eaten while I'm here. Entice people to come up here and explore the great outdoors."

"Interesting."

The way she wipes down the counter, walking away from me with that single word has me on edge. Is that a good interesting? Or a bad interesting?

I guess I'm killing three birds with one stone on this trip.

Because I'm determined to learn more about this girl.

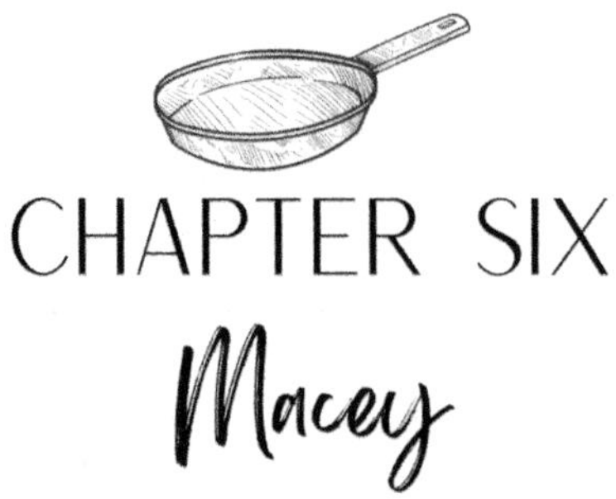

CHAPTER SIX

Macey

"Well, now you have to come back and explain that interesting comment," Oliver calls out just a few seconds after I walk away.

The first time I met him, he was like a breath of fresh air. I was drowning in anxiety and questioning my choices in life. Beating myself up with regret that maybe this was a stupid idea after all. But after a few hours with him on a plane, I felt at ease. I felt calm. I felt a sense of relief at the stranger who made me laugh when I hadn't been able to in years.

Now he's sitting in front of me.

At my place of work.

Drinking an orange freaking soda.

And looking like he walked off the cover of an outdoors magazine.

"Interesting as in…" I pause, trying to save myself the embarrassment. "Your brother's cabin. Just wondering if I know him."

"You might." He shrugs. "He's actually the one who recommended this place. He was up here in August for the first time ever with his now real fiancée that I told you about. You know, the one you're not supposed to ever say anything about if you meet them?"

There was only one couple I met so far since I've started working here that has never been in this town before.

Oh my God.

The man who tipped me three hundred dollars on a glass of champagne and a whiskey neat.

"Is her name Avery Woods?"

"The one and only." He nods with a grin. "Do you know her?"

"I do."

Over the last couple of months, there have been a handful of pivotal moments in my move here. Times that made me feel less and less guilty about uprooting my daughter's life.

The first was meeting Oliver on the plane.

The second was Samuel and Flora taking the two of us under their wing and believing in me when I barely believed in myself. They know my goals. They know I don't plan to stay here and they give me the daily encouragement that I need to keep me going.

The third was that couple tipping me the three hundred dollars that night. Making it my biggest night of tips to date. Allowing me to treat my daughter to a comforter set that she loved for the only bed we have in the cottage so she wasn't sleeping with just a throw blanket. And then I stashed the rest in our savings.

My eyes well with tears and I try to fight them back.

Oliver is that man's brother.

"Damn, you're good at remembering things." His voice stops me from full blown tears while I'm here at work. I watch intently as his thick arms cross over his broad chest. "Is it because you're that good or is it because I'm just unforgettable?"

I can't help the child-like laughter that comes out of me.

But Flora interrupts me before I have a chance to answer his question.

"Sweets, can you meet me in the kitchen really quick?"

"Of course."

I don't miss the wink she shoots Oliver and I roll my eyes as I follow her into the back.

"I'm sorry, I was talking to him for so long. I didn't mean to neglect the other customers," I start before the door is even closed.

"I didn't call you back here because you're in trouble." She moves to the order window and picks up the cheeseburger that he ordered. "Take this back to your friend and take twenty."

"It's busy tonight." I grab the plate from her hand. "I can't do that. I'm fine."

"I insist."

"But he's not *really* my friend. I met him on the flight to New York. That's all." I nervously tuck one hand in my apron pocket as my gaze falls on the cheeseburger to avoid eye contact with her.

"You should make him your friend." I look up and find her winking aggressively.

"Do you have a twitch in your eye tonight? What's with all the winking?"

"He's one fine looking *friend*, Macey. I've seen you chat with customers before. I've been watching you for months and no one has ever made you smile like that before."

"I'm not smiling any different."

"You are."

Shit. She caught me.

There's something about the way Oliver's blue eyes sparkle and match his perfectly white teeth that shine with his goofy looking smile. It's contagious, and within seconds I catch myself smiling goofily with him. He has an easy going personality that just makes everyone around him feel good.

"You're doing it right now," she prods.

"Maybe because this conversation is ridiculous. You know I don't mix work with pleasure."

She wiggles her eyebrows. "I bet that man would bring you some *great* pleasure."

"Flora!!!" I gasp.

"What? I'm old, which means I'm experienced."

I stick my free finger that isn't holding a plated cheeseburger in my ear, "I don't need to know that! You're going to make my ears bleed."

"Don't be so dramatic." She waves me off. "You need to pull your head out of those college textbooks you keep reading despite *not* being in college and open your eyes to what's out there for you. Plus, when fate deals you cards, you can't sit back and try to fight it."

Is that what this is? Fate?

"I'm not looking for anything like that though, Flora. You should already know I'm happy with it just being me and my daughter. Mackenzie is the only person I need in my life."

"I know that. But I also know that you're not happy."

Her words cut through my heart like the sharpest kitchen blade.

I swallow the lump in my throat, and whisper, "I am."

"Are you truly? You know I love you just the way you are, and I know that little girl makes you the happiest person in the world… But I know deep down you're fighting demons that you won't allow a chance to come to the surface. I also know that you can't pour from an empty cup. Your cup runneth empty, child." Her laugh lightens the mood. "Now take this cheeseburger to that fine man before it gets cold. Here's a southwest chicken salad for you. Take twenty."

"Fine," I concede as I grab the salad plate from her hands and make my way out to the bar.

It's only a twenty-minute conversation.

I can totally do that.

CHAPTER SEVEN

Macey

Once Oliver notices me on the opposite side of the bar, he swivels in his stool towards me.

He rests his hands on his broad and thick legs as he spreads them out. He's wearing a pair of dark wash denim jeans that pair perfectly with his red checkered flannel. He looks more like a local than I do.

"Wow, the customer service here is top notch."

I raise both plates in my hands. "I figured I'd join an old friend for dinner. If he's up for it, of course."

Oliver leaps off the chair, grabbing his orange soda. His body is dangerously close to mine with the sudden movement, which forces me to stumble back a step. *He's a total flirt, isn't he?* His blue eyes meet my green ones and my body trembles slightly. His hand grips my forearm to keep me in place so I don't spill the plates.

"Woah there, dragonfly."

The nickname he started using earlier echoes in my ears.

I didn't disclose what any of my tattoos mean, but something tells me this man is more intuitive than I think he is.

"I'm good." My voice comes out hoarse. "Let's grab a table."

He follows me as I guide us to the only open table in the back corner of the bar. No one ever sits here because it's close to the side door and there's a draft from this particular window that sits over it.

However, it's not bothering me one bit at the moment because Oliver's presence has me hot in every part of my body.

What the hell is wrong with me?

"You know... I never got your last name," he says.

"Evans."

"Macey Evans." The corner of his lips curves up, as he repeatedly nods his head. "Has a nice ring to it."

I shrug a shoulder, bringing my gaze to my salad as I stab the pieces with my fork.

It has a nice ring to it, but it forever ties me to my parents and I can't stand that. In fact, Mackenzie is also an Evans. Her birth father wanted nothing to do with her so why give her the last name of someone she will never know in her life?

"I have a question for you," he interrupts my thoughts.

"Shoot."

"I'm in town for just a few days before that 'big storm of the century' hits," he says with air quotes. "You think you can help me a little bit with my blog post?"

"How can I help?"

"I need someone who knows the area to show me around a bit. I want to take some scenic mountain shots. Find the best restaurants in town and try their food. Because you know"—he leans in close—"food is the way to my heart."

My heart rate picks up speed because food is also the way to mine. But that isn't the only reason... I can't spend time with this man outside of this place when I'm not working.

This conversation is already doing a number on my anxiety for missing out on some possible tips. Besides, I barely spend enough time with my daughter, so I can't spend the free time I have to be away from her with him.

To add to my list of things I feel guilty about: being a working mom.

It's truly a double-edged sword. When I'm at work, I feel guilty about not being with her. When I'm not at work, I feel guilty about not making money for us. The vicious cycle in my brain is never ending.

"I'm not sure that's a good idea. Besides, I've only been here a few months myself. The only places I know are where I live and this bar. That's about it."

"We should rectify that then, shouldn't we?"

"I have a lot going on right now here with…" I stop myself because Oliver doesn't know I have a daughter and I'm not sure I'm ready to disclose that information. "With work. I'm on schedule for the next week every single day," I lie.

"Hmm," he mumbles, wiping his mouth with a napkin after taking a bite of his burger. "Maybe I should extend my trip then."

"Oh, you're persistent." I can't help but smile.

"For some reason, I am with you."

I feel my cheeks heat up at his admission, making it feel like a summer day in this corner of the bar.

"You never told me *your* last name."

"Ford." He reaches his hand across the table for me to shake it as if we're meeting for the first time. My hand cups his and the electricity that courses up my arm at his touch is enough to shut the entire city down. "Oliver Ford."

"Wait." My eyes widen in shock. "As in… *Notes from Oliver Ford*?"

"You've heard of my blog?"

I lift one shoulder in a shrug. "Here and there."

I try to hide my embarrassment that I actually follow the blog. Religiously. I'm constantly blown away by the foods he shares and wanting to learn how to create each one he posts. Wishing like hell I could visit all the places he's been to. My foodie heart is obsessed with it.

Then, throw in the incredible scenic views he captures with his camera.

Like Oliver said before, he wants to entice people to explore the great outdoors with little notes from his travels. He does just that with every single post. He's added to my bucket list an insane number of times.

I can't believe I finally get to put a face to the name. The photos he posts of himself usually have his face cut off. I always assumed it was for privacy reasons.

He's the shirtless man with the chiseled abs that's enough to cause you to drool over your laptop.

He's the rugged outdoorsman who can rock a backwards baseball cap and pair of Levi's that perfectly showcase his incredible ass.

He's the man who, without a doubt, would want nothing to do with a washed up, single mom like me.

CHAPTER EIGHT

Macey

I'm pretty sure I got a full forty minutes of sleep last night.

That's probably exaggerating a little bit, but it felt like I tossed and turned on the couch all night long while my mind spun with thoughts of everything under the sun.

That's the issue when dealing with my anxiety. I worry so much about anything and everything. Mostly, it's things completely out of my control but my brain doesn't seem to realize that.

It's full of intrusive thoughts of things that could possibly go wrong and I can't stop them from coming. Generally, it leads to full-body shakes, a spiked heart rate and breathing I struggle to control.

One night a while back, Dr. Google told me those feelings are signs of a panic attack coming on. Unfortunately for me, it wasn't something I could seek help or obtain medication for since I lived under a microscope with my parents. I was too scared that they would deem me too unstable to care for my daughter.

I learned over the years that a lot of my problems stem from my relationship with them. Not a single scar on my heart came from an enemy. They came from people who were supposed to love me and support me no matter what happens in life.

People who are supposed to lift you up and encourage you to do better, people who are supposed to stand by you through thick and thin.

Tears prick at my eyes for probably the tenth time since last night. I stopped keeping track. This wasn't the life I had planned for me and this *definitely* wasn't the life I had planned for my daughter.

I wonder if she thinks less of me as her mom because I can't afford nice things.

I wonder if she resents me for taking her away from the life we were living.

Was she happy?

Is she happy now?

I shake off any of those thoughts before I spiral and I pull out my old laptop that has a crack right down the middle of the screen to creep on the *Notes from Oliver Ford* blog page. He doesn't post often, but when he does, it looks like it takes off like wildfire.

His most recent post was about his trip to Montana and the first thing I notice is the thousands of comments on the page. Not only does this man have a keen sense of how to make someone smile when it's the last thing they want to do, but he can capture the beauty of the world through a lens perfectly.

I can confidently say that because I've seen those mountains and scenic views in person, his images make me feel like I'm right there again. We must have been in the same area at the same time when we were there because I recognized some of the restaurants he showcased in the blog and his honest review of them.

The Den was one amongst them and he rated it the lowest. He's on point with that because that place is a total shithole and not worth the time or energy to eat there.

The last photo on the bottom of the post has me doing a

complete double take on my screen. Despite the crack cutting through the image, I see all of him.

He's advertising a brand of outdoor attire on top of a mountain during the sunset. He's modeling the khaki pants by lifting his shirt just the slightest bit as if he's about to lift the bottom of it to wipe his face like most guys do with their shirts outdoors. A move that allows people to see the brand name at the waistband of the pants he's influencing people to buy.

But my eyes land on the chiseled V-cut abs peeking out of the top.

I'm not on the hunt for a relationship of any kind, but I have two weaknesses when it comes to men. When they're in a pair of mountain boots with a flannel and a backwards ball cap, or when a man is dressed in a pair of dark gray dress pants and a button down shirt with the sleeves rolled up just enough to expose their forearms.

Unfortunately for me, I'm staring at a picture of weakness number one.

"Good morning, Mom." Mackenzie's tired voice causes me to jump in my seat, which startles her too. "Jeez, relax. It's just me."

"You just scared me, that's all."

I close my laptop quickly, guilt immediately reaching my stomach that I lost track of time and don't have any sort of breakfast ready for her.

"I'm sorry I didn't make anything for breakfast yet." I move quickly to the mini kitchen, assessing what we have that I can make. "I can do eggs and bacon or French toast today."

"What are you sorry for?" She lets out an amused laugh. "I'm actually happy you didn't make breakfast yet."

"You are?"

"Yeah." She nods, jumping up to sit on the small kitchen counter. "I was hoping you can teach me how to make French toast myself."

I give her a side eye. "You're a little too young to work the stovetop yourself, Mackenzie."

"I'm eight. Not two. I can handle French toast on the stove top. It's like three ingredients."

The straight sass from her. Lord help me when she's actually a teenager.

"You're eight going on eighteen it seems." I laugh. "Too smart for your own good."

"I get all of my bests from you."

Lack of sleep plus my daughter saying things like that has me blinking back tears. I move quickly around the kitchen to gather the supplies, hoping that she doesn't see me getting emotional on her.

I *hate* the idea of her seeing me at my weakest because I'm supposed to be the strongest person she knows.

"Let me get the stuff." She hops off the counter.

She moves around the kitchen with ease grabbing the eggs, milk, cinnamon, and a loaf of bread before she pulls out the only flat pan we have that we make do with because we don't have room for anything bigger.

I don't remember much from when I was a child, but she reminds me of me when I was younger. Always in the kitchen and trying to bake or cook something. She moves like she was born to be in here. While I don't think she dreams of being a chef like I do, that's okay.

I want her to chase her own dreams.

I give Mackenzie step by step instructions while I let her do all the work to make French toast, and I decide to figure out what we're doing tonight to celebrate the New Year.

"What do you want to do tonight? I should be off work before the ball drops."

"You're not working tonight," she says with certainty.

"I am, babe. I'm sorry."

"But you're not." She laughs. "Samuel told me they are forcing you to take the day off to spend it with me."

"What?"

"His exact words were "that girl works too damn much."

Sorry for cursing. But you do work a lot, Mom. I know why you're doing it, and trust me—I'm really thankful. But take the break he's giving you. You need it."

Shit, Samuel's right. Mackenzie is on winter break. It's the happiest I've seen her since we moved here because she hates her new school, classmates and teachers. It's not like our small town at home and she says people look at her as an outsider. And since she's been off, she's spent more time with Samuel than she has with me.

I've picked up every shift I could to make as much money as I can since it's the busiest season at the bar. We have been flooded from travelers coming to ski for the weekends and people getting away for the holidays.

Just as I'm about to apologize, yet again, for working so much, my phone rings on the couch.

"Hello?"

"Macey, it's Samuel," he answers, practically screaming.

"I figured that." I huff out a laugh. "The caller ID told me it was you. Also, you don't have to scream, I can hear you perfectly clear on this end."

"Always a smart ass," he scoffs, but keeps his voice raised. "Listen, you're off the schedule tonight."

"So I heard."

"Mackenzie beat me to it?" he questions.

"She did. But isn't it supposed to be busy tonight?"

"We've been doing New Year's Eve since we opened this joint in the dinosaur ages. We've got it handled. You spend some time with that sweet girl of yours."

I swallow past the dryness in my throat. "Okay."

"Gotta run. I'll see you for the lunch shift tomorrow." He hangs up before I can respond.

"Well I guess I'm off," I tell Mackenzie as I walk back into our kitchen again. "What do you want to do tonight?"

"I'm good with doing nothing, honestly. I know money is

tight right now. I really am perfectly okay with just snacks on the couch and watching everything on TV."

"No," I stop her. More abruptly than I planned too. "Don't you worry about money being tight. You're way too young to even be saying that. Besides, it's not your responsibility. Let's make it the best New Year's Eve ever."

"Okay?" Her tone is laced with uncertainty because she doesn't want to have to put us out more than we already are. "What if we get dressed up and go to dinner, and *then* come home and wear jammies?" she suggests.

"Are you sure that's all you want to do?"

"I'm sure. As long as we're doing it together, I'm happy."

She turns around to place the French toast on the pan, but my eyes remain locked on her back. Her words ring in my ear about how she's happy as long as we're doing it together.

Who knew one sentence could take a small amount of weight off my shoulders?

Dinner ended up being exactly what the two of us needed together.

There's a small pizzeria on the mountain that is on the more upscale side of places here in town. We got dressed in nice jeans and pretty shirts and made our way there. It wasn't as busy as I thought it would be, but it was just right for us.

We chatted about everything, including her not wanting to return to school and begging me to homeschool her when they go back mid-January, to laughing about the latest show that she and Samuel have been watching at night.

Having a foodie for a daughter has its ups and downs. Since I wanted to spoil her tonight, I settled for a bowl of chicken corn chowder soup so that she could order her filet mignon with a side of mashed potatoes.

Only my daughter would order a steak from a fine dining pizza place.

She almost picked up on the fact I only ordered a cup of soup because she's way too smart for me, but I lied and told her that my stomach wasn't feeling the best and I wanted to keep it light.

The second we got home, we tore off our jeans and got into our jammies.

Because fuck jeans.

An hour later, Mackenzie was passed out in my arms. I can't even begin to describe the feeling that came over me. As your child grows older, you never realize that the hug you just gave them or the time you picked them up will be the last time until you have moments like this where she's nestled under your arm and sound asleep.

I've missed so many moments like this.

When the New Year's Eve host on the television announces that the ball will drop in three minutes, I wake her up from her sleep because she told me she didn't want to miss it.

"Here we go, babe." I sit on the edge of the couch intently watching the screen project to the ball in Time Square.

"Don't forget to make a wish when it drops, Mom."

"What?" I chuckle. "You don't make a wish when it drops. You just cheer and say Happy New Year."

"I don't make the rules, okay? You *have* to make a wish. Please." She presses her hands together in prayer as she begs.

"Okay, fine." I throw my hands up in defense. "I'll make a wish if you do."

She taps the side of her head. "I got it right up here."

We both countdown and watch as the clock reaches the new year. The people over the TV scream and cheer. I glance over at Mackenzie who has a serious look on her face and her eyes closed, wishing harder than she ever has.

I wonder what's going on in that head of hers.

I do the same and the minute my eyes close, an insane feeling of hope washes over me. Sending goosebumps down my arms, and water to pool behind my closed eyes.

I don't believe in wishes like this. I never make a wish when I blow out my birthday candles because they are just that... wishes. But the feeling taking over my body right now is like an out of body experience.

I do as she asked and make a wish.

I wish for a year of opportunity.

I wish for a year of chasing my dream and giving my daughter whatever she just wished for.

This is going to be the year that everything changes for us.

And for the first time since I was a child, I actually believe it.

CHAPTER NINE

Oliver

"Happy New Year," Marc says on the other end of the phone.

"Happy New Year, brother. How's Paris treating you?" I glance down at my watch and I see it's almost five in the evening here which means it has to be close to midnight over there. "It's probably almost January 2nd there by now."

"Close," he laughs. "That's why I'm calling now before I lose the actual day."

"How nice of you."

"Yeah, yeah. How's the cabin?"

"Well… last night we had a small kitchen fire. But I got it conta—"

"That better be one of your sick jokes, Oliver," he says, interrupting me.

"Caught me." Now I'm the one laughing despite the silence on the other end. "Everything is in tip top shape here. I took the patio furniture into the ginormous garage thing you have off the side of the property. What do you plan to do with that anyway? It's large enough for a small aircraft."

"It came with the house."

"Makes no sense but whatever." I shrug despite that he can't see me. "I saw that the water line outside was exposed so I went ahead and insulated those for you and I'll shut the water down before I leave."

"You're the best, despite your stupid jokes." This causes us both to laugh. "So, how's it going with Macey?"

"How do you know her name?"

I hear Avery chuckle in the background. "Lucky guess. We assumed you went to the bar we recommended the first night you got there and that was the night you sent the text. So we put two and two together."

"You little smarty pants over there," I say in a tone that sounds like I'm talking to a two-year-old.

"Whatever you do, do not christen my house before I get the chance to," he warns.

"Is this a bad time to tell you we already did? Three times in the kitchen, once on the couch, another in that massive shower and the last time was right in your king-size bed."

"I'll fucking kill you."

"No you won't, because you already know I'm joking."

He sighs. "One can *never* tell with you. Besides, it's your thing to bang someone everywhere you go."

"It's not like that," I correct him before continuing, "I mean it's not like I don't want to. She's a smoke show. But there's something about her that has me intrigued. I'm actually more desperate to just get to know her."

None of that's a lie.

Don't get me wrong, the thought of laying Macey in bed and claiming every part of her body has absolutely crossed my mind since I saw her at the bar again. But she's the first woman who has crossed my path that I just want to learn more about and find out who she really is under that armor she seems to have up.

It's a totally new feeling for me.

"Careful. You're starting to sound like you want a relationship."

"Nah. It's a strictly platonic friendship."

"Riiiight," he drawls out.

"Get your head checked while you're up there, Ollie," Avery bellows from the background. "This doesn't sound like you at all."

"I'll add it to my to-do list."

"What's your plan for the rest of the day, anyway?" Marc asks.

"On my way in, I saw a small cottage style home at the bottom of the mountain. I only have three more days here and I still need a few more things for the post. I feel like I haven't gotten enough pictures so I'm going to knock on their door and see if they'll let me take some pictures of the sunset for the main image."

"Spoken like a true extrovert."

"Yup. Have no fear, Ollie is here."

He barks out a laugh. "Whatever you say. Good luck with that. We're headed to bed. Have a good rest of the day and Happy New Year."

"You too, brother." I end the call and pocket my cell phone.

Once I step out the front door, I suck in a deep breath, letting the crisp mountain air engulf my lungs. God, it's perfect up here.

The snow stopped falling a few hours ago, leaving the perfect amount of snow covering the grass and keeping the roads clear. *This* is the type of snow I can work with, fuck the other heavy, life consuming shit.

When I finally arrive at the little cottage style home, I look up and see that the sky has transformed into a perfect cotton candy pink hue. I pull out my camera before I even turn the truck off because I refuse to miss a second of this.

A fleeting sunset is proof that no matter what happens during the day, or how bad it was, every day can end beautifully, leaving behind whatever weighed you down.

I aim for the spot between the main house and the other small house on the property and snap at least a dozen.

God, it's beautiful.

I turn the truck off quickly and jog up to the front door of the main house.

Within seconds, an elderly man answers the door.

"Good evening, sir. My name is Oliver. I'm a travel and lifestyle blogger from the city."

He smiles and extends his hand to greet me. "I'm Samuel."

"Pleasure to meet you." I nod. "Listen, I wouldn't normally do something like this on my travels. But when I arrived in town, something about this spot, this house and this view pulled me to come down here and snap a few scenic images of the mountains for my next post showcasing the town."

"Okay?"

"Would you mind if I went into your backyard and took some pictures? You have the perfect view, by the way. But I will keep the house and the little cottage off to the side out of the images."

"That's a super nice camera." A little girl comes up to the door, her eyes locked on the camera around my neck.

I say little girl, but she looks to be about eight or nine years old. I'm not good with kids and ages, so maybe I'm completely wrong about this one.

However, I am intuitive when it comes to kids and who they look like. She doesn't look anything like the man who I want to assume is her grandfather. She's got bright blonde hair that lays off one shoulder in a braid, and bright green eyes.

Familiar, bright green eyes.

But how many people in the world have green eyes? Honestly, I think I just can't get a particular set out of my head.

After Macey and I enjoyed some lunch together when her boss forced her to take a little break, I realized quickly I can't get enough of her, which sounds nuts. Besides our flight, I haven't spent more than thirty minutes with her.

Yet she's had a chokehold on me since.

I even found myself at the Bar and Grill of all places for New

Year's Eve in hopes she would be working since she seems like a workaholic. But she wasn't there.

Talk about a disappointing way to end the year.

"You like taking pictures?" I finally ask the girl.

"I'm not good at it, but I do love it. I just use my phone." She shrugs.

"If it's okay with your grandpa, you can come out back with me and snap a few if you want."

The girl looks up at Samuel, her hand covering her mouth as she lets out a chuckle.

"You calling me old, boy?" He joins her in laughter.

"Shit—I mean shoot," I stutter. "I'm sorry. I just… assumed."

"You know what they say about assuming?"

"I do." My eyes trail down to the girl. "But I won't say it. I've already let one bad word slip."

"It makes a donkey out of you and me," she finishes for both of us.

I point down to her, bringing my gaze back up to Samuel. "What she said."

Samuel scans my body up and down. My guess is he's assessing to make sure I'm a normal human being. He gives me a side eye, but jerks his head. "Head on back. I'll be watching from the kitchen window. You only have a few minutes. Dinner is almost ready."

"Okay." She jumps up and down, following me outside.

"Let's make it quick," I tell her.

We round the house and I take notice of the fact that I didn't miss the sky changing colors. It's still the most beautiful hue of colors I have ever seen. If anything, it's more vibrant than it was before.

I lift the camera to my face to take a few shots for myself.

I feel her eyes on me as I do.

I look down and confirm she is looking up at me in awe. Like she's fascinated by the camera.

"Are you ready to give it a shot?"

"I'm scared I'm going to break it," she admits.

I pull the loop off my neck that was keeping it in place, and bring it down over her head. She smiles wildly as she looks down at the giant camera now in her hands.

"This is so cool," she says. "This is probably a million-dollar camera."

"Not quite," I assure her. "You won't break it. That's why the loop is there to put around your neck. You just have to look into this little hole right here, and aim it into the direction you want to shoot for. Then when you're ready, press this button to take the picture."

She's clearly a quick learner because within seconds, she's shooting the camera up to the view and snapping away. I'm willing to bet they will come out just as good, if not better, than the ones I just took a little bit ago.

I'm instantly drawn to her for some odd reason. The only thing I can think of is the fact that she's a little bit like me. A curious mind that wants to learn all the things and finds any opportunity to do it. Like this opportunity right here, no matter how short on time we are.

"How old are you anyway?" I ask curiously.

"I'm eight. But I'll be nine in June."

"Mackenzie." Samuel stands at the sliding screen door before I can reply. "Dinner."

"I have to go," she says in a more somber tone. "That's really so cool. Thank you for letting me use it."

"How about I put these on a hard drive for you and drop them off tomorrow morning to Samuel."

"That would be freakin' epic!" She stops herself, covering her mouth. "Don't tell anyone I said freakin'."

"I wouldn't dare." I put out my fist to give her a little fist pound. She does a little explosion at the end without me even saying anything as if it's our own little thing. "By the way, I'm Oliver. But because you're really cool, you can call me Ollie."

"See you tomorrow, Ollie." She skips away, leaving me to

wonder what the hell just happened and when children started thinking I was cool.

I mean my nephew, James, seems to think I'm pretty cool. Despite Thomas thinking I'm trying to corrupt him.

I decide to make my way off the back deck and down to the little pond in the backyard for just a couple more shots before I get out of here. Here in the mountains, each home has a mini pond in the backyard. I'm told it's because if there was ever a fire, that's where they would get the water to put the fire out. I learn something new everywhere I go.

Minutes later, the sound of a throat clearing startles me.

"Man, you are persistent," she says.

I turn quickly and the grin that takes over my face is one I *did not* intend to happen as fast as it did. But something about Macey causes me to feel so giddy inside. And just looking at her standing in the grass in a pair of skinny jeans, a peacoat and a beanie has my smile that much brighter. The little bit of sun that's left and the white snow makes her tanned skin glow even more.

Fuck, she's beautiful.

"Who? Me?" I point my fingers at my chest. "It seems to me like *you're* the one following me here."

"What are you doing here?"

"I thought the camera around my neck would kind of give it away."

"Oh, he's got jokes." Her smile grows as she nods her head.

I take this moment to bring myself closer to her. The magnetic pull between us forces my feet to move and put myself in her bubble. "You're not the only one."

"Mmhmm. So, I heard you met Samuel."

I nod. "I did. Is that your dad?"

"He's not." Macey shakes her head at the same time her arm extends to showcase the small cottage on the side of the property. "Why don't you come in and I can make us some homemade hot chocolate. I'll even be extra nice and tell you a good place to eat that isn't the Bar and Grill."

She turns to walk toward the place, and I follow like a puppy.

"I definitely have to hit the gas station after this for a lottery ticket. Because Macey Evans is being extra nice."

She doesn't reply but keeps walking down the gravel walkway until we reach the house. Once we get inside, I take in how tiny this place really is. From the outside, it looks way bigger than it is. The kitchen is packed with cooking gadgets that take up the little bit of counter space and small appliances.

On the floor next to the couch, I notice a pile of culinary education books stacked taller than the back of the couch. One would look at that pile and immediately assume a college student lives here.

"Are we learning how to cook?"

"I know how to cook."

I point to the stack of books. "*Someone* here is learning."

"Oh, yeah." She pulls off her beanie. Running her hands through her hair. Despite it being jet black, it shines in any light it touches. "That would be me."

"Really?"

"Remember those goals we kept talking about? Well, that's my number two goal in life."

"Number two?"

She releases a long drawn out sigh like she's hesitant to continue. "When I was in high school, I knew I wanted to become a chef. I had big plans to go to culinary school after graduation. Then after that, try and make it to the big city and work in one of those fancy five star restaurants to become the greatest female chef."

Confusion washes over me and I can't help but be curious to know more. "*Had* big plans?"

"I heard you also met Mackenzie inside," she says, ignoring my question.

"The little girl? I was showing her my camera a little bit ago up at the house. I think I totally scored brownie points because she thinks I'm really cool." I laugh.

It all dies down when I notice that Macey is *not* laughing back with me. I can't read the expression on her face, but if I had to guess it looks like… worry.

She clears her throat, averting her stare to the ground.

"That's my daughter," she finally says.

Everything in my chest tightens. I can't move. I can't breathe. All I can do is stare at her.

She has a daughter?

That can't be what I just heard, because she's too young to be a mom, right?

"Let me get you that hot chocolate," she says, breaking me out of my state of shock.

"Yes. Chocolate. Hot," I stammer.

She doesn't say anything else as she works around the kitchen grabbing two mugs from the cabinet and boiling hot water on the small stove. My head is *spinning* right now. Not in a bad way, but I'm just really shocked. If anything, this new revelation makes me like her even more.

I want to ask her more about her and her daughter, but I settle for small talk not wanting to push her to reveal more than she's comfortable with. "So… can you tell me anything more about this town other than the Bar and Grill?" I ask in an effort to relieve some of the thick tension in the air.

"I wish I could tell you more, but I don't get around much. It's a small town." She laughs at that. "I mean, compared to where I lived in Montana it's small. It's actually something like eighty miles long. But I've only explored the five-mile radius from this house."

"Do you ski?" Now I find myself asking her mundane questions when I want to be asking about her daughter.

What the hell is wrong with me?

"Absolutely not. I don't have a death wish," she says.

"I have to agree with you on that one." I laugh.

Macey finishes making the hot chocolate and places the mug in front of me. I look down at it, nervous and unsure of what to say next.

"It's getting late, I'm going to head out," I say.

She nods, but doesn't reply. I feel like an asshole but there's some things I want to work out before I open my mouth anymore tonight.

She has a dream to make it to the city and become a chef.

If anyone knows restaurants in the city, it's me.

I think I know just the thing to do.

CHAPTER TEN

Macey

For a man who makes my cheeks hurt from smiling so much when he's around, Oliver sure is doing a number on my sleep patterns.

I don't think I've slept a normal amount since he came into my life.

It's as if he tilted everything on its axis for me.

Except, I don't have time to be tired right now. Apparently it's a busy travel day for people leaving town and they all want to get a quick lunch in before they hit the road. So the Bar and Grill is packed today.

I feel less guilty working than I normally do because Flora has Mackenzie for the day. She is taking her downtown for lunch and to see the horses.

There's two different types of spoiling she's experienced. The kind from my parents that includes monetary things and gifts that get shoved in a closet or are given to her with an ulterior motive. And then there's the type of spoiling that two people who don't hold a grandparent title give her—love and experiences.

Just as the lunch rush finally dies down and I get the bar area cleaned up, I hear the bell ding, signaling someone is coming in.

Just as my eyes land on the entrance, I see Oliver walking toward me like a man on a mission.

I prop my hand on my hip as I stare at him. "How did I know you would be coming in today?"

"Something about this place…" His eyes trail my body. No doubt I look a hot mess right now after that rush we just had. I also probably smell like grease and booze. "I would much rather be here than anywhere else. Plus, we need to talk."

I feel like when a man tells you *we need to talk,* that's when the break up happens. But we're not even remotely on that level, so why does my stomach flip when he says those words to me?

Anxiety wins instantly because I wonder if I did something wrong by telling him I had a daughter. When I did, I watched as the wheels spun in his head while he processed the information I unloaded on him.

Twenty minutes later, he claimed he had to get back and left rather abruptly.

I don't blame him, honestly.

Dropping a bomb like that one will cause anyone's head to spin.

Is he ending our friendship because I have a daughter?

This is it. This is where the judgment comes from me being a young, single mom.

I should be used to this from living with it for so long. I learned how to brush it off after my parents would throw it in my face any chance they got. But it feels different with Oliver. There's something about him that makes me care about what *he* thinks more than anyone.

Even if once he leaves for the city, I'm likely never going to see him again.

"Come back to the city with me."

It's a statement, not a question, one that quite literally knocks me off my feet and I drop the glass I was holding, letting it shatter into pieces.

"Excuse me?" I fire back, ignoring the glass shattered around my feet.

"After I left your place, I got to thinking."

"That's usually not a good thing."

This grown man chuckles, and there's just something I love about the sound. "I'm a big supporter of people who set goals and want to do something big with their life. I called a friend of mine in the city and I got you an interview at one of the restaurants there. If you want it, of course. It's a five-star restaurant and they are actually looking for some help because they want to add a second location across town by the summer."

What? That wasn't where I saw this going.

There's a part of me that's shocked but the other part feels like he might have hacked my computer while I looked at the New York City ads last night after he left to see if anyone is hiring anytime soon. I even shot off three emails to see if they would be willing to set me up with a virtual interview in the next couple of weeks so I can start in the summer.

As much as I *want* the job and the interview he's offering me, I also can't afford a place there just yet.

"I can't do that. I'm not ready," I finally reply.

"Why do you say that?"

"I have to study more. I have to practice more." I frantically start wiping down the counters as nerves spike inside of me. Clearly I'm a stress cleaner. "I'm not ready."

"Practice in the city."

I stop abruptly and watch his ocean blue eyes bore into mine. "I'm not sure if you noticed or not, but I work a lot here. I live in a small one-bedroom place on someone else's property because I'm broke as a joke, Oliver."

I hate admitting my financial struggles to someone who looks like he doesn't have to worry about a thing. I'm sure he picked up on it by now after seeing my place and how much I'm at work. But it stings more admitting it out loud.

I continue, "Plus, how can I find somewhere to stay on such short notice?"

"Short notice? I'm giving you two days' notice," he jokes. "That's when I head back to the city."

"That's short notice last I checked."

"Is it?" He smirks.

What's it like to be so carefree about life? I envy him right now.

"I can't accept. I appreciate it, but I just can't."

"If money is the biggest factor stopping you from chasing what sounds like your life long goal, then stay at my place." He says it so casually as if we've known each other for years. "Besides, I'm heading out of town for two months to backpack Europe."

"You don't know me. What if I'm a serial killer?"

He rolls his eyes. "Don't be dramatic. You don't have a mean bone in your body."

"What if *you're* the serial killer?"

"I'm not going to lie; I can fuck up some fruity pebbles."

I ignore that while he laughs at himself as I press on, "What if I'm messy and leave my laundry out everywhere?"

"I saw your place, and you're *not* messy."

"I cook a lot, but I hate cleaning up. What if I leave a mess in the kitchen when you're home?"

He laughs again, rubbing his hand in a circle over his stomach. "Good, I like to eat. So if you're cooking, I'll gladly do the cleaning."

"God," I cry out. "You're impossible."

"All you have to do is say yes."

If I wasn't in the position I'm in, I probably would say yes in a heartbeat. But the list of people I trust is very small, so small I don't even need all the fingers on one hand to count how many people.

I have one very important person to think about when making decisions now.

I swallow past the lump clogging my throat. "What about Mackenzie?

"What about her?"

"I can't go to the city without her."

Oliver takes two steps towards me, closing the distance between us until he's only inches from me. My body ignites at his proximity and I feel myself gravitate towards him as if he's going to embrace me in his thick arms.

"You think I'd tell you to come to the city with me and leave your daughter behind?"

I shrug a shoulder before Oliver places both hands on each of them, bending down low enough to where his eyes are level with mine. His breath directly on my face takes over my senses with the strong smell of peppermint.

"Clearly we need to spend more time together because you've lost your mind if you think for one second that she isn't coming with us."

"Lost my mind? When I told you about her last night you barely said three words about it. No thoughts are equivalent to negative thoughts, Oliver."

"I was a little shocked." He grins down at me. "But believe me when I tell you, I couldn't stop thinking about it when I left. From the few minutes I spent with her, I can tell we'll get along great."

"Now *you've* lost your mind. Plus, you're a hot, single guy." I wave my hand up and down his body silently saying what I'm thinking about his looks. "You don't need a little girl in your house."

He holds up his pointer fingers. "First of all, it's an apartment." Then he brings up his middle finger with it. "Second of all, you think I'm hot?"

"That's not the point I'm making here."

"Third of all," he continues, ignoring my comment, and bringing up his thumb to join the other two fingers. "She's a part of you, which means I like her already."

I don't have the words to reply to that.

I don't have any more argument in me that this is a terrible idea.

I made a promise to myself when the ball dropped, that I would make this our year…the year of opportunities and to finally go after what's always been mine, to live out the dream and make a better life for us.

Am I really considering his offer right now?

CHAPTER ELEVEN

Oliver

I do one last sweep of the cabin before I load my things into the enclosed truck bed. I turn off all the lights, make sure the water is shut off and lock all the doors and windows.

I'm not ready to head back to the city if I'm being honest. I just love it up here. But I'm also not about to get stuck up here in this cabin alone when the snow storm hits any day now.

It's about a two-and-a-half hour drive back into the city, so I first stopped by Samuel's house to drop off the disc of photos I was supposed to deliver yesterday. No one was home, so I just dropped it in the mailbox.

Once I pulled out of that driveway, I made the executive decision that I should probably eat before I hit the road to avoid unnecessary stops. Whenever it's time to leave somewhere, I battle the urge of not wanting to go and also the feelings of 'just get me the hell home'.

I'm downright exhausted too.

I barely slept the last two nights while my thoughts were consumed by Macey.

It *was* crazy for me to ask her to come back with me. I know this.

But why wouldn't I use the connections I have to get her a step in the right direction of the goals she has for herself.

Once I step foot inside, my eyes immediately find Macey standing off to the side of the bar, talking with Samuel who gives her a hug and whatever he's saying to her has the biggest smile plastered on her face.

God, that smile.

As if Macey can sense me standing there, her head turns and that same smile stays as she makes her way over to me. My feet refuse to move from the place I'm rooted in. I can't help but notice she's not in her normal work attire. She's wearing a pair of black leggings with short fur booties and an oversized sweater.

Something about the way she wears her hair down in those loose curls and how radiating her smile is right now has the ability to bring me to my knees for her.

Fuuuck me.

What the hell is wrong with me today?

"I was hoping you'd come in today," she says, breaking my spell on her. "I have no way of getting in touch with you since I don't have your number or anything."

I take one step that brings me closer to her, a grin splitting my cheeks. "You want my number, Macey Nicole Evans?"

"That is not my middle name," she scoffs playfully.

"Are you going to make me guess?" I ask.

She laughs and opens her mouth as if she's about to say it, but Mackenzie coming out of the kitchen interrupts her.

"Ollie!" She beams before bulldozing me with a hug around my waist, a hug I did *not* expect after only spending about five minutes total with her.

"Hey there, killer." I wrap an arm around her shoulder to return the embrace. "Getting some lunch today?"

"Nah." She shakes her head. "We're waiting for someone mom knows to show up and take us to the city to live with them."

I smirk down at her before bringing my gaze up to Macey. Her cheeks turn fire engine red with embarrassment and shock. "Are you now?"

"Mom was *not* wanting to go. At all. You know, the whole stranger thing." She leans in close to whisper to me, but her voice is a normal volume. "She gets a little bit of anxiety about things. She worries a lot."

"Hey! I heard that," Macey exclaims.

"Sorry, Mom. But you know I'm right. You also know that this is such a good idea and I'm so happy I talked you into it."

"Did you now?" I raise a brow to answer Mackenzie, but keep my eyes on Macey.

"Yup! I just know that we're going to thrive so hard out there."

"Who are you?" Macey cuts in.

"I told you." She turns to face her mom. "I get all of my bests from you. That includes my brain." She taps the side of her head.

"She's not wrong," I say with a wink.

"I don't know who we're meeting or anything," Mackenzie continues. "They might show up. They might not. But we're freakin' ready!" She covers her mouth. "Sorry for the curse word, Mom. I'm just so excited. Like, I'm not excited for the whole switching schools thing again. But I did some research on some schools there and they are just seem so much better than this place. Their curriculum is… chef's kiss." She emphasizes her rambling words with a kiss to her fingers before throwing them in the air. "I bet I'll make so many new friends too."

I blink at her, unmoving. "Who are you? And did you just say curriculum?"

"I'm Mackenzie. Duh." She rolls her eyes and lift her chin. "And yes. I think it means the classes you take. And the word sounded really cool to say out loud."

The three of us pause for a brief pause before we all burst out in laughter at her antics.

"Why don't we grab some lunch before we head out," I announce. "I'm starving."

Mackenzie's eyes bounce between Macey and I. "Wait. Are you coming too? Do you think they have room for all of us?"

"Last I heard, I was the lucky guy taking you back to the city."

"You are?" Her eyes widen with excitement like a toddler on Christmas morning. I know what that looks like from being around James on the holidays. "Oh my God, MOM!! This is so amazing! Ollie is so cool! Have you seen his awesome camera yet? He let me use it and it was just so awesome! Oh my God!" She squeals in excitement.

I lean into Macey to ask her in a hushed tone. "Did she have coffee or an energy drink or something today?"

"I need to pee," Mackenzie announces before she races off to the restroom.

Macey laughs. "She had zero caffeine. But she's very excited about this next adventure."

I throw my arm around her shoulders, forgetting that whenever I make contact with her, my body lights up. I half regret it and half welcome it the second we make contact. I feel her shoulders tense under me and I wonder if she feels it too.

I lean in, bringing my lips dangerously close to her ear. "So… what's this I hear about you saying yes?"

"I don't know what the hell I'm doing. But I made a resolution, a wish, if you will, when the ball dropped. Whatever you want to call it." She shakes her head, waving off the thoughts. "But I told myself I would be open to more opportunities this year and finally stop sitting idle and chase what I *think* I deserve."

"Not what you think." I turn Macey's body around, tipping her chin the slightest bit. God, what I would give to feel her lips on mine right now. But I won't cross that road with her. "It's what you *do* deserve, dragonfly."

Her eyes flutter closed. "Are you absolutely sure this is okay?"

"I wouldn't have offered it if it wasn't."

"I can't believe I'm doing this."

I can't believe I'm doing this either. I can't believe I'm allowing someone who affects me this much, to enter my space, my home. But there's something inside me that wants to be the one to give Macey everything she deserves in life.

Our spell is broken when Mackenzie comes barreling out of the restroom with a small backpack on her back, ready to go.

For the next half-hour, we eat lunch, talking about all the things Mackenzie wants to see first in the city. Once we're all done and the truck is loaded with Mackenzie comfortable in the backseat, I put the truck in drive and hit the main road.

"I have one very important question for the ride," I ask Mackenzie through the rear view mirror.

"Hit me."

"What's the playlist for the drive?"

"Taylor Swift! Duh!" she says at the same time I toss her the auxiliary cord and allow her to plug in her music.

"A girl after my own heart."

I keep my eyes fixed on the road in front of me, fighting like hell to avoid this dangerous feeling swarming my gut that these two might already have me wrapped around their fingers.

CHAPTER TWELVE

Macey

Oliver caught me completely off guard when he started belting more than half of the Taylor Swift songs that Mackenzie played. The last thing I expected was this man to be a total Swiftie, but here we are.

Mackenzie saved the best song on the entire playlist for last, she says, "Welcome to New York."

The decision to leave Roxbury with Oliver did not come lightly. I barely slept going through the pros and cons of doing this. He's technically a stranger to us, and I mean, what if he is a serial killer?

I replayed every interaction with him and tried to see if there were any red flags, but I couldn't find a single one. My stomach didn't do any weird flips like it normally would when I get a bad energy from someone, and I know that feeling all too well. My body can immediately pick up when someone feels off. Call it mom instinct.

After spending hours upon hours of debating if this was the right decision, it felt like the right thing to do.

I was nervous and a total ball of anxiety when I got in his truck though. All of that changed once we got on the highway.

We talked about all the things we can do in the city and a little bit about his brothers and sister, who sound so fun. I kept my past to myself because it's not something I wanted to scare him with.

Thankfully, Mackenzie didn't mention grandma and grandpa or our life in Montana. She was more fixated on talking about Flora and Samuel and learning about Oliver's life. I'm thankful for her curious brain, because hearing about him relaxed any fears I have about temporarily moving in with him.

The sound of her belting out the chorus is drowned out by the lights blinding my vision in front of me as we enter the heart of the city. I sit up taller in my seat and lean forward, rolling the window down to look out and scan every direction I can as the lights flash, people walk and cars buzz by.

The cold air hits my face and the city is much louder than I expected. People talking and screaming, horns blaring because someone didn't go through a yellow light.

I turn around to see if Mackenzie is seeing the same thing I'm seeing, and sure enough, she has the biggest smile plastered on her face as she looks up in wonder.

Such a small girl in the big city.

It's one thing to see this place online or in photographs, but it's a whole new thing to see it for yourself. My insides swirl with anticipation and any exhaustion I was feeling is gone, with the wind flying through my hair. My mouth parts and tears sting my eyes that after all these years, after never being able to stop thinking about this.

I'm here. *I'm finally here.*

In the concrete jungle. The big apple. The city of dreams.

New York City.

I don't know how long I spend taking it all in, but next thing I know we're pulling inside a parking garage of what looks like a massive skyscraper.

"What is this place?"

"This is home," he says.

Home.

Maybe to him this is home. This is where he's planted his roots, built a life for himself and what I assume from the first time I met him—a successful one.

I can only hope to do the same here someday.

"This is where you live, Ollie?" Mackenzie asks.

He nods, steering the car into a spot that reads *Reserved for Oliver Ford* on it. "It is."

"This is wild," she says to him. "I feel like this is a place where rich people live. Are you rich?"

He shrugs to brush it off. "You can say that."

Hold the phone. He *what*? No way. I mean… I assumed he was successful after seeing the very expensive watch he wore on the plane and the fact he ordered whiskey on the rocks not sitting in first class.

But to be… wealthy?

"You don't look rich," Mackenzie says before I have a chance to say anything.

"It's not something I like to flaunt around. I'm grateful for it, but it's not what makes me, me," he says.

"Interesting…" she says in a very questioning tone like her little brain is spinning with what to say. But because she has absolutely no filter, she continues. "You know…my mom has a weakness for guys in gray suits though."

"Is that so?" He raises a brow in her direction, pulling our bags out the back seat.

"Yup. That and guys who dress like they're going on a hike in the woods or something like that."

I cover my eyes in complete embarrassment. "Who are you and what have you done with my daughter?"

"What? You always told me to be honest."

"Except there are *some things*"—I say the last two words through gritted teeth—"that should be kept to ourselves, babe."

Completely ignoring me, she walks over to Oliver to grab her backpack from his hands. "Does your place have cool purple walls and like a big window that you can sit on as you look out into the city streets and spy on people? You know, like that show my mom is always watching? I feel like all places in the city look like that."

He lets out an amused chuckle. "I have no idea what you're talking about."

"It's called *Friends*. It's so, so funny. Joey is totally my spirit animal. And he loves food as much as I love food. Come to think of it"—her fingers graze her chin—"you kind of remind me of him, actually. Tell me you have a pet duck. That would be epic."

"I wish I did." He laughs. "That would be the coolest pet. But now I need to watch this show to see for myself about this Joey guy. I'm one of a kind, Kenzie."

I internally cringe at him for calling her Kenzie. I know that she loathes when people use a name on her that is anything other than her birth name. She knows she has a long name, but can't stand when people shorten it. She's also bold enough to call people out on it so they don't call her—

"What about tonight?" she replies back to him, Which is not the response I was thinking she was going to say. I truly believed she was about to school him and give him hell for the nickname like she does everyone else.

"Not tonight," I tell her. "It's really late and you need some sleep."

"No way." She shakes her head, fighting back a yawn. "We're in the city that never sleeps."

As we grab our bags and head toward the elevator to the apartment, Mackenzie yawns at least a dozen more times. But my mind can't stop thinking about how she just so casually let someone she barely knows call her a nickname that she hates.

While confusion continues to swirl, a smile of relief crosses my lips.

She's comfortable with him. She's excited for this and she trusts him. Kids are the best judge of character, after all.

Once the elevator doors open, anything I did want to say is gone. Poof.

This place is massive. This isn't an apartment. This is a house stuck inside a skyscraper. That's the only way to really describe it.

I step into the entryway as I scan the room and take it all in. There's a living room with an oversized sectional sofa, as well as a loveseat off to the side. A massive television hangs over the electric fireplace built into the wall. I take a few more steps in, and then quickly falter as the kitchen comes into view.

If I had any dream for a home that would be all mine, it would include this kitchen. There is a panoramic window that overlooks Central Park covering the stretch of the kitchen counters with the sink sitting right in the middle of it all. Parallel to that counter is an oversized island completely clear and begging to be cooked on.

"This kitchen…" I release my shaky breath as I say it.

"It's pretty bare," Oliver says, walking up behind me.

"It's… perfect."

"I'll have it stocked for you tomorrow." He rounds the kitchen island. Standing across from me, Oliver places both hands on the counter to hold up his body weight. His muscular arms showcase his forearm veins with the weight and I can't help but stare.

"Are you ready to see the rest of the place?" he asks, pulling me out of my thoughts.

I nod.

He shows me the two hallways on each side of the living space. One leads to the master bedroom where he stays. On the opposite side of the apartment, closest to the kitchen, a hallway leads to three bedrooms.

It almost makes me feel relieved that we have our own space separate from him because my nerves are already heightened at the thought of living with someone who has a weird effect on my body when he's around.

But for some reason, my gut trusts Oliver as if I've known him my entire life.

Mackenzie hurries past me and finds a queen size bed in one of the rooms. Claiming it as hers almost instantly.

"You know, that's the one I was going to suggest for you," Oliver says.

"You have good taste, Ollie," she says. "This bed is ginormous and so comfortable. I feel like a queen!"

My heart gallops in my chest, while it simultaneously feels tighter.

Watching her right now, full smile on her face and making herself comfortable in the bed and… happy. It's everything I've ever dreamed of and then some.

Oliver leaves us to get settled. Once I tuck Mackenzie in, despite her protesting that she's *too old for that,* I make my way back to the kitchen where I find him again. Leaning against the marble countertop, arms crossed and a serious look on his face. He looks like he's deep in thought.

When he senses me enter the space, he stands up quickly and puts a smile on his face.

"So I spoke to Frank, the owner of the restaurant, and he said everything's all set for you to interview with him on the fifteenth. That gives you a little over a week to get all prepared if that works for you."

"That sounds great. I can't thank you enough for that."

He nods. "Listen. I hate to do this when you just got here minutes ago, but I have to leave before the sun comes up tomorrow for a few days."

"O-okay."

"I'm really sorry, Macey."

"Don't be. It's okay. I just… feel bad. I feel like we're already invading your space here."

"None of that." Oliver shakes his head as he takes long

strides around the island to close the space between us. His arms wrap around my head in a warm, comfortable, yet unfamiliar embrace, forcing my body to tense under him.

When was the last time someone just stopped and hugged me like this?

When was the last time I felt comfort the way I do in his arms?

"I want you to make yourself at home. I'll drop to my knees and *beg you* to make this feel like your home if I need to," he jokes.

My arms wrap around him at his words, a silent answer to his statement telling him that I'll try.

His one hand cups the back of my head, holding me to where I land on his chest. My heartbeat thunders in my ribcage while feelings I'm not used to swarm in my gut.

"I'll be home by Wednesday night. I have to head down to Florida to help with a new product launch for one of the companies that sponsor me for a new men's beachwear line."

Anddd now I'm thinking about Oliver in swim trunks and the fact I can't wait to creep on that post.

But before my body can react, he pulls away. I watch intently as he grabs a piece of scrap paper out of a junk drawer and scribbles something on it.

"Here's my number. I figured since we're roommates, but more importantly *friends*." He winks. "It's only right I give this to you. You can use it as you wish. Oh, and your interview is scheduled for next Saturday. I know it's a weekend but that's what worked best for him."

He doesn't allow me a chance to respond or even try to come up with one of our witty comments that we always give each other before he's grabbing a glass of water off the counter and making his way to his bedroom.

I watch as Oliver walks away, stuck in the same spot he left me in the kitchen with a phone number in my hand when he pauses at the last minute and turns around, his eyes meeting mine.

"Treat this like your home, Macey."

His words play over and over again in my head as I finally get settled into my room. I eventually fall asleep with the biggest smile on my face for the first time in years.

Home.

CHAPTER THIRTEEN

Oliver

UNKNOWN

Why are there bags and boxes all over the kitchen?

Who's this?

UNKNOWN

Funny guy.

I told you I would stock the kitchen for you, Macey Ashley Evans. If that's who this really is.

You should probably open them all and make sure everything is good.

MACEY

First of all, still not my middle name. Nice guess though.

Secondly, did you SERIOUSLY buy an All-Clad Copper Core cookware set??

Is that the wrong one?

MACEY

Uhhh… It's a crazy expensive cookware set for someone with nothing but a collection of empty takeout containers and Pop-Tarts in the pantry. Even the rats were starving.

First of all, there are no rats in the apartment. Where do you think you live? Second of all, those takeout containers are quite useful.

MACEY

That's beside the point. Why is this here? It's too much.

I googled it and they said this was the crème de la crème of cookware sets.

MACEY

Are you ignoring my question?

I'm going through a tunnel.

MACEY

That only works when you're talking and not texting.

Well I can't talk right now because we're shooting for the new line.

MACEY

Just as I expected, no tunnel.

Funny girl.

MACEY

…

Seriously, Oliver. This is all too much. What are you planning to do with this?

I wanted to make sure you had everything you needed to do what you love.

CHAPTER FOURTEEN
Oliver

I can't remember the last time I felt this exhausted.

The plane rides, car rides and long journeys to get to and from each place is downright exhausting. I mean Florida isn't that long of a flight, but the fact that I have a black-haired beauty occupying my thoughts every minute of the day has me eager to get home to see her again.

We've been texting non-stop since everything I ordered for overnight delivery showed up at the apartment. I probably went a little overboard, but if it makes her feel more at home then I'll buy her whatever she wants.

Despite my urgency to head home, I'm making a pit stop at Moore's for our weekly Wednesday night drinks with the boys.

A few years ago, we started meeting on Wednesdays here since it's the day of the week they are the least busy. With how high profile my brothers are, we like to keep it somewhat low key.

Prior to the two of them meeting the loves of their lives, they were some of the most eligible bachelors in the city. Women would flock to them anywhere they went. So when we found this place, we realized it was the best option for all of us.

Logan also joins us more times than not, providing he's not picking up overtime as one of New York City's finest officers.

"You're a sight for sore eyes," Thomas teases as I take my seat in the back corner booth with them.

"Been a little busy. And don't give me shit. My flight from Florida was delayed and it's been the longest day."

"Oof, that's rough," Marc adds.

The server comes by and takes my drink order. It's been way too long since I had a whiskey on the rocks and I'm straight up craving it right now. Not to mention I need it to calm the nerves I have about seeing Macey soon.

"How's the wife?" I ask Thomas.

"Peyton is great. Last week was the grand opening for her daycare downtown. Needless to say, she's been pretty swamped."

"No shit." I nod. "Congratulations. How happy is she?"

He shakes his head and a wicked smile stretches across his face. "You have no idea."

"Good for her."

Logan slaps the table, drawing our attention towards him. "For the first Wednesday in forever, I finally have some news for everyone and something exciting to share."

"You finally got to sleep with your one and only celebrity crush?"

"Why do you have to keep bringing that up?" He pouts. "You and I both know that will never happen."

"Continue on with the news, Logan," Marc urges him.

"I had a meeting with the chief today. We discussed a possible promotion for me this summer. If all goes well"—he throws his arms out to the side—"you're looking at the next Chief of Police."

"No way!" Thomas starts.

"Good for you, brother!" Marc slaps his shoulder.

"I'm not sure I'm ready for it, but I'm excited."

As one of Logan's best friends, I worry about him constantly.

Being a cop in the city isn't for the weak. It's constantly being alert for what's lurking around every corner.

"Careful, you're starting to show your age," Thomas jokes.

"I'm still a fresh, young, and feisty thirty. Relax."

"Anyway." Marc shuts that conversation down. "Was everything good with the house when you left?"

"Tip top shape. I checked the weather the other day and the storm didn't hit as bad as they thought it would. But it was better to be safe than sorry."

"Are you still in contact with the bartender?" Logan asks.

I grin. "She has a name you know."

"Eww. Fix your face." Logan wrinkles his nose in disgust. "Why are you smiling like that?"

"Here we go," Thomas says as he leans forward on the table, eager to hear more.

"Should I tell you now or later that she's here in the city?"

"I thought she lived there?" Marc questions.

"She did. But…" My eyes scan each of the boys before I spill. "I may have kinda-sorta… brought her home with me."

"Jesus Christ." Marc runs his hands down his face.

Logan extends his fist across the table for a fist bump. "My brother."

"Where the hell is she staying? Did you just put her up in the *Marriott* or something?" Marc asks.

"My apartment is big, but we don't need to call it the *Marriott*."

"She's staying with you?" Marc exclaims.

"She is." I bring the glass of whiskey to my lips before I whisper the next words over the brim, "Her and her daughter."

Logan practically sprays his drink across the table. "Come the fuck again?" he asks at the same time Marc says, "She has a kid?"

Listen, I was as shocked as these guys when Macey dropped the news on me about her having a daughter. Not just any daughter, but the girl that I took photos with outside of Samuel's place.

When she told me, my brain swirled with so many questions. My initial reaction was that Macey does *not* look old enough to have an eight-year-old.

I've never been involved with a single mom before but it only elevated my curiosity more than it already was.

"Would you three stooges relax? You know I'm not looking for a relationship. That's not why I brought her back."

Logan leans forward to whisper just to me, "Is she hot?"

I shake my head. "She's fucking beautiful."

"You're so done for," Thomas snickers.

"How so?"

"You already sound like she has you wrapped around her finger."

She absolutely does. That's for sure. Don't get me wrong, I've thought about it more times than I want to admit to these guys. I've thought about what it would feel like to touch and devour every single part of her body and be consumed by her.

But I refuse to go there.

Macey doesn't seem like the girl you fuck to get her out of your system.

She's the type of girl you want to stick around for.

"It's not like that. I brought her back here to help her out. She has this wild, yet amazing dream to be a chef in the city. I have the connections to help her, so why not use them?"

"That's so very noble of you." Thomas rolls his eyes.

"Oh hush. You know I'd give someone the shirt off my back if it meant making someone's day. I'd do it for you guys, too."

They remain silent because they know I'm right. It's who I am.

"Anyway, I got her set up for an interview with Frank over at Mollie's."

"Oh, that place is amazing," Marc says. "I'm there at least

once every other week. No one makes mashed potatoes the way they do."

"I was thinking the same thing. Even if it's just a stepping stone for her to get her foot in the door, I think it's the perfect place."

"Absolutely," Marc agrees.

Thomas and Logan have nothing else to say to that, but I can see Thomas giving me weary eyes like he's worried about this entire situation.

"Listen, I have to head back home. I haven't been there yet since I landed and I want to make sure both the girls are still in one piece."

"Riiight," Marc says in his signature drawn out tone. "Good luck with that."

Laughter erupts around the table as I stand to pay my tab and leave.

I've never been more eager to get home.

CHAPTER FIFTEEN

Oliver

Once the elevator doors open to my apartment, I notice that it's eerily quiet. But that only lasts a few seconds before I hear sniffling coming from the direction of the kitchen as if someone is crying.

I enter the space and see nothing but a gigantic mess that's taken over every piece of space in the kitchen. There's flour everywhere, brand new pans filled with red sauce and bowls scattered all over the place and random pieces of kitchen tools and food to prep with.

Once I round the island, I see Macey curled into a ball on the floor, leaning against the kitchen cabinet.

She doesn't lift her head, which tells me she doesn't know I'm here yet.

"Macey," I whisper her name in an attempt not to startle her.

"Oliver," she gasps, standing quickly off the floor as she brushes the mess off her apron. "Oh my god. I'm so sorry. This wasn't how I wanted you to come home. I'll get everything cleaned up. I'm sorry."

She moves quickly around the kitchen to clean up her mess as if I didn't already see it. When she tries to rush past me to grab a bowl off the island, I grip her wrist to stop her.

Macey's eyes widen as they bore into mine, but her body relaxes under the palm of my hand.

I grip her chin with my fingers, forcing her eyes to stay fixed on mine. "What happened?"

"I'm so sorry," Macey repeats again.

"I don't know what the fuck you're sorry about, but if you say it one more time, I'm going to lose my mind." I instantly regret my tone, but it's been a long day and the last thing I need is her being sorry for doing something here.

"I'm so—"

I cut her off by placing a finger on her lips. Her soft, plush pink lips press against my pointer finger and all I can think of is what they would feel like against mine.

She clamps her lips shut, and I move to swipe the tear that broke free from the corner of her eye with my thumb. One simple move sends sparks racing across my skin at the contact while she works to regulate her breathing from crying as hard as she was.

Craving more contact with her, I run my hand to the side of her head to bring the stray pieces of hair falling from her wild bun out of her face.

I offer her a smile, praying like hell it forces one on her face.

"You look good in my kitchen, Macey Evans."

She groans. "I don't feel good. I'm just so frustrated right now."

Fail on the smile part.

I take a step back from her, and lean against the counter behind me, crossing my arms over my chest. "Talk to me."

"I'm working on a recipe that I've been dying to try for a while now. I didn't have the space in the mountain house to figure it out, so I thought I would try it here with all this space and new pots and pans. I also knew you'd be home sometime tonight and I didn't want you to come home to a complete disaster. But I just couldn't figure it out. I wanted it to be perfect. And I'm stressed about this interview. I don't think I'm ready."

"Tell me about the recipe," I urge her.

She pauses, averting her gaze to anywhere but me. "You don't want to know about the recipe."

"Why not?"

"Because if I tell you, you're going to laugh and then probably tell me how simple it sounds."

I narrow my eyes at her.

She groans again. "Fine. It's homemade spinach and ricotta raviolis."

I can't help but smile at her. Raviolis do seem like a very simple thing to make, but I only know the frozen kind. Even a child can heat that up if they know how to work a stove. I can only imagine how difficult it is to make homemade ones and making sure they come out perfect.

"Each one I do pops open and everything falls out of it before it's even done cooking. The first one I did I put too much filling in. The next one didn't have enough. The next one was over cooked. And the sauce. I just can't fucking get it just right. It's just… been a disaster."

I practically choke on a laugh. "Did you just curse?"

"Now is *not* the time to make fun of me for my use of profanity."

I quickly move away from her, laughing on my way to the pantry.

I reach in and pull out an old apron that was given to me as a gag gift one Christmas by my sister. She knows that I *never* cook. Quite frankly, I don't have the first clue how to cook.

I'm a Pop-Tarts, leftovers and takeout kind of guy. Which Macey figured out pretty quickly.

"What are you doing?" she asks.

I pull the apron over my head, giving her my best smile in another attempt to put one on her face. It works, because now she's downright giggling on the countertop where I left her.

"Why are you wearing that? And does your apron say *Snaccident - When you accidentally eat all the bacon*?"

"Yup. And I'm wearing this because we're going to figure out your recipe. Right here. Right now." I point toward the ground in an over-exaggerated motion to make sure she understands.

She brings herself directly in front of me, placing both hands on my chest to stop me from tying the back of the apron. "No. You don't have to do this."

"I don't ever do anything I don't want to do."

"You've been traveling all day. Go to sleep." She pats my chest. "I'm going to get this stuff put away and I'll try again another day."

She tries to walk away, but I stop her by wrapping a hand around her wrist.

"I don't ever do anything I don't want to do," I repeat. "And right now, there's nothing I'd rather be doing than helping you make this happen."

Her green eyes glisten as they stare into mine.

Fuck, it's like those eyes have a spell on me. I can't ever look away from them.

But, the way she's looking at me right now, tells me that she's not used to getting help from anyone.

No one has ever taken care of her before.

The realization makes me equally angry and eager to change that.

"Now, tell me what I need to do and where you need me."

I don't care how exhausted I am or what kind of day I had, this is exactly where I want to be. I meant it when I said I don't do anything I don't want to do.

Macey stares at me and blinks three times before finally snapping herself out of her state of shock that I'm offering to help her. "Uhh," she starts. Her eyes land on a bowl and she picks it up and puts it in my hands. "How about you start by cooking the spinach?" She says it like it's a question.

"Done," I say firmly, making my way to the stove

Damn, I haven't turned this thing on in years probably. Okay, I might be exaggerating, but it feels like it. I notice there's already a pan on the stove with remnants of spinach from her first attempt at making it.

"You just want me to dump this bowl in this pan?" I ask. Macey lets out a soft chuckle and I can't help but do the same. "It's nice that someone finds humor in my lack of cooking abilities."

"I'm not laughing at you; I'm laughing with you."

I turn on the stove and pour the bag of spinach into the pan. Within seconds, it starts to sizzle. I turn to face her and use my pointer finger to tap on her nose. "For your information, I was only laughing because you made me."

She blushes at my words.

My smile grows. It just can't help it when I look at her.

"What next, chef?" I ask.

"You can use this to move the spinach around a little in the pan." She hands me a wooden spatula. "This way, all of it gets cooked thoroughly," she adds.

I finally look down at the pan to start mixing it around and my eyes go wide. "Woah. Woah. Where did all my spinach go?"

Macey covers her mouth with her hand to hide her amusement, but fails miserably when my eyes meet hers. She snorts out a laugh I've never heard before. This time I'm not laughing with her.

"Are you playing jokes on me, Macey? Did you take half my spinach?" I point the wooden spatula at her.

Her body bends over and the sweet song of Macey's laughter fills the kitchen.

God, that laugh.

"Oliver," she huffs out, trying to catch her breath from laughing so hard. "Spinach shrinks when you cook it. You put that whole bowl in there and you end up with a quarter of the amount, it seems."

I take a step back. "I never knew that."

Macey moves to take her place in front of the stove, stirring the weird vegetable a few more times before putting it in another bowl with a bunch of other ingredients already mixed together.

"What's that?" I ask over her shoulder.

As if she didn't expect me to be standing right there, her body stiffens and I can't help but place my hands on her shoulders to help her relax. As soon as my palms make contact with her skin, her chest rises and falls slowly as if she's breathing a sigh of relief.

"This is the filler that goes inside the ravioli," Macey finally says as she mixes the spinach into the white-filling.

She takes a step away from me and I find myself following her just to be near her. I never liked the idea of cooking. It's always a mess to prepare and cook the food, and then there's the cleanup of all the pans and plates you used.

It's always sounded so tedious to me, until now.

She moves to her next station that's set up on the island, where she has what looks like the outside of the ravioli laid out. She takes small teaspoons of the filling and places them onto the dough before folding it over and flattening it over the filling.

She whips out a weird-looking contraption that looks like a mini pizza cutter with ridges on it. Then, she slices her filled raviolis into a square shape.

"Well, I'll be damned," I say with amazement. Because that's just about the coolest thing I've ever seen. I'm not sure I'll want to eat frozen raviolis again after this.

"Pretty cool, huh?" She smiles up at me.

I don't have any words to say back to her other than a nod, because right now her eyes are boring into my soul. I'm fighting every urge in my body not to lean down and place my lips on hers and kiss her the way I've thought about one too many times already.

As if she's fighting off the same thought, she quickly averts her gaze back to the raviolis, bringing each piece next to the water already boiling on the stove.

"This is the part I keep screwing up," Macey admits.

As if she's channeling her inner badass, she takes a long deep breath and releases it before scooping the raviolis gently into the water. She doesn't take her eyes off the pot for one second.

My eyes stay on her, watching her every move. The way she so delicately drops each stuffed pasta into the water. The way she concentrates on the boiling water to make sure none of the raviolis break open while she stirs.

"Can you turn that burner on for me?" She nods to the top right corner of the stove, not taking her eyes off the pot. "It's for the sauce. If these come out as good as I think they will, we will need that sauce."

I fire up the burner at the same time she scoops them out one by one into the strainer in the sink. I don't know much about all of this, but I know I should be stirring the sauce so it gets hot evenly. I think I saw it on a TV show once.

As I stir the red sauce with the wooden ladle that was sitting to the side of it, I look over to see Macey almost crying over the raviolis in the strainer. "Macey?"

She shakes her head to bring herself back from wherever her head just went. "I'm good. I'm really good." Now she's smiling so wide that I *really* want to walk over to her, wrap my arms around her body and claim her lips as mine.

"They came out okay?" I ask.

She looks up at me, eyes glassy and filled with pride. "They came out perfect. Thank god, because I'm starving," she says with a groan.

The noise goes right to my cock, and that's when the ladle slips from my hands and falls into the pan and splashes over the front of me. My face burns from the heat of the red sauce and I can't help but scream out from the initial contact.

"Oh my god, it burns!" I bellow, frantically turning the heat off and moving around the kitchen to find a dishrag.

Macey can't stop laughing. She's doubled down and almost on the floor in tears from laughing so hard.

I find a rag and wipe my face before I develop third degree burns. "I'm on fire, Macey Evans, and you're laughing at my pain."

"I'm–I'm…" She tries to speak, but can't find the breath to do it. When I finish wiping my face, I find her on the floor with her back against the cabinet and still in a fit of hysterics. "I'm sorry. I don't know why that was so funny." She attempts to school her features. "I'm sorry you're hurt." As soon as the last word leaves her lips, she snorts out another laugh like she just can't hold back.

Now *I'm* laughing.

I notice the flour sitting on the counter above her head. She's laughing so hard that she doesn't notice when I pinch some between my fingers. I crouch down until I'm eye level with her and she looks up at me with happy tear soaked eyes.

That's when I flick the flour at her.

"Oh, you did not," she gasps. "You realize what you've just done right?"

I smirk and shrug a shoulder at the same time she stands up to reach for the flour. "Game on."

My eyes go wide as I run away from her and round the kitchen island. She chases me around the kitchen with flour between her fingers. Then she does what I least expect her to do. This woman climbs onto the kitchen island and cuts me off on the other side, successfully throwing the flour into my face now.

My hands grip her biceps holding her in place so she can't escape.

Fuck, I want to kiss her.

Macey doesn't move away. Instead, she looks up at me with lust-filled eyes. No doubt, she sees the same look in my eyes. My tongue grazes my bottom lip and her eyes track the movement and she doesn't make a move to break away from my hold.

Her face softens. "Thank you for helping me tonight."

"Anytime. Although I didn't do much. It was you that did all the work. *You* made it happen," I say honestly.

She nods, and that's when she finally steps out of my hold. My body feels coldness creep from not having her close anymore, and I hate it.

Macey Evans is quickly becoming a weakness I'm not sure I can fight off.

CHAPTER SIXTEEN

Macey

I'm going on my third night in a row not being able to fall asleep at a reasonable hour.

Oliver had to go and be the most perfect human when he got home from his trip a couple of days ago. Not only did he make me feel better when I was super emotional over my recipe not working out, but he proceeded to stay awake until an ungodly hour to help me make it perfect.

Just having him in the kitchen with me gave me a sense of comfort that I've never felt before. It's a feeling I'm struggling to deal with because I was never comfortable cooking when I lived with parents for fear of being scrutinized over my decisions and love for food.

I was never comfortable there, *period*.

I felt like my entire life was spent walking on eggshells, waiting for a bomb to just drop while simultaneously trying to prove that I was a good mom.

Now here I am, on a Friday night curled up in bed while the rain pours against the windows with my laptop in my lap trying to get ready for this interview. I leave the window slightly cracked because there is something so refreshing about the smell of rain.

But I can't focus on the interview because I can't stop thinking about the man who's flipped my world upside down, the man who's made me feel very unfamiliar feelings in the best way possible.

My roommate, of all people.

When smelling the fresh rain water through the crack in the window doesn't seem to ease my anxiety, I grab one of my culinary books off the end table and make my way to the kitchen.

After rummaging through the pantry and refrigerator, I settle on a tub of Ben & Jerry's for a midnight snack.

There's only one way to eat this kind of ice cream, and it's sitting on the counter with a spoon, enjoying it right from the carton. If you actually scoop it out into a bowl, you're doing it wrong.

I hear a door creek open from the other side of the living room and nerves spike inside of me.

Was I too loud?

Did I wake him up when the freezer door slammed shut?

Dammit.

My nerves quickly change to desire when I see the man I can't get out of my head walking into the kitchen in nothing but a pair of black sweatpants hugging the curve of his waist, his chiseled cut abs on full display and his hair going in every which direction like he just woke up.

And is he wearing… glasses? Oh, dear lord. I've thought this man was good looking from the moment I laid eyes on him, but nothing beats Oliver right here with the black large frames covering his light blue eyes.

Would it be awkward if I lifted my hand right now to return my jaw back to where it belongs? Or should I just leave it there on the floor? Because oh. My. God.

"Hey, dragonfly," he says, before throwing me a wink.

I'm done for. I'm a goner.

How am I expected to live under these conditions?

He notices me staring and quickly looks down to assess what has me in a trance.

"Shit. Sorry. I'll go grab a shirt."

"You. Uh. No. Don't need. It's—" Now I'm rambling and can't form a proper response.

When did I turn into the girl who can't talk to someone of the opposite sex.

This isn't me.

A smile curves his lips, just before his eyes roam every inch of my body heating everywhere his eyes touch. Oliver's tongue brushes along his bottom lip in what feels like slow motion. My things clench with need.

Again… another new feeling for me.

I haven't been with a single person other than Mackenzie's dad when he knocked me up.

I'm a twenty-four-year-old inexperienced woman staring at a man who looks like he could be on the cover of *Sports Illustrated*. I mean, he doesn't play sports but looking at his abs right now tells me that's where he belongs.

Which makes all these things I'm feeling out of my element.

"So…" I attempt to guide the conversation to something other than the fact he's not wearing a shirt. "You're supposed to be leaving for that Europe trip soon, right?"

Oliver shakes his head, grabbing a spoon from the drawer before jumping to sit next to me on the counter. He scoops a heaping spoonful of ice cream from the carton in my hands and brings it into his mouth. "Actually, no. I found out late last night when I was checking my emails that the backpacking trip was canceled. Something about the weather? Who knows. But all the places I was planning to stay at along the way canceled on me."

"You seem like you're always on the go. Maybe this will be a nice break?"

Oliver's shoulder brushes mine as he reaches for another spoonful, sending an electrical current through every part of me only making the desire I felt moments ago enhance.

"For the first time in as long as I can remember, I would rather be home."

Why does the way he says that, make me smile an uncontrollable amount?

Is it because I'm here? My mind wonders, but I brush it off.

For the next hour, we talk about what I did while he was gone for work.

Mackenzie and I walked around Central Park on one of the days and got pretzels from some street cart which was fantastic.

The next day we headed to her new school to get her enrolled and they told us she could start first thing Monday. She even got a chance to meet her teachers and her new classmates.

Her excitement for this school is such a stark difference from when she started at the one in the mountains. She's actually *eager* to go and wanted to stay that day.

Oliver radiates excitement for her when I tell him about all of it.

After that, our conversation shifts to more mundane things, mostly about how shitty the weather is right now and how he's happy it's not snow because that would be a disaster for the city.

Even these little conversations we have about something as silly as the weather make me realize more and more how comfortable I already feel in his space.

Just as I feel like I'm finally ready to head back to bed, Oliver stops me. "Hey. I forgot to tell you. I know your interview was supposed to be on Saturday but I rescheduled it for a week."

"What? Why?"

"He was all set for it but he called me today to tell me that his wife and kids all have a stomach bug. I forced him to reschedule it."

"You didn't have to force him to reschedule. I would have gone since it sounds like he's fine."

Dare I say that part of me is glad? As much as I want to get this interview over with because my nerves are shot, it does give me a little bit longer to prepare for it, which is a relief.

"Yes, I did." Oliver pauses as he turns his head to look at me, adjusting the brim of his glasses. He has the most serious face I've ever seen on him before. "I wasn't about to risk you or Mackenzie getting sick. I don't think I'd be able to handle it. Food going in versus coming back up are two very different things." He chuckles.

Thank god I'm sitting down, because that admission makes me feel weak in the knees.

"So, speaking of the restaurant. Do you go to Millie's often?"

"*Mollie's*? Yes," he corrects me. "It's a very well-known, high end restaurant in the city. It's been on many blog posts featuring the top five restaurants that are must visits. They specialize in fine dining. You know the type of place where the servers wear all black and fancy aprons."

"Wow." *That sounds like a dream for me.*

I pick my book back up, trying to fight off the feelings he's got me spiraling into.

"Are you going to tell me what's with all the college culinary school books?"

I feel my cheeks heat up that he caught me. "I'm kind of a book nerd," I admit.

"When I think of a book nerd, I think of my brother's wife who reads those romance novels." He laughs. "Isn't there a difference between reading books for pleasure and reading school books when you're not in school?"

I nervously laugh. After I told him about Mackenzie, Oliver never once asked me for more information about her or my past. People would think he didn't ask because doesn't care, but I felt more relief than worry about him not caring because I'm so used to being criticized and the last thing I wanted was that from him.

Now's as good a time as any.

"Well, I don't immerse myself in a fictional world like most people do. The day I found out I was pregnant, I was sixteen years old and I knew with certainty that the track I had set for myself would never happen. A few years ago, I started aggressively reading culinary education books that were part of college curriculums to teach myself. I can't afford to go to college, and besides, I would have no idea how it would even work with Mackenzie and being her sole provider. Being a single mom doesn't really work with school. So I found these on some second hand thrift website for a fraction of the cost."

My stomach does somersaults on repeat as I wait for the judgment to come. It always does...

"I like that. You're goal-oriented and when things don't work out, you take it upon yourself to fix it."

Just like that, relief floods my entire body.

He's *not* judging me?

I've just become so accustomed to it that I didn't expect this.

"The next best thing," I continue. "Was studying on my own so that when I finally made it here, I would have learned so much along the way, things I can implement into work and be the best damn chef I can be."

"From what I saw the other night and the way you moved around this kitchen, you were born for this, Macey. And I'm not just saying that because I like you." Oliver smirks when he bumps my shoulder. "But you truly know the way around a kitchen, and you fascinate me."

His words vibrate through my body. I've never had someone say these things to me. I've always wanted to believe I was born to be a chef, but I thought it was always just because my dreams pushed me to believe it.

Hearing it come from someone else... Correction, hearing it from Oliver, truly makes me feel like all of this could be possible.

"I just have one question, and I hope you're not offended," he says before I can respond.

"Shoot."

"Why bartend when you want to work in the kitchen?"

I sigh. "I started doing that just to get into the industry back home in Montana. I wanted to make some cash and get my foot in the door with some experience to put on my resume. My thought at the time was that having a restaurant listed there, regardless of what position it was, might help me in the future."

Oliver doesn't respond, but keeps his eyes locked down on the spoon in his hand that he swirls between his fingers.

"One day…" I pause, averting my gaze from him while I try not to let my emotions get the best of me. I've never said this much out loud before. "One day, I'll prove everyone wrong. One day, I'll give my daughter the life she deserves."

I refuse to look at him right now, but I can sense his stare boring into the side of my head.

"You're an amazing mother. She's really lucky to have you."

I huff out an amused breath. "You don't know me *that* well."

Oliver leans in, his lips grazing the shell of my ear. "I think we're doing a good job getting to know each other though. Don't you?"

I'm completely unable to fight back the smile anymore when my eyes land on the clock above the microwave and I notice that it's almost midnight.

"Hold on. It's almost midnight. What are you doing at home?"

"What do you mean?" He tilts his head in question.

"I mean… don't you normally go out or something? Isn't that what attractive single guys do on Friday nights?"

He smirks. "That's two times you've made a comment about my looks."

"Oh my god." I cover my face with my hands. "Don't let that get to your head."

"I'm sorry, Macey Brittany Evans… but that one is staying right here." He taps the side of his head as his lips slowly rise. "But to answer your question, I had some editing to catch up on for my blog. I didn't realize how long I was staring at the computer screen until my stomach started growling. Besides"—he pauses his thoughts as he looks down at my body—"I'm perfectly fine being home tonight and every night if it means you're here."

I blush and can't help the giggle that comes out of me.

God, this man is the most perfect man I've ever met. He knows all the right lines to say to make a girl smile or completely change her mood around.

I know it doesn't say much because I don't have a good history with men. But is this how they all are? Sweet talkers and full of swagger?

"You're smooth. Also, still not my middle name."

He grins and I can't help it when my lips match his. It's a fun little game he's playing trying to guess. I would hate to spoil it and tell him.

He leaps off the counter, tossing his spoon in the sink telling me he's done with the midnight snack.

"I have to ask you one more thing." I nod and he continues, "Would it be okay if I had my brothers, and some friends over next week since my trip was canceled? I'd like to introduce you to everyone. Maybe a chance for you to meet some girlfriends in the city so you're not just stuck with me."

"Who says I don't like being stuck with you?"

I regret my words almost as soon as they cross my lips. Being around Oliver causes me to have no filter—one I usually have. It feels like the walls I've put up around my heart so no one gets close to me are completely invisible and I'm just here welcoming him in with open arms.

"Trust me, dragonfly… I'd love nothing more than to keep you to myself. Especially knowing that you think I'm hot. But I think it would be good for you too."

My heartbeat revs with every word that pours out of him.

"I'd like that a lot," I say softly. "Meeting everyone. I'd like that a lot."

"Tuesday," he fires back. "It's Taco Tuesday, and apparently the girls are big fans of that day. Unfortunately, my sister has a big exam the next day so she won't be here."

"Exam?"

"She's in nursing school and will be done at the end of June.

So she's been swamped lately. You will get to meet her soon though, don't worry."

"Would you mind if I cooked?" I hesitantly asked, not wanting to invade on these girls' taco night. "I haven't had a chance to cook for people in a really long time."

"If you're cooking, I sure as *hell* am eating."

With those final words, Oliver leaves me alone as he retreats back to his room.

My brain is spinning at everything that just happened.

I have to be dreaming.

CHAPTER SEVENTEEN

Oliver

There's a nagging feeling deep in my gut that I may be falling for my roommate.

Macey has only been living here for a few weeks, but every encounter with her has me learning more about who she is and desperate to just be in her space.

I don't have the slightest clue what these feelings are.

I don't do this shit.

Something shifted on Friday night when we had our midnight snack run in. It wasn't the first time I was so close to her, but sitting on the counter and sharing a tub of ice cream together just *felt* different.

And let's not discuss how many times I've had to jerk off in the shower at the thought of her just to get some form of release. There's no part of me that wants to head to the bar on a random night and find someone because the woman in my apartment is taking over every part of my life. In the most surprising way possible.

I'm definitely not mad about it.

"Should we get the hard or soft shells?" Mackenzie says, holding up two boxes of taco shells while we decide which ones to buy for dinner.

"Your call, Kenzie."

"I've never had the hard shell ones." She shrugs. "So I don't want to waste money and get these. What if I don't like them?"

I've heard Macey talk about how she's *'broke as a joke'* but it wasn't until coming to the grocery store with Mackenzie that I realized they struggled a lot more than she let on. I asked her if she wanted any snacks for the house and she denied them all.

What kid *doesn't* want snacks?

I get it though. It's not something someone wants to showcase to everyone. Although our situations are different and I'm grateful for what I have, I hate people knowing. When you have money, people look at you differently. You find that people are nicer to you because they need something from you. Quite frankly, her situation doesn't bother me. It doesn't make me look at either of them any different, but rather makes me want to give both of them the entire world.

They deserve it.

However, doing so runs the risk of Macey feeling like she's less than who she really is and in need of a handout. Which she isn't.

She's so much stronger than she thinks she is and I have front row seats to watch her make it happen.

"Let's get both," I finally reply back. "If you don't like the hard shell ones, I'll eat them."

"Are you sure?"

"One thing you'll learn about me is that I don't do anything I don't want to do. I told your mother the same thing. And right now… I want to buy *all* the tacos."

She giggles. "You're really nice. You know that?"

"I've been told that a time or two," I laugh back with her.

I was really happy when Mackenzie asked to tag along for my grocery store trip to grab a few things for dinner tonight. I feel like I haven't spent enough time with her since they moved here because I was gone for work and she's been busy starting school.

She's also obsessed with her new room and rarely comes out.

She asked if we could walk because she's learning to really love exploring the city on foot. She's fascinated by the fact that most people don't have cars and walk everywhere they need to go.

"How was school today?" I ask her.

"It was really good," she emphasizes. "Like really good."

I raise a brow. "Really good as in, you got an A on a math test? Or really good as in, they gave out free pizza for lunch?"

"Neither. Really good as in I made two new friends. It was amazing."

"You're a likable kid, Kenzie. Of course you made friends."

Her face falls. "I didn't have very many friends when we were in the mountains. You were my first friend there."

I… what?

"What do you mean?" I ask as we move down the dairy aisle to grab some cheese.

"It's just… I don't know how to explain it really. Everyone kept treating me like the new girl. From one small school to another. The other kids looked at me funny." She wrinkles her nose. "One boy made fun of the bun I was wearing in my hair. So I haven't worn my hair in a bun since that day."

I grip her shoulder lightly, stopping Mackenzie in her tracks.

"You mean to tell me you haven't worn your hair in a bun since a little asshole, excuse my French, made fun of you for it?"

Her shoulders lift in a shrug to brush off the question, but she remains silent.

"Put it up now," I urge her.

She does as I ask, but I quickly regret it. I don't know much about Kenzie but I can tell that she doesn't want people to not like her. She wants people to be happy with her decisions.

Within seconds, her hair is in a messy bun perched on the top of her head. Her bun matches the one I first saw Macey wearing on the flight, except hers is bright blonde.

"Do you like wearing your hair in a bun?"

She gives me a small nod. "It's easy to do and keeps everything out of my face."

"Do you know why I asked you to put it up?"

She shakes her head.

"Because I want you to remember that from this moment on, you're not going to give a hoot what anyone thinks about you. If it's something *you* like, then you do it. If it's something *you* feel good about, keep it. Don't dim that sparkle you have inside of you for anyone."

She doesn't answer me as she tries to process all the words I just threw at her. But after a few heartbeats, she jumps to me and wraps her arms tightly around my waist. James has hugged me tons of times, but I've never felt the tightness in my chest that I feel right now when Mackenzie hugs me.

"Thank you, Ollie," she murmurs into me. "You're the best."

"Anytime, Kenzie. You know I've always got your back."

And that's turning into the damn truth.

I'll go to bat for this girl. There's no doubt about it. I knew there was something so insanely special about her from our first interaction together, not just because she's a part of Macey, but because she's quickly becoming one of my favorite humans.

Mackenzie pulls back and I look down at her, into familiar green eyes. "So, are you ready to head out of here and eat some tacos?"

"Let's do it!" She fist pumps the air. "I'm excited to meet your family. You think they'll like me?"

"I think they'll *love* you. I know James is going to love you the most."

"Who's James?" she asks.

"My nephew. He's a little younger than you, but he's funny as all hell. As a matter of fact,"—I tip my head to the side to give her a knowing look—"he's a lot like you. He acts way older than he really is. Too smart for his own good." I tap her nose with my pointer finger, earning me a chuckle.

"Does he like puzzles?"

"He loves puzzles! But they have to be the ones with bigger pieces. He's not ready for the ones with tiny pieces and he gets flustered when there's too many at once."

"Perfect. I'm going to pull out the one Flora gave me before we left. I think he's going to love it. It's the solar system and the pieces aren't super small!" She beams as she talks about it as if it's the greatest gift she's ever received.

"You're right. I think he will love it." I wrap an arm around her shoulder, guiding her towards the check out.

"One more thing." She stops me.

I give her a questioning glare as I narrow my eyes.

"You probably shouldn't tell my mom you cursed in front of me. I mean, I'm not a baby." She rolls her eyes like a teenager. "But she won't like it. Especially that you called that little boy a donkey butt."

I blink a few times before a laugh breaks free. "I probably shouldn't have said that, right?"

Mackenzie shrugs. "Probably not."

"Noted. Now let's get you home, smarty pants."

"Yes! Let's go home."

The way Kenzie says the word home has warmth filling my chest, something I am just not used to. The way she says it makes me want to make my place their permanent home and not a temporary one until they get their feet on the ground.

I swore I would never settle down.

But Macey bulldozed into my life and is making me want things I've never wanted before.

The elevator to my apartment dings as we enter with grocery bags filled with different kinds of taco shells, fresh lettuce and blocks of cheese. I absolutely snuck in a package of chocolate chip cookies that Mackenzie clearly wanted but was too afraid to ask for.

Mackenzie runs ahead of me to go get her puzzles ready for James to play with as well as various things she thinks he would love.

I immediately find Macey moving freely around the kitchen.

There's many ways I like Macey. But this right here, her in the kitchen doing what she loves, takes the cake. Watching her doing what I know she is meant to be doing, she looks the happiest. It makes me want to give her every hope and dream she has if it means her looking the way she does right now.

My heart pounds wildly in my chest as my eyes scan her up and down. It has to be about thirty degrees outside and she's wearing cut off jean shorts and a tank top, exposing the curve of her breasts for the first time to me.

But that's not all I'm seeing for the first time. The rest of her tattooed sleeve is on full display now. Cherry blossom branches cover her entire upper arm, shades of black, gray, and pink cover every inch above her elbow.

"Hey, you," Macey murmurs softly when she notices me.

A grin spreads across my face as I drink her in.

"Hey, dragonfly."

"Come here. I need some help before everyone gets here."

I round the island with a little pep in my step because I'll do anything at this point to be near her.

"Can you take the cheese block you just got and use the shredder to shred it up?"

"Do we have a shredder?"

She tilts her head and smirks at the same time her fists land on her hips. "This is your kitchen and you don't even know you have a shredder?"

"I don't need to shred Pop-Tarts. They're perfect just the way they are."

Macey laughs and moves to a random drawer on the other side of the kitchen. My eyes wander to her ass without thinking. I would give anything to have my hands on her right now.

Except I should *not* be looking at my roommate this way. So I snap my eyes up just in time for her to turn around.

"Here. I had to wipe the dust off it the other night, but it works just fine," she jokes.

"Huh." I nod. "Didn't know I had this fancy contraption."

She shakes her head as she laughs harder. "You're something else."

"One shredded block of cheese coming right up, chef!"

She beams… she fucking *beams* when I call her that. And damn, do I love it.

Just as I'm halfway through the block of cheese, she makes herself comfortable next to me as she chops the head of lettuce into fine pieces.

"So I made enough ground meat to feed at least ten people," she says. "I know your brothers are coming, and if they eat the way you do, I should have more than enough."

"Shit, I forgot to tell you." I sigh, dropping the block of cheese and hanging my head. "My brother's wife is a vegan. Dammit. I fucked up. I should have grabbed something from the store for her when I was there."

Apparently that doesn't faze her. She grabs the wash cloth and wipes her hands as she makes her way to the refrigerator. After scanning the inside of it, she pulls out some kind of white brain looking thing from one of the drawers.

She brings it to the cutting board and starts working on it as if she was prepared for this exact situation.

"What is that?" I ask her.

"Cauliflower. Mackenzie is obsessed with it. I mean, all vegetables really. She's not a vegetarian, but she has a soft spot for animals. So, if the option is presented to her to eat something that isn't meat, that's what she will choose."

"I thought Peyton was the only vegan I've ever met."

"Oh, don't get me wrong." She stops me. "She will eat meat here and there. But it's rare, more like special occasion meals. She's weird about being called a vegetarian or vegan. She thinks…" She pauses. The smile falls from her face as if she remembered something from her past. I can't quite pinpoint it. "She thinks that people will judge her for her choices or something."

My heart stings at her words.

After my short grocery trip with Mackenzie, I can see her thinking that exact thing. Especially because she was hellbent on never wearing a bun anymore after being judged by the kids in her school.

"I hate that for her," I finally say. "She's such a good kid. She's smart and funny as hell."

Macey stops chopping the cauliflower and angles her body so she's facing me. "Thank you," she breathes out. "For being so good with her. And for being okay with the both of us invading your space."

"I like her, Macey. She reminds me so much of someone else that I know." I shoot her a wink, hoping she's picking up that I mean her. "So, what's not to like? Besides, neither of you are invading my space. I'm happy just the way it is around here."

She offers me a smile and turns back to finish prepping the cauliflower with the taco seasoning.

The aroma of Macey's cooking pulls me closer to her. I bring myself to stand directly behind her, looking over her shoulder as she tosses the vegetable in the skillet. I can't help but inhale her scent standing so close to her.

The entire apartment smells like tacos, but her… she smells like vanilla and sugar.

Sweet. Intoxicating. *Addicting.*

"That smells amazing."

I can't tell if I'm talking about her or the food.

Macey shivers at my touch when I place both hands on her shoulders, but her body relaxes into mine at the same time. Her petite frame melting into the front of my body is officially my new favorite feeling.

I can feel the rise and fall of her chest with my hands still in place and it's taking every bit of willpower I have in me not to lean in and kiss the exposed skin my hands are touching.

"Oliver," she whispers.

"Are you going to let me try some?" I lean in to whisper, dangerously close to her ear.

Her head tilts to the side, allowing me access to explore her neck and feel the bounding pulse beneath my lips if I wanted to. But I won't cross that line with her.

I *can't* cross that line with her.

"Try what?" she asks flustered.

I laugh. "The cauliflower. Unless there's something else you want me to try?"

Macey pulls away from me. Clearly this is new territory for her too. She's conflicted on how her body is reacting and it shows with how uneven her breathing is, and the widened look in her eyes when she turns to face me.

This should be one interesting dinner.

CHAPTER EIGHTEEN

Macey

After I finish making dinner, I quickly run to the bathroom to freshen up.

My nerves and anxiety are through the roof right now at the thought of meeting new people.

I've always thought I was pretty good at making friends and getting to know people. But that was about eight years ago. When I was still in high school before my world changed completely. Losing everyone close to you because of what they deemed a 'mistake' really fucks with your head.

I hate even saying that. I never once—since the second I laid eyes on my daughter—thought she was a mistake. But to outsiders, that's exactly what Mackenzie was.

The goal was to get to the city and make a life for us. This *has* to be one of the steps if I'm going to survive. You can't go through life without ever having friends. That shit gets lonely.

Trust me.

I hear female laughter erupt from the living room, telling me that they are here. I allow myself a few deep breaths as I give myself a once over in the mirror.

"You got this," I whisper to myself.

Once I step out and round the corner, I see the girls sitting around the couch, still full on laughing with each other. My immediate thought is that this is a tight group of girls. You can tell they blend well together and have the best time just from watching them be with each other.

My eyes land on Oliver who's looking at me intently. He doesn't speak yet or move an inch from where he's standing, but he's looking at me like we're the only two people in the room right now.

Like he doesn't care if anyone catches the way he's looking at me.

He snaps out of his daze quickly, before clearing his throat. "There she is."

All three girls snap their head in my direction, the smiles never leaving their face from the previous laughing fit they were just in. I immediately recognize one of them from the time we met at the Bar and Grill. I remember how fun and free-spirited she was that night and think this might not be so bad after all.

The really pretty blonde is the first one to jump off the couch and rush to me. She doesn't even say hi or give me her name before she's wrapping me in her arms for a hug.

"It's so nice to finally meet you, Macey." She releases me from her hold. "I'm Peyton. This is Kali." She points to the last girl with the cowboy, copper-orange hair before pointing to the girl I already recognize. "And this is Avery."

"Yes, I remember you. It's nice to see you again." I offer Avery a smile. "And it's so nice to meet you two."

"I was so excited to hear you finally made it to the city." Avery claps her hands together, gushing in excitement.

I actually had forgotten that I told her that this was where I wanted to end up. She was one of the first people—outside of Flora and Samuel—that I admitted my future plans to out loud, which is weird now that I think about it.

But you know how you come across people who you just feel comfortable around? I got that feeling within seconds of meeting her.

"I'm really excited to be here."

"Oliver told us you made a bomb ass taco dinner," Avery starts.

"I mean… It's just tacos. You can't really screw that up." I nervously laugh.

"You don't know Avery very well yet," Kali scoffs. "This girl can screw up a peanut butter and jelly sandwich."

Avery pops her hands on hips, giving Kali an evil eye. "I take offense to that. And I've gotten a whole lot better since moving in with that guy over there." She hikes her thumb over her shoulder, causing me to direct my gaze to the two other men sitting on the couch with Oliver. "Plus, you're obsessed with my apple crisp recipe."

As if the men can sense Avery's talking about them, they both stand from the couch and make their way over to us. I recognize Marc from the bar, but if I had met the other brother on the street, I would think they were twins. Oliver doesn't look like either of them so I would have never guessed they were brothers.

"Nice to see you again, Macey." Marc extends his hand for me to shake it before gesturing to the man standing next to him. "This here is my brother, Thomas. Peyton's husband."

"Nice to finally meet you, Macey," Thomas says.

My eyes find Oliver and my brows pinch together in accusation. Has he been talking about me with them? What has he told them?

Marc leans in to whisper in my ear as if he can sense exactly what I'm thinking. "Trust me, he's only said good things about you."

"Good to know." I nod.

Oliver hasn't moved from his spot in the middle of the living room. He's just standing back and witnessing everything unfold in front of his eyes. He looks happy but also anxious, as if me meeting his family and close friends is something he's equally excited and nervous about.

The way the two of us keep our eyes locked together also tells me that neither of us want to screw this up.

He finally breaks the spell to ask, "Where's Kenzie?"

I shake my head and smile, because I can't believe we've been here for as long as we have and she still hasn't told him she hates that nickname. I think it's adorable, but I know deep down she doesn't care for it.

"I'm here," she announces as she enters and eyeballs the crowd of people. "Hi! I'm Mackenzie."

For the next few minutes, everyone goes around in a circle and introduces themselves to her. Their faces light up to match hers with how happy she is to be surrounded by so many new people.

Peyton finally introduces James to us and that's when Mackenzie's eyes brighten. She loves kids so much and I just know this is making her so happy.

Oliver leans in to whisper in my ear, "I think they like her already."

I didn't even realize he was standing next to me. Arms crossed over his chest, eyes fixed on the crew with my daughter, and a wide grin on his face like a proud…

Why did my brain automatically go to the word *dad*?

Oliver and I aren't together and we won't be ever. Maybe it's the sting in my chest remembering that Mackenzie will never know what it's like to have one. I want to be able to give her that someday, but my heart is just not open for that kind of commitment right now.

I know deep down that I have to fix my own life and get my feet planted firmly before I allow anyone to break down these walls.

"Is everyone ready to eat?" I announce, ignoring this feeling swirling around my gut.

For the past hour, we sat around Oliver's giant kitchen table, laughing so hard that my stomach actually hurts, which is such a damn good feeling.

I've learned a lot about these girls during that time. Peyton just opened her daycare center and has been so busy but she's loving every second of it. She even offered Mackenzie to come and hang out there whenever she wanted, which she was over the moon with the invitation to go 'volunteer' there… aka play with the other kids.

She's always had a soft spot for them.

Avery and Marc are engaged but don't have a single plan in place for the actual wedding despite Peyton's protest to just 'get it over with already.' Avery says she just wants to elope and call it a day because she's never had the desire to even have a wedding, but Marc feels the complete opposite.

Kali is definitely the more level-headed one in the group for sure. She will tell it to the girls straight and put each of them in their place, but I can also tell she's a great friend. She does it all strictly out of love.

It doesn't sound like she's got a boyfriend or anything. She even mentioned in conversation how she might want to write a book one day.

Once dinner is done, Mackenzie and James run off to her room for the puzzle she had set up for him to work on together. She didn't care about anything else today other than doing that with him, despite having never met him.

But that's who she is. *My sweet girl.*

"Did it hurt?" Avery asks Marc. "When I told you to google it and I was right?"

"You literally had me google *why can't I own a red panda*. Which was stupid to begin with," Marc tosses back.

"But I was right when I said they are protected by the law in the countries that they originally come from."

Marc just shakes his head in disbelief as the table roars in laughter at the wild things she comes up with. I can't help but laugh too. Avery is most definitely that wild friend that every friend group needs.

"Macey, those were the best damn tacos I have ever had," Avery says, changing the subject as she sits back in her chair and rubbing her stomach like she's full.

"I agree," Peyton adds. "Probably the best vegan tacos I've ever had."

"Way better than Old Jose," Kali says.

"I don't know what that is, but thank you. I'm glad you all enjoyed them."

"Oh my god," Peyton groans. "Old Jose is like the best Mexican restaurant here in the city. We go every week for girls' night for tequila and taco Tuesday."

"Tacos and tequila solve all life's problems," Avery adds.

"You should go with them one night," Oliver interjects.

"You took the words right out of my mouth, Oliver!" Peyton exclaims. "You have to come hang out with us."

I shake my head. "I appreciate that. But I can't. I don't have any family or anyone here in the city to watch Mackenzie for—"

Oliver cuts me off, "You have me."

My head snaps in his direction, everyone goes silent and my throat all of sudden feels extremely dry. I swear I even hear a fork drop against a plate as if someone was mid-bite and just as shocked as I am right now.

It wasn't an offer. It was him volunteering himself to hang with her, no questions asked. If there was a single part of me that felt like she was a burden on him, it's out the window because those three words just told me he *wants* her here.

"Yeah?" The only word I can manage to get out.

He sighs. "Yeah, Macey."

Shit. I feel like I might have just offended him. I know he's told me he likes having us here, but my anxiety gets the best of me most of the time and I always think the worst of everything.

I can't help I'm in a constant state of worrying about what others think or that I'm a problem. Feeling like a burden when you live under the roof of two people who are supposed to love you unconditionally no matter what will do that to you.

"That settles it." Avery claps her hands together, breaking the tension. "You're freaking in for girls' night, babe."

Peyton pulls out her phone, swiping it open. "We need your phone number. We're going to add you to our *Girl Gang* text chat we have going."

"Emiline is in it too," Avery says. "I don't think you've met her yet but she's just as cool as us."

"It's a shame she has to study tonight. I would have loved to meet her," I say.

"Studying," Avery scoffs at the same time she throws up air quotes and shoots me an exaggerated eye roll.

"What does that mean?" Marc asks her as concern washes over him.

"It means nothing," Peyton hisses at her through gritted teeth. "It means she needs to go to bed early because she's tired from work."

My eyes bounce around to everyone at the table, trying to figure out what that's all about.

So… is she not studying?

Marc and Thomas pull out their phones and begin texting a mile a minute when a few seconds later, they both groan.

"Logan isn't answering his phone," Thomas starts.

"I'm going to fucking kill him," Marc rasps.

Kali leans in to me. "We all think that their friend Logan has a thing for Emiline. Avery *assumes* they're together tonight and that's why they aren't here. I, for one, really do think she's studying but Em tends to keep some of her life hush-hush."

"Ooh. That's… interesting." I lightly chuckle.

"It's actually hysterical how much these guys get all wound up over it," Kali says.

"Let's go," Marc announces. "I'm going to his apartment right now."

"I'm in." Thomas stands next, grabbing his jacket off the back of the chair.

"I'm not," Peyton announces. "I'm going home and going to bed. Let those two live their lives. Plus, I doubt they're even together right now. You need to stop being the big bad wolf and let her study in peace."

"That's my baby sister, Pey." Thomas kisses her forehead. "He knows she's off limits."

"I'm going home too," Avery adds next, not allowing Peyton to get another word in. "Leave her be. Girls have needs too."

Oliver's fingers find his ears, and he makes a cringe face. "This is all too much for me."

Both men stand up and grab their jackets, ignoring both Peyton and Avery's protest in leaving them alone. Except, I can't see either of them winning this argument and actually going to Logan's apartment because these girls have these guys wrapped around their fingers.

"It was so nice to meet you, Macey." Thomas gives me a goodbye hug. "Thank you for dinner. It was perfect."

"Sorry we have to rush out of here." Marc hugs me next. "I agree with him. Dinner was perfect."

"Are you heading out too?" I ask Oliver.

"Nah." He laughs as he makes his way to the kitchen to start doing the dishes. "They have it handled."

The girls hug me and say their goodbyes and warmth fills every part of me when they squeeze me like I'm officially their new best friend. A group of people I just met a few hours ago, hugging me goodbye. This might seem so minuscule to people but having no one hug me for so many years other than my daughter, it's like being wrapped up in a warm, heated blanket.

And these people mean it.

They love with their whole heart.

They accept me just the way I am, confirming even more that I think I've found the place I want to permanently call home.

CHAPTER NINETEEN

Macey

"Can we *pleaseeee* have breakfast for dinner?" Mackenzie begs.

"Of course." I can't help but laugh. Doesn't she realize I will give her whatever she wants, whenever she wants? "What did you want me to make?"

"*I* want to make my famous French toast." She beams. "I haven't made it since we moved here and this kitchen is screaming for me to make it."

She's right, this kitchen begs to be cooked in any chance it can.

Next to working in a five-star restaurant, this kitchen is a dream.

"Alright, babe. You're on." I take a seat on the bar stool. "Show me what you got."

"Yes!" Mackenzie pumps her fist in the air as if she's succeeded in persuading me.

She asks Echo to play songs by Taylor Swift and within seconds, the *Reputation (Taylor's Version)* album blasts through the speakers that Oliver has placed all around. It almost sounds like a concert here when they go off.

I watch as she dances through the kitchen, pulling out the

pan she's going to use before she pulls out her ingredients. If anyone ever found out my eight year old is using a stove and cooking French toast, I might get some judgment again.

But she's good at it, and I fully trust her.

Besides, she has so much life in her lately and I've never seen her happier than she is here in this new environment.

"Samuel called me this morning to ask how my first week of school went," she says as she pulls a loaf of wheat bread out of the pantry.

Guilt creeps into my chest because I haven't called either Samuel or Flora since I've been here. They've played such a pivotal role in my life in accepting us and helping us get our feet on the ground, and now it's been almost three weeks since we left Roxbury and I haven't called them once.

"I feel terrible I haven't called them yet."

"He knows you've been busy getting ready to interview for your job." She shrugs. "I miss watching *Friends* and his TV shows with him each night, but I don't miss that school. I love it here."

"That makes me so happy." I force a feeble smile. "They were really good people to help us out. We'll have to go up there and visit them sometime."

"That's what I said to him! He said they will make a trip down here one day soon to visit wherever you get a job. He said he wants to see the best chef in the city work her magic. His words, not mine."

I offer her a soft smile. "I have to get the job first."

"You're *going* to get the job, Mom. I think everyone knows this but you. Duh."

I laugh at that.

But I also hate myself for it.

I'm so sick and tired of not believing in myself when everyone else does. I've been wired all the wrong ways. I've been made to believe I'm not worthy of having anything I want in life.

But Mackenzie believes in me.

Flora and Samuel believe in me.

Oliver believes in me.

All the most important people in my life.

"You're right, babe." I rise from the chair to round the island before I bring her body into mine for a long embrace. "Thank you for that. I needed that kick in the butt to remind myself."

"I won't actually kick you in the butt." She laughs as she returns the hug.

"You little jokester. Back to cooking. It's almost dinner time and I'm willing to bet you're starving because I know how you get when dinner time rolls around."

"Yeah, I get *hangry,*" she retorts. "Is this pan big enough?"

"It's perfect."

She continues her prepping and my phone dings in my pocket with a text.

OLIVER

On a scale of 0-10, 10 being absolutely... How ready are you for your interview Monday?

I can't help but smile down at my phone.

I'm beyond ready for my interview, but it doesn't lessen the anxiety I have in my gut that I might not be good enough and that they might see I don't have enough experience for the position. As annoyed as I was about it being pushed back a week, it worked out for the best.

I give myself a 6 on that scale.

OLIVER

We need you at a 10.

My plans tonight actually include a deluxe breakfast for dinner made by Mackenzie and then looking up interview questions they might ask me on my laptop for the rest of the evening.

Then I should be at a 10.

It's true.

As far as the cooking aspect of the interview goes, I'm as prepared as I can be. I've been practicing and studying fine dining cooking for years. I even downloaded the restaurant's menu and studied it from top to bottom. Everything on it is fairly easy to make and I'm eager to learn how they put their own spin on each item.

It's the questions part of the interview that has me stumped.

What will they ask me? How will I answer them?

Will they ask me why I didn't attend a famous culinary school?

Will that be why I don't get the job?

OLIVER

Just be yourself. They're going to love you if you just do that.

I stare at the words, unable to find anything to reply to that.

Just be yourself. They're going to love you.

His words of encouragement are everything I've ever wanted in life. Only further confirming the tightness in my chest filled with feelings I might have for my roommate. It's only been three damn weeks and he has a complete chokehold on my life.

"Mom," Mackenzie cuts through my thoughts. "How many pieces do you want?"

I've been in my own little texting bubble, I forgot she was even making dinner.

I'm lucky she didn't burn the place down while I wasn't paying attention.

"I'll have two." I smile up at her.

She gapes at me as she places a plate of French toast in front of me. "What's with that weird look on your face?"

"I don't have a weird look on my face."

"You do. You're all… smiley and giddy. Is Ollie texting you?"

"What? No. I mean. Yes. No," I stutter, because this is new territory for us. I've never been in a relationship since having her. I've never had a situation like this arise around her.

"I hope it was." She winks and she takes the seat next to me at the counter to eat her dinner.

My freakin' *eight-year-old* daughter just winked at me.

"Do you like living here with him?" I ask reluctantly.

"I love it," she says without an ounce of hesitation. "I really like Ollie too. He's so funny to be around. I hope we get to stay here for good."

"We can't stay in his apartment for good."

"Why not?"

"Because he's being really nice by helping us get situated and our feet on the ground until I get a job. I'm sure he'll want his space back."

"Doubt it." She shrugs before putting another massive bite of food in her mouth.

I don't ask her what she means by that because I don't want her confirming more feelings I already have for him, feelings I've been dodging left and right because I shouldn't be feeling them.

Instead I just focus on finishing the dinner she made for us. After a few minutes of silence and the two of us finishing dinner, she goes to put her dishes in the sink and retreat to her room.

"Hey, Mackenzie?" I call out.

"Yeah?"

"I just want to tell you that I love you."

She offers me a beaming smile. "I love you more, Mom." And then she's off to her room to do her own thing.

I find my place on the couch and watch reruns of *Grey's Anatomy*, my guilty pleasure, and pull out my laptop to research some questions.

I must have fallen asleep about two episodes in because I'm woken up by my laptop being removed from my lap and a thick warm blanket being draped on top of me. My eyes never fully open to see who it is, but a smile spreads across my lips anyway.

"Sweet dreams," Oliver whispers.

I snuggle into the blanket, and then feel his lips on my forehead.

Something tells me that nothing I do can stop me from falling for my roommate.

CHAPTER TWENTY

Macey

PEYTON

Good luck on your interview today, Macey!

AVERY

OH MY GOD. THAT'S TODAY. YES YES!!

PEYTON

Relax.

AVERY

YOU'RE GOING TO NAIL IT!

KALI

But really why are we screaming like this.

AVERY

I WANT TO MAKE SURE MY EXCITEMENT FOR HER IS SHOWING THROUGH TEXT. FUCK RIGHT OFF. BOTH OF YOU.

KALI

Please do what we do and just ignore her. You don't need luck because they'll hire you on the spot. You got this, babe.

EMILINE

Yes! You got this, Macey! The job is going to be yours!

PEYTON

We're so proud of you.

Ever since the girls added me to their group chat at dinner on Tuesday, my phone has been going absolutely haywire all day, every day. At first, it was weird because I use my phone so little that my battery can last for about three days. Now it's dead by two in the afternoon.

But something about this group of girls has me feeling more and more at home.

I finally feel like I might fit in somewhere.

I finally feel like my past isn't at the forefront of my life filled with people criticizing me.

The group chat is called *Girl Gang* but they should really consider renaming it to *Hype Squad* because these girls are constantly lifting each other up.

One day, Kali barely got any sleep and she sent a text about how she's pulling herself out of bed to go get coffee down the block. Everyone hyped her up for just getting out of bed to get coffee. I couldn't help but laugh. *That's* who these girls are.

I eventually learned through texts that Emiline works at the hospital in the Emergency Department, and when she has a rough shift, the girls are right there listening to her and making her feel better about whatever it is despite not understanding a damn thing she's talking about with her medical jargon.

It took a few days for me to open up. I felt weird and out of place in the group still, especially since I haven't met Emiline in person yet. But a few days ago, I finally opened up about this interview and my nerves surrounding it. Since then, I've been bombarded with nothing but positivity from them.

It makes me feel… at peace.

It makes me feel like this could possibly be a long term friend group for me.

It makes me feel like I have some type of family here.

I fire off a quick thank you text to them and begin to rummage through my closet to try and find something somewhat presentable to wear for this interview. Unfortunately, I don't own many clothes since I didn't leave Montana with much to begin with.

It's a five-star restaurant, so how bad is it going to make me look when I show up in dark wash jeans and a floral t-shirt? I mean, I'll likely be wearing a pair of black work pants and a shirt they provide for me anyway.

This is what I hate most about our situation.

The only money I have right now, is everything I saved up from working at the Bar and Grill, nothing more since I haven't been working since I got here. Things in the city are not cheap. So heading out to spend our savings to find an outfit I'll likely only wear one time was not happening.

Oliver has been a true blessing when it comes to making sure the two of us are fed. I've been great about walking everywhere with Mackenzie, even to and from school so that we aren't paying for taxis.

A knock on my door startles me and I jump at the sound, hand grasping my chest when I look down and realize I'm not even wearing a bra. The only thing I have on is an oversized tee that hangs low enough to cover my sleep shorts making it look like I have no pants on.

"Yeah?" I call out nervously.

The door squeaks open and Oliver stops dead in his tracks as soon as his sight lands on me. Hand still gripping the door, he trails his eyes down my body. All of a sudden, I'm having trouble breathing and I feel my nipples harden under my shirt despite the heat being on in the apartment.

Slowly, his tongue slides along his lower lip as he wets his lips, swallowing before he says, "Well… good morning."

The man staring at me now is doing something to me that I just can't explain. A strong desire pools in my gut, wanting his hands all over me. My brain fires off thoughts of what it would feel like if he pressed his lips to mine.

Stop, Macey.

Turn it off.

That's your freakin' roommate!

"It's customary to say good morning back when someone says it to you." Oliver smirks. "Or I mean… say anything at all."

"I'm sorry. Yes. Hi. Good morning."

A soft chuckle escapes him before he finally steps fully into my room.

"What are you doing?" I ask.

"I came to see what *you* were doing."

A smile stretches across my lips. "I'm just trying to get ready for my interview."

"Do you have something picked out yet?"

I shake my head. "I'm trying to figure that out now."

"Perfect."

Oliver runs out of my room and I'm left standing there, staring at the open door wondering what the hell that was all about. One minute he's there, the next he's gone with no context whatsoever.

I finally snap myself out of the trance and get back to my closet to look for the nicest shirt I own when I hear a throat clear. Like a magician, he's standing in the same spot he just was but this time holding a black garment bag.

"Stop looking. I got you something."

My gaze dances back and forth between him and the bag he's showcasing in the air. "A ball gown isn't what I need for this interview," I joke.

"Damn. Really? So you think I should return it."

I blink without being able to find the words to answer him.

"It's not a ball gown," he tosses back. "I had a custom-made suit made for you."

"A what?"

"It's a suit. For your interview."

"Why did you do that?"

"Because I wanted to." He shrugs. "And you know that I—"

"Don't do anything you don't want to do," I finish for him. "But Oliver, you really didn't have to do that. Besides, you're already doing more than enough letting us stay here and I'm not paying for anything yet. I don't want to be your charity case."

"Is that what you feel like you are?" He takes small, slow strides as the words come out of his mouth.

I can't reply. I can't fill my lungs with enough air to even breathe with him closing the distance between us. My palms feel sweaty, my heart galloping in my chest at an uncontrollable speed. I feel like I'm going to pass out.

How does *one man* have the ability to affect me the way he is right now?

Oliver's hand rises to grip my chin between his fingers. "The last fucking thing I ever want you to think you are, is a charity case, Macey Evans." He practically growls it and that does it. My insides summersault and goosebumps race across my skin. "I didn't buy this for you because that's what I thought you were. I bought it because I want you to feel good going into your interview. I drove you here with a single suitcase for you and one half the size of that for Mackenzie. I had a gut feeling that there wasn't anything in either of those that would make you feel ready to nail this interview."

I shake my head while his fingers still have a grip on my chin. "That's all we had."

"And that's all you needed."

I blink back the tears that are fighting like hell to break free. "It feels wrong to accept it when I'm already living here rent free."

"Unfortunately for you"—he offers me a smile—"I don't take no for an answer when I'm giving out gifts. No take backs."

"Did you just say, 'no take backs'?"

"I did." Oliver nods before lifting his chin in defiance. "And I stand by it."

Before I can even reply, he's out the door. Leaving me there shocked by his generosity.

Something I'll never get used to.

Whenever I received a gift in the past, there was always an ulterior motive behind it.

One time my parents gave me the gift of a night to attend a special cooking class in town. I remember so vividly how excited I was and how hopeful I felt that maybe they wanted to see me achieve the dream I set when I was a young girl.

Instead, they wanted me out of the house so they could convince Mackenzie to go with them to get a haircut. They cut off almost all of her hair to shoulder length when I was dead set on letting her grow it because it was *her* wish to keep it long.

My little five-year-old girl cried in my pillow for hours that night and ended up sleeping in my room for a month. I will never forget that night and how broken I felt for my baby girl.

Except Oliver isn't them. There's no part of me that believes he has a motive behind this gift. He's doing it because he cares, because he wants to.

I finally shake off the thoughts of my past that tend to send me down a spiral and quickly jump in the shower so I'm not late for my first interview. That would probably be the worst first impression ever made.

I can't stop thinking about my roommate though.

The hot water cascades down my back while I think dangerous thoughts about his hands all over me, about how it would feel to have someone like him touch me in places that haven't been touched in a very long time.

The thing is, I know this man knows his way around a woman's body. Call it judging a book by its cover or whatever you want. But just looking at Oliver, I know he would know what to do if he was given the chance.

My fingers brush over my hardened nipples and I groan in

pleasure at the sensation. I've never really touched myself like this before because when you live under your parents watchful, narcissistic eyes, you're very careful about anything you do under their roof that they could hold against you.

These thoughts about Oliver while my hands brush across my nipples are very new to me. But it's also a boundary I don't want to cross. With every day that passes, it's becoming more and more difficult to stop thinking about him as if something more will ever come out of it.

My fingers graze over my stomach. A stomach that created life, and kept my girl safe for nine months. A stomach that was stretched to the max with a nine-pound bundle of love. A stomach that is littered with tiger stripes as a testament to all I've been through, reminding me that I did it all on my own.

I don't hate my stomach. At least, not anymore.

I've learned to love and embrace every single mark that I've earned.

But what would a man like Oliver think about the imperfect scars scattered around my midsection? My guess is that it's a far cry away from the woman he's used to.

Before I find myself inside an emotional bubble, I turn off the water and step out. Only to realize I forgot my stupid towel in my room. I call out for Mackenzie and she doesn't answer. It has to be those stupid headphones she always has in.

I grab a small hand towel on the sink and use it to cover my lady bits as best I can. The door creaks open slowly as I peek out to see if I have a clear view to my room to run quickly so no one sees.

I cover my chest and take three giant steps in the hallway when a body collides with mine. Strong hands that I was just fantasizing in the shower about, grip both of my biceps while his eyes bore into mine. He's refusing to look anywhere but my eyes, knowing damn well I'm completely naked.

"Macey," Oliver says my name like he's in pain standing here with me.

I press my body harder into him in an effort to hide my naked front. I guess my brain thought the harder I pressed against him, the more he wouldn't be able to see me.

I regret it the second I feel a bulge press into my stomach.

"What. Are. You. Doing?" I whisper-shout.

"What are *you* doing? And why the hell are you naked in the hallway right now?"

"I forgot a towel. And keep your voice down. Mackenzie is in her room."

His head falls back, his eyes shut and his hands grip my biceps harder. "You're killing me, Macey."

The feeling is so mutual.

"Please don't open your eyes," I plead with him.

"As much as I'm dying to open them right now." He smirks. "I won't."

Slowly Oliver takes a few steps back and I notice he's bringing me towards my room. I stay pressed into him, mirroring his footsteps.

"I'm going to keep my eyes closed and you're going to scurry your pretty little ass into that room and get ready for your interview. Got it?"

I nod, despite that he can't see me. However, my body can't help but become reignited from the words that come out of his mouth. *Pretty little ass.*

He releases me and I run into my room, closing the door and pressing my back against it as I let out a sigh of relief. I'm still struggling to control my breathing because I don't know how much he saw.

I was on the verge of touching myself in the shower and then *he* touched my very naked body.

"And Macey?" he calls out.

"Yeah?" My voice cracks as the word leaves me.

"I came to wish you good luck. I didn't tell you when I was in here before and I just wanted to be sure I told you before you leave. You're going to kill it and the job will be yours."

My heart fucking soars.

He came here to wish me luck at my interview.

"That really means a lot, Oliver." I clear my throat as I swallow past the dryness. "Thank you."

"You're amazing. Just remember that."

Then I hear his footprints take off down the hall.

I can't help but think that he just walked away with another piece of my heart in his hands for the keeping.

CHAPTER TWENTY-ONE

Oliver

I think I'm just as anxious as Macey about waiting to hear about whether she got the job. Mostly because I've never wanted to see someone achieve their dreams the way I want to see her do it. It's been four days since her interview on Monday, and I just want today to be the day she gets the call.

Now that I'm showered and shaved for the day, I head to the kitchen to find her in, hopes we can do something today while Mackenzie is at school.

Once I step foot in the living room, I find myself rooted in place, staring at her in the same way I have been doing way too much lately. Since I slammed into her in the hallway after her shower incident, my brain shifted into wanting to be even closer to her.

My body lights up when it's in contact with hers. Even if it's just a shoulder bump.

Something I've never had with *any* woman I've slept with before.

Something I've never *wanted* this much with another woman before.

The women I've been with before were always a one-and-done type of thing. I'm not ashamed to admit that—it was my past. We never kept in contact and I rarely exchanged numbers with any of them. For the most part, I met them on my travels anyway.

Since Macey walked into my life, I've had no desire to look at another woman. Having her in my thoughts with my hand around my cock has worked. For now.

And to think... I haven't even slept with Macey.

She moves freely around the kitchen. She's dressed casual today in a pair of black leggings with an oversized, charcoal-colored sweater that covers almost all of her legs because of her petite frame.

Unfortunately for me, it hides the curves of her body that I would give anything to have my hands on again. But there's something about the way she wears dark colors that brings out the bright green color in her eyes.

I bring my gaze to Macey's face and her hair falls down her back in loose, shiny curls.

What I would give to have that hair wrapped around my fist.

I finally break myself out of the hypnotic trance she has me in, adjusting the brim of my glasses. I didn't bother with contacts this morning since I've been editing pictures all morning.

"Let me ask you something," I start as I enter the kitchen. Macey jumps slightly at my lack of introduction. "Have you had a bagel in the city yet?"

"I've had bagels before."

"But have you had a *New York City* bagel," I emphasize.

"No?" Her eyebrows pinch together.

I swipe my wallet off the island and stuff it in my back pocket. "Grab your jacket. Let's go."

"What? I just had a coffee. I don't need a bagel. Really, I'm fine," Macey continues to protest.

I grab my camera bag next because I rarely leave the house without it. "Would you just trust me?"

Her eyes slightly widen just for a heartbeat before they

soften. A smile creeps up her cheeks and watching her relax for me has my pulse skyrocketing.

"Okay," she agrees, grabbing her jacket from the back of the chair at the counter and triple checking to make sure she has her phone on her.

I knew the exact place I wanted to take her for her first city bagel and it was about a ten-minute walk from my apartment. Strangely, we walked in silence which is sort of new for me. When did I start getting nervous around a woman and had nothing to say?

Macey makes me worry for the first time that something I say might mess everything up or scare her away.

She grabs us a small booth in the corner of the deli while I grab us the bagels. Once we sit down, she dives into her bagel like it's the first meal she's had in days, devouring it like her life depends on it.

And fuck, a woman who loves food the way I love food is one after my own heart.

"This is without a doubt the best bagel I've ever had," she says through a mouthful of cream cheese goodness.

I hit her with a wink and smile before taking another bite of mine.

"I'm sorry. I probably look like such a slob."

"Impossible."

She blushes, but her phone vibrates and she jumps to grab it and see if it's a phone call. But the look of disappointment takes over when she realizes that it's just a text message.

I lean in, resting my elbows on the table to get close to her. "Relax, Macey. You have to know you're going to get the job."

She sighs. "You don't know that. The interview went really well. I answered all the questions that Frank asked me honestly. I met the staff and even saw the kitchen. And how cute that it's named after Frank's wife, Mollie. My god, Oliver…" She beams through her ramble. "You should have seen this kitchen. You were right about how fancy it is. I've never wanted something as bad as I want this. I'm absolutely terrified that I'm going to screw this up the way I always screw everything up."

She can't mean that.

Since I've known her, there has been nothing she's screwed up. Our first encounter left me wondering what was going on in her life. She had this sad look in her eyes and was in a state of worry the entire flight. I've slowly watched her free herself from whatever had her locked up in chains and kept her from her fullest potential.

"I don't know what to say because I don't know what you're talking about when you say you screw everything up."

Macey wipes the corner of her mouth with a napkin and finishes her current bite. "I know you don't know me well enough…"

"After our Monday morning run-in, I think I know you a little better now," I interrupt her with a wink.

"Very funny." She gives me a cheeky grin, playfully slapping my forearm. "My past isn't something I've come to terms with yet. But it's what's shaped me into the person I am today."

I swallow, sitting back in my chair. "I really want to ask more, Macey. But I don't want you to talk about things you're not comfortable with or anything that is going to bring you down. That's not what this morning is supposed to be."

"Is that the reason you haven't asked me about why I left Montana? Or about Mackenzie's dad? Or about my parents?"

Macey rattles off the questions as if she's offended that I haven't asked about any of those things yet. I didn't think we were on that level with each other and the last thing I wanted was to make her upset.

"Listen. Ever since I walked on that plane a couple months ago and started talking to you, I've made it my mission to make you smile because it's so fucking beautiful when you do, Macey." I can't help but smile just thinking about it. "So yeah, that's why I don't ask and don't bring it up. Not because I don't want you to talk about it, but because I see the sadness in your eyes most days. I don't want to be the person to put any more hurt in those eyes."

"You don't?"

I shake my head. "I don't. I never want to be that person."

A few heartbeats pass before she finally speaks again. "I left Montana to run away from my parents and the life I had with them."

My breath catches in my throat as my nerves stand at full attention.

Was she in trouble? Was someone hurting her?

"I pray you never have to meet them," she continues. "They're the epitome of controlling and manipulating. The day I found out I was pregnant, I was basically disowned as their daughter. Yet, at the same time, I was in total lockdown with no freedom to grow into who I wanted to be. They had to make sure I was living how *they* wanted me to live."

I raise a brow in confusion.

"I know that really doesn't make much sense." She lets out a nervous laugh. "But the day before I found out about the pregnancy, was the last time I ever heard the words 'I love you' spoken out of their mouths to me. That was the last hug I ever got from them. They stopped being my parents and just became my keepers. They made sure I did everything they told me to do, and that included raising Mackenzie to their expectations."

I don't answer.

I can't answer.

How could anyone ever do that to their child? It makes me sick.

"It shaped me into this person that I never wanted to be. I now live in fear. I live with anxiety. I walk on eggshells waiting for rock bottom to strike again." She pauses, exhaling a long draw out breath. "I told myself that *when* I make it to New York City, I'll never let myself get back to that again. Needless to say, the fear of me not getting this job is real. This job has the opportunity to catapult me into the direction I so desperately crave to reach, to finally give us the life I've always dreamed about. One that Mackenzie deserves. So the thought of never getting there makes me sick."

"This all makes so much sense."

"What does?"

"Your parents and how they've treated you." I reach across the table, taking both of her hands in mine in hopes that she feels comfort in the words coming out of my mouth. "You've never had anyone believe in you. You've always had to believe in yourself and sometimes that's just not enough."

"Wow… uh. Yeah. That's. Yeah." She's completely stunned speechless.

"And I've eaten food you've cooked, remember? You're fucking good. Like really good, Macey. But there's a lot more to that industry than just making good food."

"What's that?"

"Passion," I fire back quickly. "You love being in the kitchen. I've seen first-hand how your face lights up when you enter mine. I see the shift in your entire day when you're making something. Anything. And that right there is why you're going to become a top chef in this city."

Macey blinks back tears I can tell she's fighting to hold in, just as she averts her gaze out the window to the busy sidewalk. "I want that," she says barely above a whisper before she turns to look back at me. "I love cooking and everything about it."

"Then screw anything that's ever happened before today and keep doing what makes you happy."

"I mean not everything. You happened before today and I can't screw that."

My eyes widen, and a sly smirk causes one side of my lip to tip up. "I mean…"

Her hand covers her mouth almost instantly. "Oh my god. I didn't mean it like that. Jesus, what is wrong with me?"

"Just know the invitation is always there."

"Oliver!" Macey swats my arm.

"It's a joke. It's a joke." I laugh. "Roommate things. Wink-wink."

She laughs with me, but doesn't acknowledge my joke. "On a very real note… thank you, Oliver. For letting me get all of that out with you. I didn't mean to unload all my life on you and spill about all my rock bottoms."

"I'm always here to listen." I nod. "But while we're on the topic… what's the situation with Mackenzie's dad?"

"He's completely out of the picture."

I release a breath I didn't realize I was even holding. Thankful that he isn't like some deranged stalker that she's running away from.

"He's been absent since the day after I found out I was pregnant. He wanted nothing to do with her. He's never even met her."

"He's really missing out," I say

"He is. I really thought I loved him, you know. That stupid high school love. Then again, what the hell do I know? My own parents couldn't love me," she huffs out an annoyed breath. "If there's one thing my life has taught me, it's how to love someone properly. Which is basically doing everything they didn't. She is the definition of real love."

Every moment I spend with Mackenzie, I understand exactly what she's saying. She's not my daughter, but I've grown a super soft spot for her. Dare I say, I'll protect her at all costs while she's living under my roof? She's smart, witty, funny as hell and easy to talk to.

"He did you a favor. Fuck that guy."

Macey laughs. "You're right, he did do me a favor. I can't imagine what life would be like if he stuck around. What Mackenzie would be like." She shakes her head. "Last I heard, he went down a really bad path of drugs and alcohol right out of high school. I'm not sure anyone has heard from him or knows where he is."

"Yup. He definitely did you both a favor."

I want to be a selfish asshole right now and admit that he did *me* a favor too. If he never walked out of their lives, she wouldn't be living in my apartment. The entire trajectory of her life wouldn't have put her on that plane and our paths crossed in the first place.

Macey doesn't answer, so I continue, "I didn't mean to make breakfast turn into such a deep conversation. I'm sorry if I brought you down at all today by bringing up your past. It wasn't my intention. I just really wanted to distract you today."

"Yeah?" Her smile comes back. "That was your motive?"

I grab the camera off the booth next to my lap. "Yup. And to see you smile more." I raise the camera and shoot it directly at her and snap a picture before her body has a chance to respond. Capturing the most candid, perfect smile from her.

"You know… Mackenzie is obsessed with your camera. She never stops talking about it."

"One day, we'll have to get her one."

Something washes over her and I'm not sure what. But the smile falls the smallest bit, leaving her with a reluctant, almost fake one. Maybe it's the way I've worded what I said, or maybe it's the talk of spending money like that. I don't know, but I'm also not about to find out right now.

"One day," Macey finally says before she takes the last bite of her bagel.

It's time to turn this day around.

"I meant what I said, Macey. I want you to forget about everything that happened before today. Except me of course." I wink again. "You're on track to do something really fucking big. I'm insanely proud of you."

"You're a really good guy, you know that?"

Only for you, I want to say.

I stand from the booth, looping my backpack over one shoulder and reaching my arm out for her to take my hand. "I want to show you something."

Macey's eyes move from my hand to my eyes like she's questioning if she wants to trust me on this.

"Trust me?"

She doesn't say the words, but her hand clasps mine and she stands from the booth.

I don't release her hand for the next twenty minutes because it's a physical touch that I've craved lately. It just feels too good to have her hand in mine.

She still has no idea where we're going as we ride the elevator seventy stories up at the Rockefeller Center. Honestly, this place is one that everyone needs to visit if they ever make it to the city.

I've even blogged about *The Top of the Rock* when I first started. I know she hasn't been here yet in the small exploring she's done with Mackenzie because most people new to the city don't know unless they look it up.

Once the elevator doors open to the panoramic views of the city, Macey steps out, her eyes wide as she slowly circles and takes in everything she can. Her hair dances angelically in the cool breeze and this is the freest I've seen her since she got here.

Like she just stepped into her future.

I pull my camera from my backpack and I snap a few photos of this moment because I want to remember it. I want her to remember it.

"This is incredible," Macey finally says.

"It is." But my eyes haven't looked anywhere but at her. I don't need to.

She's perfect.

She's beautiful.

Without thinking, I step behind her and wrap one arm around her neck. She immediately rests her jaw on the crook of my elbow, relaxing her back into my front as she stares out into the city. Her hands come up to hold my forearm, and she breathes out a sigh of comfort and relief.

My heart is beating so loud that I swear she can hear it.

I lean down to whisper into the shell of her ear. "No more rock bottoms, dragonfly. Welcome to the *Top of the Rock*. This is where you stay for good this time."

She grips my forearm tighter as a silent agreement.

The same way she's slowly gripping my heart.

CHAPTER TWENTY-TWO

Macey

I'm not used to the amount of rain that New York City seems to be getting lately. Oliver says it's unusual for this time of year, but never misses a chance to mention that he's happy it's not snow.

We laugh, the way we do every time he says it.

The way we do so much more lately over just about everything.

On Thursday, he successfully took my mind off the fact that I still hadn't heard about the job. He brought me to the top of the Rockefeller Center to show me the best views of the city, the city that I've dreamed about for so many nights.

Seeing it from that perspective changed something inside of me. I started shifting my mindset and really making this place feel like a home instead of acting like a temporary tourist.

It was the dreamiest day.

From bagels, to the top of the rock, to picking up Mackenzie from school together and the two of them bonding over his camera. They took pictures of the most random things during the walk back to the apartment as I walked a few steps behind them and watched intently.

Feeling my armor slip more and more around him.

I still haven't heard about the job and it's now Saturday. I forced my brain to rewire itself to believe they will call me on Monday, that management is out on the weekends and I'll have an answer for sure at the start of the week

Look at me talking myself out of anxiety.

I sit up from Mackenzie's bed where we are watching one of her favorite movies for the millionth time to check my phone out of habit. I've been in her room since I woke up because her stomach has been bothering her on and off all night.

She might be getting too old to cuddle, but when she's sick, it's exactly what she needs.

"Mom, stop checking your phone every two seconds," she scolds me. "You're going to get the job. Just relax."

I snuggle back into the pillow with my phone in hand, swiping away the notification that reads thirty texts from the girls' group chat. They are likely asking for an update the way they have every day since the interview. I'm so damn thankful for this new found friendship in these girls and their support.

"I'm just nervous, babe," I admit to her. "I want it more than I've wanted anything before."

"I know. But you're going to get it. You totally deserve it."

"You think so?"

"I know so." She nods with conviction. "I'm old enough to know things now. You seem a lot happier here."

There's a heavy pit in my stomach wondering what Mackenzie means by that statement. I just stare at her, hoping she keeps going without me having to ask.

"I know how Grandma and Grandpa treated you. It really bothered me and it hurt me a lot. I just kept it all inside because I didn't want to fight with anyone. But I hated seeing you hurt, Mom."

I run the back of my finger along my cheek to catch the tear that escaped. "I didn't want you to know I was hurting."

"I could tell."

"I wish you would have said something, Mackenzie. We would have left sooner."

"I wanted to, a few times." She shakes her head. "I was kinda hoping it would get better. But it didn't."

I've said it before and I'll say it a hundred more times, I am the luckiest mom in the world to have such a smart and intuitive daughter. Moments like these make me feel like I did something right in life.

For once.

"I'm sorry for having an attitude when we left that day. I was tired and grumpy and hungry," Mackenzie says with sincerity.

"So you weren't mad about leaving your school and friends?"

"Nope." She grins with the shake of her head. "I miss them. But I don't miss that life."

"God, I love you so much, babe." I pull her in for a hug. "Thank you for supporting my decision and taking this journey with me and for being so wise beyond your years that we can talk about things like this."

"Always, Mom. I love you too. To the stars, the moon and Jupiter and back."

We both laugh at that as we hold each other tighter, while rain pounds on the windows.

Suddenly, my phone vibrates aggressively on the edge of the bed. I leap up and notice it's not a number I have saved, but it is a New York area code.

"Hello?"

"Hello. Is this Macey?"

I suck in a sharp breath when I hear the female voice. "Yes."

"I'm so sorry to call you on a Saturday afternoon. This was the first chance all week that I've been able to take a minute to call you. I regret to inform you that our position for a new line cook has been filled."

My stomach sinks and my heart breaks into tiny pieces with every word.

"But…" She pauses and I wait intently despite the overwhelming disappointment. "I wanted to offer you a position as sous-chef."

My eyes widen in complete shock. "You want to offer me a sous-chef position?"

Just like that, the same heart that cracked pieces itself back together and beats faster than ever before. They filled the entry-level position, but they want to offer me a level up position.

As a fucking sous-chef.

Holy. Shit.

Mackenzie begins violently jumping up and down on the bed in excitement before she eventually falls on top of it, kicking her legs in the air as she squeals quietly in excitement despite the fact that she has no clue what that even means.

"Yes." The woman on the other end of the line says. "Frank loved meeting you and the work you showcased for us. Oh, I'm Mollie by the way—his wife." She chuckles. I probably should have said that sooner. Anyway, it was a no-brainer to give you the sous-chef position."

"Wow," I breathe out. "Yes. Oh my god, yes. I would be honored to accept the position, Mollie."

"Great! We'll be in touch with you later this week to get more details from you, as well as send you over our more detailed menu so you can familiarize yourself with it. We'd like you to start around the first weekend of March, give or take. Does that work for you?"

"Whatever you need."

"Excellent. Congratulations, Macey." She hangs up before I can process the news fully.

I drop the phone, Mackenzie sits there waiting for me to speak.

"You got the job?"

"I did it." I pause, letting it soak in completely. "I did it. I DID IT!"

She leaps into my arms, wrapping her long legs around my

middle and squeezing me the tightest she's ever hugged me. "I'm so happy for you. You finally made it happen."

I squeeze her back just as hard.

This all started because I wanted to show her anything is possible, and that it's never too late to chase your dreams. Her being here and able to witness it first-hand warms my heart.

I'm overwhelmed with every emotion under the sun.

"You have to go tell Ollie," she says, releasing me.

I kiss her on the forehead and spring out of the room. I round the corner quickly and find Oliver standing in the kitchen before my eyes travel to a small suitcase and his camera bag sitting next to the couch.

I won't lie when I say disappointment engulfs me the same way it did when the lady on the phone said *I regret to inform you.*

I've learned that I don't want to spend time away from him. Especially not right now.

But I have no right to feel that way, this is his job. He doesn't have to tell me where he's going or what he's doing. I'm just his roommate.

"Hey," I say, announcing my presence in the room.

Oliver lifts his head, and a smile hits his lips. "Hey, dragonfly." His eyes never leave mine as he watches me bounce my head from him to the suitcase in the living room. "I'm sorry. I forgot to tell you. I have to leave for two nights to attend a blogger conference."

"A conference," I repeat, trying to process what he just said.

Maybe it's because my mind is still reeling over the fact that I just got my dream job. Or maybe it's because he's standing here in his signature look, this time pairing his dark washed jeans with a long-sleeve Henley. He's rolled the sleeves just enough to expose his corded forearms, making my mouth water at the sight.

"I have to speak at it," he interrupts my thoughts. "It's like a training for bloggers everywhere who are getting started or looking to grow their accounts. People who want to really take off and see success with it. Since my blog has done so well, I was asked to speak and share some tips with the group. It's an opportunity of a lifetime in this industry."

I inhale and exhale once. "That's really awesome."

"Are you alright?" he reluctantly asks.

I can't help but smile, wildly as he stands across the room from me. "I just got a very interesting phone call."

I hold up my phone like I'm the host of a game show at the same time he rounds the island and rushes towards me.

"Yeah?"

"I didn't get the job I interviewed for."

His smile falls and I watch as his jaw hardens. He looks almost… angry for me and I can't help but chuckle.

I clench my fists together, bringing them to my mouth to emphasize my excitement. "They offered me the sous-chef position instead!"

His face morphs into confusion as he reads my expression. Then his eyes widen and I watch as the wheels in his head spin to the words that just came out of my mouth. I almost feel bad for putting him through this small rollercoaster of emotions.

"You're joking!" Oliver says, still trying to read me.

"I'm not," I squeal. "I got the job, Oliver. I got the freakin' job!"

His arms wrap tightly around my waist as he lifts me in the air. My legs wrap around his waist and the contact of his strong arms holding me is enough to make everything inside me explode.

My body feels like a spark, and his touch just set me on fire. I can't help but wrap my arms around him and hold on tight as he buries his head in the crook of my neck.

"You fucking did it," he speaks into my skin and I can feel the heat of his breath only building the fire inside me.

Oliver reluctantly releases his hold on me, and both my feet are planted back on the ground. I immediately feel cold without his touch, which causes me to avert my gaze from him down to my hands nervously.

"I couldn't have done it without you."

"That was all you."

"You brought me here." I look back up at him, his blue eyes searing me. "You made a call to get me an interview in the first place. I owe you so much."

"You don't owe me a damn thing. But…" he drawls. "I'll never turn down one of those epic meals you like to make," he finishes, giving me a wink.

"Consider it done."

Once the words leave my mouth, something in the air shifts. It almost feels as though a window is wide open and the cold, rainy breeze is making its way through the apartment. Or maybe it's that Oliver is still rooted in the same spot, not moving away from me. Not making an effort to go anywhere when he very clearly needs to leave for his trip.

"So you're leaving, huh?"

"I *really* don't want to," he admits without skipping a beat.

"Why not?"

"You won't be there."

That does it.

Desire courses through my veins. I've been fighting the way this man makes me feel since the day he showed up at the bar in the mountains. I knew I felt something on the flight, but seeing him show up there just confirmed so much for me.

Every moment since then has just built up to this moment right now.

Oliver's fingers slowly brush along the apple of my cheek, until he reaches the shell of my ear and trails the tips down to the pounding pulse in my neck.

"Can I tell you something?"

"Anything." My voice is hoarse with emotion.

"I really want to fucking kiss you right now." Oliver waits a few breaths for me to respond, but the only thing I can do is look up at him and smile. "I know it's crossing a line. I know you're technically just supposed to be my roommate and you're trying to get settled in the city. I know I shouldn't"—he steps closer to me and I feel the rate of each breath pick up—"but fuck, Macey. I want to."

I can't find a single word to answer him. I just keep my eyes locked on him while his remain locked on my mouth. I'm unsure what to do or how to navigate this moment since the last time I kissed another man, I was sixteen years old.

Oliver's eyes darken from baby blue to a deep ocean blue as cups my cheeks and brings my face close to his. The smell of peppermint on his breath causes my pulse to skyrocket.

"Fuck it."

His lips crash onto mine, and I feel an explosion happen the second they do. He kisses me with need, like kissing me was the air he needed to breathe. My body melts in his as his hand skates around the back of my head, tangling in my hair as he pulls me closer, closing every inch there is between us.

His tongue swipes along my lips and I open up for him, pressing up on my toes to allow me better access. One he notices, he scoops me up with one arm around my waist and my legs wrap around him again. My core throbs when I feel his muscular stomach between my legs.

Oliver doesn't release his mouth from mine when he places me on the kitchen counter, not letting his body separate from mine for a single second.

Just as he's about to pull away, my hands clasp the sides of his face to hold him there.

I want this moment to last longer.

I don't want this to end with him.

Except we both let go, a smile curling his lips, before he presses one more to my lips.

"What the hell was that?" he asks breathlessly.

Heat builds in my cheeks as I shrug a shoulder.

"Now I'm pissed that I have to leave because I *really* want to keep kissing you."

I don't know why I pick this time to become as bold as I do, but I bring my hand up to his tousled blonde hair and run my hands through it. "Now you have something to look forward to when you get back."

"I'm going to be thinking about this the entire time I'm gone."

"I think I will too," I admit.

"Fuck, you're killing me, Macey." Oliver presses his forehead to mine, his body hasn't left the spot between my legs. "Tell me I didn't ruin everything and you'll be here when I get back."

Do I want to dive into a relationship when I haven't even got my feet planted here yet? When I haven't even started my new job?

I don't know the first thing about being with someone and how to maneuver this. It's not a question I can answer right now.

"I'll be here," is the only answer I have for him.

He presses one more quick kiss to my forehead before he steps away from me. "I'm going to say goodbye to Mackenzie and then I have to head out. Will you two be okay? Do you need anything before I leave?"

I think I need you is the only thing I can't stop thinking about in my head, but I decide against it right now.

"I think we can handle it. Go crush your speech."

Ten minutes later, Oliver is out the door leaving me with an aching sensation between my legs and thoughts of what the two of us could be swirling in my mind.

CHAPTER TWENTY-THREE

Macey

I've been floating around the apartment like I'm on a cloud since Oliver kissed me.

It's been three hours and I already can't wait for him to come back.

I don't know who I've become or who he's turning me into.

I haven't been able to bring my heart rate down since that kiss either. I never in my life thought I would want more with someone after being hurt as bad as I have.

I made it my life mission to focus on Mackenzie. At one point I even said to myself, *'I'll try dating when she goes off to college or something.'* But Oliver has thrown a complete plot twist in my life plans.

My phone buzzes on the kitchen counter and I think it's going to be Oliver but Flora's name flashes on the screen.

"Hey, Flora," I answer.

"You've been gone for a little over a month and you choose *now* to answer the phone all happy and cheery?" she says.

I can't help but laugh. "Nice to hear from you too. How are things going up there?"

"Oh, sweets. You have no idea," she scoffs.

My stomach bottoms out. Did I ruin everything for her when I left?

"Your silence is very loud, Macey dear. Trust me, it's been *very* good."

I breathe out a sigh of relief. "Yeah?"

"We've been so busy in the best way possible. The man who is clearly more than just your friend... made a blog post and our Bar and Grill was featured in it."

"What?" I gasp.

I realized now that since I've been here, I haven't stalked *Notes from Oliver Ford* once. Maybe it's because I'm now living with the blogger extraordinaire? I'm not sure.

"Yup!" she says as I scurry to my broken laptop and flip it open to see what she means. "He said we have the best double bacon cheeseburger in the entire town, that our service is the best he's had in his travels and that it's a must visit restaurant when you swing by town for your skiing adventures."

"He said that?" I click through the windows on my screen to open up his blog. There it is. His entire blog post about Roxbury, New York. Complete with a featured image of the backyard of Flora and Samuels property.

The caption under the image reads '*Image taken by the coolest local girl, Kenzie.*'

My daughter took that picture.

And he featured it on his blog as the header image.

"He sure did," Flora says, cutting through my thoughts. "I saw the perfect post snow sunset photo Mackenzie took with his camera too. She captured the cotton candy skies so perfectly. I'm going to have it printed and framed into a canvas for our living room."

"It's beautiful," I reply in a breathy whisper while my eyes remain locked on the image.

"Enough about work," she says. "How's my girl doing?"

For the next ten minutes I fill her in on how Mackenzie is loving her new school and her new friends. She's made so many since coming here and her grades are better than they have ever been.

She's a true testament of being able to thrive in the right environment.

She was right about what she told Oliver before we even left the mountains.

"We're going to thrive so hard there."

And she is.

"And how about you, sweets?"

"Well…" I pause, my face lighting up with the cheesiest smile despite the fact that she can't see me through the phone. "I got a job."

"Oh, dear," Flora screams. "That's wonderful! Tell me it's a cook position."

"I'm sorry, I wish I could." I giggle. "It's a sous-chef position in one of the city's top-rated restaurants!"

Silence rings through the phone for a few seconds. Just as I'm about to ask if she's still there, I hear sniffles on the other end.

"You did it, baby girl," Flora finally says through a shallow whisper. "I've never been more proud in my entire life."

Tears sting my eyes. Flora isn't my mom, or my grandma, but she's taken me under her wing and loves me as if I was her own. That causes every emotion I've always wanted to feel bubble to the surface.

I catch my tear before it lands on the laptop still sitting on my lap.

"I love you, Flora."

"Oh, sweets. I love you so much. You have no idea how happy this makes me to hear. You chasing your dreams is everything I've always wanted from the moment I laid eyes on you."

I swallow. "I did it."

"You sure as hell did," she exclaims. "Now tell me about the blonde hottie. Is he treating you right?"

My lips immediately twist into a smile at the thought of him, while my eyes remain fixed on a selfie he posted on the back deck of another house I vaguely remember while traveling along the mountain street. It must be Marc and Avery's new house.

"He's one of the good ones, Flora."

"That's all I need to know dear." I can hear the smile in her voice and it warms my heart.

"I have to head back to work, but don't be a stranger," she scolds. "Keep me updated on work! I'm so excited to see you kill it down there."

"Thank you. Tell Samuel we said hi!"

With that, I hang up the phone to finally get to making dinner for us.

Since Mackenzie's stomach is still bothering her, I decide to make some chicken noodle soup for her and a sandwich for myself. I turn on some music and find myself bopping around the kitchen with a smile on my face when Mackenzie enters the kitchen crying.

She's in full on hysterics, clenching her stomach and screaming out in pain.

I rush to her. "What's wrong?"

"I don't know," she cries out louder. "It hurts so bad. I can't take it."

"Where does it hurt this time?"

"Here. Same as before." She holds her lower right stomach. "Ow. Mom. Please help me."

I've never felt so helpless in all my time of being her mom. In the eight years since she's been born, she's never had to go to the hospital or had any type of emergency. The worst we've ever dealt with was some allergies that turned into a cough.

"Do you think we need to go to the hospital?"

"Yes. Please. It hurts so bad I can't stand up. This is so much worse than earlier today."

I don't even bother to clean up the lunch meat I left out before I swipe my bag from the table next to the couch and pick her up bridal style to carry her downstairs. Her tiny arms wrap around my neck as sobs wrack her body harder.

I want to cry myself because there's nothing worse than seeing your baby in pain.

My first thought as the elevator brings us to the first floor is it's her appendix.

Did it rupture? Does she have an infection?

We hail a taxi and take her to the closest emergency room which is four minutes away.

Thank God.

Her pain never once lets up and as soon as we enter the waiting area, she vomits everywhere. The pain is so intense for her little body that it forces her to expel everything she's eaten all day.

"Someone please help me," I cry out now.

A nurse rushes to us, throwing her on a wheelchair and bringing her immediately back into a room. I'm struggling to see through tear filled eyes as I stand in the corner and watch the nurses and the doctors hook her up to monitors and give her a quick assessment.

She pukes again, but this time her body turns white as a ghost like she's on the verge of passing out.

"Is she okay?" I ask the nurses.

No one answers me as one draws her blood and another takes a set of vitals on her.

"Macey?" A blonde runs over to me, wrapping her arms around me as if she's known me forever.

"Yeah?"

"I'm sorry. I saw you come in and thought it was you and Mackenzie, but I wasn't sure since we've only met through texts. I'm Emiline."

"Oh my god." I cry harder as I squeeze her into me. "I'm so happy you're here. Mackenzie. She's sick. I-I don't know what to do. She's never been this sick before."

"Shhh." Emiline holds the back of my head to her chest and my tears stain her scrubs. "It's okay. She's in the right spot to figure out what's going on."

She's right. I know she is. But that's my baby girl.

"Can you stay with me for a little longer? Or do you need to get back to your patients?"

"I asked my manager if I could sit with you for a little bit because you're family."

Family.

That's the only way to describe the friendship I've found in these girls. Despite only ever speaking to Emiline via text messages, she and those girls are more like family to me in my short time here than my own parents were in all the years I lived with them.

"T-Thank you," I choke out.

For the next ten minutes, the doctors and nurses keep checking her and run even more vital signs on her. They ask me if they can give her some pain medication that will help her feel more comfortable while we wait to see what the doctor wants to do next.

I ask Emiline what she thinks and went with her best judgment since she's the one almost graduating nursing school and knows a little more than I do about all of this.

There's a knock on the door and the woman announces herself as registration.

"Can I come in?"

"Sure."

"I'm just filling out your paperwork and I noticed two things were missing. We don't have health insurance for you and we don't have an emergency contact."

"I... uh... don't have health insurance."

"That's no problem." She smiles. "We can get that squared away at a later date. Do you have an emergency contact I can put on file?"

"I don't have one of those either."

"It doesn't have to be family. It can be a friend. I just have to put someone down," she says.

I think about it for a second, wondering if Oliver would be

okay with it if I used his name for that. I mean, we're roommates so I don't think he would mind. It's not like they'll call him or anything unless something happens to me.

"My roommate. Oliver Ford," I finally tell the woman. I reach into my bag to pull my phone out to get his number and realize I must have left it on the counter when I ran out the door in a panic. "I just don't have his number on hand. I left my phone at home."

"I have it," Emiline announces before she writes it down for the woman.

After she gets all the information she leaves us be.

"Does he know you guys are here?" Emiline asks.

I shake my head.

"You should let him know. I know he's going to be worried."

"That's exactly the reason why I shouldn't," I reply quickly. "He's getting on a plane as we speak for his conference. He's so excited for his presentation and to have this opportunity to help other bloggers out. I'll tell him about it the second he gets home."

She doesn't reply, and just nods her head in understanding.

Before I can continue, the doctor enters the room.

"Good evening, Ms. Evans. I'm Dr. Stark, your daughter's doctor for tonight."

"Nice to meet you."

"After looking at her assessment and lab work, I want to send her down for a CT scan on her abdomen to rule out a ruptured appendix. I'm going to have them come shortly to get it done so we can confirm and go from there with treatment."

"Oh my god." I cover my eyes in disbelief. My first thought when he says that is surgery. There is no way in hell I'll be able to afford the bill when that comes in. But I can't think about that right now because the first priority above everything else is making sure Mackenzie is okay.

I'll work for the rest of my life to pay this off if I have to.

I learned quickly how much I hate emergency rooms.

All I want to do is go home with my baby girl and shower. It doesn't help that my face feels puffy and swollen from crying so much.

They gave her some more medication to keep her comfortable while we wait for the results. They got her back surprisingly quick despite how busy the Emergency Room is tonight and they told us it would be about twenty minutes or so before we got the results back.

I've never been so thankful that Emiline was on shift tonight because I've never felt more alone than I do here waiting.

I hold Mackenzie's hand as I sit next to her bed, refusing to let it go even for a second. I finally allow myself a moment to breathe and lay my forehead down on the bed beside her. I wish I could take even just a small nap, but I also don't want to go to sleep in case she needs something.

Just as I close my eyes, strong hands grip my shoulders.

I startle, almost leaping out of my seat as I look up to see wondering who's here. I'm in complete shock when standing next to me is the man who's supposed to be on a plane right this minute.

"What are you doing here?" I ask, bewildered.

"Em called me," Oliver says nonchalantly as if it's nothing.

"She did? But. You. Here," I ramble on, trying to find the words. "You have a plane to catch. You have to do your presentation."

"I do." He takes a small step, closing the distance between us. "But Mackenzie is sick so I can't leave."

Oliver's admission just flipped my world upside down.

He stayed.

He didn't get on the plane.

For Mackenzie.

"You're going to skip your conference? You're going to skip the opportunity of a lifetime for her? You can't—"

Oliver cuts me off when he presses his pointer finger to my lips, before he crouches down next to my chair. Delicately, he uses the same finger to brush the hair away from my face, sending goosebumps across my skin.

I still can't believe he's here.

In front of me.

"I'd skip every opportunity ever given to me for my girl, Macey Evans."

CHAPTER TWENTY-FOUR

Oliver

The past two weeks have gone down as the scariest time of my life.

Mackenzie ended up needing emergency surgery for a ruptured appendix. I paced the hallways of the hospital for hours waiting for her to come out. Anxious as hell wondering what would happen and praying she would be okay.

The only relief I felt was seeing the girls show up for Macey. Peyton, Avery, and Kali have become such good friends to her and warmth spread through my chest seeing her become part of our group.

They all came to the hospital to sit with her and brought her an iced coffee and one of their books for her to read to help pass the time. Not that she was in any frame of mind to read a book, but I caught glimpses of her here and there with it opened in her lap.

I, for one, couldn't sit still if I tried.

In the end, everything turned out perfectly fine. Mackenzie only had to stay in the hospital for one extra night as a precaution. By the time she was discharged, she was so excited to get back home to her own bed.

Besides some pain she was experiencing, she was given one hundred percent clearance for us to take her home.

I've learned through Mackenzie that children are resilient. It's almost like the whole thing didn't happen now that the time has passed. She's back to feeling like herself with only a small scar.

I missed the blogger conference, but I couldn't give two shits about it at this point. I stayed back for what's important and that's all that matters to me.

On the other side of things, every single interaction with Macey has me falling for her more than I ever thought I could for a woman…this overwhelming need to claim her, this desire to make her mine.

I can't quite pinpoint when it was that I tipped over the edge and completely fell for her.

Was it when I decided I needed to kiss her? Was it a few days ago when we went to her new favorite bagel shop again for breakfast and did nothing but laugh at the dumbest things? Or was it this morning when I walked in on her making scrambled eggs in a pair of silk pajama shorts and a matching tank top?

I feel like it was long before today, but my hands itched to run my fingertips across every inch of exposed skin this morning.

I want to devour her.

I want to worship her.

I want to give her everything.

As if my thoughts brought her to me, she walks out of the hallway and into the living room, pulling me from staring out into space.

"Next time, Peyton," Macey says through the phone. "I'll see if Mackenzie can have a playdate next Tuesday with one of her friends from school and then I can come."

"What's going on?" I leap off the couch in an effort to interrupt her conversation.

She covers the speaker on the phone. "Peyton's begging me to go to girls' night."

"Go," I tell her.

"I promise. Next time," she tells Peyton, completely ignoring me.

I swipe the phone from her hands, smirking as I do when I bring the phone to my ear.

"Peyton?"

"Hi, Ollie," she says on the other end.

"She's going. She'll meet you there."

I hear Peyton squeal in excitement before I press end on the call.

"What the hell?" Macey laughs.

"You made some really good friends here. I think you should spend time with them. I think you *deserve* to spend time with them after the last week you had."

"But… Mackenzie."

"I don't have plans to go anywhere tonight." I throw myself back on the couch, kicking my feet up on the ottoman. "I was planning to kick back and watch a movie anyway. She's fine here with me."

"I can't ask you to babysit."

I scoff. "Babysit? There will be no babysitting. She's a grown girl, not an infant."

"She's eight," Macey fires back.

"Semantics." I shrug. "Regardless, she's not a baby. And if you haven't figured it out by now, I actually like hanging out with her."

A beat passes where Macey no longer has anything to come back at me with for why this is a bad idea.

"Kenzie," I shout.

"Ollie," she shouts back through her laughter. It's sort of our thing now.

"Want to hang out with me and watch a movie?"

"Heck yeah," she screams as she barrels into the living room like a bull in a China shop. "Oh, sorry for cursing Mom."

"Heck isn't a curse word," Macey tells her.

"What she said," I add for fun, pointing to her mom.

Macey gives me a little side eye, but she's doing a *terrible* job at hiding the smile she's fighting like hell to hold back.

She turns to her daughter. "Mackenzie, are you okay if I go out to dinner with Peyton and the other girls for a little bit? I won't be home too late."

"Of course, Mom. And tell Mrs. Peyton I said hi!"

Macey's mouth falls slightly open as if she's shocked Mackenzie is saying she's fine with her leaving.

"See." I raise a brow. "Now go get changed. I'll call you an Uber."

Her eyes bounce between her daughter and me as she takes a few steps backwards toward the hall. After about three steps, a smile forms on her face as she shakes her head and turns to go get ready.

"What movie will it be, Kenzie?"

"Dealer's choice."

"Did you just say… dealer's choice?" I can't help the full belly laughter that comes out of me. "I don't think that's how it's supposed to be used."

"I heard it in a TV show once and thought it was funny."

"You're something else." I put out my hand for a fist bump and she meets me there with a bump and an explosion. "*Princess Diaries* tonight?"

"Ew, no." She wrinkles her face. "How about *Harry Potter*?"

I give her an impressed nod. "Well, okay. I'm down for a marathon movie night."

Just as I finish clicking through apps on the smart TV and bringing up the movie, I hear heels clink behind us on the couch. My head snaps in her direction and I think I just died and gone to heaven.

Macey's outfit choice for the evening is *not* helping the temptation I have for her right now.

I leap off the couch, meeting her more than halfway to stop her from walking anymore into the room.

"Woah, woah there," I say, stopping her in her tracks. My grin is uncontrollable at this point as I scan her body up and down. She's wearing a leather skirt that barely reaches halfway down her thighs, paired with a black body suit that shows every curve of her breast to me. "Is this what you're wearing?"

"That's all I have."

"Fuck, Macey," I breathe out, barely above a whisper. "You're killing me in this."

Pink hits her cheeks instantly. "It looks okay?"

"More than okay." I lean down to speak into her ear, my lips barely grazing the skin there. "There's a chance I'll be thinking about you in this outfit later tonight too."

Macey laughs, brushing me off to grab her jacket from the coat rack. Almost as if she's not picking up what I'm putting down with my comment.

"Thank you again for watching over her."

"Anytime." I wink.

I don't move from where I'm standing as I watch her walk out the door.

I already can't fucking wait for her to get home.

"I almost forgot, I got you something," I tell Mackenzie while we wait for the timer on the oven to ring.

After our first *Harry Potter* movie ended, she was craving a sweet snack. I can't make much and also don't know how, but Peyton gave me her recipe a while back for her chocolate chip cookies.

After scouring my pantry, I realized I had all the ingredients to make them and she was so excited to give it a try with me. With her baking abilities and me being able to work the oven for her, we made the best batch of cookies our duo could make.

I rounded the kitchen island, and grabbed a box from when I was at the store the other day. "Here. It's not the color I wanted to get you, but it's all they had."

"You got me something?"

"Open it up and see for yourself."

Mackenzie tears the box apart like it's Christmas morning and we're sitting around a tree opening gifts. She doesn't realize what it is until she opens the box inside of it, revealing a sage green polaroid camera.

"You got me a camera, Ollie?" She beams with so much excitement that it makes my heart explode.

"I remember how much you loved my camera, and I thought this would be the perfect starter camera for you."

Mackenzie lifts the small device up, examining every square inch of it and testing the buttons before she finally turns it on. She whips out the directions to see how to insert the instant film.

Once she figures it out, she shoots it directly at me and I give her my best kissy face, and hold up the peace sign for her. She laughs wildly at my silly face as she watches it process.

"You really got me a camera? What for?"

"Just because. You're doing really well in school so far and I'm really proud of the transition you've made here and making so many new friends."

And because I wanted to see her face light up the way it is right now.

Mackenzie lifts the instant film to see if it's done at the same time the oven time announces that the cookies are ready. She hovers over me as I take them out, snapping a photo of the tray of fresh baked goods.

"You're a natural with the camera," I laugh.

"I learned from the best."

I can't help but chuckle at that comment because I've barely taught her anything in those five minutes in the mountains she held my camera. But I'll let her have that.

I plate each of us a few cookies and we sit on the island together.

"Where did you find this amazing recipe?" Mackenzie hums in appreciation as she takes a bite of the cookie.

"Peyton. These happen to be one of her most popular recipes in the family."

She pauses mid-bite as if something just crossed her mind. I watch intently as her gaze falls to the counter where she places the cookie down. Her smile is quickly replaced with a frown.

Fuck, I hate seeing her upset.

Did I say something wrong?

"Are you okay?"

"Yeah," she whispers.

"You know you can talk to me about anything right?"

Another pause before she lifts her head, green eyes glisten as they stare at me.

Please, don't cry.

"I'm a little jealous of you, Ollie."

I swallow, trying to process what she would be jealous about at such a young age.

"Your family. Your brothers and your sister and the other ladies. Everyone is really just so cool and so funny. I wish… I wish I had that. I wish I had more people in my family to love the way you all do."

My heart cracks.

For the first time in my life, I'm left speechless, unable to find just the right words to comfort Mackenzie and make her feel accepted. I want to tell her that she will always be a part of our family, that she can have a spot with everyone. She can call them Aunts and Uncles, for all I care but it's not something I should be saying unless Macey says it's alright.

"Do you like my mom?" Mackenzie asks, cutting through my thoughts before I have a chance to respond to her first confession.

I nod. "She's a really good person."

"Not like that. Do you *like her* like her? Like, do you have a crush on her?"

Talk about being completely caught off guard.

It's like this girl can actually read my mind, like she was in my head earlier tonight when I was staring off into space at a blank TV screen thinking about my roommate being more.

Being in the first relationship of my life.

"Can you keep something between us?"

"Yeah?" Her eyes narrow in suspicion.

"I *like her* like her. But… it's kind of a new feeling for me," I admit.

"How come?"

"I've never actually dated anyone," I say then pause, realizing I'm talking to an eight year old about my nonexistent relationship history. But I continue anyway because she's clearly wise beyond her years. "I haven't done the relationship thing before and I'm not sure I'm that type of guy."

"I don't know." She shrugs. "I think you're a pretty cool guy."

The corner of my lip tips up in a half grin. "You think so?"

"I *know* so."

My heart thunders in my chest that this girl is growing on me. I'm not just falling for Macey, but I'm caring at rapid speed for Mackenzie too.

"Why do you ask all of this?"

Mackenzie takes another bite of her cookie, staring at it deep in thought. "I just really want to see my mom happy."

Something she and I have in common. I find myself in a constant state of trying my damndest to make Macey as happy as I can, especially after learning so much about her past and how she lived back in Montana.

"Has she ever told you about Grandma and Grandpa?" Mackenzie says, despite me still being unable to say anything.

All I can do is nod, not wanting to divulge too much info to her for fear that I'm going to say something she doesn't know.

"They were never really nice to her." Her smile falls even more. "She's always tried to hide it from me because she didn't want me to know she was hurting or having a fight with them, you know? But as I was growing up, I saw a lot more than I should have. I'm a pretty smart kid."

"I'm sorry you had to see anything like that at all."

"I know I'm still young, but I'm not dumb. I saw it all. I heard it all. I can put two and two together that all of my mom's problems were that she had me so young."

I'm left stunned.

Speechless.

Blinking down at her small frame.

"You don't think… I mean, you don't feel like you're to blame do you?"

"I used to," she says without missing a beat. "I used to hear the little comments Grandma and Grandpa would say but I know that Mom wouldn't trade me for the world. The same way I wouldn't trade having her as my mom for anything. I love her so, so much."

There goes my heart.

"You know… you really are too smart for your age."

She lets out an amused laugh. "So I've been told."

For the next fifteen minutes, we silently eat the cookies, clean up and still have a few leftovers for Macey for when she gets home.

My mind doesn't stop thinking about all the things these two have been through, along with all the things I want to do for these girls.

I don't just want Macey.

I want Mackenzie to be a part of my life too.

I want everything that comes with them both because no matter how much money I have in the world or how many places I've traveled to, nothing could ever compare to being right here, right now with my girls.

"Hey, Kenzie?"

"Yeah?"

"I don't ever want to see your mom hurt either. I hope you know that."

She smiles up at me. "I can tell."

CHAPTER TWENTY-FIVE

Macey

Oliver offering to take care of Mackenzie, despite my reluctance, is the best thing that could have happened. Being with these girls tonight is exactly what my heart needs.

I can't think of a single time that I've felt completely comfortable with a group of girls before. I had friends back in Montana, but the more I get to know these girls, the more I feel like that was never genuine or real. Like much of my life, it seems.

I've spent so little time with them, but feel connected on a level that I can't quite explain. Maybe it's the fact that we text all day, every day. But from the first night I met them until now, they've welcomed me with open arms.

Then Emiline sat with me during her busy shift and held my hand as if we've been friends forever. Staying at my side did nothing to benefit her, but she still did because she cared.

I was so damn used to people using me until they didn't need me.

These girls are not that.

"I think it's time for a round of tequila shots to celebrate Mackenzie feeling better, Emiline passing her big test last week, Macey getting her new job and the five of us finally fucking being able to get together!" Avery cheers.

"I'm so down for that," Emiline says.

Shit.

Every muscle in my body tightens hearing the girls talk about taking shots. Fear creeps in that the group of friends I finally have, one that I've craved for so long, are about to judge me for not drinking. It makes me wonder if they won't want me around after today.

"Oh, none for me guys." I wave my hands. "I actually don't drink."

"Really?" Peyton asks. "Shit, sorry. I didn't mean for that to come out as judgmental as it did."

I relax my shoulders. "I take no offense. I'm used to it if I'm being honest."

"Can we ask why?" Em reluctantly questions.

"I've watched too many people from my hometown in Montana fall into a bad habit when it came to alcohol. I've watched people's lives change from it. So when I had Mackenzie, I told myself that I'd never allow it to potentially have control over me and wanted to just focus on being the best mom I could be."

"I can respect that," Avery says.

"I agree with Avery," Peyton says. "How is Mackenzie feeling?"

I breathe out a sigh of relief. I should have known these girls wouldn't be like everyone else in my life.

"She's so much better, like it never even happened. But it truly was one of the scariest days of my life."

Peyton shakes her head. "I can only imagine. There was one time when I was still nannying James and he got really sick. I felt so helpless. It was horrible."

I'm confused by her statement. I had no idea she was ever their nanny. I actually assumed she was James' mom with the way he adores her and the ways she is with him.

"Nanny?" I ask.

She chuckles. "Fun fact, I worked for Thomas before I ever

became his wife."

The table erupts in a fit of laughter. I nervously smile as I look around the table wondering what everyone is laughing about and why it's so funny.

"It was straight out of one of her romance books," Kali says first.

"The single dad falls for the hot nanny," Avery says. "Gets me every single time."

My eyes continue to bounce to each girl at the table in confusion. "I have no idea what you're talking about."

"I'm sorry, Macey." Peyton's laughing fit finally dies down. "We're avid readers here. Do you read at all?"

"I love to read." Everyone stops moving as if I just said something wrong. "What?"

"How do you love reading and have never heard of this particular romance trope?" Avery asks.

"What's a trope?"

"Oh, babe. We have a lot to teach you." Avery laughs.

Emiline leans in to whisper in my ear, "Don't worry. I don't get it much either but some of their books aren't bad."

Kali leans in, elbows on the table as she clasps her hands together. "First, we need to know what type of books you *do* read?"

"Mostly culinary education books I find in the library."

"Yawn." Avery emphasizes by stretching her arms out in the air. "Girl, you need some spice in your life.'

"I mean… I'm a chef. So I have plenty of that."

The girls laugh. "That was a good chef joke, but that's not what we mean," Peyton says.

"Adult romance books," Avery says. "You need romance books with spice."

Wait, are these girls talking about reading books with people having sex in them? I've heard about these before but I never knew people actually read them. It's not something I can relate to since I've never even watched porn myself, let alone *read* it.

"Woah, woah." I hold up my hands. "I don't know about all of that. That's a little... weird?"

"Sex is a totally normal thing. Reading it just elevates the actual act. Really gets you going if you know what I mean." Avery winks.

"Reading spicy books is like a drug," Kali adds. "Once you start, you literally can't stop."

"I agree with them." Peyton nods.

This entire conversation has me very curious about what's inside these books. I won't sit here and try to deny that I *have* thought about watching porn once or twice to see how to do things. But something about watching it in the same house as your parents is just uncomfortable.

So, out of fear, I never even attempted it. I mostly didn't want to get caught and give them leverage on something that it would get my daughter taken away from me.

But I'm not there anymore.

I'm here, on track to living out my dreams, free from the chains of them.

"Okay," I sit up straighter in my chair. "Color me curious here. Give me one of these books and I'll give it a shot."

"Yes!" Avery punches the air.

Kali grabs my phone and downloads an app where I'll be able to read. She adds me to her unlimited plan without even asking questions.

I can't help but smile again at this group of girls who just do anything for each other.

A sisterhood I've only ever dreamed of.

"Okay, I put a cowboy romance on there. It's one of our all-time favorites."

"You all read it?" I ask.

"I read it twice," Peyton says, holding up two fingers. "It's that good. The spice is immaculate."

"When he says, *'crawl to me,'* I just die every time." Kali emphasizes with fluttering eyes.

Crawl to me? I think I'm very much out of my element here, but, strangely, I also feel comfortable enough with them to be vulnerable for a moment despite how experienced these girls are.

"I feel like we're all good enough friends now, right?" I ask, wringing my hands together with nerves. My heart thunders in my chest at the fear of judgment.

"Obviously," Avery rolls her eyes.

"I need to admit something to you guys. But I don't want you guys to judge me for it."

"We'd never judge you," Peyton says sympathetically. "This is always a judgment free zone for you, babe."

I inhale and exhale preparing for the shock that's about to come.

"So I have a daughter—"

"What? No way? That's who that little girl who looks like she can be your twin but with blonde hair is?" Avery chuckles.

Kali smacks her arm. "Would you let her speak?"

I let out a nervous laugh. "So I'm obviously not a virgin. But I'm very inexperienced in this realm of things. When I say I'm nervous to read this stuff, I mean it. The only man…" I shake my head of the thoughts, as I release another sigh. "The one and only man I've ever been with was the one who got me pregnant."

I look around the table, and the girls just sit there. Stone faced and repeatedly blinking.

"Are you serious?" Peyton speaks first.

I groan. "You said no judging."

"No. That's not what I meant. It's just that"—her eyes trail me up and down—"you're so fucking beautiful, babe. When I first saw you, I pictured men lining up on their knees for you."

"God, we love a man who gets on his knees for a woman." Avery brings her fingers to her lips and kisses them before releasing them in a chef's kiss.

"We do?" I ask.

"Hell yeah, we do," Avery exclaims.

"I wouldn't know the first thing," I add.

Avery sits up in her chair as if she's gearing up to give a big presentation. "Okay, since it's been so long, when the opportunity is presented to you, you have to let the guy take control of the situation. Let him guide you to where you need to go, and what you need to do. Guys love when they are in control too."

"Okay." It's the only word I can think of to process any of this.

"Are you asking because you have someone in mind?" Peyton says with a cheeky grin.

I crinkle my nose. "No, no. Nothing like that at all."

"Not even a particular *roommate*?" Kali asks with the same grin.

Emiline groans. "Guys, please. How many times do I have to remind you… they're my brothers?"

"Don't act like you're not used to this already," Avery scoffs.

"Fine." Emiline rolls her eyes. "Continue."

"Seriously, you guys." I laugh now. "Definitely not Oliver. I can't cross that road with him. It's bad enough we already kissed once."

"You didn't," Peyton screams.

I can't help the smile that takes over my face just thinking about it again. It was unexpected but beyond perfect. If I'm being honest, I wanted more of it.

"I won't lie and tell you that I don't have feelings for him. Something is brewing, but I don't know how to navigate it or do anything about it. I also have my daughter to think about."

"He seems really good with her," Emiline says.

"He really is," I reply. "She's loving living in the city, her new school and hanging out with him."

"If the whole inexperienced thing," Peyton says, squiggling her finger in the air. "Is what's holding you back from pursuing things with him, you have nothing to worry about there. Oliver is as experienced as they come."

What the heck does she mean by that?

"Yeah, he doesn't stay put for long. My brother is a typical playboy who's never been in a relationship before," Emiline adds.

What?

"Actually, come to think of it," Peyton starts. "Thomas told me the other night that he hasn't talked about any girls he's been with since his birthday trip to California at the start of the summer."

"Logan said he's been ditching boys' nights on Wednesdays too," Emiline adds.

"I bet he has been saying that, huh?" Avery snickers at her comment.

"Don't even start," Emiline scolds.

"When did you two meet?" Peyton asks, ignoring their bickering with each other.

"In July. On my flight here from Montana," I answer.

"Yes, that's right." Peyton snaps. "Thomas said Oliver was obsessed with a girl he met on that flight. He would *not* stop talking about her and wished he could find her again."

"And he found her." Avery throws her arms out towards me like *Vanna White*.

"He totally found her," Emiline repeats with a grin.

My eyes land on each girl, one by one. Each of them with a shit-eating grin on their face as if they just put the pieces of Oliver's puzzle into place just now.

My brain can't stop thinking about all the information I just received in such a short time frame.

Oliver, a playboy? I really don't know how because he's rarely gone out since I moved in and he definitely hasn't brought any woman to the apartment. At least that I know of.

But the most blaring thought from their revelation is the girl he met on his flight from Montana.

It's me.

I'm the girl.

He thought and talked about me after our flight? I mean, half of that sticks for me too. I thought about him a whole lot after that flight.

He was the man who made me feel at peace on that flight. He made me feel like this was the right decision after all.

"Fate is a funny thing, isn't it?" Avery interrupts my thoughts.

Yeah… it really is.

CHAPTER TWENTY-SIX

Macey

I've never been more anxious to get back to the apartment than I am right now.

My leg bounces in the Uber as the driver approaches the building and I can feel my clammy palms against my exposed thigh. I can't exactly pinpoint what I'm so anxious for.

But for once, I know it's not the bad kind of anxiety. It's more exciting than anything else. I can't wait to get home and see Oliver again.

I pray he's still awake.

Once I make my way up the elevator and enter the living room, my excitement turns to disappointment quickly. It's dark except for a small lamp next to the couch that I assume he left on for me, and it's quiet as if everyone is already asleep.

Even though I'm in a different place than I was months or even years ago, my routine is still the same. I come home and head right to Mackenzie's room to see her and make sure she's okay.

She's *always* sleeping, but it brings me peace just to say good-night to her even when she can't hear me.

Before I head to my room and get ready for bed, I decide to

make one more pass in the living room thinking that *maybe* he heard me come in and wants to see how the night was.

However, it's still quiet.

I grab a bottle of water from the refrigerator and just as I turn to make my way toward my room, I hear a loud "*fuck*" come from his bedroom and a loud bang like something fell.

I rush to his bedroom door to make sure he's okay, but I freeze when I hear moaning coming from the other side. I can't tell if it's a moan of pain or pleasure from where I'm standing.

My first thought is… did he invite someone over after Mackenzie went to bed?

No. He wouldn't.

"Oliver?" I say through the small crack in the door, but there's no answer.

Since the door is already slightly cracked, I gently push it open a little more so I'm able to peek my head into the room to assess the situation. But the minute I do, the moans grow louder.

The only light in his bedroom is coming from the en suite bathroom off to the side shining just the right amount of light into the room that I can tell he isn't in here.

I should leave.

I should turn around right now.

I shouldn't invade his space.

I take in the enormous primary suite as I tiptoe my way through the room. Dark blue curtains that match the dark bedding on the king-size bed. Even with the little light in the room, I don't miss the random stuffed bear in the middle of the bed. It even has a small bandage wrapped around its foot.

I feel like that's something Oliver would do to a stuffed animal if it had a hole in it. If I had to picture his room and what it would look like, this would most definitely be it. The bear certainly adds a touch of his personality to the space.

Just as I'm in the middle of scanning the room, I hear a "*Jesus Christ*" come out of him. This time, his groan sounds more painful, like something might really be wrong. I still don't hear a female moaning which has me thinking that maybe he really doesn't have anyone over.

But what do I know?

I take tentative steps toward the light shining through the crack of the door. It's only when I'm inches from the door that I hear it.

My name.

Coming out as a painful moan off his lips.

Is he… Oh. My. God. I can't help but gasp and cover my mouth with my hands as I stand there, stuck in place outside of the door.

"Macey?" My name now comes out as a question as if he's heard me.

My head moves forward to see if I can see him through the crack in the door. I clear my throat, swallowing past the lump that's formed. "Yeah. It's me."

Without any rational thought, I push the door open a little more to find Oliver standing outside the shower with the water running as if he was just about to get in. My eyes widen when I take in the tanned, muscular man standing before me. His backside is built like a brick. From his shoulders, to his lower back and right down to… his ass.

Bare and exposed.

My eyes come up to meet his through the mirror.

"You're home," he says, a smirk forming on his lips.

I only nod, unable to find the words to say because of what I'm looking at right now.

"I was…" Oliver looks from me down to where his hands are in front of him, before he brings his eyes back to meet mine. "I was just thinking about you. Is that okay?"

I swallow before I nod again.

"Open the door all the way, Macey Evans. Let me see you."

My stomach clenches, and my nipples harden. There's no doubt in my mind Oliver was just taking care of business with my name on his lips and, for the first time in my life, I want to witness it.

So I do as he asks. I take a tentative step into the oversized bathroom. Oliver's head falls back as he closes his eyes. Then, his hand slowly begins moving up and down as he starts stroking himself again.

He maneuvers his body at just the right angle for me to see and that does it.

I can't help it when my eyes widen as I look down and see him pleasuring himself.

He's… huge.

He's hard as steel, and I'm not just talking about the muscles that cover every part of him. His cock is standing straight in attention as he strokes himself from shaft to tip. The veins protrude along the sides while the tip glistens with precum.

My thighs clench together as wetness pools between my legs. And because Oliver is intuitive, he picks up on my small movement and his eyes darken to the color of the deepest parts of the ocean.

"I want to be real upfront with you, Macey. I've thought about you so many times when I've done this," he admits with a low, guttural groan. "But seeing you standing here, in my bathroom… a picture fucking perfect fantasy come to life."

My body moves me forward by one step. I'm not sure where it wants to go or what it wants to do, but curiosity is winning right now. I went from wanting to be a part of this, to *needing* to be a part of this.

"Are you going to…" I stop myself. Not wanting to sound as inexperienced as I am.

"Finish that sentence."

"Are you going to come?" I ask nervously, barely above a whisper.

His strokes slow, eyes never leaving mine before a grin forms on his lips. "Do you want to watch?"

I nod my head with eagerness wondering who I've just become in a matter of seconds.

"Sit," Oliver orders, jerking his head to the large bathroom counter.

I take slow steps, keeping my eyes fixed on his as desire courses through my bloodstream. I give myself a little jump to sit, and as soon as I do, I cross my legs. Right now, my pussy is *throbbing* and in dire need of attention. I've never wanted to touch myself more than I do right this second.

His gaze lights me on fire before he says, "Uncross those legs for me, dragonfly."

I let out a small groan, but do as he asks.

"Good girl," he praises. "Now lean back. Let me see you."

My legs open the smallest amount. My leather skirt does not allow me much room to widen, but it's just enough that I'm sure he can see the wet spot through my bodysuit. I use my hands to hold me up as I sit back and watch him.

Strangely enough, sitting here under his eye, is making me feel every bit of sexy I've never felt before. And I'm not even doing anything other than watching.

"Fuck." He bites his bottom lip. "You're so fucking perfect. I want to see more of you."

I remain silent. I can't even form coherent thoughts to even nod in agreement.

A spark of confidence courses through me and I answer his question by reaching for the hem of my shirt and pulling it up over my head. I feel my nipples harden under my bra at the rush of air hitting my skin.

"Beautiful," Oliver murmurs as he continues to stroke his cock. "What I would give to have my hands all over your body, Macey. To trail kisses up your thigh until I give you exactly what you crave."

My hand finds my ink covered thigh as I run my hand along the art. A scene of wildflowers, sunshine and raindrops cover my left thigh, a reminder for me to live like a wildflower, searching for the sunshine and growing after the rain.

My fingertips skate along the ink right above my knee until I reach the hem of my skirt. I lift it just the smallest amount to give me more access to open up for him. There is something so insanely hot about knowing that I'm what's going to get him off right now.

Not another girl.

Not some porn on TV.

But me. Sitting here for him.

"Picture. Perfect," Oliver growls. "You're going to make me come and my hands haven't even touched you."

I prop myself up on my hands one more time, keeping my legs spread for him. As I do, I can see the muscles in his stomach contract as he picks up the pace. Within seconds, Oliver's breathing becomes wild and frenzied while his intense glare continues to light me on fire.

I watch in shock as cum pours out of the tip and into his hands.

"Fuck, Macey," he groans my name as his release takes over.

Oliver slows his strokes until his breathing regulates. Then, he releases his cock from his hands and walks next to me to wash up in the sink directly to my right without saying another word.

That was the hottest thing I think I've ever seen.

And it was my name on his lips.

As soon as he's done, he moves to stand between my legs. Naked from head to toe as he cages me in. His breath is hot on my face as he leans in close.

"I didn't overstep, did I?" his voice pained, and almost full of regret.

"Not at all," I choke out. "That was… hot."

A few heartbeats pass, he doesn't move from where he's standing.

"Good," he finally says. "You terrify me."

My eyes narrow. "How so?"

"Never in my life have I had a fear of screwing things up. But with you, I lose all control. I don't want to scare you away. I..." he pauses, as if he's trying to process his thoughts. "I don't want you to leave."

My hands cup the side of his face on instinct. "I'm not going anywhere."

No matter how much this scares me, I don't think I could leave if I tried.

Oliver Ford has made me want things I didn't think were possible.

CHAPTER TWENTY-SEVEN

Oliver

I've barely seen the woman I've become obsessed with after she caught me fantasizing about her over a week ago.

It's helped that Macey has been busy with new hire orientation and training all week. She leaves early and isn't home until after the sun sets. I could be a selfish asshole and ask why they're such long days, but she walks in the door with a smile on her face…and I couldn't ask for more. She's doing what she loves and it makes me happy to see her this way.

I don't know what came over me that night in my bathroom, but after seeing her looking like that, I couldn't get her out of my head as I waited for the water to run hot.

Next thing I knew, my hand was wrapped around my cock and I was about to come when she showed up. I've never come so hard in my life with her sitting there watching me. She's beautiful, in every sense of the way, but it was sexy as all hell seeing her sitting on my bathroom counter in nothing but a skirt and her bra.

Mackenzie has been busy with school this week. On top of that, she's been heading to Peyton's daycare center immediately after school. It just so happened to be on the same street as her school, so Peyton has been picking her up and walking Mackenzie back with her.

Mackenzie *loves* kids despite being one herself. She likes the idea of 'working' and helping Peyton with the little ones. I think it has a lot to do with the circumstances she grew up in and she's so damn good with them too. She holds more patience than most adults.

Needless to say, I've barely seen both of my girls.

I've turned down a number of trips since Macey walked into my life. I want to go on them, trust me. But I hate the thought of leaving her and Mackenzie. They both have this insane chokehold on me and it makes me want to stay put for the first time in my life.

My phone buzzes on the end table next to the couch, and I pick it up to see Logan's name flash across the screen.

"What's up?" I answer.

"Eww. What's up with you?" he snaps. "No, hi. No, how are you? What am I, chopped liver now?"

I can't help but laugh. "You're so dramatic, you know that?"

"Can't help it. I'm losing all my friends here."

"You are not losing all your friends." I roll my eyes even though he can't see me. "Miss me, Logan?"

"Whatever," he scoffs. "What are you doing tonight? Do you want to head out for drinks? I have a Saturday off for once in my life."

There's a part of me that really wants to take him up on that offer. Trips aren't the only thing I've skipped on since she's been here. I've missed the last few Wednesday's with the boys because I'd rather be here.

"Not tonight. It's Macey's first night working."

"And?" he says. "It's not like she's going to be there. What are you going to twiddle your thumbs all night while you stare at the front door waiting for her to come home?"

"I might."

"How am I still friends with you Ford brothers?"

"Because we're the only ones you have in the city beside those guys you work with."

He groans. "You're so annoying. If you change your mind. Call me."

He hangs up on me, and I just laugh.

Typical Logan.

Just as I place the phone back down on the end table, Macey catches my eye as she walks into the kitchen. My eyebrows furrow in realization that she's not dressed for work. She's wearing sweatpants, an oversized tee, and slippers.

I jump off the couch before I can think of anything else. "What are you doing?"

"Getting a drink of water?" Macey says as she fills her glass before making her way over to the couch and sits down. She tucks her legs under her small frame and grabs the remote.

"Don't you have your first night in the kitchen tonight?" I ask.

She shrugs, clicking the TV on. "I have to call out but no one was picking up when I called ten minutes ago. So I'll try again in a little bit."

"What? Why?" I blurt out, harsher than I intended. "It's your first night. You can't call out."

"I have to. Peyton called me earlier to tell me that James has the stomach bug and she doesn't want to risk Mackenzie getting it. I appreciate her for that."

Wait… she's calling out of work because she has no one to watch her daughter?

"Okay?"

"I can't go to work and leave Mackenzie here alone."

"She won't be alone. I'm here," I assure her.

"Oliver," she breathes out. "You have a life. You need to get out and hang out with your friends."

Fuck. She must have overheard some of my conversation on

the phone with Logan. It's not like I said anything about her or Mackenzie being the reason I don't go out. I don't know how many times I need to tell her that I don't do anything I don't want to do.

This is all I've wanted lately.

Her. Mackenzie. Being here.

"You heard me on the phone, huh?" I smirk.

"Yes, and I feel really guilty. I feel like we're taking over your social life. I hate being the reason you're not doing anything. I think I'm ruining your life."

She's cute when she rambles and shows her true feelings.

I take a seat on the couch next to her, throwing my arm around the back of the couch where she sits.

"I'm right where I want to be, dragonfly."

Macey throws herself off the couch, almost aggravated. "You're a guy, Oliver. You have needs. You need to get out there." She's talking a mile a minute with arms flailing all over the place.

The corner of my lip tips up even more as I cross one leg over the other, resting my ankle on my thigh. "I'm pretty sure you witnessed me taking care of my needs just fine last week."

She blushes at that.

Bingo.

"That's just because I was there at that moment."

"No." I stand from the couch now, bringing myself directly in front of her as I close the distance between us. "That's because you're the center of every fantasy I have when my hand is wrapped around my cock, Macey Evans."

Her chin lifts to meet my eyes and they widen almost instantly.

I can't think about anything else when I'm alone in my room. Every thought I have when I'm not sleeping is her. I'm consumed by her.

"With that being said." I bring a finger under her chin to

make sure her gaze stays locked with mine. "Mackenzie stays with me. No questions asked."

She sighs. "Are you absolutely positive that's okay?"

"Do I really need to repeat myself again?"

"I know, I know." She steps out of my hold to grab her glass of water as she makes her way to the kitchen. "You don't do anything you don't want to do."

"Good girl."

The cup tumbles into the sink as soon as the word leaves my mouth like she's caught off guard by my praise. The night she walked in on me in the bathroom was without a doubt, the hottest fantasy I've ever had come to life.

I could tell it's not something she's used to with the way her body reacted to me.

I could also tell she's never been praised properly.

"Now go get ready for work and tell Mackenzie that I'm going to kick her ass at *Monopoly* tonight." I laugh. "I mean, I'm going to let her win, but just leave that part out for me, will ya?"

Macey runs her fingers along her lips as if to zipper them shut. "My lips are sealed."

She retreats to her room to get ready for work and I move quickly to get the board game out, two cans of orange soda and some chips. I've learned from hanging out with Mackenzie that she loves sour cream and onion chips so I make sure to keep some on hand at all times for her.

As soon as I set everything up and open the box to the game, both girls emerge from the hallway. Mackenzie throws herself onto the couch in her buffalo plaid checkered pajamas and a fresh braid on the side of her hair from after her shower.

Macey looks perfect as always.

She's wearing her black kitchen pants and a button down chef shirt that has the restaurant's logo on it with her hair pulled back in a tight bun on the back of her head.

Macey surprises me when she walks up to me, wrapping her

small arms around my waist and whispering, "Thank you," into my chest. "I owe you one for this."

"You owe me nothing. Have the best first night in the kitchen, chef."

I lean down and press a kiss to her forehead.

Macey blushes before she's out the door without a passing glance.

———

Mackenzie lets out a yawn from the spot next to me on the couch. She's turning into quite the night owl when she's with me at night.

Monopoly didn't last long for us because I let her win. I love a good board game but who has the time and patience for this particular one? So I let her buy all the big name blocks and she won the entire game about an hour later when I went bankrupt.

"Why don't you head to bed. You seem tired," I tell her.

She groans, but stretches her arms out above her head. "I don't want to go to bed. I'm not ready."

"It's almost ten."

"But I like hanging out with you," she admits.

Talk about making a grown man feel all the feels. Kids are so funny because they don't hold back their feelings. When they say something, they usually mean it and they mean it with their whole heart. Hearing Mackenzie admit this makes the grip she already has on me only tighter.

"I like hanging out with you too, Kenzie," I say giving her a little shoulder slug.

She laughs at that. "Can I tell you something, Ollie?"

"Anytime. You can always tell me anything."

"I *hate* when people call me anything other than Mackenzie."

She what?

I've seriously been calling her a name she hates since the day we left the mountains and I'm just learning now that she actually hates that nickname? Fuck.

"Why didn't you tell me? You should have said something the first time. I would have called you by your full name."

Mackenzie shrugs her shoulders. "I didn't want you to."

I stare at her, blinking as I try to understand what this means.

"You're so cool," she continues. "And the fact that you made that nickname sound so awesome made me want you to keep calling me that."

"I think you're pretty cool too," I tell her the honest truth.

She smiles but another yawn quickly follows after that.

"How about we make a deal? Fifteen more minutes of this show and then it's bedtime. Does that work for you?"

Mackenzie nods. "That's a deal I can work with."

She settles into me and I can't help but think about how my life has drastically changed in the last few months. In the best way possible.

I get it now. I do.

Why Thomas would drop anything and everything for his son.

Why Thomas was head over heels for Peyton as quickly as he was.

Why Marc couldn't stay away from Avery even if he tried.

The woman I met on a flight home from work had to go and change everything. I'm not afraid to admit that it scared the crap out of me when I heard Macey was a mom. I've always tried to avoid them at all costs because I knew I wasn't built for a relationship. I never once had plans to stick around long enough with anyone and I couldn't do that to a kid.

On top of my transient lifestyle, no part of me has felt like I had any fatherly instincts. It all came so naturally for my dad, being able to balance work and family life. Marc grew up always wanting to be just like dad. Thomas was a little more career driven. But I just never stuck around long enough for anything more than a quick weekend fling. I thought there was no way a family would happen for me.

Up until her orientation began, finding new little breakfast nooks with Macey has become a regular occurrence. We started ordering multiple plates and splitting everything, just so we can try more food together. This has actually resulted in me creating a whole new base on my blog just dedicated to NYC content. There have been a few times I've needed to go out and take some pictures for the blog and both girls will come along with me to see a little more of the city. Mackenzie loves it because she brings her camera and we take the pictures together.

This new normal is bringing me a sense of peace I had no idea I was missing.

I've never been more comfortable with the direction of this life and staying put with my girls. I don't know for sure how either of them feel about it, but that's what they are to me.

My girls.

The ones I would protect at all costs.

The ones I would drop everything for if they needed me.

A few minutes go by as these thoughts swarm in my head when Mackenzie interrupts them.

"Hey, Ollie?"

"Yeah?"

"I just want to say again that you're really great. I don't know if I ever actually said thank you for my room. It's really amazing." Mackenzie yawns again. "And this place. And for bringing us here."

She's sitting right next to me, but she scoots herself closer and wraps an arm around my waist causing me to drape an arm around her shoulder to hold her into me.

"I really love you," Mackenzie confesses.

And there it goes.

My heart. Gone.

Completely lost for the taken by a little girl who's flipped my world upside down in the greatest way possible.

No child has ever said that to me other than James who has known me his entire life. Loving your family is something you naturally learn when you grow up surrounded by healthy relationships. I beamed when he first told me *"I love you, Uncle Ollie,"* but there's something so special about hearing it from Mackenzie.

After taking a minute to process it, I give her a tighter squeeze on the shoulder.

"I love you too, Kenzie."

And I mean it. I really fucking do.

CHAPTER TWENTY-EIGHT

Macey

"Macey, you completely killed it in the kitchen tonight!" Kevin says, holding out his fist for me to meet him in a fist bump.

"Yeah?" I question him. "Thank you. It was way busier than I anticipated it would be."

"It was one of our busier nights for sure," Jan says as she brings a stack of pans to the dishwasher.

Kevin is the head cook here who I work directly under and Jan is one of the other cooks working alongside us. Kevin has to be in his fifties but you can tell he looks younger than he is. His gray hair definitely gives away more of his age. Jan looks to be about my age which is nice to have someone close to work with.

Since it was my first night behind the line, I took some time to intently watch the way each person does things, learning that they each work together as a seamless team. Most of them don't say many words when we're slammed. If they do, it's one word and everyone else just knows what needs to be done. Kevin says "broccoli" and Jan knows exactly which plate needs it. Otherwise, it's light conversation between rushes.

I like to think I'm a pretty quick learner. Once I picked up on some things, I jumped myself right into their groove.

"You fit in perfectly." Jan smiles as she comes back to help clean up.

Pride takes over every single part of me.

I did it.

My first shift.

I still can't wrap my head around the fact that the goal I set myself when I was just a young girl is finally happening.

"I still feel awful about that order I messed up. Who messes up a baked potato for a sweet potato?" I shake my head.

"If that's your only mistake, then I would call this the best night." Kevin laughs.

"Ugh. I just hate to see people unhappy."

"If they are unhappy over a potato mix up that can easily be fixed, that's on them, girl," Jan says.

Kevin stops wiping the counter to turn to me. "Most people fail miserably on their first shift here. They aren't fired or anything, obviously. But first shifts are the hardest for new employees and you were kind of thrown into the deep end with a busy weekend shift."

"And you didn't serve a well-done steak to someone who wants it rare. That kind of mistake costs a whole new steak. You fucked up potatoes. That's nothing." Jan waves her hands.

Dream job. Check.

Supportive coworkers. Double check.

"Thank you guys for making me feel better."

"It's the honest truth. I don't know about Jan over here, but I'm honored to work with you."

"I agree with that." Jan nods. "Now get out of here and go celebrate a successful shift."

"No. I can stay to help clean up." I pick up an empty container that once held the potatoes that will haunt me for shifts to come.

"Nah." Kevin grabs the bin from my hands. "We got this tonight."

I thank them and say goodbye before moving quickly to hang

up my jacket for the night in the little locker they gave me in the employee lounge. I can't wait to get back to the apartment to tell Oliver all about how amazing this night was.

Mackenzie is likely sleeping because she's one of the few kids who loves their sleep and likes to go to bed early. But knowing her, she's going to wake me up at the crack of dawn to hear all about it. She was just as excited as I was for all of this and there's truly no better feeling in the world.

When I made the decision to chase this dream, I was nervous about how it would affect her. I've quickly learned there's no better feeling than having the person you love more than anything in the world cheer you on and be just as excited as you are to watch everything unfold the way it should.

Once I make it back home and step foot into the apartment, my eyes widen. It's bright as hell here. Like every single light is on which is different from the last time I was this excited to come home.

My eyes scan the room before landing on the kitchen where I find Oliver. He's leaning on the counter, using his hands to anchor him there as he reads a book that's laid out in front of him. His black frame glasses thick with white dust sit on the bridge of his nose. He has that ridiculous apron on that I can't help but chuckle at every time he brings it out.

My eyes land on the mess that's scattered everywhere.

Flour. Sauce. Pans. Open cookbooks. A random assortment of kitchen appliances that I'm confident he has no clue how to operate.

Then I notice smoke coming from the oven.

"What… in the world… is happening right now?"

He jumps at my voice as if he didn't hear me come in. "Oh good. You're home."

"What are you making?" I ask, stepping foot into the kitchen as I circle the island and notice the crumbs and disaster everywhere. It looks like a tornado ripped through here. "Or killing?"

"Well…" A nervous chuckle escapes him. "I don't have a damn clue."

Is he… nervous?

My eyes move from him and back to the counter. I can't even begin to try to put the pieces of this puzzle together to figure out what recipe this is all supposed to be.

I notice the very expensive KitchenAid mixer is out and I laugh.

"What were you doing with this KitchenAid?"

Oliver scurries to a cookbook he has placed on a different countertop. Licking his finger tip before flipping the pages aggressively like he knows exactly what he's looking for. "Something about whipped potatoes."

God damn potatoes. I can't escape them tonight.

"I really love potatoes," he rambles. "And you know what a good potato pairs well with?" Oliver stops himself, finger to the lip as if he's trying to remember what he's doing.

This is a whole new light I'm seeing Oliver in and I truly can't wipe the smile off my face. It's hysterical watching him move around the kitchen and attempt to figure anything out. It's adorable how nervous he seems.

"The bacon! Shit." He runs to the oven. The second he opens the door, smoke pours out. "I burnt the bacon," he deadpans.

Now I'm curled over, hands on my knees, laughing.

He said that with such a serious face, not an ounce of panic or emotions.

"Stop laughing. I burnt bacon, Macey! This is a tragedy of epic proportions."

That only makes me laugh harder. Oliver moves quickly to slide open the window above the sink to air out the room in an effort to avoid the smoke detectors going off, waving a used dishrag around the kitchen to force the smoke outside.

He attempts to scurry past me, and I stop him with two hands to his broad chest.

"Oliver!'

He stills and his eyes meet mine. I watch his body visibly relax in front of me.

I offer him a smile. "Tell me what's happening here."

Oliver releases a long drawn out sigh. "I was trying to teach myself how to cook."

"Why didn't you just ask me to teach you?"

"I wanted to surprise you."

"Why?" I ask hesitantly.

"Because…" He takes a step to me, closing any distance that was left between us. "I wanted to learn how to do the thing you love to do the most."

This man has been taking pieces of my heart over the last few weeks. Little by little, breaking through every invisible wall I've built up to protect myself from any more hurt in my life.

"If you haven't picked up on it by now… I kinda like you, Macey Evans."

I think Oliver just took all of my heart for the keeping.

I'm silent because I can't find the words to even respond.

This mess. Him being so flustered. It was all so he could learn how to do my most favorite thing in the entire world.

"First things first." I clear my throat, fighting back any emotions that are fighting to reach the surface. "Let's get this cleaned up. Next time, you wait for me and I'll teach you all you need to know."

Oliver responds with his signature grin and a nod.

We move seamlessly together to clean up the dishes he's used and appliances that he had out that he did *not* need for any of these recipes he attempted to make. He has successfully snapped out of his flustered state when he settles next to me at the sink to take over drying duty.

"How was your first night at Mollie's?"

I smile wildly as I scrub the pan. "It was amazing, Oliver. You have no idea. Not to be dramatic or anything, but it was probably the best night of my life, next to giving birth to Mackenzie."

"That's amazing. I'm really proud of you." He bumps my shoulder as he picks up the next dish to dry.

"Don't be too proud." I laugh. "I messed up potatoes tonight."

"How in the world do you mess up potatoes?"

I drop the pan, propping one hand on my hip and the other pointing to the Kitchen Aid still nestled on the island. "I don't know… why don't you tell me?" I smirk.

Oliver looks in the direction of my hand and nods. "Touché"

"But if you must know, I served a sweet potato instead of the baked potato the customer wanted."

"Honest mistake. All potatoes look the same to me when they aren't cooked and cut open."

We both pause at how ridiculous that sounds before we fall into a fit of laughter together.

I vividly remember how nervous I was to take this man up on his offer of coming back to the city with him, but it's slowly turning into the best decision I've ever made. He makes everything so easy and carefree. He makes me forget about my past mistakes, and he makes me want to be a better version of myself.

Once the kitchen is spotless, Oliver throws the dishrag on the counter before removing his glasses to sit next to the sink and props a hip against it. "Now what?"

"What do you mean?" I narrow my eyes.

"You said first things first before. So now what?"

I smile spreads across my face remembering what he said when Oliver admitted what he was doing here in the kitchen.

"So… you kinda like me, huh?" I ask with full confidence.

"Kinda. Sorta. Maybe." He shrugs.

"Then I guess the second order of business is that you should probably kiss me again. You know since I had such a great night at work."

His lips curve up as he hums. "You want me to kiss you again, dragonfly?"

"Kinda. Sorta. Maybe."

He doesn't waste a second before his lips crash into mine.

Fervently.

Wildly.

His fingertips slide through my hair as he grips the back of my head, angling me just the right amount to give himself better access to my mouth. My hands grip his biceps as I press my body into him. My body lights up even more and I moan into his mouth just as his tongue swipes my bottom lip.

I open up for him instantly as our tongues dance eagerly together. I press up to my toes, wanting to be as close to him as possible, craving the oxygen in his lungs to bring me back to life.

As soon as I do, Oliver lifts me up, never breaking free from my mouth as if we're glued together. I wrap my legs around him and instantly feel his hardness press into me. It forces another moan of pleasure out of me right before he places me on the counter.

"You can't be moaning like that," he says out of breath as he breaks free from our kiss. "I don't think I'll be able to control myself any more than I already have if you keep that up."

I answer him by cupping his face and bringing his lips back to mine.

I can't help it when my hips begin to slowly rock into him through the kiss. I fight back the moan that's sitting in my throat because… fuck, this feels incredible. I *want* him to lose control with me.

My clit is throbbing between us and the friction sends a surge of endorphins through my body that has me begging for more from him.

Oliver stops kissing me again.

"Macey," he breathes out. His hands move from my hair to my thighs, gripping them with a force that tells me he's holding back with everything he has in him.

I grip his forearms and feel the veins protruding under my palm as I beg. "Touch me, Oliver. Please touch me."

"Where do you want me to touch you?"

I have never admitted to anyone other than my new girlfriends that I'm inexperienced. If the situation ever arose, my plan was to let them take the lead and follow along with that. But I trust Oliver. More than I've trusted anyone before.

If we're going to do this, I have to tell him.

"I don't know," I finally admit. "But I need you to make me feel things. I need you to show me how to do this. I've never…" I pause as his eyes bore into mine, urging me to continue. "I've never been with anyone other than Mackenzie's dad."

His eyes widen at the same time he takes a tentative step back in shock.

Disappointment swarms me.

Talk about a mood killer.

"What are you telling me, Macey? Did he hurt you? Did he force himself on you?"

I place my hands on his chest. "No, nothing like that. We were young. I later found out that it was just a 'fun time' for him in high school. Hence why he's not in the picture. He wanted nothing to do with the both of us."

I spit the words out in rapid fire, and pray to God he doesn't judge me for this.

Oliver's gaze travels from my eyes and down my body as I sit perched on his kitchen island. My heartbeat pounds in my chest. One… two… three long beats pass before he lifts me up and I wrap my arms and legs around him. I cling to him for dear life while my mind races wondering what's going through his.

"What are you doing?"

He doesn't answer me, but kicks open his bedroom door with what feels like rage before my ass quickly falls onto his king-size bed.

He turns around to close and lock the door behind him.

I stand up. "If you brought me in here to scold me so that Mackenzie doesn't hear, then save it. I've had enough of that the last eight years of my life."

"Is that what you think?"

I wave my arms out to showcase the room. "What do you want me to think?"

He takes slow fluid steps towards me, no ounce of smile or amusement on his face.

"I brought you in here because it makes me completely rage inside knowing you and this body have never been fucking worshiped before."

I inhale a sharp breath and trap it in my lungs.

"That *no one* has ever touched this body properly before." Oliver's fingertips brush my skin from my hand to my shoulder. "That no one has tasted you before."

"I—" He cuts me off with a finger to my lips.

"I brought you in here because when I touch you how you deserve to be touched, I don't want it to be on the kitchen counter. Because when I touch you, Macey Evans… I know that you're going to be screaming my name when you come. We shouldn't be waking Mackenzie with that kind of noise, right?" Oliver smirks.

I release the breath I forgot I was holding, unable to answer him with any sort of words or movement of my head in agreement. My body is reigniting in flames as a shiver runs down my spine at the idea of him touching me the way he says he will.

I want that. I want *him*.

"Touch me, Oliver," I repeat the same words I begged in the kitchen.

He answers by reaching for the top button of my shirt. Slowly and intently, he unbuttons each of them one by one before he untucks it from my pants. His eyes never once leave mine as he does it. The anticipation builds inside of me and I'm eager for what's next.

Oliver pushes the shirt off my shoulders and I stand there exposed to him in nothing but a light pink lace bra and my work pants.

"Fuck," he drawls out when his eyes land on my chest. "Do you know how many nights I've dreamed about this?"

His hands move to palm under the swell of my breasts, and that does it for me. My chest jolts forward into his palms as the sensation of pleasure spirals out of control through every part of me. I don't know how I'll be able to handle him touching me anywhere else, because this feels wild.

Oliver's head dives into my neck, and his lips press against the pounding pulse that I know he feels. He presses kiss after kiss to every part of my neck, trailing down to my exposed shoulder before he reaches behind me to unhook my bra and freeing my breasts for him.

I swallow past the lump in my throat as nerves spike for this man seeing me in this light for the first time. I've never been a self-conscious person. But having a baby changes your body. Your breasts are no longer as plump and your stomach has a little extra stretch to it. Things I've learned to love and embrace. I only hope he feels the same way.

"Fucking. Perfect," Oliver says, as if he can read my thoughts. "You're so perfect."

His hands find my breasts the second the word leaves his lips. Rolling my hardened nipples between his fingertips turning my breathing almost erratic.

"Jesus," I pant through breaths.

Oliver bends down, taking one of my nipples into his mouth and I'm slightly embarrassed with the moan that comes out of me. My thighs clench together as my hands dive into his blonde, tousled hair. I grip the strands while his tongue flicks back and forth before he sucks hard.

"Fuck." My head falls back.

"So responsive, baby." His hot breath against my nipple with his words. "I can't wait to see how you react when I touch you... here." His other hand reaches between my legs, cupping my now soaked pussy on the outside of my pants.

I jump with the brief touch between my legs. Craving more, I hook my thumbs inside the waistband and begin to bring my pants down my legs slowly and tentatively as his heavy gaze remains fixed on each move I make.

Oliver makes a sudden movement, and my eyes land on him palming the growing erection between his legs, forcing my lips to twist into a grin at knowing that I have that effect on him.

Once I step out of my pants, the only remaining piece of fabric touching my body is the pair of black lace panties I decided to wear tonight. I should feel cold, but every part of me feels on fire under the weight of his stare as he skims every inch of bare flesh.

I reach up and pull the clip from the back of my hair before tossing it off to the side, letting my hair flow messy and wild down my back.

An unrecognizable sound comes out of Oliver from somewhere deep in his chest before he lifts me in his arms to place my back against the soft comforter of his bed.

My chuckle is stopped short when Oliver lands a searing kiss to my lips.

His body pressed on top of mine as my hands claw at the muscles on his back, pulling him closer to me to erase every single bit of space that separates us. I feel the bulge behind his sweatpants between my legs and without thinking, my hips buck up to meet him.

"Macey." He releases his lips from mine, his minty breath against my lips. "Don't."

I groan. Partially annoyed because I want to feel this.

I want to feel this with *him*.

Oliver laughs. "You're so cute when you're begging for me." He kisses the shell of my ear, his smooth jawline brushing my cheek. "I promise I'm going to give you exactly what you need." He presses a kiss to my collarbone. "As much as it pains me to not be inside you right now, I'm going to take my time with this body." He trails a kiss down to the swell of my breast. My back arches as his mouth clamps around my nipple. "I'm going to learn and explore every inch of you." Oliver continues moving down to my striped stomach. The area I'm most nervous for him to see so close. His lips touch every single stripe as he moves closer to the line of my lace panties. He growls against my skin. "Every fucking inch of you."

Just as I'm about to beg him to touch me, his hand comes up to pull the panties down, allowing him access to an area even I'm unfamiliar with.

My body shakes with a mix of nerves and *need*. I've never wanted anything more than this.

Oliver removes them from my legs, tossing them to the side as he stares down at my bare pussy open and on full display. I watch every feature on his face to try and figure out what he might be thinking. But any amount of nerves I had are washed away when he pulls his bottom lip between his teeth at the same time his lips curve into a grin.

"I don't have to touch you to know you're dripping for me." His voice deep with desire. "Your pussy is begging to be touched, isn't it?"

I nod eagerly as I lift my head to meet his stare.

Oliver reaches between my legs and runs a single finger between my wet slit. My back completely arches off the bed at the contact as I moan in pleasure.

"So. Fucking. Responsive."

His finger reaches my clit and I swear I've never in my life felt a feeling quite like this. It's intoxicating and overwhelming in the best way possible. My hips buck into Oliver's hands while he rubs slow circles around the throbbing bundle of nerves. I want him to give me everything he's got.

"Fuck," I say through a breathy moan.

Just as the words leave my lips, his one hand grips my tattooed thigh while his finger dives inside of my pussy. I scream. I fucking scream out in bliss as he slowly pumps in and out of me.

"You're so tight, baby. I can feel every single muscle clamp around my finger."

"More," I beg through ragged breaths. "Please. I want more."

"Only because you asked so nicely," Oliver says before removing his finger from me and replacing it with two fingers while his thumb finds my clit. Only enhancing the euphoric feeling taking over my body right now.

I don't know what having a real orgasm feels like, but if I had to guess… I'm pretty damn close to seeing stars from Oliver's fingers working my pussy as he plunges in and out of me. I know I'm wet, but I can hear it with every thrust.

"I'll give you everything you want, Macey. But I need something from you."

I lift my head to meet his eyes but can't form coherent words. My mouth is parted and my breathing is rapid as I try to maneuver the feelings lighting me up right now.

"I want you to come for me. I want you to soak my fingers so I can lick off every last drop of your pleasure."

That does it.

My legs quiver around him as he fucks me with his hand harder and faster.

"I think I'm going to…" I pant.

"Yes. That's it," he urges me. "Bring yourself over the edge for me, baby. Let me see you fall apart for only me."

And I do. I shudder around him as my orgasm takes over.

I scream out his name over and over again as my hands grip the sheets around me. The most powerful feeling takes over my body and I've never felt sexier than I do under his watchful eye with his hands touching the most sensitive parts of my body.

As I come down from the wild high I just experienced, Oliver removes his fingers from inside of me. I prop myself up on both elbows, my chest rising and falling rapidly as I watch him bring his fingers between his lips. Sucking them clean.

"The sweetest thing I've ever tasted." He hums in approval.

"Jesus. Christ," I whisper.

Oliver leans forward, pressing a kiss to my forehead before he retreats to the en suite bathroom. As he walks back into the room, I notice a washcloth in his hands. But I also notice the painful erection he's trying to hide behind his sweatpants. He doesn't say anything as he reaches between my legs, pressing the warm cloth to me.

I hiss at the contact and his eyes widen. "I didn't hurt you, did I?"

I shake my head.

"I need words, Macey. Tell me I wasn't too rough with you."

"No," I say quickly. Not wanting him to feel one bit of guilt over this because I wanted this the same way he did. "It was… wow. It was incredible."

Oliver runs a palm over my sweat soaked hair, planting another kiss to my forehead.

Which has me soaring every time his lips make contact.

Once he stands off the bed, I follow suit and grab my clothes that are littered across the floor. Anxiety creeps back into my gut because why didn't he want more? Did he want me to return the favor? This new territory has me unsure of what to do next.

And I don't want to screw things up with him.

I dress in my panties and bra, sliding my pants on, trying to avoid eye contact with him.

Tears sting the back of my eyes.

"Macey," he cuts through my thoughts. "What are you thinking right now? Why are you rushing out of here?"

"I'm not," I snap back, quicker than I intended.

He grips my wrist, stopping me from putting my shirt back on. Silently pleading with his eyes to tell him how I'm feeling.

"I'm sorry," I admit. "I've never done this before. I feel like I need to return the favor."

He laughs. "You don't need to return anything. Whatever happens after this is on your pace and wherever you want it to go." He cups my cheek. "I've told you once, and I'll tell you again. You make me nervous and I don't want to do anything that would scare you away."

I swallow through what feels like thick air and nod.

"But," he starts. My heartbeat revs with the words, impatiently waiting to hear the rest of what he has to admit. "You may have just become my newest addiction, Macey Evans. I'm not sure I'll be able to get enough of you after watching you fall apart under me. After tasting how sweet your fucking pussy is."

My lips part in a gasp before Oliver takes three steps away from me, smirk plastered on his face before he spins and makes his way into his bathroom.

When I hear the shower turn on, I realize I'm still rooted where he left me.

I can't help but think, Oliver just became my newest addiction too.

CHAPTER TWENTY-NINE

Macey

I finished that first book you let me borrow, Peyton...

PEYTON

Well???

AVERY

So good right? I'm such a sucker for a dirty talking cowboy.

EMILINE

DON'T GIVE ME ANY DETAILS. I haven't had any time to read that one yet.

AVERY

If you pulled your head away from Logan's crotch for a few hours, you might have time to read it.

KALI

L M F A O

EMILINE

I don't understand why you're all so hellbent that that's where I keep my head. They have been in school books for your information.

PEYTON

Leave her alone, Ave. You say it all the time... a girl has needs.

AVERY

I'm just getting tired of her trying to deny it.

EMILINE

If you must know… I prefer my head face down in the sheets and ass in the air instead of in these textbooks. Happy?

AVERY

That's my girl.

I know I'm still new here... but are we safe to assume that you're admitting things with this Logan guy?

EMILINE

There's nothing going on…

So you liked the book, Macey?

KALI

Deflection. I love it.

The book was so hot. I don't know how you guys read that stuff, but I'll tell you… I'm definitely addicted and need another one after this.

AVERY

At least you have a super hot roommate to help you out when they get you all hot and bothered 😉

Not sure that's such a good idea.

PEYTON

Avery, you can't call your fiancé's brother hot, that's weird.

And Macey, I don't see it being a bad idea at all.

KALI

I agree with Peyton. There's nothing wrong with roommates with benefits.

EMILINE

I'm really so done with this group chat.

CHAPTER THIRTY

Oliver

"Alright, Kenzie. Bedtime," I tell her.

"Come on," she tosses back. "It's only nine. And it's a Friday night."

I give in again because I just can't say no to this girl. "Fine. Ten more minutes."

"Okay," she squeals. "Can we play with your camera? I took a picture of the puzzle I finished with James on my polaroid but it didn't come out as good as yours do."

I laugh. "Of course," I say as I go to grab my camera from my bag.

As I do, my mind wanders to thoughts of how this life is so completely different than the one I used to live. My weekends were for going out and drinking with the boys. Now, they're consumed with Mackenzie or Macey if she's not working.

But it's everything I never knew I needed.

I can barely remember the old me and how I used to be.

It's like they lit a fire inside of me, making me dream of more things.

Like… having a family one day.

Once we step foot into her room, I hand her the camera. "Here you go."

She eyeballs the camera. "I still can't get over how cool this is. I want to get one of these when I'm old enough to have one."

"When you're a little bit older, I'll make sure you do."

Her amazement staring at the camera washes away quickly, like something I said has struck a chord unlocking feelings she doesn't want to think about. Mackenzie frowns down at the large, black camera as she fiddles it between her palms. She looks like she's assessing the device, but she's likely processing something in her head.

Mackenzie lifts her head. "Will you still be around when I'm old enough?"

Damn. That stings.

I sometimes forget Mackenzie doesn't have a father figure in her life which makes me wonder if she believes that no one will stick around long enough. I also question how much she knows about her dad and the story behind that.

After Mackenzie told me she loved me and then having that explosive night after Macey's first work shift, I knew I wanted them to stick around. I want these girls in my life for the long run. Despite not knowing how to approach this, I want it.

I clear my throat. "I want to stick around for as long as you both will let me," I admit.

She smiles up at me. "I think mom would like that too."

I raise a questioning brow. "What makes you think that?"

"Ever since her first day at work, she's been much happier. She smiles a lot more now. You can't tell her what I'm about to tell you though," she whispers as if someone else is in the house and might hear her.

I lean down and match her tone of voice, "My lips are sealed."

"The other night…" Mackenzie lowers her voice to a whisper. "I caught her dancing in the kitchen while she cooked breakfast. She was *dancing,* Ollie. Like what?" She giggles, waving her hands in the air the way I would picture a teenage girl gossiping.

She's not wrong, though.

I noticed too.

Macey has been smiling so much more this week. She's been getting out of the house to explore the city on her days off too. I've watched with my own two eyes how much brighter she gets every day.

It's almost like the weight of her past has lifted and she now looks ahead for what's to come, as if she's had a massive shift in her atmosphere. Whether it was the crazy hot orgasm I gave her after her first night of work, or the fact she's actually working.

While I had to organize my life and plan my trips for the second half of the year, I noticed a shift.

Doing that used to excite me before Macey.

Now, I just dread leaving.

"I think her new job is definitely making her happy," I finally answer Mackenzie.

She lifts the camera, tapping on the button on the top right corner. "I press this button to take a picture, right?"

"Yup. One click."

She lifts the large camera to her small face and snaps away at the puzzle she created, something she and James worked on that makes her really damn proud. I love that for her. Because she needs that boost. Something to feel good about.

Just as Mackenzie pulls the camera away from her face, bouncing up and down in excitement, it slips from her grip and tumbles to the ground with a crash.

Her hand comes up to cover her face and she turns to stone.

"Oh my god. Oh my god," she repeats over and over. The color has drained from her face at this point and I can't even tell if she's breathing. "Tell me it's okay."

"Shhh," I say, trying to calm her as I can hear the panic breaths coming from her. I pick up the camera and notice that the lens is now slightly bent with a crack in the side where it hit the floor. The lens is supposed to retract in and out when the camera is turned on. But it can't do that when it's curved like that. Meaning, it's definitely broken.

"It's fine," I lie, offering her a smile in hopes that she calms down.

That's when she breaks.

Mackenzie starts crying uncontrollably, her body shaking with sobs.

"I broke it. I'm so sorry, Ollie. I'm so sorry. I didn't mean-"

"Shhhh." I pull her small body into mine, wrapping her tightly between my arms. "It's fine."

She breaks free of my hold and starts pacing her room. "No, it's not! I broke it. The same way I break everything. The same way I ruin everything!"

"Don't say things like that."

"I ruin everything," Mackenzie screams back at me. Her face is red, tears streaming down her little cheeks and rage coursing through her blood. "I ruined your camera. I ruined my mom's life."

I crouch down at her level, gripping her wrists in my hands. "Don't you dare say that, Mackenzie," I scold her between gritted teeth, my voice growing louder.

From watching James grow up, I know that kids can be extra emotional when they are upset. I know he's much younger than her, but I can't imagine it's anything different.

Both hands grip her shoulders now, forcing her body to relax under my touch. "Stop it, Kenzie. You *do not* ruin everything and it's not broken. This is an easy fix and I have extra lenses. It's perfectly fine."

Despite me trying to reassure Mackenzie that it's okay, she just sobs harder.

I wrap my arms around her again in another attempt to bring her some comfort. This time, squeezing her tight so she can't pull herself away.

"Please stop crying. My heart can't handle this right now."

Her body relaxes at that, her head resting on my shoulder as she wraps her arms around me, matching my tight squeeze.

"Can I do something to make it up to you? Do you want me

to clean your apartment for you?" She pulls herself free from me, looking me in the eyes. "I can take out the trash. Mop the floors. Whatever you want."

What the fuck?

"Absolutely not," I snap back. "Why would I make you do any of those things?"

"Isn't that what I'm supposed to do when I'm in trouble?"

I shake my head. "But you're not in trouble."

She cries again, wrapping her arms around me as she buries her head into my neck. "I'm so sorry."

My heart cracks.

I hate that she's feeling like this.

I hate that she feels this guilty over something that can easily be replaced.

"There's nothing to be sorry for. It's something that can easily be replaced. Your happiness means more to me than this camera and right now I want you to stop beating yourself up over it."

Mackenzie nods as she climbs into her bed and covers herself up with her blankets.

"Wait right here. I have something for you to help you sleep tonight."

I run down the hall and across the living room until I reach my room. Swiping the teddy bear with the broken leg from my bed to let Mackenzie have tonight.

"This is Bert," I announce, holding up the teddy bear.

I successfully make her giggle through her tear soaked cheeks. "That's a funny name."

"I've had him my entire life and never go to sleep without him. He has a hole in his foot though, so he's got a permanent cast on so the stuffing doesn't fall out."

"How will you sleep without him if you're giving him to me?" Mackenzie asks.

"I think… I'll be okay knowing he's still in the apartment being looked after by the best little girl I know." I wink.

She smiles as she snuggles back under her sheets with Bert tucked under her arm.

"I love you, Kenzie." I lean down to press a kiss to her cheek. "Get a good night's sleep."

"I love you too, Ollie," she whispers before her eyes fall closed.

I hear the front door open and I don't move from my spot on the couch.

For the last hour, I've been staring at a blank television screen hating how Mackenzie went to bed, how she was so torn up over the camera.

I didn't like how she was still so upset when I told her it could easily be replaced. But she's so young that she doesn't fully understand that yet.

"Sorry, I'm late," Macey announces, placing a bag on the kitchen counter.

"What is with everyone being sorry tonight?" I groan, standing from the couch.

I make my way to the kitchen, avoiding eye contact with Macey as I round the island across from her. When my eyes finally land on her, my body relaxes. Fuck, she's so beautiful even after working in a hot kitchen all night. Even without an ounce of make-up on, she's the most captivating woman.

"Oh no," she exhales. "What happened?"

I place both hands on the counter, muscles flexing under my weight. "I'm going to tell you, but you have to promise me you won't say anything."

She swallows before she nods.

"Mackenzie went to bed pretty upset tonight."

Before I can continue, Macey moves quickly toward the hallway that leads to her room.

"No, stop." I rush to her, stopping her in her tracks by gripping both of her shoulders, forcing her body to face mine. "She's asleep now, but she wanted to play with my camera and take a better picture of the new puzzle her and James have been working on. She accidentally dropped it and the lens broke."

She covers her eyes. "Oh my god, Oliver. I'm so sorry."

I pull her hands away from her eyes, leaning down to level with her. Her green eyes widen as they bore into mine. "None of that. I'm not upset or mad *at all*. It's replaceable. I was right there with her when it happened. It was just an accident."

"But it's your work!" Macey interrupts me. "It's your business. It's your camera. You don't go anywhere without that thing."

"Again… it's replaceable." It's my turn to stop her. "I don't care about any of that shit. But it fucking killed me how upset she got over it. She cried and cried and her face turned sheet white. I didn't know how to handle it."

Her body deflates as if it was a balloon and someone just stuck a needle in it.

Macey releases a long drawn out sigh. "She's a lot like me. She doesn't like to disappoint anyone."

"Explain."

She moves to take a seat on the couch. There's no doubt in my mind that she's trying to figure out how to say the next thing she needs to say. I take a seat next to her and watch while she tucks her legs under her and positions herself facing me.

"Ever since she was born, there's been this pressure to prove everyone wrong. You already know my parents were harsh and manipulative. I spent my teen years trying to make everyone around me happy. I spent *years* doing everything just to please other people. Specifically, my parents, which meant putting my own happiness aside."

"You should've never had to live like that," I quip.

"You're right. No one should have to live like that. I'm happy I finally realized that and got the hell out of there, but I hate the lingering issues we have to deal with and work through. I know

Mackenzie is old enough to where she's picked up on the habits, trying to please everyone the way I've always had to."

On instinct, both of my hands grip the side of her face, pulling her close to me until we're a breath apart. "I hate more than anything that the two people who are supposed to love you until the end of the earth have made you feel like this. But it's done. It's fucking done. Do you hear me?"

Macey's eyes widen, and I swear I see her eyes glisten with emotion.

She nods.

"You are one of the strongest and most resilient people I've ever met. You are sunshine, Macey Evans. Don't ever dull that shine for anyone else ever again."

She nods and a single tear escapes from the corner of her eye. I quickly brush it from her cheek with my thumb before pressing a kiss to the spot where it just fell.

"Now..." I stand from the couch to make my way to the kitchen. "Let's make something to eat. I'm starving."

She huffs out an amused laugh as she follows me into the kitchen.

"I actually made us dinner before I left," Macey says while opening up the bag she brought home with her from work. "I made you a steak with mashed potatoes."

I groan in delight. "Fuck. Can I keep you?"

Macey chuckles but doesn't reply.

There's a part of me that wishes she would say yes. That she would agree to stick around.

As she moves around *my* kitchen, my mind wanders to what's next for her. We never actually talked about the next step for her. Is she really only going to be staying here temporarily? Once she earns enough from her new job, will she leave to get her own place?

There's a fear in the pit of my stomach for the first time in my life.

"I can't help but notice you haven't left for any work trips in a while," Macey cuts through my wandering mind as she plates the food. "Is the blog suffering at all?"

I shoot her a grin. "Are you trying to get rid of me?"

"Definitely not." Her cheeks flame.

Damn, she's so cute.

"The great thing about blogging is that the internet always works in your favor. My posts from years ago still show up in the top ten when someone searches a place I've written about. I also strategically placed ads throughout the pages so I can get paid from that as well."

"Wow, that's amazing," Macey says as she places both plates on the kitchen counter. "It fascinates me hearing about how all that works."

"Yeah?" I tip my head in question.

"Yeah," she nods. "You've learned a lot about the kitchen and it's only right that I learn about your blog and how it works."

Butterflies swarm my stomach as we sit there and eat.

For the next half hour, Macey tells me about her night at work and I tell her about how I worked today answering emails and planning brand collaborations.

We sit next to each other, eating dinner as if we're a… family, just two people catching up on each other's days while we enjoy a meal together.

I want this for the long haul.

I want this with her.

"You know," Macey starts. "I don't think I've properly thanked you for all you've done for Mackenzie and me. And all you *continue* to do."

"You thanked me enough last week when you were screaming my name over and over again in my room," I joke.

"Oliver!" Macey swats my arm.

"I'm just saying." I laugh, shrugging a shoulder.

"I'm being serious here." She contradicts herself with a laugh. "I don't know if any of this would be possible without you."

"You would have made it here. I believe it with everything inside of me," I tell her the truth.

"You gave me the push. You gave me confidence."

"Dragonfly," I breathe out, reminding Macey of the tattoo on her forearm that she still hasn't told me about. "You've always had the confidence inside of you. It was just masked by the armor you kept to protect yourself and your daughter."

"I..." Her words fall short. She's left stunned and speechless that I figured her all out.

Macey should know by now that she's taken over my life enough that I've learned everything about her.

I've learned about her good days and her bad days.

I've learned what little things make her smile and the things that make her sad.

Dragonflies symbolize our ability to overcome hardships. They are a reminder to take time to connect with your own inner strength, courage and happiness.

Maybe she got the tattoo because it was pretty.

Or maybe she got it because it's the reminder she always needed.

But I'll call Macey dragonfly everyday if I need to, just to remind her.

"Listen," I continue, attempting to change the subject. "Emiline texted me earlier today. She wants to take Mackenzie out to lunch and for a girls' day tomorrow? They want to go pick out a birthday gift for James too."

Macey's mouth parts in shock. "She does?"

"Does that surprise you?"

"I... I mean. I don't know," she stutters her words. "I'm not used to that. She doesn't have people like that in her life who want to do things with her *just because*. Besides Samuel and Flora. Usually there's always an ulterior motive."

"You should probably get used to it. None of us are going anywhere."

I rise from the table, grabbing both of our dishes and begin cleaning up.

"Also, are you off Sunday?"

"I am."

"Good. You're coming with me to the birthday party. Another thing you should probably get used to." I wink.

Macey doesn't reply to my comment. She doesn't need to.

I know she's going to be there Sunday.

"Are you going to be up for a bit?" she finally asks.

I try to fight back a yawn, because if Macey wants to stay up I will *gladly* stay up with her.

But she catches me and tries to backtrack. "Because I'm pretty tired," she says.

That's a lie.

She quickly turns to leave, taking four giant steps toward the hallway. It's honestly really adorable how nervous she is around me. I get the feeling because everything with her makes me nervous. Especially these new feelings I have for her.

"Hey, Macey. Before you go to bed," I call out.

"Yeah?" She turns around, her hair whipping around behind her at how quickly she turned to face me.

My cheeks split with a wide grin as I stare at her. Her green eyes glaring back at me in question. But I don't say anything, I just keep smiling.

Waiting for her to match it.

And she does.

Slowly the corner of her lips twist up and I have successfully done what I wanted to do before she went to bed—put a smile on her face.

"Goodnight."

With that, I turn and head toward my room, wishing like hell she would spend the night lying beside me in my bed, wrapped in my arms.

CHAPTER THIRTY-ONE

Macey

Mackenzie was not herself when she woke up today.

The sun wasn't even over the horizon enough to peek through the blinds before she was in my room and crying to me about everything that took place last night.

She feels so awful for what she did.

I talked her through it and made sure she knows that it was just an accident, making sure she understands accidents happen and it doesn't make you a horrible person.

It helped that Oliver was so good about it.

The relationship Oliver and Mackenzie have developed is something special. Oliver's happy and relaxed personality allows Mackenzie to let her guard down, just like it does for me. I spent so much of that first car ride to the city worrying if suddenly having a man around would put her on edge. But it turns out I didn't need to stress because the friendship that blossomed between them has been incredible to watch. I see every day that Oliver puts in the effort to grow and nourish their relationship. Mackenzie has started to mirror his cheerful, yet calm, demeanor, but what I really think is happening is that she's allowing herself to finally be a happy kid.

I let her take over the kitchen after that where she made her famous French toast and it lightened the mood a lot. Oliver even came out and she insisted on making a giant plate for him as an apology. He kept saying over and over how it was completely unnecessary, that she didn't need to apologize, but Mackenzie's heart is too big for her body and I know she's going to live with this for a while.

The conversation over breakfast shifted to Mackenzie telling us about Samuel and Flora. She spoke to them on the phone yesterday and they have been doing well and have been *really* busy since the blog post.

When we finished, I was reluctant to let Mackenzie go with Emiline after what happened yesterday. I know it was still eating her up, but it made her happy to go spend time with her. She was extra happy to help pick out a birthday present for James.

Who am I to deny that?

Once she left, I spent the entire day snuggled with another book I borrowed from Peyton while the rain hammered against the windows. This used to be my favorite time to read my educational books, but getting lost in a fictional world is a whole new level of relaxation.

But these books… good lord.

Talk about dirty and hot. I now understand why this genre is so addicting and the girls don't stop talking about it. Avery once told me through text message, *once you're in, you won't be able to stop*. She was right, I read the entire book in one sitting.

The rain finally stopped and the sun set so I made my way into the kitchen to make something to eat. The house was strangely quiet so I assumed Oliver was gone for the day.

I won't lie, reading dirty romance books doesn't help the feelings I keep having about him. It brought me back to the night he gave me my first ever orgasm. I don't think I'll ever stop thinking about it…the way my body trembled at just the use of his fingers, the way I want more of it.

More of him.

As if I thought him into existence, Oliver walks in the kitchen.

He looks like he just walked out of the book I just read. Dark wash jeans, and a Henley tee paired that hugs his muscles deliciously. His blonde hair is tousled as if he ran his hands through it a few times and was content with that.

That book got me way too worked up.

"Good you're here," he breaks through my trance. "We're going out."

I look down at my outfit. I'm wearing a pair of oversized sweatpants and a crop top. My hair is a literal mess perched at the top of my head in a bun.

He can't be serious.

I look up at the clock and realize it's already 9 PM.

"I'm not really dressed to go out right now. And don't places close soon?"

He hits me that irresistible smile that I don't think a soul could say no to. "It's a Saturday night in a city that never sleeps."

"Touché."

Oliver laughs before nodding his head towards my room. "Run and get changed. You don't have to get dressed up if you don't want to. But I want to take you out."

My lips part. "You… want to take me out?"

"I do."

"But why?"

He rolls his eyes. "I won't repeat myself, Macey Evans."

I don't do anything I don't want to do, replays in my head. Clearly I'm having trouble grasping that concept. But I can't help it, he's mesmerizing. He makes me forget simple things when he's around.

"Right." I hop off the counter. "Got it."

He smirks. "Good girl."

Fuck. My thighs clench together. I never knew I would be such a praise kind of girl. Maybe it's the books I've been reading or because he's the one saying it. Reading the words in a book leaves me all hot and bothered, and now hearing it from those lips… oof.

"On a serious note," Oliver continues. "I really do want to take you out. I just want you to enjoy a little break from work and mom life, and have some fun."

Mackenzie decided to have a sleepover at Emiline's apartment. I've never been away from her overnight before so it's a new feeling for me. My plan was to stay awake, staring at my phone, waiting for her to beg to come home to me.

However, I don't see that happening with how happy she is with all these new people loving on her.

"So, what should I wear?"

"Nothing works for me," Oliver proposes with a wink. "But I don't want to share your body with anyone. So, casual? Jeans work fine."

He's really not helping the throbbing feeling building up between my legs that I've been feeling since he walked in here. Part of me wants to stay here and let him devour me and give me another orgasm to relieve some of this tension built up inside of me, but another part of me really wants to get out and do something fun.

"Well then… let me go get dressed, sir."

He growls. "On second thought, maybe we should stay home."

"Too late. I'm going to get dressed."

I leave Oliver with the same wink he just shot me.

Tonight should be interesting.

Oliver brought me to his favorite restaurant for dinner. It's a small place, but the atmosphere is perfect for a late night dining experience. He secured a spot on the rooftop terrace that has space heaters strategically placed everywhere. It doesn't feel one bit like you're sitting outside in the cool February air.

"This place is beautiful," I say to him as I stare up at the night sky. Stars twinkle in the distance now that the rain has completely cleared out. The dim lighting allows us to get the best view from here. Leaving us with the fresh scent of rain after it's fallen—my favorite smell.

"It's cozy, right?"

I wouldn't mind being cozied up next to him, if I'm being honest.

The thought reminds me to send a text to the girls later about how I need to lay off the books for a bit because who am I tonight? Why can't I stop thinking like this?

The server comes over and introduces herself before I can give it more thought.

Oliver orders an orange soda and I laugh the same way I did on that first flight where I learned he loves it more than any other soda.

After I order a water, she leaves us to look over the menus.

"Let me guess," I joke. "A double bacon cheeseburger for you?"

His menu falls to the table and he shoots me a knowing look. "It's like you know me or something."

"When I see bacon, I just assume that's what you're going to get now."

Oliver pauses before he breaks out into laughter and I can't help but join him.

Everything he does is infectious.

His smile is like a sudden beam of sunlight, illuminating the darkest parts of my heart.

He feels like home.

"I love it when you do that," Oliver says just as his laughter dies down.

"What? Know what you're going to order before you order?"

"No." He shakes his head with a grin. "Laugh."

Now it's my turn for my laughter to die down, but the smile doesn't leave my face.

I truly believe that I've laughed more in the few weeks I've been with Oliver than I have in my entire life. I really wish that was an exaggeration, but it's not.

The thought alone confirms leaving Montana was the best decision I've ever made.

"I'm… I'm happy."

"It looks fucking good on you." Oliver's cheeks dimple and I feel heat creep up my neck.

Once we order, we fall into comfortable small talk. Our food arrives twenty minutes later and we talk as if we are two people in a long term relationship just catching each other up on our days over dinner.

"I think I might get a new tattoo here in the city," I say.

"Yeah?"

"Yeah. I think so." I nod repeatedly. "I like my tattoos to have meaning. You know, if I'm going to live with them for the rest of my life, I want it to be something worth having. This fresh start here, the happiness I'm feeling, makes me want to get one to celebrate that."

Oliver offers me an encouraging smile. "I think you should do whatever you want to do."

The live music from the band begins to thrum in the background interrupting our conversation. My head snaps in the direction the band is starting to play and I see people getting out of their seats to dance.

I look back at Oliver. "Dance with me?"

He taps a finger to his chest. "Me?"

I look around to see if there's anyone else I might be asking. "Yes, you. Dance with me?"

Oliver pauses for a beat before he looks down at my extended arm and then clasps his hand in mine as I tug him towards the makeshift dance floor they have set up.

I don't have a drop of alcohol in me, but being wrapped up in

Oliver's bubble has me feeling drunk for the first time in my life. It's a high I never want to come down from.

He wraps his arms around my waist, pulling me close to him as we sway to the upbeat music playing around us. My body molds perfectly with his despite our height difference. It's not until Oliver looks down at me, his blue eyes turning gray with desire that the music begins to drown out around me.

It feels like the people around us disappear too.

It feels like it's only us in this crowded space.

As if Oliver senses it too, he pulls me in tighter despite the fact the front of my body is already closing every bit of distance there could be. My body feels weak from his touch, while my heart pounds with every breath I take.

"I can't get any closer, Oliver," I tease.

He leans down and I feel the stubble on his jaw line brush my cheek before he whispers, "You're never close enough."

CHAPTER THIRTY-TWO

Oliver

The feeling of Macey's body pressed up against mine has me ready to go full caveman on her. I'm ready to throw her over my shoulder and not let her go until she's flat on her back in my bed.

When I sent her to her room to get changed earlier, I didn't expect her to be ready as quickly as she was. And I definitely didn't expect her to walk out looking as hot as she did.

She changed into a tight pair of black skinny jeans paired with boots that came up to her knees. And she was wearing the same body suit that still haunts me from the night she walked in on me fisting my cock in the bathroom. It's so tight that it looks like it was painted on her, exposing the swell of her breasts just for me.

I had to palm my dick just so she didn't catch on to the fact that simply looking at her gets me hard.

I really believe from hanging out with Peyton and Avery long enough, that it takes light years for women to get ready for a night out. But Macey successfully went from a messy bun, to loose flowing curls that dangle freely down her back in a matter of fifteen minutes.

Now here I am, with her wrapped up in my arms in the middle of a crowded restaurant.

I take a moment to stare down at her, forcing her head to lift up to meet my gaze. Her thick lashes flutter, while a smile permanently stretches across her face as we sway side to side.

I need her in ways I've never needed someone before.

Coming home to her has me more excited than hopping on a plane to travel ever did.

And it's so much more than in an intimate way.

I need her the way I need oxygen to breathe.

I meant it when I said she's never close enough.

My throat feels tight at the realization while she's in my arms and the delicate smell of her shampoo engulfs my senses.

"Want to get out of here?" I ask, but it comes out as if I'm choking on my own breath for some reason.

"Are you trying to take me home, Oliver Ford?" Macey shoots me a cheeky grin, not realizing how wound up I am over her right now.

Not to mention the way she coos my full name. I'm completely feral for her.

"I'm definitely trying to take you home, Macey."

I watch on bated breath for her reaction as her cheeks flame.

"I like when you call it home." She pauses, green eyes twinkling under the night sky above the open terrace. "You make it feel like I'm home."

That does it.

All restraint is out the window when I grab Macey's face between my palms and bring her lips to mine in a searing kiss, one I need to survive the rest of the night, one I've been desperate for since the last time our lips touched.

This kiss feels like more though.

It feels like the spark that ignites everything I want with her.

It feels like I'm making Macey mine.

I run my fingers through her hair, taking every bit of air from her lungs she wants to give me as her tongue swipes between my lips and dances with mine. She angles her head higher, allowing me better access as I hold her close to me. My cock swelling behind the zipper of my jeans.

Some intangible sound erupts from deep in my chest before I say, "Let's go."

One single night out, and Macey is floating on cloud nine.

When I say floating, that's exactly what she did on the entire walk home. Her arm hooked with mine and laughing like tonight was the best night of her life. If I didn't know any better, I would think she even had a few drinks in her. But she's stone cold sober and just… happy.

"This night was so fun," she exclaims as we enter the apartment.

Yup. Confirmation it was, in fact, the best night.

Macey stops spinning around laughing when she turns to me in the kitchen. The smile wiped clean from her face in a matter of seconds. *What the fuck.*

"This night was just… it was perfect, Oliver." She pauses as if she's trying to think of the words she wants to say next. "Being around you, being in this city… It makes me feel alive. I've never felt more myself than I did tonight."

I take slow, tentative steps toward her while she remains rooted in place.

Begging me to touch her again.

Hopefully, begging me to kiss her again the way we did at the restaurant.

When I get close to Macey, her hands fist my t-shirt at the waist line, forcing my body to press into hers.

"That night," she breathes out on a shallow whisper. "When you touched me."

"Do you want me to touch you again?"

She nods aggressively. "But…"

I raise a brow. "But?"

"I want to touch *you*, Oliver."

My heart thunders in my chest at her admission and the muscles in my back tighten at the thought of her hands all over my body, hands I've envisioned touching me more times than I care to admit.

I grip her chin with my thumb and finger, forcing her head upright. "Tell me what you want to touch, Macey."

"Everything."

My cock jerks at that, pressing into her stomach, and I hear her suck in a breath.

Her hands travel down to my chest as her nails dig into my skin through my shirt while her chin still rests between my fingers. I bring my face down until I'm practically grazing her lips. "So touch me."

"I… I've never done this before."

Fuck. I forgot about last week when Macey told me she's never been with anyone other than the guy who ditched her when he found out she was pregnant. I couldn't sleep that night thinking about that. What kind of person does that? Mackenzie doesn't deserve that, and neither did Macey.

Macey's hands moving along my shoulders to my biceps have me swallowing down any thought I was just having. She pushes her body into me, closing any distance that was just there.

She sucks in a sharp breath, no doubt feeling what she does to me.

My hands land on the counter behind me, allowing her to roam her hands over my body freely. I let her take control of the situation and move at her pace. With the silent invitation, she rakes her nails down my chest and stops at the waistband of my jeans.

My head falls back and I moan at just her touching me there.

I can feel her unbuttoning them, before she pulls the zipper down.

I should get a medal for holding as much restraint as I am right now.

But then Macey's hands are no longer on me and my eyes land on hers as I snap my head down. She has her bottom lip between her teeth and her cheeks are glowing red.

I brush a stray strand of her hair behind her ear before pressing a quick kiss to her lips. I wrap my hand around her wrist as I guide her hand back to the waistband of my jeans. "Take out my cock."

Macey sucks in a sharp breath, but pushes my jeans to the ground and reaches into my boxer briefs to grip my cock. I groan out in pleasure at the feel of her soft, delicate hand wrapped around the shaft. I could actually come right now from just that.

I help her out by pushing my boxer briefs down to rest on the floor with my jeans. stepping out of them to allow her full access to me. Macey's eyes never leave my dick. She just stares down at it, wide eyed.

"Jesus," she breathes out. "It's thick."

Macey doesn't allow me a chance to respond because she begins stroking me up and down with a cautious speed. I can see her brain swirling with all sorts of thoughts as she keeps her eyes fixed where her hand works.

My chest rises and falls as my cock swells in her hand.

Macey swipes the bead of precum from the tip and I moan as my hip involuntarily thrusts into her. "Fuck, that feels so good."

"Yeah?"

"Do you feel how hard I am under your touch?" I say through gritted teeth.

She moans in agreement as her pace quickens and I hear the roar of my own blood in my ears. "You do that to me. Only you."

And I mean that with everything in me.

I watch as Macey wiggles her thighs where she's standing. I know her pussy must be throbbing with need right now. Bump me up to the top of the podium and put the damn gold medal around my neck for holding back restraint.

My chest rises and falls at the feel of her pumping my cock, and then she does what I least expect her to do.

She drops to her knees.

"Fuck, Macey," I groan.

"I've never done this before. So I need you to talk me through this. Okay?" She sounds confident in her question, and eager to have me in her mouth.

I can't even find the words to answer before Macey brings her tongue to the base of my shaft, slowly trailing up to the tip, as if she was tasting me. She swirls her tongue around the head of my cock.

I can no longer breathe as I watch her soft pink lips wrap fully around it before I disappear inside her mouth.

"Fuuuck," I growl.

Macey hums around my throbbing length and it's taking everything in me not to come down the back of her throat.

"That's it, baby. Bob your head up and down for me."

She does as I say, her lips wrapped tightly around me as she moves up and down. She tentatively sucks the tip as she comes to the top and then diving back down until I reach the back of her throat.

I can feel her throat constrict around me, and she gags softly.

Macey picks up speed after that, adjusting herself to my girth as she bobs up and down like a starved woman despite already eating dinner.

"Look at you on your knees for me," I rasp. Her eyes flutter up to meet mine. They glisten as a single tear comes out the corner of her eye. "You look so fucking pretty with your mouth wrapped around me and taking me so well."

She moans, the vibration of her around me has me ready to combust.

"You keep making noises like that and I'm going to come down the back of your throat."

Macey's eyes widen and she aggressively nods her head.

"Is that what you want?"

She nods again.

My hand flies to the back of her hair, holding her in place as I gently buck my hips in and out of her mouth. "Suck, baby. I want to feel my cock hit the back of your throat," I say through gritted teeth.

She moans again and it feels too good to release now. I need another minute with her.

"Relax your throat for me," I say through a breathy moan. "I'm going to come, baby."

Macey slowly sinks lower and lower until I feel the tip deep in her throat. My stomach tightens as I pour myself into her. Grunting as I pump in and out, releasing everything that's been built up over the last few weeks of her being in my presence.

My hand is nothing compared to the feeling of her mouth.

"Jesus Christ." I release a long, drawn out exhale.

She swallows down the last drop, releasing my cock from her mouth with a pop before she wipes the corner of her mouth with the back of her pointer finger. Then, she brings it into her mouth to suck it clean.

Macey stands, eyes meeting mine and god, she's fucking perfect.

I rub my hand along her swollen, red lips before claiming her mouth as mine again. Kissing her with enough force so that she *knows* she's fucking mine. I keep my lips to hers as I yank down her jeans in a feverous rage. Eager to get the taste of her on my tongue.

"What are you doing?" Macey gasps.

I smirk, tossing the jeans to the side before hoisting her up on the counter. I waste no time before I'm unsnapping her damn bodysuit and ripping off her panties. I press a hand to her chest, forcing her back flat against the surface, but she props herself up on her elbows to watch what I'm doing. "You had your dessert, now it's time for mine."

I don't wait for her response as my head dives between her legs. I swipe my tongue through her already wet pussy until I reach her clit, flicking my tongue up and down as I lap her arousal with my tongue. Macey's back arches off the counter and she screams out my name.

I feel goosebumps rise on her thighs as her legs grip my face. She falls to her back as her hands cover her mouth to muffle her screams and moans.

"Let it out, Macey. It's just me and you. I want to hear every moan and every scream come from those perfect lips."

Macey does as I ask, withering beneath me as I suck her clit hard. I want to taste everything she has to give me. I keep my tongue on her clit while one finger finds her pussy and plunges inside.

Her head flies up to look down at me, and our eyes lock. I keep mine on hers so she can see how much I love doing this. How much I'm enjoying tasting her.

"God, that feels so good," Macey flutters. "Please don't stop."

"I have no intention of stopping until your cum is dripping down my chin."

"You really know how to talk dirty." She giggles through her erratic breathing.

I insert a second finger with more force than I intend, causing Macey to buck into my hand. Her back rises off the counter again and I love how responsive she is to my touch. I fuck her hard with my fingers while I suck on her swollen clit. Her pussy pulsates around me and I can feel she's close to reaching the edge.

"You're close, baby. I need you to come for me."

"I think I'm…" Macey's words fall short as her legs begin to tremble around me. I remove my fingers but keep my mouth on her pussy and I suck up everything she's giving me as she comes.

And she comes hard.

"Oh my god," she continues to scream out through her orgasm.

There's nothing hotter than Macey Evans coming for me.

I'll die on this hill.

Once I know she's successfully come down from her release, I rise from between her legs. She lifts herself up until she's resting on her hands.

I lean forward until I'm close enough to her lips. "You taste like heaven."

Macey grins in euphoria before she says, "That was… unreal." Her chest rises and falls rapidly as she works to regain her regular breathing pattern.

Every single thing about this night only confirms all the feelings I've been having for her.

She's become my drug of choice.

My addiction.

My weakness.

Macey Evans is my everything.

CHAPTER THIRTY-THREE

Macey

I wake up with a beaming smile on my face despite Oliver no longer being in the bed.

I don't know what came over me last night.

Was it the book I spent all day reading that got me worked up?

Was it just being around Oliver?

I can't help the flutters in my chest when he's near, the smile that forms on my lips when he walks into a room, the shiver that racks my body when he touches me.

His hands.

Damn, he's good with his hands.

The way Oliver touched me and devoured me was something I've seriously been missing out on. I've never craved sex or anything like that before, but I wouldn't complain if he wants to do that again.

He also makes me want so many things that I didn't think were in the cards for me.

When the world shut me out for having my daughter so young, I knew I was destined to be a single mom for the rest of my life. Because who wants to jump into someone's life and accept the baggage that comes with another man's kid.

But Oliver makes me feel like he wants this too.

We haven't talked about more than what happened in the kitchen and I want to, but today isn't the day to bring it up. We have to get ready for James' birthday party.

I fire off a text to Emiline to see how Mackenzie is.

How's Mackenzie doing? Did she sleep ok?

EMILINE

She slept like a rock. LOL. She actually just woke up a few minutes ago and is begging us to let her make her famous French toast?

It's her favorite meal to make.

wait... Emiline...

EMILINE

Yeah?

What do you mean by 'us'?

EMILINE

Me and the dog.

I can't help but laugh because dogs probably shouldn't be eating French toasts, but whatever.

I make my way into the kitchen to make myself a cup of coffee. My steps falter when I see Oliver standing over the stove in nothing but a pair of sweatpants. His back is on full display for me as I admire at every rigid muscle painted along his tanned skin.

As if he can sense me, he turns to face me and an irresistible smile is painted on his face.

"Hey, you." The way the words are said, I swear I melt on the spot. "Come sit. I made you breakfast."

"You made me breakfast?"

"I did. Mackenzie taught me how to make her French toast.

She said it's your favorite thing she makes and I wanted to make it for you."

Swoon.

Oliver learned how to make my daughter's favorite breakfast food so he can make it for me.

My throat feels tight while I take a seat at the bar stool.

"I wrapped our gift for James already this morning too," Oliver says as he puts a plate of French toasts topped with powdered sugar in front of me.

This man really takes advantage of mornings. It's nine in the morning and it sounds like he has an entire day of tasks completed already.

"Our gift?" I ask.

"Yup. We got him a plethora of puzzles that I know he's going to love. I hope it's okay that I put the gift is from both of us."

"That's..." I pause, trying to find the words. It's more than okay. Is this the confirmation I was looking for not long ago when I opened my eyes and immediately wondered what we're doing together? "That's fine," I choke out.

"You good?" Oliver laughs at me.

"Yeah. I... uh... I guess my mind is spinning a little bit this morning about what happened last night and what this all means for us."

Oliver's movement in the kitchen halts. He slowly turns around as if he's a video that was being played in slow motion. A wicked grin plays on his mouth and I watch his cheeks dimple.

"It means whatever *you* want it to mean, Macey. I don't know the first thing about relationships and what to do or how to do them. But there's no denying that I want something with you. Anything you're willing to give me. I want to figure everything out *with* you."

I straighten under the weight of his gaze on me and my muscles tighten.

Do I want this? Yes. God yes, I do.

But I have another person to think about with every decision I make.

"But I have a daughter," I blurt out.

"Is that who that other girl living in my apartment is?" He smirks. "I had absolutely no idea."

I snort out a laugh. Leave it to Oliver to take every bit of tension in a conversation and completely evaporate it in thin air. I can't help but relax with his sarcasm.

"You know what I mean."

"Actually, I don't."

"It means I have *baggage*, Oliver. Are you sure you want to get involved with that?"

He rounds the kitchen island before he swivels my bar stool until I'm facing him. With a small nudge, Oliver spreads my legs open and steps between them. He grips my chin between his fingers, forcing my gaze to meet his.

"Lucky for you." He presses a quick kiss to my lips. "I like to travel."

Then he walks away to continue cleaning the pan in the sink, leaving me frozen in place. Mouth parted like he didn't just tell me he wants all of me.

The broken and bruised parts.

The past I've been fighting so hard to be clear from.

And my Mackenzie.

He wants all of it.

"We have to leave in a little bit," Oliver breaks the silence. "Thomas and Peyton live in New Jersey, so we have a little bit of travel. Apparently there's an accident in the tunnel too, so we might have to take the long way."

"I'll go get ready now then," I say as I bring my plate to the sink. "You know, I heard Mackenzie also made French toasts for Emiline and her dog this morning."

He raises a brow in question. "Emiline doesn't have a dog."

Well that's… interesting.

It took us an extra half hour to get to Peyton's house due to traffic. But it didn't feel like it took us long to get here at all with Oliver belting *Today's Top Hits* over the radio while I laughed uncontrollably in the passenger seat.

If there's one thing I've learned, I love being around him for this reason alone.

By the time we arrived, everyone was here already. We walked through the door hand in hand as if we do it all the time. No one batted an eye as if everyone expected this from us.

The weather was perfect for James' party, despite it being the end of February. It was a cool day with a mild breeze in the air, allowing him to have the bounce house he wanted in the backyard.

I remember when Mackenzie turned five, but her party was nothing like this. I wish I was able to give her something like this, but my parents were dead set on keeping things more elegant.

I'm not even sure that's the word I'm looking for, but they acted like it was a thirty-year-old's party filled with a five-course meal and she couldn't even pick the cake she wanted.

I'm convinced that's why she acts so much older than her age. She was forced out of her childhood.

That's why I find myself on the verge of tears as I stand on their back deck, looking out into their massive backyard as Mackenzie laughs like the child she is with James and his friends in the bounce house.

She's having the best day ever.

"She loves spending time with James," Peyton says next to me. I didn't even hear her coming.

I shake off the emotions, not allowing them to bubble to the surface. "She really does. She loves kids so much. I wouldn't be surprised if she becomes a teacher in the future."

"I wouldn't either," Peyton agrees as she stares at the kids with me. "She's so good with them at the daycare center. We love having her come hang out with us after school. The kids actually look forward to it and wonder when she's going to be there each day."

My head snaps in her direction. "They do?"

Peyton nods. "You raised a really bright and smart young girl, Macey."

That does it. The emotions bubble and I can't control it. "Thank you."

"None of that today." She wraps an arm around my shoulder. "It's a day of celebration. For all things."

I give her a curious eye and she just laughs at me.

"Come inside. We have cake."

I follow her inside and I'm curious why we aren't calling James and the kids for cake.

"You ready, babe?" Thomas says from the kitchen.

"Ready," she squeals as she bounces into his arms.

I watch intently as she wraps her arms around his waist and he wraps his arms around her head. He looks down at her with so much love in his eyes and I get weepy all over again. Their love is something so special. I'm so thankful that this group of people were brought into my life and that I get to witness their love.

My eyes scan the room and I see Marc with his arm draped over Avery's shoulder as she wraps her arms around his waist from the side. It's crazy to hear the story about how they were actually *faking it* when they were in my bar over the summer. As an outsider looking in, there was nothing fake about the way they interacted with each other.

"Want me to call the kids in?" Logan asks from the couch.

I notice Emiline sitting on the armrest of the couch right next to him. Not quite touching him, but my brain can't stop thinking about those two. I've always been Team Emiline in the group chat. I feel like she would say something is going on with them, but after our conversation this morning, my curiosity peaked and I wonder even more what's happening there.

"We will call them in soon," Peyton says. "It's been damn near impossible to get us all together the last few weeks. So we figured we would steal some thunder from James for a moment."

Avery gasps as her hand covers her mouth.

Is this what I think it is?

"Welcome to our gender reveal," Thomas announces.

"Shut up!" Avery bellows. "Are you kidding me!"

Peyton giggles as she shakes her head, and her hand flies to her stomach that doesn't look any bigger than it did a few weeks ago. "Surprise! We're expecting!"

"Wait..." Emiline says with furrowed brows. "But we had tequila shots a couple weeks ago at girls' night."

"*You guys* had tequila shots," she scoffs. "We were so wrapped up in conversation that no one noticed that I didn't actually take my shot."

There are a few beats of silence before Emiline, Avery and I all break out into a fit of laughter as we hug and congratulate Peyton on the news.

"Congrats, brother!" Marc reaches for Thomas, giving him a brotherly hug.

"That's amazing news!" Oliver follows and does the same.

"So are we going to find out what the little gummy bear is or what?" Logan announces.

We all take our place around the table. Avery takes her place back in Marc's arms while Logan and Emiline stand next to each other with a matching stance of elbows propped on the counter. Oliver finds his spot on the bar stool next to me, spreading his legs and moving me to stand between them.

My heart rate picks up at the small display of affection in front of our friends. There's no part of him that wants to hide whatever the hell we are and that alone makes me beam with happiness that he wants *me* that way.

Peyton and Thomas pick up the knife and slice the cake like it's their wedding day, pulling a piece out on a plate.

"It's blue!" Thomas yells. "Another boy!"

"Oh my god," Peyton gasps. "I knew I was destined to be a boy mom!"

We all clap and scream in excitement as they embrace their own happiness.

"When are you due?" Avery asks

"Not until September," she says. "Probably a Christmas-made baby."

"We really don't need all those details." Emiline scrunches her nose.

"You don't want to know the positions we used?" Peyton jokes.

"Please don't," she begs. "It's bad enough I have to hear about my brother's sex lives through a group chat."

The girls start laughing and tears spill from my eyes because it's so beautiful to be a part of this news with people who have now grown into my family, to be so happy for someone who's become one of my best friends in such a short period of time.

"You okay?" Oliver whispers in my ear.

"It's just so beautiful. I'm really happy for them."

He nods. "Me too," he says before he presses a kiss to my cheek.

"While we're on the good news train." Avery clears her throat to the side of me. My head snaps in her direction and I watch as her eyebrows raise in a wiggle.

"Oh, no news here." I giggle.

Oliver wraps his arms around my waist. "Yet," Oliver adds. "I'm just waiting for Macey to realize she's actually head over heels for me."

A shiver courses through me at the feel of his lips against my shoulder.

But Oliver is wrong.

I'm already head over heels for him.

It's just taking my heart a minute to catch up to my brain.

CHAPTER THIRTY-FOUR

Oliver

"How the hell is it March already?" Logan asks.

"I said the same thing," Thomas adds from the seat across from me.

"Listen, I'm just happy that we haven't had any big snow storm hit here," I chime in.

It's our typical Wednesday night out with the boys. We haven't met up in weeks because Logan has been working overtime and before the gender reveal, Thomas was busy taking care of Peyton and hiding the fact that she's pregnant from us. As for Marc, he's just been doing his own thing with Avery.

Which is why we agreed that this was long overdue.

"I don't understand why you hate the snow so much." Thomas laughs.

"I don't understand how people like it," I quip.

"I like it." Logan shrugs. "It's a nice excuse to sit inside and do nothing."

"You already do that," Thomas snaps.

"Among other things." He stops himself as he eyes Thomas over the brim of his whiskey glass.

Thomas rolls his eyes. "I'm not even going to entertain the look you just gave me."

"Good." Logan nods with a shit eating grin.

"Anyway," Thomas starts. "Any trips coming up, Oliver? I feel like you haven't been away in a while."

"That's because I haven't."

"Is there a particular reason for that?" Logan raises an eyebrow. "Does the reason happen to have black hair and a kid by any chance?"

My lips curve over the brim of my glass. "Maybe."

Logan's gaze snaps to Thomas before he puts his hand out for him. "You owe me fifty dollars."

"I did *not* shake on that." Thomas swats his hand away.

"Hold up. Did you guys make a bet on us?"

"He did," Thomas defends himself. "I said I wasn't betting on my brother's soulmate."

Logan wrinkles his nose. "And I said, soulmate sounds like something satan puts in his coffee. But I proceeded to bet that you would be in love with her by the summer."

My mouth parts in shock. "I can't stand you both. Where the hell is Marc when I need him."

"He's closing a deal in Brooklyn with Avery," Thomas says.

I groan.

"You know you can talk to me about anything," Thomas adds.

I release a sigh before I admit, "I just don't know what I'm doing. My mindset has always been *'don't settle down'* and *'you don't need to plant roots anywhere to be happy.'* Which is why I've always lived the way I have because that's what made me happy. Then Macey came into my life and I swore I wouldn't get attached. But I did. I can't get enough of her and find myself wanting more in life."

The words hang in the air between us as Thomas keeps his gaze locked with mine.

"You love her," he says.

Love? There's no way that's what this is.

I know to an extent what love is. I love my brothers, my

sister, my mom, and my nephew. I love the friend group we've created with Logan and the girls too. It's become a bond between all of us that can never be broken.

But in love with Macey?

I huff out a breath. "I wouldn't go that far."

Thomas laughs. "I vividly remember saying the same thing about Peyton. I denied the feelings I had for so long. Mainly because she was my son's nanny. She was there for James. It was never supposed to be more than that."

"We all knew you were head over heels for her after that first night at the charity event where you two met." I say.

"Exactly." Thomas nods. "I know Marc isn't here to speak for himself, but look at him and Avery… Those two fought their feelings hard. Remember those stupid rules she set?" He laughs again. "She had three. We knew Marc would be the one to break her most important one."

"We also knew he fell for her after that first date," I add. "Despite it being fake, it was definitely real from the outside looking in."

"See what I mean?" Thomas offers me an encouraging smile. "You can deny your feelings for her all you want, but you just have to ride it out and see what happens between you two even if you have no idea how to do this. I should also add, it's *okay* to change the direction of your life. If you've never wanted to settle down before and you find yourself wanting to now… that's okay too."

Logan sniffles next to us, wiping a fake tear from his eye. "Gosh, that was beautiful."

"Fuck off," Thomas and I say in unison.

"I just *really* don't want to mess it up with her. I find myself nervous that if I say the wrong thing she's going to run for the hills."

"You can't mess up what's right for you." Thomas shrugs.

His words ring in my ear as I sit in silence.

I never knew the first thing about what was right for me. But now that I have Macey, is this what was always meant for me? I don't know… but what I do know is that I can't deny the way I feel when I'm around her or the way I crave to be with her so much that I've put off trips.

Or the way I haven't just fallen for her, but for her daughter too.

I can't picture a life without either of them in it.

"Since we're on the advice train…" I pause. "I do have a trip coming up."

"That's great," Thomas exclaims.

"I was thinking about asking Macey if she and Mackenzie wanted to come with me for the weekend."

Logan spits out his drink while Thomas looks at me with wide eyes unblinking.

My eyes bounce between both of them. "What?"

"It's just…" Thomas starts.

"You never travel with other people," Logan finishes for him.

"I do too."

"Name one time," Logan counters.

I stop to think about it. I've taken trips with people. I don't like it, but I've had to take trips with others. That one time I went to California… wait, no. Oh, that time I went down to Texas for a week to help a hotel chain open a new location. Logan came… Shit… no, he didn't.

"Okay, fine. You have a point."

"You know how many times I've asked to tag along?" Logan says.

I throw my hands up in defense. "Okay. I get it. This is weird, isn't it? Now I'm even more nervous to ask her."

"Do what I do when you're afraid to ask a question." Logan straightens in his chair. "Text it."

"I can't do that. That's so impersonal."

"Just do it," he groans. "See what she says and you can finish talking about it when you get home. And then bang it out together."

"That's... no." I shake my head before pulling out my phone.

I start typing in my open text thread to her and show it to them before I hit send.

"What are we in, high school?" Thomas laughs. "You need someone else to analyze a text to your crush before sending it?"

"Just fucking send it." Logan rolls his eyes.

Hey. You think you can get next weekend off?

"Smooth," Logan deadpans.

I sit back in my chair with a huff. "This is too much for me."

"Oh, stop. You're fine." Thomas rolls his eyes.

"While I wait for a response from her. I wanted to ask both of you where you get your tattoos done here in the city."

"Are you finally getting one?" Logan raises a brow.

"No, it's for Macey."

"I'll text you my guy's contact information," Thomas says as he pulls out his phone to swipe through his contacts. "He's the best. Logan uses him too."

I nod. "Awesome, thank you."

My phone dings on the table, cutting off that conversation as quickly as it started. I think it's Thomas sending me the contact info, but when I look, it's from Macey.

MACEY

I'm already off actually. I'm working a few lunch shifts during the week to help cover for someone. So they gave me that weekend off.

Why, what's up?

Butterflies dance wildly around my stomach as I read her reply. There's nothing I want more than to whisk her and Mackenzie away for a weekend. There's nothing I want more than to give Macey everything she's ever wanted in life. She's got the job of her dreams, and now she deserves a little getaway to celebrate.

I nervously type out my response and hit send before I second guess myself.

I was wondering if you and Mackenzie wanted to take a weekend trip with me.

CHAPTER THIRTY-FIVE

Macey

OLIVER

I was wondering if you and Mackenzie wanted to take a weekend trip with me.

My stomach drops and my heart gallops in my chest as I stare down at the phone in my hands reading the text that just came through from Oliver. He wants to take me on a trip. With him. With my daughter.

"You look like you just saw a ghost." Peyton laughs beside me.

Peyton and Kali are here for the night to have an impromptu girls' night at the apartment while Oliver has a guys' night.

I was reluctant to have them over at first because this isn't really my place. It feels weird to have people over when Oliver isn't here. However, he insisted they come over. These girls remind me time and time again that they aren't just friends anymore.

They are family welcoming Mackenzie and me with open arms.

Mackenzie is sucked into a *Harry Potter* marathon on TV in her room and can't seem to bring herself away from it because "it's just getting good," she says.

So we've spent the last hour talking about the last book we all read over a charcuterie board full of a variety of cheeses. Kali made sure to include vegan options for Peyton and I love how these girls look out for each other.

"Oliver just asked us to go on a trip with him," I finally answer.

"He what?" Peyton practically screams.

My eyes widen at her reaction, as if that was truly the last thing she expected to hear.

"It's just... wow," she says, shaking her head but also has a smile plastered on her mouth.

"Oliver doesn't travel with anyone. *Ever*," Kali says for her.

"He doesn't? Why?"

"Who knows?" Kali shrugs as she goes for another piece of cheese and crackers.

"It's sort of his thing," Peyton adds. "He likes traveling alone because he feels at peace, or something like that. And he can do things without worrying about what other people want to do. He just likes doing his own thing."

That leaves the question swirling around my brain... Why is he asking me to go on a trip with him? And not just me, but Mackenzie too.

With that thought, I can't help but smile down at my phone.

I don't care how crazy I look when I do it because this man has grown to be more than I ever imagined he would be. This should terrify me, but it doesn't. There's something about him and how careful he's been with my heart that makes me want to *scream* yes.

I've noticed a massive shift in myself from the time I got in Oliver's pickup truck to leave Roxbury, until now. I no longer feel on edge. In fact, I feel more carefree than I ever have. I have everything I've ever dreamed of now. Mackenzie is happy. We have a roof over our head. I have the job I've always dreamed of. And...

Oliver.

I know they say you don't need a man to make you feel complete, that you don't need a man to realize your worth. But it's nice to have a partner who pushes you to be better in all aspects of life.

Is that what we are? Together? I don't know where we stand.

But Lord help me, I want it all with him.

"I think I'm going to say yes," I finally tell the girls.

"I think you totally should," Kali agrees while Peyton giggles and kicks her feet in excitement on the couch next to me.

"Yes. Yes. Yes," Peyton bellows. "I love this so much. Do you know where the trip is?"

"Let me ask."

Where are we heading?

OLIVER

The way you just worded that makes me want to come home right now.

I wouldn't be opposed to that.

OLIVER

You're absolutely killing me.

And to answer your question, we're going down to Wilmington, North Carolina.

"He said Wilmington, North Carolina." I tell Peyton.

"Oh my god. First of all, that place is adorable. Second of all, did he say when?"

"His first text said next weekend. Why? Am I missing something?" My eyes bounce around the girls, clueless on what's happening.

Peyton throws herself back on the couch with a groan. "God, I'm so jealous. I wanted to go down there that weekend so badly. Avery did too, but our schedules didn't work out."

I look at her in confusion. "Is something going on that weekend?"

"Yes! Only the most epic romance readers retreat ever!" Peyton says.

I laugh. "I have no idea what that is."

"It's just to get together for a weekend and talk about all things books. Obviously romance," she says with certainty. "We wanted to go so bad."

"How fun. But I doubt that's where Oliver is taking us."

"I heard it's kind of romantic down there." Kali winks.

"Is it?"

"Wait." Peyton stops us. "You should leave Mackenzie with me for the weekend. This way you two can have some adult-only time."

"Oh absolutely not." I shake my head. "I can't go on a trip and leave her behind."

"Why not?" Peyton asks.

"I just can't. The one and only time she's ever been away from me is when she stayed over at Emiline's last weekend. Even that was a lot for me."

It was hard to deny her that night. Mackenzie *wanted* to go because she loves having these people in her life. Besides I was in the same town as her. I was right down the street from her and felt at peace with knowing she was still close if she needed me.

The thought of taking a flight to an entirely different state while she stays behind makes me feel like I'm abandoning her.

"I understand that." Peyton's soft tone cuts through my thoughts. "Being a mom is the hardest thing in the world. You question your worth just about every day and wonder if you're doing the right thing in how you're raising them."

I nod because that's so spot on.

"But it doesn't make you a bad mom to do something for yourself. You're allowed to take time away from your kids. You're allowed to have adult-only time and step out of the role of being a 24/7 parent." She stands to take a seat next to me, placing her hand over mine. "You're a good fucking mom, Macey. I look up to you so much...your strength and how you've overcome so much, how you fought to get here and achieve your lifelong dream. I'm willing to bet Mackenzie sees that too. She's such a smart, *amazing* girl. She's more advanced than any eight year old I've ever met. And guess what... *you* did that. She's the way she is *because* of you."

I blink away the tear that's threatening to spill over.

Emotions I fight so hard to keep down so often bubble up inside of me. The days where it's so hard, I have my daughter.

Peyton's right. Mackenzie is such an amazing girl and I'm so damn lucky that I get to call her mine.

"You're right," I whisper. "About all of it. I just love her so much."

"We know you do," Kali interjects. "We love her too. It wouldn't mean you love her any less if you decide to take a weekend off."

"I seriously love having her over," Peyton adds. "She and James really get along so well. I like to think of her as a bonus niece to the family."

Her confession does it for me.

I swipe a hand across my cheek, brushing away the tear that escaped. Nothing warms my heart more than having people love Mackenzie the way I do. She deserves that kind of love. Every kid does. And she finally has that unconditional love from people who have welcomed us with wide open arms.

Am I seriously considering this?

"Okay." I nod. "How about I ask her? Let's see what she wants to do and we can go from there."

"That's a perfect idea," Peyton agrees.

I make my way to her room, taking a deep breath before I knock.

"Yeah?" Mackenzie calls out.

"Hey, babe. How's your movie marathon?"

"It's so good," she says, keeping her eyes fixed on the TV.

"I have a question for you."

She pauses the TV and sits up in her bed. "Yeah?"

I make my way to her bed to sit on the edge of it. I don't know why I'm so nervous.

"So Oliver texted me and asked if we wanted to take a trip with him down to North Carolina."

"Wow," Mackenzie interrupts before I can say more.

"I know." I let out a light laugh. "I was telling Peyton about it and she said you can hang out with her for the weekend instead if you wanted. He invited both of us but we want to leave the decision up to you. Do you want to go on the trip or do you want to stay with Peyton for the weekend?"

Mackenzie doesn't answer me back right away and I can tell the decision is swimming around her mind with what she wants to do.

"Would you be mad if I stayed with Peyton?"

"Absolutely not, babe. I'm leaving the decision completely up to you. But are you okay if I go away?"

"Yeah." She nods. "I'll miss you a lot, but you kinda need a vacation."

"Oh, do I?" I offer her a smile.

Mackenzie giggles. "You do. You've always worked too much. Plus, I love hanging out with Mrs. Peyton and James. And it'll only be for a weekend."

"Okay." I nod. "Then it's settled. We both will get a fun weekend out of it."

"It's settled," she agrees.

"Go back to your movie," I say as I stand and leave her room.

"Hey, Mom," Mackenzie calls out.

I turn around, standing in her doorway and my eyes lock with hers. "Yeah?"

"I love you."

My heart flutters in my chest. "I love you too, baby. To the moon, stars and Jupiter."

I retreat back to the living room where I find Peyton and Kali laughing about whatever they were just talking about. I plop down on the couch next to them.

"So, are you sure you're okay with Mackenzie staying with you?"

"One hundred percent." Peyton smiles widely. "This will be so good for all of you."

My nerves dance around my entire body.

A weekend with Oliver. Alone.

I can't deny that I want that alone time with him more than anything. I want a chance for us to get closer than we already are, a getaway from the hustle and bustle of work and the city.

It's time to finally stop fighting these feelings I have for him and take action.

I pull out my phone to send him a quick text.

How do you feel about just us two going on the trip?

CHAPTER THIRTY-SIX

Oliver

MACY

How do you feel about just us two going on the trip?

I keep reading the text over and over again as the taxi drives me back to the apartment.

I really wanted the three of us to go on this trip, but there's something about the idea of having Macey completely to myself that has me wanting to jump out of my own skin in all the best ways possible.

She's mine, and I'm ready to claim her in every sense.

The same way she's already unknowingly claimed me.

When I finally arrive at the apartment, my leg is bouncing in the elevator in anticipation of seeing her and asking her what her text message means. I pray it means what I think it means and that she feels the same way I do about everything.

When I finally enter the apartment, the only light on is the small one over the kitchen sink where Macey is washing dishes.

I stalk over to her like I'm some kind of feral animal because seeing her in *my* kitchen makes her look like she belongs here for the long run. All thoughts I had of asking her more about her text vanish and I can only think of having her in my arms.

Macey doesn't hear me until I'm right behind her, gripping her waist and spinning her around until her wide eyes meet mine. Her wet hands grip my biceps and I'm too wound up to give a shit.

I crash my lips to hers with a need I've never felt before.

I mold my lips to hers as she kisses me back with the same desire, angling her head just the right amount to gain me better access as my tongue swipes along her bottom lip. She easily opens for me, allowing me to taste everything she has to give.

My body hums at the feel of Macey's body relaxing into mine while her hands circle my head. Her fingers grip my hair, holding me there for dear life to ensure I never stop.

Trust me, I couldn't stop if I tried.

My hands find her round ass and I grip tight. Lifting her into my arms, Macey easily wraps her legs around my waist, not once breaking the kiss between us to speak a single word to each other as I bring her to my bedroom.

She doesn't release the kiss to even protest.

She wants this the same way I do.

I kick my door shut behind me before I turn her around and press her to the back of the door at the same time I turn the lock.

She releases the kiss with a gasp as I press my painful erection into her.

"Oliver," Macey pants.

I don't reply, I just crash my lips to hers again. Her hands are everywhere, winding through my hair, holding my neck, and clawing at my shoulders as she presses herself into me. We're just two completely unhinged people who have been fighting this for entirely too long.

"Tell me what you want," I choke out.

"You," Macey says without an ounce of hesitation.

I pull my head back, holding her body to me as tight as I can. For fear that if I let go of her even the smallest amount, she will slip away from me.

"You have me," I whisper over her mouth. "From the moment we first met, you've had me."

Both of her hands palm the side of my face, her thumbs brushing the stubble on jawline as her green eyes bore into me. I feel like I can't breathe and my mouth feels dryer than the Sahara Desert. Every breath I take is dependent on her.

"So take *me*, Oliver."

I spin around, keeping my tight hold on her as I bring her to my bed. I lay her down on her back as gently as possible while I press kisses to every part of exposed skin I can. I reluctantly release her and she props herself up on the bed.

Her pink lips are perfectly swollen and her eyes scream with desire for me.

I reach behind my head with one hand and pull my shirt up over my head in one fluid motion. Macey pulls her bottom lip between her teeth as her eyes scan me up and down. Then she reaches for the hem of her oversized tee and brings it up over her head.

Her ink-covered arm is the first thing my eyes land on before I scan the rest of her fully exposed to me.

I quirk a brow. "No bra?"

"I don't normally wear a bra to bed."

"Fuuuck," I groan as I bring myself to hover over her again. My mouth is only a breath away from hers as she wraps her hands around me. Her touch sends shivers through my body and blood rushes straight to my groin. "I don't know what I did to deserve you, Macey. But right now, I need you in ways I've never needed anyone else before."

Macey lifts her hips the smallest amount, pressing herself against my erection while her lips twist into a grin.

"I feel the same way," she breathes out.

I dive into her neck, peppering kisses along her pounding pulse before I'm hovering over her hardened nipples. My eyes lift and I see her watching me intently, waiting for my next move.

I cup one breast in my palm and suck the nipple into my mouth. We both moan in unison. The sounds she makes has me both rushing to be inside of her, but also eager to take my time and live in every second of this.

"That feels so good," she says on a sharp inhale.

"I know." I smirk up at her, bringing my hand between us and cupping her pussy over her sleep shorts. "But I have a feeling I know something that will feel so much better."

Macey's back arches off the bed and her eyes flutter closed at the feel of me between her legs.

My need to feel every bare inch of her intensifies. I pull myself up before I hook a finger into the waistband of her shorts and in one quick movement, I have them pulled off. She props herself up on both elbows as she lays there for me.

Macey keeps her eyes fixed with mine as she slowly opens her legs for me. I move my gaze to her bare pussy and it glistens in the dimly lit room.

"Are you already wet for me, baby?" I tease as my tongue runs along my bottom lip.

Macey's cheeks flame and my body stills when I see her reach a hand between her legs. Her body jolts at the contact of her finger on her clit before she lifts her fingers up for me. "You tell me." She smirks.

Seeing this whole new side of Macey feels like I'm watching her come alive.

Like she's been trapped inside walls she built but she's finally letting them down.

For me.

I lean forward, my hand gripping her wrist as I bring her pointer finger into my mouth and suck the delicious taste off them. My eyes roll back in my head because Macey tastes like the sweetest sin.

"I need more of that." I lower myself to the edge of the bed, gripping her hips as I pull her down with me for better access. I push her legs open wider for me as I bring myself a breath away from her. "In fact, I need you to come on my face."

"But…" She lifts her head, glossy eyes meeting mine.

I chuckle. "Don't worry. This won't be the only time you come tonight."

Macey sucks in a sharp breath and my tongue is on her. I swipe through her wetness as I lap up her arousal. I make contact with her clit and her hips buck into my face. I can hear her breathing become more erratic with each suck on the bundle of nerves.

"I can't believe how good this feels," Macey moans.

My mind flashes for a brief moment remembering that she's not used to this. No one has ever tasted her the way I have. No one has ever *had* her the way I have her now. No one has ever taken the time to worship this body the way I am now.

It sparks something inside of me. A flash of adrenaline and need to take care of her and make this good for her. To show her how she deserves to be treated.

I slide one finger into Macey's pussy while I continue to flick my tongue across her swollen clit. I drive in and out of her as she writhes beneath me. She's close. I can tell by the way her walls pulse around me.

I want to see her fall apart. Only for me.

I insert a second finger as I pick up the pace. I fuck her with my hand, feeling her arousal coat my fingers until I'm feeling it drip down my palm.

Fuuuck.

"I'm close. I think I'm going to…"

"Come for me, Macey," I say against her pussy.

And she does. Her legs shake on each side of my head as her orgasm takes over her body. I take my fingers out of her, and bring my mouth to her and lick up every last drop she has to give me.

Once Macey has successfully come down from her high, I bring myself on top of her, pressing my painfully hard erection into her. At this point, I'm surprised the zipper of my pants hasn't ripped open yet.

"In case I haven't said it before—I press a quick kiss to her lips—"you are absolutely stunning when you come."

Macey giggles under me, wrapping her arms around my neck forcing my body to lay on top of hers as she nuzzles her face into my neck. My forearms cage her face and my fingers wrap themselves in her hair.

I don't want to press her for more, I'm not that kind of guy. When she's ready she will tell me but as if she can sense my thoughts, her hips rock into me.

My eyes widen as I pull myself up and look into her gorgeous eyes.

"You said that wasn't the only time I would come tonight," she reminds me.

"I did, didn't I?" I grin down at her.

"So, what are you going to do about that?"

I growl as my lips find the shell of her ear. "Are you craving my cock, baby?"

She drives her hips up in response, rubbing herself on my cock. I feel her hot, panting breaths on my neck.

"I want you, Oliver," Macey admits, pulling my face back to look at her. "I wasn't sure what I wanted. I wasn't sure if this was a good idea and I've been fighting off these feelings longer than I care to admit. But if I'm correct…" She pauses, bringing her bottom lip between her teeth. "I think you feel it too."

"I fucking do," I answer without an ounce of hesitation.

"So why don't you do us both a favor."

I raise a brow. "What's that?"

"Make me yours."

CHAPTER THIRTY-SEVEN

Macey

I don't think I've wanted anything more than this.

My head is in a dizzy haze from the orgasm he just gave me, but no amount of brain fog can stop me from wanting this with him. As someone who's had sex once in their life, this feels real.

Intimate.

This feels like it's confirming every feeling I've had about this man over the last few weeks.

"Are you positive in what you're asking me?" Oliver questions as he looks down at me. "I would never make you do anything you're not ready for."

I swallow past the dryness in my throat. "I'm ready."

He lifts himself off me and makes his way to his dresser to grab a condom from the drawer. I watch every move intently as he stands in front of me again and unzips his jeans, pushing them to the floor. His baby blue eyes are now a dark ocean blue as they reignite my body with his gaze.

I don't take my eyes off Oliver as he hooks his finger into his navy blue boxer briefs and pushes them to the ground with his jeans.

I can't help when my eyes travel to his cock standing at attention. Oliver gives himself two languid strokes before he tears the wrapper open with his teeth, discarding it to the floor before he rolls it on his thick length.

My eyes widen without even thinking about it. I've seen it before. I've had it in my mouth. Maybe I'm just wondering how *that* monster of a penis is going to fit—

"It'll fit." Oliver grins as if he can read my thoughts. "I'm going to take it slow. Okay?"

I nod in response, my body feeling like it's going to combust at any minute.

He lowers himself on top of me, nudging my legs open with a tap of his fingers. I open them, eager to feel this between us.

I keep my eyes fixed on where his hand grips his cock. Oliver strokes it from base to tip before pressing the head against my sensitive clit. I suck in a sharp breath, anticipation buzzing as he swipes in through my wetness slowly.

"Fuck, you're still so wet for me," he groans.

The tip of his cock sits right at my entrance and the feel of that alone has me ready to explode.

"Please," I beg.

"So eager," he hums. "But here's the thing… I know you've never been fucked properly before. That no one has taken their time with this sweet pussy." He slowly pushes himself into me. Not completely, but just enough that I feel myself stretch around him. A whimper that's mixed with pain and pleasure comes out of me. "And after this, no one will ever have this pussy but me."

With his words ringing in the air, Oliver pushes even more into me.

"Jesus Christ," he draws out. "You're so tight."

"Oh my god, Oliver," I practically cry out. "That feels. Wow."

He leans down to press a kiss to my lips before whispering, "I'm not all the way in, baby. Arms over your head," he orders. "Grip the bars of the headboard and don't let go."

I do as he says. I feel hot in every single part of me, but I'm shivering with need, with desire.

The quick pain I felt morphs into pleasure as Oliver sinks

himself completely into me, and I cry out his name. My back lifts off the bed, my knuckles white from holding on. I feel so completely full.

"Are you okay?" he asks.

"Yes," I assure him. "So much, yes."

Oliver laughs as he pulls back slowly, just enough that the tip stays in before he pushes himself back into me. He hits a spot I didn't even fucking know existed because I suck in another sharp breath.

"You're a dream, Macey," Oliver grunts as he repeats the same tentative movements. He's clearly taking his time with me as he makes sure I'm okay. "Your pussy was made for me."

"I need more," I plead. "Please."

"Because you asked so nicely." Oliver pulls back and thrusts into me. He picks up his pace as he leans into me, taking my bottom lip between his teeth with a teasing bite.

I release my hold on the headboard and I palm the sides of his head just before he's about to pull away and bring my lips to his. He takes anything and everything he's willing to give me. My tongue sweeps past his lips as he drives in and out of me.

"Oh my god," I moan on a shaky breath.

"You keep making noises like that and I'm going to come before I'm ready," he hisses. "And I am *not* ready to be done with you."

His eyes glaze over. The blues are gone and I'm about to see a whole new side of Oliver as he pulls out and flips me onto my stomach faster than I can let out a breath. "On your knees."

I rise to my knees, leaning down on my forearms as I lift my ass into the air for him.

"Such a good girl for me," Oliver praises as his strong, calloused hands squeeze my ass before he lines himself up with my entrance and plunges in as far as he can go.

I can't help but gasp. I'm unable to breathe as the feeling is so intense that I can't even think straight. This new position has him hitting spots that I didn't even know existed as he drives into me over and over again with rapid movements.

Suddenly, without warning, his movements slow and I look over my shoulder and I see his eyes closed and his head back as if he's trying to maintain control for me. I've realized that there is nothing sexier than a man who loses control. And watching him lose control with me, has me closer to the edge.

"Oliver," I cry out. "I'm close. I need you to move."

"I need a minute, babe." His voice is soft. I can feel the energy under his palm as he holds onto my hips for dear life. Like if he lets go, I'm going to slip away. "You're everything, Macey," he whispers under his breath. "Everything I never knew I needed." He says the words so softly that if I wasn't paying attention I would have missed them.

I push back into him, his cock hitting the sweet spot as I bounce myself against him. A flood of adrenaline rushes through me like a drug, and I've never felt so alive.

"Jesus Christ," he rasps. "I'm going to come, baby. I need you there with me."

"I'm there," I scream out.

Oliver thrusts into me harder and faster, as if he's snapped out of his own resolve.

My orgasm hits me like a rocket. I take off into outer space as stars dance across my vision. My entire body shudders as Oliver's name crosses my lips over and over again. My head dives into the sheets to mask my scream and the only thing I can think of is that I'll never be able to get enough of this feeling with him.

Once my body decides to come back to reality, Oliver pulls out of me and I fall to the bed. My body feels taut and jelly-like from the explosion that just occurred. I turn my head and watch him, his bare ass full of muscle on full display for me as he discards the used condom in the trash before making his way back over to me.

He climbs into bed beside me, wrapping his arms around my

waist and pulling my back into him as he holds me in a warm embrace.

"I didn't hurt you, did I?" Oliver asks as he kisses my shoulder.

I can't help but let out a soft laugh as I turn to face him in the bed. "Not at all. That was… I didn't know it could feel like that."

Something washes over his features and the smile falls from my face.

"I'll be honest with you… it's never felt like that before for me. I've never been with anyone the way I am with you," Oliver says while he brushes a strand of hair out of my face. "I know that makes me look like an asshole talking about it, but I wasn't the type of guy to settle down."

"We all have our pasts, Oliver." I place my hand on his forearm. "You don't have to talk to me about yours. But if you do, you won't see any judgment coming from me. Besides, wasn't it you who told me to forget about the past and anything else that's happened before all of this?" I ask with a grin.

Oliver laughs as he pulls me into him, tightening his hold on me. I can hear him inhale once his face leans into my hair as if he's also soaking in this moment.

It's a moment I don't ever want to forget.

"I meant what I said, you know…" He pauses, pulling back to meet my stare. "You're everything, Macey. And I don't plan on letting you go."

CHAPTER THIRTY-EIGHT

Oliver

We leave today for our trip and it's been a week and a half of Macey sleeping in my bed every other night. She doesn't stay the whole night, but I understand why. Mackenzie doesn't know anything is going on with us and she wants to be in her bed if Mackenzie wakes up.

Something shifted the night I came home from the bar with the boys.

Everything I've felt for Macey over time was confirmed when I had her in my arms.

It's not just about the mind-blowing sex. It's so much more than that. I've felt a connection with her since the very first time I met her, and then I felt it again when I showed up at the bar she worked at and saw her again.

Call it kismet. Call it whatever the hell you want to call it. The universe put both of us in the same place at the same time more than once, and it's something that's hard to deny no matter how much I planned to avoid it.

The aroma of breakfast food creeps into my senses and I'm pulled out of bed. I mean, come on… I'm a total foodie. And you know the smell of breakfast equals the smell of bacon.

I run my hands through my hair a few times before making

my way to the kitchen where I find Macey over the stove. I can't help but admire her from behind.

God, she's breathtaking.

In every sense of the word.

Looking at her, touching her, kissing her, thinking about her… all of it steals the air from my lungs.

Macey radiates beauty, even at eight in the morning. She stands there in her oversized t-shirt that hangs past her sleep shorts and messy hair that looks like it probably hasn't been brushed yet. But it's still perfect.

"Good morning," she coos when she notices me.

"Well, good morning to you too, baby," I reply as I make my way to stand beside her. It's hard as hell to avoid touching her because I don't want Mackenzie to walk in on us. I've avoided asking more about us being an actual couple and how we should act around Mackenzie. But I plan to bring it up soon because I'm done trying to hide how I feel.

"You made enough food to feed an army here," I say as I eyeball the assortment of French toast, pancakes, and bacon.

Macey laughs. "You are the army, big guy. I know you like to eat."

"I bet you do." I shoot her a wink. "But this isn't my favorite meal as of recently."

She swats me with the dishrag as she continues laughing. "You're incorrigible."

"Only for you." I lean in and press a fast kiss to her forehead right above the brim of her glasses. I don't miss the way her cheeks turn pink and the little dimple that I love forms on her right cheek.

"Eat," Macey urges me. "We have to pack for the trip."

A shiver runs through me at the reminder that today is the day she and I leave alone for a trip. At first, I was disappointed that Mackenzie wasn't coming because I really do love having her around and she's always got something funny to share. Plus, she dominates board games.

But I'm excited for this time I can spend with Macey. Technically, we're going down because a really nice young couple offered me a free weekend stay at their new rental property to help promote it on my blog.

They are just starting out with the vacation rental industry, and there's nothing more I love than helping people make their hustle work for them. So if it's a place I love and enjoy, I fully plan to help promote it for them to kick start their endeavor.

"Are you one of those people who packs for three weeks when we're going to be gone for three days?" I ask.

"I've never left Montana." Macey shrugs, letting out a soft chuckle. "So I'm not sure what type of packer I am. But if I know myself, I already know I'm going to be the minimal type. Who wants to carry that much on the plane for just a few days?"

"Right? I feel the same way," I agree.

We spend the rest of breakfast talking about what we have planned for the trip. I tell her all about the place we're staying, things we can do in the area and places we can go out to eat if that's what she decides she wants to do.

While this trip is for my work, I want Macey to take the reins. I want her to tell me what she wants to do. Especially after learning that she's never taken a trip for herself before.

"Wait, where is Mackenzie?" I ask as I bring my dish to the sink realizing she's still not awake.

"Peyton came to pick her up early. There's a St. Patrick's Day parade that's happening in her town and she wanted to bring Mackenzie with them."

"And you wait for now to tell me," I growl as I wrap my arms around her waist and my face dives into her neck. She giggles under my touch but wraps her arms around my head. "I've been dying not being able to have my lips on yours."

"Well, what are you waiting for?"

I slow my movements because I want to feel this particular one down to my bones. Macey's hands move to my waist as I bring my hands to the side of her face, lifting her head so she's staring directly at me.

Her thick lashes flutter and a smile curves my lips. I feel her fist the hem of my shirt before I lean down, claiming her lips the way I have been doing so much this last week.

But this time feels better than the last.

That's how it always seems to be with her. Each kiss is better than the last. Each touch feels more electric than the last. Each time we have sex it's more powerful than the last.

Every part of her body is ingrained in my brain like a tattoo.

I press my body into her and Macey angles her head just the right amount, allowing me better access to explore her mouth. And I do. I taste everything she's willing to give me.

I know without a doubt that this is the last woman I will ever kiss for the rest of my life.

CHAPTER THIRTY-NINE

Macey

PEYTON

Have a safe flight!

AVERY

Enjoy all that... alone time.

KALI

We can't wait to hear every single detail.

EMILINE

I mean... we don't need every detail.

AVERY

Yes, we do.

Thank you! We just boarded the flight! I hope Mackenzie is ok for you.

PEYTON

She's an angel! As always.

AVERY

Unlike you this weekend...

This flight feels so much different than the first.

Coming to New York was the first flight I ever took. But

knowing I'm actually traveling *with* Oliver for this one and knowing we're going away for fun makes me way less anxious than the first time.

Oliver hasn't let go of my hand since we boarded the plane.

To my surprise, we're flying first class.

It feels like a whole new world up in the front of the plane. He told me on the ride over that he rarely flies first class because it screams *money*. He has it, but deep down he hates it.

It's something I admire about him but also something I would love to understand more. He's not one of those uptight people who flaunts their money and shove it in someone's face so I wonder why he feels this way about it.

When I asked him why he decided to fly first class for this trip, he said it's because I deserve to be spoiled.

I won't lie… my heart soared.

I've always known that I've been broken. My past broke me. My parents broke me. I forced myself to believe that I never needed anyone to fix me. Hell, I still don't. I don't want anyone carrying my baggage with them.

But Oliver become a supportive staple in my life in terms of lifting me up anytime I'm feeling down, has been everything a girl could ever dream of.

I don't want his money. I don't want him *thinking* I need his money. I've taught myself to be independent. That's what being a single mom will do after all.

"What's going on in that head of yours?" Oliver asks at my side. "You have a ten-mile stare in your eyes."

I shake my head. "Nothing. I'm just thinking about how we were in a similar situation last summer."

"You mean when I landed a seat next to the most beautiful woman on the flight?"

I look up at him and smile. I can't help but shiver from his words. They have the same effect on my body that his touch does. "I think you must have been overtired, because that wasn't my finest moment."

He turns to look down at me before his palm lands on my thigh before giving it a tight squeeze. "Every moment with you is the finest moment."

Swoon.

The walls around my heart have been broken down for god knows how long at this point when it comes to this man. I fought it as hard as I could. *Clearly* not trying hard enough because he's completely in now.

He has me.

Every part of me.

He's like the tattoos on my body—imprinted with no way to be washed away

I've spent so much of my life wondering what it's like to have that all-consuming love. To have a real family. To have a partner in the journey of life. To not feel so fucking alone. Apart from Mackenzie, I don't know what love is. But if I had to guess… this would be it.

More often than not, I find myself missing Oliver when he's not home. When he's on his way home, I'm anxious for him to walk through the doors. When I'm at work, I can't wait to get home and see him and Mackenzie.

The two people who are the center of my world.

The flight attendant cuts through my thoughts and it feels like déjà vu but with a new woman. Her eyes take their time to scan Oliver in his seat, shamelessly flirting with her eyes. Every muscle in my body tightens.

"Good morning, sir," she purrs. "Can I get you anything to drink?"

"Ladies first," he says as his eyes land on mine. His infectious soft smile relaxing the tension I was just feeling.

"I'll take a soda. Thank you."

Oliver looks back at the woman. "And I'll have an orange soda."

She nods and winks at him before retreating to the back of the plane.

"Some things never change." I laugh.

The grin on Oliver's lips never falters when he looks at me. He picks up my hand, clasping it between his palms. I'm sure he can feel how clammy they are under his touch.

He lifts my hand to his lips and presses a delicate kiss to the top of my fingers. "And some things do."

My heart beats like a drum in my chest because I get exactly what he means.

"The last time we were in this spot," Oliver continues. "You were a stranger to me. Someone I was insanely intrigued by, might I add. I don't know how the stars aligned for me. I don't know what I did to deserve them putting you back in my life, but I'll always be thankful that some things have changed for the better."

I swallow past the dryness forming in my throat. "I'm not so sure I deserve it either."

"One day, I'm going to change that mindset of yours." He huffs out a laugh.

I tilt my head to the side in question. "What do you mean?"

"When you say you don't deserve it. Because, Macey Evans" —he releases a long drawn out sigh—"you deserve the entire fucking universe. It makes me see red when I think that anyone in the world made you believe you didn't. It makes me want to go on a rampage when I think of anyone that made you feel less than who you really are deep down."

Tears threaten to spill as I stare unblinking at him before I finally mutter, "Thank you."

"For what?"

"You've never made me feel less than. You've never made me feel… broken."

"That's because you're not, babe."

The word *babe* slips off his lips so easily and coincidentally the same time the flight attendant returns with our drinks. This time her uniform shirt a little more unzipped in the front to make a show of her chest for him. But from the look in her eyes, she heard him call me babe and realized that she's lost her shot.

She hands us our drinks with a fake smile and not a word spoken before she scurries away.

"She was totally checking you out." I laugh.

"Was she?"

My eyes widen. "I don't know how you could've possibly missed that. Even the zipper on her shirt was extra undone."

Oliver runs his hands down his face and lets a groan slip free. "Jesus, that's hot."

My stomach does a flip despite all the words just poured out of him before this. I can't help but wonder if I'm reading everything all wrong. Anxiety that I haven't felt in a long time comes rushing back in.

Feeling his words is like a stab to the gut and the tears I kept at bay now pool in my eyes, forcing me to avert my gaze out the window.

Oliver whips my head back to him by gripping my chin. I blink rapidly, hoping he doesn't see the jealousy in my eyes.

"You, Macey. Your possessiveness and jealousy over me." He grins. "*That's* what's hot."

"That's… not what I was thinking," I lie.

"You forget that I've spent an ungodly amount of time watching you. Mesmerized by every single move you make. I've become so in tune to what you're thinking without you even having to say it."

"Fine." I lift my chin. "I was a tad bit jealous."

Oliver's grin grows wider. "There's no need to be." He leans to the side, pressing a kiss to the side of my head. I can hear him inhale as if he's soaking in every moment the way I always do. "I only have eyes for you."

I melt. Physically, my body relaxes next to him.

When Oliver came back into my life, I vividly remember thinking there's no way a man like this would want anything to do with a washed up single mom like me.

He's proven me wrong every step of the way.

I clear my throat and adjust myself in the seat, because I don't know what else to say that wouldn't be prematurely having a slip of the tongue and uttering three words I'm not ready to say out loud.

I'm not even sure if he's reached the point of hearing them. I know myself enough to know it would sting if he wasn't ready to say them back.

"So what's on the agenda when we land?" I decide to ask.

"We're going to check into the little house we're staying in first. The only thing I really need to do before we get settled is snap some pictures of the house since the post is sponsored by the owners and the plan is to sell people on visiting the location and staying here."

I nod. "Okay. That sounds fun."

Oliver leans down, bringing his lips to the shell of my ear. "I can think of other things that are fun. Every single one of them includes you naked."

Are we stuck in a lightning storm up here? I swear I just got struck because everything feels hot in this small space. Everything he's saying settles right between my thighs.

"Oliver," I gasp.

"I only speak the truth," he whispers before he pulls away. "After that we can explore the town. Whatever you want to do."

I nod and my smile matches his before I turn to look out the window.

The sky is full of clouds and even if I wasn't on this plane with Oliver right now, I would be feeling every bit on cloud nine as I feel right now.

On top of the world with my hand in his.

"This is a lot different than that first flight we took, huh?" I tell him, keeping my eyes on the sky.

"So much different, dragonfly."

CHAPTER FORTY

Macey

It's official. I'm obsessed with this little town.

Since I've never traveled outside of Montana before New York, I've never seen a coastal town like this before. Only on the internet, which always seemed so unrealistic to me. I've lived and breathed mountains my entire life and I've found myself sucking in the salt water air more times than I care to admit.

Wilmington is so cozy.

As nervous as I was to leave Mackenzie, it's been a refreshing break from mom life. Peyton has texted me updates all day and they are having the time of their lives. It's unfortunately raining there so they started a movie marathon with James and even built massive blanket forts in her living room.

Oliver took all of the pictures he needed when we checked in, right before we got settled. It took everything in me not to jump him after the conversation we had on the flight.

I've had an ache between my legs all day and he is one hundred percent the source of that.

We spent the afternoon visiting a few shops downtown and Oliver got so many amazing photos of the town. I know he's going to paint this town as the perfect destination for a getaway because it really is. From following him on the site for a while now, I know he will do this town the justice it deserves.

My feet have been killing me since we got back an hour ago, so I decided to curl up on the couch with a book while I wait to see what the plans are for the rest of the night.

"I have a question," Oliver says as he enters the living room wearing nothing but a pair of jeans.

Nothing.

But a pair of jeans.

That sit *really* low on his waist and showcases the V-shaped curve that runs down to what's under those jeans.

A curve I would love to run my hands over at some point tonight.

Who the hell have I become? I think these books are ruining me.

"Yeah?" I choke out. It comes out hoarse because I'm still staring at his stomach.

"Eyes are up here, dragonfly."

And... I've been caught. "Hard not to stare."

The corner of his lips twist up as he leans against the door frame, crossing his arms over his chest and one leg over the other. Jesus, that's so hot. It forces my eyes back down his body.

"I might have to take back my question if you keep looking at me with those 'fuck me' eyes, babe. I don't know how much restraint one person can have."

Now it's my turn to smile. "What's your question?"

I don't realize that I'm still staring or that he's moved off the wall until he's crouched down in front of me to level himself with my eyes. "Do you want to go on a date with me tonight?"

"You want to take me on a date?" I ask.

"I want to do a lot of things with you, but this is a good start." Oliver shrugs.

I rise from the couch and he stands with me as I wrap my arms around his bare waist and my body warms at the contact. The smile has never left my face as I look up at him. "I'd love to go out with you, Oliver Ford."

The air leaves Oliver's lungs as his body relaxes into mine and I hear a groan under his breath. "*Please* don't say my name like that."

"I'll try to keep my tone in check for dinner."

"Please," Oliver emphasizes before he leans down and presses a kiss to my lips. It's not a kiss we can get lost in like we've had before, but he stays there just long enough that I feel it in every part of my body. He pulls away before he says, "I can never get enough of your lips on mine."

"Same."

Oliver takes a step back, and I realize how much I hate that feeling. But I know if I stay any closer, I'm going to want to skip dinner the same way I think he wants to.

Before my brain can lead to anymore dirty thoughts, he spins me around and gives my ass a little smack. "Go get dressed. We have reservations at six."

I raise a brow. "You just knew I was going to say yes, huh?"

"I'm goal-oriented. I knew I'd find *some* way to make you go out with me." He winks as he turns on his heel towards the bedroom.

I stare at his backside as he walks away and take in the way his muscles curve every part of his back before I retreat to the shower and get ready for dinner.

I already can't wait to get home.

This isn't the first time Oliver has taken me out to dinner, but this time feels more intimate.

I chose to wear a silk thin strapped dress that reaches mid-thigh that Peyton told me I had to bring. She said she hadn't worn it yet, and that it was made for me. It's not the warmest weather since March is so hit or miss, but sitting under the watchful eyes of Oliver Ford, I feel like I'm sweating bullets.

Maybe it's the location, or maybe it's how much things have

escalated since he last took me out. I'm not complaining either way. Oliver was such a gentleman when we got here and ordered dinner for both of us. He got the surf and turf and after telling him how amazing the seafood fra diavolo looked, he ordered that for me.

We spent dinner reflecting on our day and how we can't wait to see how the pictures that he snapped came out.

"That was amazing," I say, patting the corners of my mouth from my meal. "And this place is so beautiful."

Oliver's eyes scan my body for the millionth time tonight. "It doesn't hold a candle to how you look tonight."

My cheeks heat up at his compliment. "That was smooth."

"It's easy when you look like that."

I tuck a curtain of hair behind my ear and offer him a soft smile. I wonder if there will ever be a time that I don't smile uncontrollably when he's around. Probably not.

"So I have a question for you," I say as I bring my elbows to the table and rest them under my chin.

"Shoot."

"Can you tell me about this bear that Mackenzie can't stop talking about. His name is Bert?" I lightly laugh.

"She likes that old thing, huh?"

I nod. "She insisted on bringing it to Peyton's for the weekend saying that she can't sleep without it."

Oliver clears his throat and adjusts himself in his seat before taking a sip of his water. I immediately regret asking him about it because I can tell he's nervous to talk about it.

"You don't—"

"No," he cuts me off. "I want to tell you all about it. I want to tell you everything about me."

I swallow past the lump in my throat and all of a sudden my stomach churns with nerves myself. Fear creeps into every one of my senses because things have been going so well for us. I'm terrified that something he's about to tell me will change that.

"I got that bear from my dad when I was a kid," he starts. "I think I told you that he passed."

I nod, remembering the conversation we had on the flight when we met.

"I'm the man I am today because of his guidance and everything he's taught me. But I didn't want to follow all of his footsteps. He was a big wig investor and I watched it slowly kill him. Stress and work wasn't what killed him, but all of his underlying stress didn't help him recover from the pneumonia that took him." Oliver pauses to take another sip of water. "Our last conversation we had in the hospital room was him telling me *"Live life to the fullest. Fuck the money and everything else that doesn't matter. You are what matters. Travel the world and don't ever settle."* And I lived by that. Every single day. Seeing what money did to my dad, is the reason I can't stand my bank account."

"You've built an amazing life for yourself."

"I thought so too," he says without missing a beat.

I don't answer because I don't know what he means by that. I'm not entirely sure I *want* to know. I pick up my water glass and nervously take a sip of my own.

"I want to be an open book with you, Macey," he starts. "I'm not too proud of my past."

I keep my eyes locked on him, waiting for the ball to drop.

"Because I slept with a lot of women. Most of them I never called the next day." He scoffs at himself and the corner of his mouth curves up. "That's a lie. I never called anyone the next day. I treated women like they were expendable and I didn't care. Truth be told, they didn't care either."

I release a long drawn out sigh because I knew this already. The girls told me that Oliver was sort of a playboy in the past. They were shocked to hear that he hadn't been with anyone since I showed up.

"But you're different," he says.

"Oliver," I say before he can continue. "You don't have to explain any of this to me. Thank you for sharing a piece of yourself with me, sharing your past with me. I hope you know it doesn't change how I see you."

"It doesn't?"

I shake my head and smile. "Do you really think I would judge you for your past when mine isn't any better? Mine just has a little less females." I wink.

Oliver laughs at that and his smile grows wider.

I reach across the small table, taking his hands in mine. "You're a good man, Oliver Ford."

He lifts my hands that are in his and presses a kiss to my knuckles.

"So that's why you keep the bear?" I ask.

"I kept it as a reminder every night to live life to the fullest. To live with no regrets. It sounds so dumb when I say it out loud."

"It's definitely not dumb. I think it's very sweet."

The waiter interrupts me before I could say anything more. "Can I get you two some dessert?"

"Not tonight," Oliver answers the server but his eyes are locked with mine, growing darker by the second. "I think we have something a little sweeter at home."

CHAPTER FORTY-ONE

Macey

Oliver hasn't taken his hands off me since we left the restaurant.

The drive to the little house was only ten minutes but was full of anticipation and nervous energy from wanting to get back as fast as we could.

Once the car stops, he practically pulls me out. My hand clasps his as he unlocks the door with the click of a few buttons on the keypad. He ushers me inside and kicks the door shut with his foot before his mouth claims mine.

Now *this* kiss is filled with need.

It's as if he hasn't been able to breathe all night long without his lips on mine.

Our mouths fuse together. The kiss is rough. Demanding.

My back lands against the door with a thud and Oliver presses his hard body against mine. His hand tangles itself in the hair on the back of my head as he angles my head just right to gain a deeper access to my mouth. His tongue brushes along my bottom lip and I open for him easily.

The kiss vibrates throughout my entire body.

My hips press into his leg because I'm craving so much more than this right now.

The minute I do, Oliver lowers himself to lift me up into his arms. My legs wrap around his waist on their own accord and his mouth never leaves mine. When I feel the bulge behind his pants press into my center, all the air leaves my lungs in a needy moan.

He pulls away. "Fuck, baby"

I cup his face and give him a searing kiss. My hips move against him. I already feel like I want to combust right here against the front door. The grip he has on my hips tighten as he lets me grind my pussy against his erection.

I moan in pleasure against his lips.

"Not here," he grunts. "I am not fucking you against this door."

"Take me to the bedroom then," I beg.

Oliver doesn't let me go. My legs stay locked at the ankles around him as he walks toward the bedroom. If he releases me, I feel like I might die.

I've never wanted this the way I do right now.

In a few long strides, he's busting into the bedroom not even bothering to close the door because for the first time, we're doing this with no one else around.

I'm hungry for so much more tonight.

Reluctantly, Oliver places my feet on the ground and I reach for the buttons on his white button down shirt. My rapid movements slow and the world stops spinning with his heavy stare on me. In a matter of seconds, we went from hungry to fuck each other to something major shifting in the air.

Love.

I know deep down that's what this is with him.

With each button I undo, our eyes remain fixed on each other while his hands fall to the side, letting me take control with slow, meaningful movements.

"God, you're so beautiful," Oliver whispers while he brushes my messy hair from just moments ago away from my eyes.

I don't say anything back but my lips twist up on their own as I push the shirt off his shoulders. I can't help but look down at his broad chest that rises and falls in front of me before my eyes trail down to his rigid abdomen carved with perfectly sculpted muscles.

My hands move to his shoulders before I brush them down his front and over every single bump, stopping right at the hem of his jeans.

"You're not so bad yourself," I whisper back.

I pause, unsure if this is right. I'm not used to being in control, but the lack of urgency on Oliver's end tells me that he *wants* me to be the one to take control here.

He's giving me all of him. He's giving me all his trust.

As if he can sense me silently questioning if I should undo it, he nods.

My hands work quickly to unbuckle the belt before I pull it out from the loops and toss it to the side. Then, I unbutton his pants and slide the zipper down. The second my finger hooks into the waistband, he sucks in a sharp breath and throws his head back. I take that as a sign to push his pants all the way to the ground.

This man really is so fucking beautiful.

I force myself to take a step back and take in every inch of bare flesh.

This man… is mine.

Oliver must sense me staring at the erection behind his boxer briefs when his words cut through. "Take my cock out, baby. I need your hands on me."

I quirk a brow up to the sky. "Just my hands?"

"It's a start." He huffs out a laugh. "I want your mouth on my cock, your pussy squeezing me. I want your cum dripping down the sides of me by the end of the night."

My mouth goes dry while a shiver racks my body.

I step to him, reaching inside his boxer briefs and gripping his length in my hand. I moan. I fucking moan just by touching it. I don't think I'll ever get used to how big he is. In every sense of the word.

His height, his body, his cock. All of it.

Oliver reaches in the waistband and pushes them to the floor with his pants as he steps out of them. My hand moves up and down his throbbing erection. Once my thumb rolls over the tip, I can feel the precum coat my finger as I move quicker.

"Jesus Christ, that feels so good," he groans. "I need to be inside of you."

I shake my head as I bring myself to my knees in front of him. Still fully clothed in my dress and eager to give him pleasure.

"You don't have—"

I cut him off when I wrap my lips around his length. Slowly pushing his cock as deep as my mouth will allow it to go.

"Fuck," he hisses.

I pull back just enough and swirl my tongue around the head, licking the bead of cum that builds before I push back down. Taking him deeper than I did the first time.

My eyes look up at him and his eyes are fixed on where he disappears inside my mouth. The fire inside of his eyes ignites energy inside of me to give him more. I pick up my pace as I bob my head up and down, taking him deeper each time.

"Look at you on your knees for me, baby," Oliver says before his hand finds the back of my head. The contact causes me to moan around him. My head moves in rhythm before I open my throat and take every inch of him in. A soft gag leaves me, but I don't let up. "That's a good girl. You take me so well."

His words land straight to my clit and I'm craving a release. I'm craving the friction and I'm craving his hands all over me.

"I'm close," he breathes out. "I don't want to come down your throat."

My hands itch to touch myself, but instead I grab his ass to keep him where he is. Because *I* want that. I want Oliver to lose control and watch him come. I want to taste every last drop he has to give me.

"Macey," he warns.

I bob up and down in rapid movements. Tears prickle my eyes as he touches my throat with each movement. I feel his hips jerk into me and it's so hot that I think I might come without even being touched.

He grips my hair tightly, his abs contract and I know I've succeeded. "I'm coming, babe. Fuck."

I pause, suctioning my lips around him as he pours himself down the back of my throat.

My name on his tongue is like a goddamn chant, while he stares at the ceiling. As soon as he releases everything he has into me, he pulls me off the floor.

Oliver brings my face a breath away from him with his hands cupping each side. "You want control, baby?" He swipes his thumb across my swollen lip. I don't answer him, but he knows. It's my turn to give him the pleasure he's always given me. "You should already know that I'll give you anything you want. You want control, I will gladly get on my knees for you. You're my weakness, Macey."

He leaves me standing there as he walks over to the bed. I stand there unblinking with a throbbing need between my legs. I take a deep breath before I turn around to face him. He sits on the edge of the bed with his legs wide open, holding himself up with both hands behind him and his cock already growing harder by the second.

I slowly kick my sandals off to the side. Oliver's eyes bore into me as he watches my every single movement. I reach for the hem of my dress before lifting it over my head and tossing that off to the side too.

A smirk grows on his lips. "You mean to tell me I just sat with you at dinner this whole time and you had *nothing* on under that dress?"

I shrug my shoulders in a very matter of fact way. "The underwear showed through the silk and I didn't have a strapless bra packed to wear with this."

Oliver groans and throws his head back while whispering

some sort of profanity under his breath. I take that opportunity to walk over to him, stepping between his wide legs and placing my hands on his shoulders.

His head snaps back up to meet my eyes as he reaches for my hips. He gives them a tight squeeze before he grazes my sides with his fingertips until he reaches below the swell of my breasts. I suck in a sharp breath and feel my nipples harden. He scans me up and down and brings his bottom lip between his teeth.

"Touch me, Oliver." It comes out as a needy plea.

"Where do you want me to touch you?" he asks with a deep raspy tone.

I point to my breasts. "Here."

His hands move up as they hover over them. He teases the area around my nipple with careful movements as he gently stimulates it with the pad of his finger. He strokes it before pinching it between his fingers. My body quakes at the movements and I can't help but whimper.

Oliver leans forward and peppers kisses from my chest and down before he takes one in his mouth. He flicks his tongue over it a few times before sucking it into his mouth.

"Oliver," I moan. An intense feeling begins to take over my body as he moves to the other breast. I've already been on the verge of exploding all night and this is just pushing me closer and closer to the edge.

I reach between us to touch myself, but Oliver senses the movement and swats my hand away. "Tell me where else you want me to touch you."

I don't skip a beat when I point to the spot between my legs. "Here."

With one mouth on my breast, his hand reaches between my legs and cups my pussy. He groans into my chest as he sucks harder, releasing my nipple with a pop. "You didn't tell me you were soaked, Macey."

I don't reply. I *can't* reply because Oliver moves a finger inside of me, making contact with my clit and it causes every nerve ending in my body to fire at rapid speed. My body heats, my chest rises and falls in more rapid, uneven movements as he works the bud with his finger in slow, delicate circles. I claw at his shoulders, unable to even stand here for much longer.

I choke out his name in a one-word plea to keep doing exactly what he's doing. I never realized that something like this could feel so damn good. But Oliver knows his way around my body and has the ability to pull every ounce of pleasure out of me.

"Oh my god," I pant, feeling closer to an orgasm than ever before.

He slides out and I immediately hate the loss of connection, but he doesn't give me a second to pout before he's driving two fingers inside of me again.

My mouth opens wide as the pleasure intensifies. My one leg lifts to rest on the edge of the bed next to his thigh, and I watch his lips curve up thanking me for easier access.

My hips grind against him on their own, chasing the high. "That's it, babe. You feel so wet. So tight," he says through gritted teeth as he hooks a finger inside of me, hitting that sweet spot he knows drives me crazy. "I want you to come so I can hear your sweet little moans."

He pulls out one more time before he adjusts his hand so his palm rests right on my clit. My body moves on its own, riding his hand faster and faster until stars dance across my vision.

"I'm going to come," I cry out.

"Such a good girl giving me what I want," he praises.

That's all I needed. Everything turns fuzzy and my body melts into his hands. Literally as my orgasm hits me full force. Despite feeling weak in the knees, I have never felt more alive than I do now in his arms.

"I knew that would be what sends you over the edge," Oliver says as he peppers kisses along the bare skin of my neck. "I love how your body responds to me."

As I come down from my high, he pulls his hands out from between my legs. His eyes are locked with mine as he brings his drenched fingers between us.

He brings them to his lips, brushing my arousal along his bottom lip before both fingers disappear into his mouth. My lips part with lust and I've learned that nothing turns me on more than the fact that Oliver loves how I taste.

His eyes roll in the back of his head and he groans before pulling them out. "So fucking sweet."

I cup his cheeks and press my lips to his, tasting myself on his tongue. Despite how hard that orgasm hit me, I want more of him. Actually, I don't think I can get *enough* of him.

"I need to be inside of you," he says in a shallow whisper before he gets up and walks over to the corner of the room where he has our overnight luggage. I can't help but stare at his perfect ass as he moves.

I feel like someone else right now.

I don't know how to describe it, but he makes me feel strong and powerful.

"What are you doing?" I ask.

"I told you, I need to be inside of you." He laughs as if I should already know just as he sits down on his knees to dig through the luggage. "I need a condom."

"No," I say quickly.

He stills just before he reaches for the zipper. He's still on his knees when he turns around looking at me full of questions.

"I don't want anything between us. I'm on the pill to control my periods," I continue before he can ask anything.

"Are you sure? My tests were negative when I got tested back in January, and I haven't been with anyone but you since then."

Blood roars in my ears at his admission. Oliver really hasn't been with anyone since me. Not that there was even a thought that he was because he never goes out anymore and he's always home with me or Mackenzie.

But something about hearing him say it sends chills through my body. Only elevating how strong I feel right now.

A smirk grows on my lips as I take note that he's still sitting on his knees besides the luggage. He hasn't moved an inch to come near me yet.

"You weren't kidding about gladly getting on your knees for me, huh?"

"I'd do anything for you, baby." He still doesn't move.

I sit down on the edge of the bed, feeling every bit of sexy with only his eyes on me. He makes me feel wanted. He makes me feel sexy. He makes me feel… loved.

I spread my legs just the slightest bit for him, holding myself up with one arm on the bed as I give him my best *'come and get me'* grin.

Oliver's eyes land on my bare pussy as his tongue swipes across his bottom lip once before he brings it between his teeth. I use my other hands to call him to me with a crook of my finger.

"Come," I tell him.

CHAPTER FORTY-TWO

Oliver

"Come," she says in a low seductive voice.

No one can bring me to my knees the way Macey Evans can. My cock pulses at the tone of her voice.

There's many ways I like Macey—when she's in my kitchen, when she's reading a book on my couch snuggled in the blankets, when she's laughing. But nothing compares to strong and confident Macey.

I don't waste another second because I meant what I said—I need to be inside of her. Especially after watching how she responded to just me fucking her with my hand. *My god.* Add that to the list of the many ways I like Macey.

I move to stand and she stops me.

"Crawl to me," she says as her eyes twinkle full of mischief.

Fucking gladly.

My face splits in a grin as I drop to both hands. I keep my eyes secured on Macey's and I'm confident she has the power to completely undo me with those eyes. The second my body starts moving across the floor, her lips part and I don't miss the way she sucks in a sharp breath while she watches every move I take.

When I reach her feet, I lift one foot to sit on my shoulder as I rise to one knee. I turn my head the smallest amount so I can still keep her eyes stuck on mine as I press a kiss to the delicate spot on her ankle and don't stop until I reach mid-thigh.

"Is this what you wanted, dragonfly? Me, on my knees for you?" I press another kiss right to the soft spot on her thigh between her legs. "Worshiping you like the queen you are?"

Macey blows out a shaky exhale as I press a final kiss to her pussy that's still soaked from how hard I made her come just moments ago.

"Yes. God, yes." She throws her head back while she holds herself up right using her hands behind me. Her nipples perk up at the sensation of my mouth on her most sensitive spot. As much as I want to devour her with my tongue right now, I need to be inside of her. I need to feel connected to her on another level.

I rise from my knees and hover over her body, forcing her back to fall to the bed. I crash my lips to hers and realize quickly that I would actually die if I didn't have this mouth on mine every day for the rest of my life.

Everything in me shifts with that realization.

My movements over her slow because I don't just want to fuck Macey Evans.

I want everything with her. A life with her. A future with her.

"Baby," I whisper against her lips. "I'm dying to be inside of you. But I can't..." I choke on my own words. Because there's so much more I want to tell her. "I need it to be slow."

Macey's eyes bounce between mine for one, two, three heartbeats, a silent understanding between us that I want this time to be more. I don't want it to be rough and demanding the way it's been so far with us.

She reaches up and kisses me again. Soft and sweet. Nothing demanding about this one. Confirmation for me that she feels this too.

My arms cage the side of her head as I rest on my elbows and Macey uses one arm to wrap around my neck and the other to reach between us. The contact of her hand around my cock causes me to buck into her hand. She guides my cock to her slick entrance and I groan at the feel of her coating me bare.

She releases me and now has both of her arms wrapped around my neck. She gives me a small nod to tell me she's ready. I take my time pushing inside of her. Pulling back with every inch before I drive in, giving her more with each thrust.

"Fuck, your pussy feels so good wrapped around my cock."

"Oliver," she whimpers under me, and with one last thrust I'm fully inside of her. Her back arches off the bed with a gasp and her thighs grip my hips. "That's... oh my god."

I pick up my pace, jerking my hips with small thrusts and it only takes a few minutes before I feel her pulsing around me. I link my fingers with hers and lift our hands, using the momentum to drive in and out of her. My movements quicken with each thrust because nothing in the world compares to her.

"Your pussy was made for me, Macey. Tell me this is all mine."

"It's all yours," she pants, clawing at my back as if she can't get close enough to me. "I'm all yours, Oliver."

"Say my name again, baby," I beg.

"Oliver. Oh my god, Oliver," Macey repeats over and over again.

My name on her lips makes me move faster. I bring myself back to my elbows and dive into her neck, pressing a kiss to the bounding pulse in her neck as her hands grip my hair.

"Baby, I—"

I love you.

I want to say it, but if I say it right now, she might think I'm saying it in the heat of the moment. I want her to know I really mean it.

"I know, Oliver," she moans louder.

I don't know if that means she already knows how I feel or she can feel the intensity between us right now. But either way, I *know* she can feel this too.

She pushes me off her chest and forces me to slow my movements and pull out of her.

"What?" I start, but she's already moving to flip me to my back. She climbs on top of me, with both legs straddling my hips as she lines herself up again. She moves as slow as I did just moments ago and sinks lower and lower onto my shaft.

"Fuuuck." I melt as I watch my length disappear inside of her. "I love when you take control."

Macey laughs before she starts to grind against my cock. Her hands that were just gripping my chest fly to her hair. I watch as she rides me like she's a rodeo champion in some kind of bull riding ring.

I don't know jack shit about what it's really called but that's what it looks like she's doing right now. Her messy hair in her hands as she picks up the pace. She's moving for her pleasure and I'd gladly give it to her.

"I need you to do me a favor," I tell her.

"Yeah?" she questions through a breathy moan.

"I need to hear you." I thrust my hips up into her. "Fucking scream."

"Ahh!" Macey screams out at that. "Fuck, that feels so good."

Her hands find my chest again as she changes her movements and bounces up and down on my cock. The way her breasts bounce with each movement has me ready to explode inside of her.

"That's it, baby. Are you close? Because I'm going to come if you keep this up."

She doesn't slow, but reaches between us and her fingers start rubbing her clit in slow circles. That does it for me. I grip her hips and thrust my hips up harder and faster as I pound into her.

Macey gasps and her lips form an O shape as my favorite little sounds she makes start falling from her lips.

"Your pussy is squeezing me. You're there. I can feel it."

"I'm..." she screams out. "I'm there. I'm coming."

I drive in and out. Harder. Faster. Wet skin slapping against each other and her screams are the only sounds I hear as her walls begin to quiver.

"That's a good fucking girl," I growl through my teeth. "Soak my cock."

"Come with me," she pants. "I want to see you lose control."

"Baby, I've already lost control with you. You own me." I thrust one more time. "You have me." I thrust again, but stop and keep my cock buried inside of her. "You're mine."

Her orgasm crashes through her at the same time mine does. I pour everything I have inside of her as I grunt through my release and she screams through hers. I've never in my life felt a connection this strong with another woman.

She's it for me. She has to know it after this.

Macey's body goes limp on top of me. Her hair falling all around us as she falls on top of me. I cup her face with both hands and I kiss her. Sealing whatever deal I have in my head and making sure she knows that she has me.

For good.

She releases herself from the kiss, our bodies still connected because I refuse to pull out of her the same way she refuses to remove herself from me.

My eyes bounce between hers and I love how Macey looks thoroughly fucked and sated.

"Shit, this is hard," I release an exhale.

The soft smile she just had, turns to a frown. Concern lacing her features before she clears her throat and tries to separate us. "I understand."

"No." I stop her with a grip of her hips. Her eyes widen with uncertainty. "It's hard because I don't know how I can live without you. I'm falling so damn hard for you it makes me sick thinking of a life without you in it."

"I…" She pauses trying to collect her thoughts. "I feel the same way."

I smile up at her because I can't help it.

"Let's get you cleaned up," I say as I lift her from me. I rise from the bed and lift her in my arms in a fireman's carry. Macey giggles before she wraps her arms around my neck. "Then we're going again because I'm not done with you yet."

Her arms tighten around my neck before she buries her head into my neck.

I'm completely and utterly in love with Macey Evans.

CHAPTER FORTY-THREE

Macey

I wake up to the sounds of birds chirping and a light breeze coming through the crack in the window. I feel the warmth of Oliver's naked body tangled with mine and there's barely any light outside telling me it has to be no later than six in the morning.

My eyes fully open as I look up at him in his most peaceful state. He sleeps with his mouth slightly parted, a hand resting over his broad chest and the other extended under my neck.

I watch as his chest rises and falls slowly with each breath he takes.

He's so beautiful.

I know it's odd to call a man of this stature beautiful, but that's what he is.

As if Oliver can sense me staring, he startles and slowly opens his eyes. "Good morning, beautiful," he says in a groggy voice as he brings himself higher on the pillow. "It's early. How did you sleep?"

"Perfect," I tell him, pressing a kiss to his bare chest before I snuggle back into his arms. "You're like sleeping with a heated blanket."

His chest vibrates as he chuckles. His fingers tickle my arms from wrist to shoulder. It's the same move I used to do when Mackenzie was younger and I would cuddle with her. The light touch causes goosebumps to pebble on my skin.

"I love when I get to see the artwork on your arms," he says.

"Yeah?"

He nods. "Your sleeve is probably my favorite tattoo I've ever seen."

I look down at the ink covering my arms as if I don't see it every day of my life. A dragonfly is drawn over my forearm and a cherry blossom scattered along my upper arm that reaches just below my shoulder.

"I got this done two years ago," I start as I rest my chin on my opposite arm and look up at him. "Things were really bad. I was at the lowest point of my life and I found myself questioning why I was still here, questioning what was the point of going forward if my parents wouldn't let me be the mom I knew I could be."

Oliver remains silent but his hands never stop tracing the ink on my skin. His face tells me he's begging me to tell him more.

"I had no friends. I had no one to talk to and was scared to admit to anyone the dark thoughts that went through my head for fear of being deemed unstable. After sleeping for three days straight," I breathe out, my stomach churning at the memory. "I had a realization that I needed to make a change. I needed to be stronger. If not for myself, but for Mackenzie."

I blink rapidly, pushing down any strong emotions because it's too early in the day for all that.

"One day I was walking around town doing some shopping for the holidays when I came across a small tattoo shop. I stared at the logo on the outside of the building for so long that I'm sure people walking by thought I was weird." I laugh at that. "I walked in and said I need something inked on my body that reminds me to keep going." I swear I see a small smile on Oliver's face, but I can't quite tell. "The guy's name was Chuck. It's a name

I'll never forget because he changed my life that day. Not because he's the one who drew up this tattoo, but because he talked to me like I was a real person. I hadn't talked to someone like that since before I had Mackenzie. I spilled my entire life to him for a few hours as if he was my therapist. I cried. He cried." I smile at the memory. "That was the day the cherry blossom was born."

"What does it mean?" Oliver asks.

"The Japanese took its beautiful, but fleeting spring blossom as a metaphor for life. The inevitable wilting decline into death always follows the full bloom. So wearing the tattoo shows readiness to live each day as if it were your last. The dragonfly was added last minute to symbolize the ability to overcome times of hardship."

"That makes me equally in love with your art and also hate it at the same time."

I huff out a small laugh.

"I hate that you've gone through what you have, but I've never been happier that it brought you to take that flight. It brought you to leave and put us on the same path."

I swallow down the emotions. "I am too."

"I mean everything I've ever said to you, Macey. I want everything with you that you're willing to give me. I'll wait until you're ready if I have to. But I'm all in with you."

This man is a dream come true.

If you told me months ago that I would fall for the funny guy on the plane who called me his *seat wife* and that he would show up and offer me a place to live in the city… I would have laughed in your face.

"I want that too. With you."

"Yeah?"

"It's getting harder and harder to deny it. I just need to talk to Mackenzie about everything. This is new territory for her. I know she loves you and is used to you being around by now. But this would be a whole new level."

"Of course." Oliver adjusts himself in bed before he cups my face in his hands. "But you should know I love her."

I've tried so hard to hold the tears back, but now, I can't hold them back at his admission. I want nothing more than having more people love my daughter the way I do.

"You do?"

"I really do, babe. I've told you before, but in case you forgot"—he offers me a beaming smile—"she's a part of you. What's not to love?"

The tears cascade down my cheek and he quickly wipes them away. "That means a lot to me."

I love you is on the tip of my tongue.

I want to tell him, but I just don't know how.

We must have fallen back asleep because I wake again when my stomach rumbles.

I glance over at the small clock on the nightstand to see that it's already nine in the morning. I slowly untangle my feet from our web to sneak out of the bed and get breakfast started.

Oliver spoiled me in the bedroom last night. Multiple times. Then he listened to me get emotional before the sun was even awake. So it's my turn to spoil him the best way I know how—with breakfast in bed.

As soon as my feet hit the floor, I feel the soreness from last night in every part of me.

My arms, my legs, my vagina…everything is perfectly sore in the best way possible.

But I already want more of it. Oliver has successfully turned me into a sex-crazed fiend. But only for him.

I scan the floor to try and find my clothes, but everything is tossed all over the place. The first thing I spot is his white button down shirt that he wore to dinner last night and decide that's what I'm wearing.

Since he's significantly larger than me in height, it hangs like a dress on me.

Just as I enter the little kitchen, I can hear my phone buzzing on the counter. In the midst of my Oliver-induced haze, I forgot for a minute that I have a child back at home who might need me.

My stomach sours that I was so negligent with my phone when I see it's Mackenzie.

"Hey, babe," I answer quickly.

"Good morning, Mom!" She beams.

I chuckle at her enthusiasm. "How are you doing? Are you having fun with Peyton?"

"Oh my god, so much fun, Mom. It rained like all day yesterday so we made blanket forts in the living room! It was massive. James and I ate popcorn under it and then we got to order pizza for dinner. It was the best time ever."

"That sounds so fun," I say as I pad around the kitchen to find things to make for breakfast. Oliver had a few groceries delivered while we were gone yesterday to get us by for our short stay.

"How's your trip?" she asks.

"It's good. Oliver got his work done and we're just planning to relax today before our flight back."

"Can you bring me a souvenir?"

"Already got you something while we were exploring the town yesterday."

"You're the best!" Mackenzie shrieks.

I pull a pan out of the cabinet to make some scrambled eggs, but the pan that was on top of it falls which causes a loud bang.

"What was that?" Mackenzie asks in my ear.

"Sorry. I'm pulling out a pan to make some eggs for us this morning and another one just fell."

I hear the door to the bedroom creek open and turn to see Oliver emerge. He's sleepy eyed and wearing nothing but a pair of boxer briefs.

"Listen, babe. I'm going to make us some breakfast. My loud bang just woke up Oliver." I laugh. "I should probably get the bear some food," I joke.

"Tell Ollie I said hi and that I miss him."

I love how much she misses him. I'm sure if I was home and he was here alone, I would feel the same way she does right now.

"Mackenzie says she misses you," I tell Oliver while she's still on the phone.

He smiles and holds out his hand for me to give it to him. I do and can't stop staring at him or even move to start breakfast. I am locked in on what's going to happen next.

"Hey, Kenzie," he says in a deep tired voice.

I can't hear what she's saying because she's not on speaker but every nod of Oliver's head with, what I assume, is her talking a mile a minute has my heart beating wildly in my ribs.

"That sounds like a fun day," he tells her. Another pause as he listens to her. "I miss you too. I'm going to hold you to that promise for that hug. It better be the biggest one ever." He smiles at whatever she replies with.

He's not even looking at me and I suddenly feel like I'm invading a private conversation between them.

There's another long pause and Oliver's eyes travel from the ground to mine. His gaze burns a hole right to my core.

"I love you more, Kenzie," he says it to her but his eyes are on me.

My breath catches in my throat and I feel like I can't breathe. *Those words.* He loves her. I know he told me this morning that he did, but to hear him tell her is so different.

I have to snap myself out of it with a small shake of my head as I turn around and make myself busy. I completely forget what I'm even doing here because he's thrown me so off guard.

"Okay. We'll call you later," Oliver tells her, and I hear the phone being placed back on the counter.

Don't get emotional. Don't cry. It's okay.

I hear him move before I feel him standing behind me. His large body takes up the air I breathe and everything stays stuck in my lungs.

"My shirt looks good on you," he says softly into my ear.

The back of his fingers feather down my neck, from my shoulder to the lower curve of my back. I shiver under his touch and everything from last night comes flooding back, sending a wave of desire to the sensitive spot between my legs.

"It was all I could find on the floor in our pile of mess," I choke out.

I hear him let out a chuckle under his breath. "How are you feeling?" he asks.

I take a deep breath before I turn around to look at him. I'm unsure how I'm feeling, especially after learning how much he loves my daughter and the night we just had.

"Perfect." I force a fixed smile.

"You're not sore? I didn't hurt you, did I?"

My muscles finally relax as my hands skate around his neck and I press up to my toes to kiss him. Oliver's large arms circle my waist, pulling me into him. I want to live in this moment with him. I never want to stop being in his arms and connected in some way shape or form.

I pull back from the kiss. "I'm a little sore, but you didn't hurt me. You could never hurt me." The last line comes out softer than the first two.

"I'm glad you know that." Oliver leans in for another quick kiss. "Because I don't ever intend to. I want to spend the rest of my days worshiping you. But fuck… your body. The way you move with me. The way your body reacts to mine. The way you take control. I can't help but get carried away in the moment with you. So if I ever get too rough, you have to tell me."

"And I love it." I cup his face between my hands. "Don't stop doing any of that."

"Macey, I…" He stops himself, shaking his head like he wanted to say something but decided against it instead.

I'm not sure I'm ready for it myself. Not until I talk to Mackenzie.

Plus, I heard how he tells someone he loves them, and I'm going to end up putty right here on this kitchen floor.

"Let's have breakfast. Even though you ruined it for me."

Oliver takes a step back and barks out a laugh pointing to his chest. "I ruined it?"

I swat his arm with a kitchen rag and my laughter matches his. "Yes, you ruined it. I was planning to make you breakfast in bed and now you're out here all"—my hand gestures up and down his body—"naked and so much skin. Oh my god, so much skin."

My core throbs again. He's turning me on just by standing there.

"Would you like me to get dressed, Macey Bethany Evans?"

"Another wrong guess." I laugh. "And please don't. I've never cooked with a hot naked man in the kitchen before. Maybe it will be some of my best work."

Oliver eyes the pan I'm holding. "Eggs?"

"Yup."

"Are you going to make the eggs some of your best work?"

"You hush." I curl over in laughter, more loudly and freely this time.

But I don't hear him. I turn to face him and he's most definitely not laughing with me. Something sobers him, but he still has a small smirk on his face.

"I love when you do that," he says.

"Do what?"

"Smile. Laugh. Breathe. Everything. Just to name a few off the top of my head."

"Oliver," I whisper.

I should tell him. Just rip off the stupid Band-Aid and not worry about what his reaction would be to me telling him I'm completely head over heels for him. At least he will know and it will allow him to freely tell me when he's ready.

Oliver doesn't say anything back.

I clear my throat. "Let's have breakfast."

"You know… I can think of something better than eggs. And it might also be some of your best work."

"Like what?"

He stalks over to me, crowding my space again. "You."

CHAPTER FORTY-FOUR

Macey

This has to be the busiest lunch shift I've ever worked.

It doesn't help that I'm downright exhausted and it's only Tuesday.

We were supposed to leave Wilmington on Sunday night but our flight was majorly delayed. A nor'easter went up the coast and we were stuck there for hours until it passed.

I was so anxious about Mackenzie but Peyton assured me they were safe and fine. Apparently they are used to that sort of thing. The word nor'easter just scared the shit out of me, but Oliver told me that it's essentially just heavy rain and wind.

Needless to say, we didn't get in until yesterday morning. I was eager to pick up Mackenzie so Oliver drove us out to where Peyton lives just outside the city. *Of course* we got stuck in traffic because what else can go wrong.

When we finally made it back to the penthouse, Mackenzie talked our ears off for hours. I think she was just as excited for us to be home as we were.

It was my first time away from her so I can see why.

The three of us snuggled on the couch with the gloomy post storm weather and watched movies all day since Mackenzie had a random day off for teacher inservice. I even read some of the book Avery let me borrow for the trip that I didn't get to finish.

It's just so good and I couldn't put it down no matter how heavy my eyes were. Those damn cowboy romances have me in a chokehold, which leaves me here dead ass tired for this shift.

"Are you good?" Kevin asks.

I bite back a yawn. "Yeah, I'm just still so tired from the weekend."

"How was the trip, by the way?" Jan asks.

I've gotten close to these two since working so closely together. It's nice to have people you work with who are easy to talk to and make working actually enjoyable. There's no drama, they care about my life outside of work, and we work as a great team.

I smile at the thoughts of the weekend before I answer her question. We barely slept while there. I don't think we ever left the bed once we got in it Saturday night. He had me completely worn down and sated.

"Oh, girl," Jan drawls. "Don't even answer that. Your smile tells me everything I need to know."

"I just had a nice, relaxing time."

"I bet you also got plenty of cardio in too." She winks.

"Stop that." I laugh as I throw a cooked pasta noodle at her. "We did not."

"You don't have to lie to me. I have a keen sense for that kind of thing. And you"—she tosses a pasta noodle at me now—"are glowing."

I want to say something back, tell her it's the glow of the kitchen lights and how freaking bright they are. But I can't deny that I even *feel* like I'm glowing.

It's not just because of the mind-blowing sex we had all weekend but everything that's happened the last few months.

It's seeing my daughter the happiest she's ever been and finally being able to be a kid. It's having the dream that I've had since I was a little girl finally come true. It's finding some of the best friends a girl could ask for that look me in without hesitation and has made this feel like home.

It's Oliver and every day spent with him that's turned into so much more than I ever expected.

"I'm really happy here," I finally say.

"Oh, we can tell," Kevin jokes.

Jan scans me up and down. "It looks good on you, girl."

"Why don't you cut out early," Kevin says. "You look beat. Lunch rush is over and there are only two tables left, both of which we've served already. Plus, the dinner crew will be here soon."

"I can't do that to you guys."

"Yes, you can." Kevin nods. "It's your turn to go out early anyway. You're always the last one here and work harder than anyone I know."

"Get outta here." Jan nods towards the back door.

"Thank you, guys."

I hang up my apron and change out of my kitchen shoes. I pull out my phone and see the *girl gang* group chat has multiple messages but decide I'll read them once I secure my Uber. A couple minutes go by and I'm still standing at the corner waiting for the car when my phone rings.

"Hey, Ave."

"Hey girl. Have you gotten any of my texts? Em and I are heading to Old Jose for Taco Tuesday. Are you down?"

"I just got out of work. I have to talk to Oliver and see if Mackenzie is okay."

I hear muffled noises in the background. Maybe a hand covers the microphone on her end? It sounds like she put me in her pocket or something. Then I hear someone say, "we're good."

"Hello?" I say.

"Yes, I'm here. You're good to go. Em was just on FaceTime with Oliver and Mackenzie anyway," Avery says.

My heart.

How did I get so lucky to have best friends who love my daughter like their own? Emiline actually saw Mackenzie over the weekend when she stopped at Peyton's house but she still can't get enough of her. I love that for Mackenzie.

"Okay. I'll meet you guys over there. But I won't be staying for long because I'm exhausted."

When I enter the restaurant, I see Avery and Emiline are already seated.

"Drinks on you," Avery says to Em after they lay eyes on me.

She rolls her eyes in response. "Fine."

"What's going on?" I ask.

"We took bets on how much you'd be glowing when you walked in here after your rendezvous with Oliver." Avery winks.

My cheeks pink as I sit down. "That obvious, huh?"

"Yes. Now spill." Avery leans forward on both elbows with her hands clasped together under her chin.

I cover my face with my hands, feeling shy all of a sudden because I don't know how to talk about it. "It was a really nice getaway. Since you already seem to know, we had sex. Lots of it."

Avery's smile grows wider.

"And I feel a lot of things... like a lot," I continue.

"Explain," Avery encourages.

"My feelings for him are growing at a rate I can't grasp. I'm feeling things that are wildly new to me in every way. I've never loved a man before or had attraction to this extent. It scares the shit out of me because it's so intense." I pause to gather my thoughts, my gaze bounces between the two girls. "And if things don't work out, I'm setting myself and Mackenzie up for major heartbreak."

Silence falls at the table. Avery has a soft smile on her face and Emiline has a look of complete shock on hers, like she didn't expect that out of me.

"Have I told you the story about Marc and me?" Avery says.

I shake my head, and hear Em let out a scoff. "This is a good one."

She releases a sigh. "Marc and I knew each other through Thomas and Peyton. He needed someone to be his fake date to this holiday gala he had to attend. I thought it was a one-time thing so I agreed to play the stupid role of a doting fiancée. Things got… interesting that night." Avery blushes thinking about it. She doesn't even need to say it for me to know what she means. "Mind you, I was also his assistant at the time. I took some time off work to help my mom because she broke her hip. When I came back, Marc told me we needed to put on the act for the whole summer to impress his boss."

"Wow." My eyes widen.

"Yeah." She laughs. "I didn't want to do it because I'd never been in a relationship. I swore off all men because of some daddy issues, which is a story for another day, but the point is, I was in a similar situation and scared out of my mind because I never had feelings for a man before Marc. It was so scary for me."

"Her admitting that is a lot," Emiline adds. "Avery doesn't do feelings."

"Facts," Avery exclaims with a finger in the air.

"You two looked so in love when I met you that time in the mountains though."

Avery nods. "That was for show. But things were already escalating quickly at that point. I was trying to fight off the feelings I knew I had for him, but just didn't know how."

"How did you handle it?" I ask.

She holds up her hand to show off the diamond on her ring finger. "I fell anyway. I let him catch me."

Ugh, that's adorable.

"It was a major chance I took to finally say those three words to him. But it was a risk I was willing to take with him because I fully trusted him with my heart at that point," Avery says.

"Knowing my brother," Emiline adds, "he won't let you fall alone either."

My insides flutter. I trust Oliver with my life. I know without a single doubt in my mind that he would never let me fall alone. I also feel like this can't be one-sided between us. There has to be more on his end.

I remember so vividly the look in his eyes on the trip when he loomed over my body just before driving into me. It was a look that screamed *I love you*, or better yet a look that said *I want to make love to you*.

"I guess I'm just nervous after hearing about his history with women. I'm not as experienced as he is so I'm not sure how to process all of it. What if he gets bored with me? What if he ends up changing his mind in a month? I don't know how the male mind works."

"I'd never lie to you about things like this," Emiline says. "Oliver was kind of a playboy for a long time. He's always lived his life carefree and like every day is his last. But coincidentally, he hasn't talked to my brothers about that stuff since his birthday trip last year."

"How would you know what he talks to his brothers about?" Avery raises a brow. "Marc says he doesn't talk to you about those things."

"I mean…" She blushes. "I'm just assuming."

"Are you assuming? Or is Logan telling you about the conversations they have at the bar when they go out Wednesday nights?" Avery says with an accusing tone.

Emiline's pink cheeks turn white like she's just been caught red-handed.

"I fully plan to circle back to this new revelation after you continue with what you were saying about Oliver to Macey," Avery says. "Because I'm sick and tired of you two hiding whatever relationship you two are having behind our backs."

"There's—" Emiline starts, but pauses quickly as her lips close with a tight seal. "Fine. I'll tell you guys everything but if I find out it gets back to my brothers, you're all fucking dead."

"Fine, continue," Avery encourages her.

"Like I was saying. Oliver changed his ways after his birthday trip. He hasn't been with anyone since he met you. I'm not just talking about when he saw you again at the bar you worked at. I'm talking about that first flight you two took to New York from Montana."

My thoughts come to a halt as I take in everything she's telling me and my stomach does a complete somersault.

I know he's said things about wanting everything I have to give and wants it all with me, but I've been burned once into thinking that someone loved me. Only to learn they didn't.

But this feels so much different with Oliver. So much more real.

"I think I'm really falling in love with him," I sigh.

"Oh, babe." Avery chuckles.

"You fell a long time ago," Emiline finishes.

I think she's right. They both are.

I don't know when or how, but I've been falling since that first flight.

CHAPTER FORTY-FIVE

Oliver

"What are you thinking of for dinner tonight?" I ask Mackenzie. Macey is working the dinner shift, so it's just the two of us tonight.

It's been a whole week since we've been back from our trip. Ever since I got a taste of what Macey sleeping in bed with me is like, I've struggled to sleep like a normal human on my own.

She would stay over but we haven't had a chance to talk to Mackenzie about it. The last thing I want to do is rush Macey into anything. This is a huge step for both of them, and I'm not about to screw it up.

"I have the best idea ever," she announces.

"Oh yeah? What's that?"

"So I never got a chance to show my mom how happy I am for her to get her dream job. And since I'm just a kid"—she rolls her eyes—"I couldn't buy her anything."

"You should have told me," I tell her. "You know I would have taken you anywhere you wanted to go and pick out whatever you wanted."

"You would have?"

I nod repeatedly. "Yes. Remember what I've always told you?"

"You don't do anything you don't want to do," Mackenzie says like a teenager and it's so damn cute. "That's really nice, Ollie. I didn't even think to ask because I've..." She looks somber and my heart folds as her smile disappears. "I've never really had anyone to ask."

Fuck. Every time she brings up her past, it's another stab to my chest. I wish I could go back in time and find a way to find these two sooner.

Except, I met these two when the universe was ready for us to meet.

Mackenzie deserves stability in her life, and I want to give her that. I want to be as good to her as my father was if Macey allows me the privilege to.

I clear my throat, swallowing any emotions I have thinking about the past. "What did you have in mind to do for her?"

"My mom really loves homemade gifts. One time in school back in Montana, I gave her an ornament for Christmas that we made in school. It was a clay mold of my hand and she cried. It was her favorite gift ever."

"I'm not crafty like that." I laugh.

"I wasn't talking about clay ornaments. It's not even Christmas, silly." She giggles. "I'm thinking of a home cooked meal. I think that's why she likes to cook, ya know. Food is the way to the heart, blah, blah, blah. I think I want you to help me make her something yummy for when she gets off work."

"Done," I say as I leap off the couch.

"Really?"

"Stop questioning me, Kenzie. I'll do whatever you want to do for your mom. What did you have in mind to whip up?"

"One day, before we moved here, I made her teach me how to make French toasts. So that way I could make her something some mornings out of love. But I'm kind of sick of it."

"Is that why you make it?"

"It's the only thing I know how to make." She shrugs.

Mackenzie is so young but she's so mature for her age and

it blows me away every time she reveals something to me. On top of that, she's got the biggest heart on the planet. Knowing she learned to make French toast for her mom as a small gesture to show her that she loves her makes my heart thump in my chest.

Food is the way to the heart.

That's why Macey loves cooking so much.

"What else does she like that's not breakfast?" I ask.

"She likes anything Italian."

I walk over to the kitchen and Mackenzie follows. I reach in the pantry and pull out my ridiculous apron and another small one I got for Mackenzie recently.

"How about we keep it simple because I can't cook either," I tell her, and we both burst out laughing.

She grabs the apron from my hand. "Is it for me?"

"Yeah. You like it?"

Mackenzie examines the pink and purple mermaid skin apron and her mouth twists with emotion. "I love it. Mom is going to love it. She's going to think I'm the best helper ever."

"We both already know you are."

She nods and puts it on.

"How about we make spaghetti and meatballs? It can't be that hard."

"Oh! I can pull a recipe from online."

"Let's do it."

While she pulls it up I grab some ground beef and an assortment of things I think might go in meatballs. I don't know the first thing about them. They taste amazing, but I've never cooked them.

"You know what drives me bonkers?" Mackenzie asks.

"What?"

"When you look up a recipe online and you get paragraph after paragraph of the person's life and why meatballs are so cool before the actual recipe. I don't need to know what inspired the recipe or your trip to Italy. Just give me the damn recipe."

I freeze where I'm standing, staring at her unblinking with my mouth slightly parted.

"Oops. I didn't mean to curse." She looks at me with wide eyes. "I'm sorry, Ollie."

"No. I mean, yes. I mean, no," I stutter in complete shock before my hands fall to my knees and I'm laughing so hard that my sides physically hurt.

"That's"—I'm actually crying I'm laughing so hard—"that's the truest shit I've ever heard, Kenzie. I think I'm more impressed at your reading skills and the fact you know it's about their trip to Italy at eight-years-old."

"I'm a whole grade and a half ahead of my class in reading, Ollie. I've read books that are harder than this mess before the recipe. Just tell me how many cups of jarred sauce I need."

I give her a questioning glare. "Your mom would lose it if she found out we used jarred sauce."

"Shh. It's out of love." Mackenzie swats my words away with her hands.

Both of us can't stop laughing, and it makes me realize just how much I love this girl. I can't tell if it's from laughing so hard, or how my feelings for both Macey and Mackenzie have taken over my heart, but I feel my chest tighten in a feeling I can't explain.

I love them both more than I've ever loved anyone in this world and I truly can't picture a life without them.

"I won't tell my mom you cursed if you don't tell her *I* cursed," Mackenzie breaks through my thoughts.

"Deal. Now let's get back to that recipe you found."

An hour later, the kitchen is a complete disaster.

Dishes are piled in the sink, there's red sauce splattered everywhere, but we truly had the best time ever making dinner. I look over to Mackenzie as she stirs the pot of spaghetti. I pulled out a stool for her so she could get a better angle since the pot was so big.

"What's got you smiling over there?" I ask her, noting the huge grin on her face.

"I was thinking about the wish I made on New Year's when the ball dropped."

"A wish?"

She rolls her eyes. "Yes. You're supposed to make a wish. I don't make the rules."

I hold my hands up in defense. "Whatever you say. Did it come true?"

"It did." Mackenzie nods. "Do you want to know what it was?"

"Sure."

"I wished for someone to make my mom really, really happy." She turns her head to look at me.

My chest feels tight as she keeps her stare locked on me. From the look in her eyes, I know she means me. I want to say more. I want to tell her how happy her mom has made me.

I want to tell Mackenzie how happy *she* has made me.

I change the subject before I can say anything more before Macey is home. "Your mom should be home any minute."

"Yes!"

"I think the fact that we didn't burn down the kitchen calls for a celebration, don't you?"

She nods enthusiastically.

"Alexa, play "Wonderland" by Taylor Swift," I say to the system in the kitchen.

"My favorite," she practically screams at the top of her lungs as the music starts.

I swear the entire city can hear her excitement.

We both bounce around the kitchen as the song belts over the speakers. Mackenzie sings every single word as if she's already had this song on repeat for months. We each grab a spoon and pretend it's a microphone when the greatest bridge of all time comes on.

Then I pick her up and put her on top of the island to let her really have the stage.

We both laugh uncontrollably when I move to the light switch and start flashing them like concert lights. Mackenzie can't even sing the words through our hysterics but a throat clearing loudly makes us both stop abruptly.

Macey stands just outside the kitchen staring at us in shock.

But she's smiling.

"Mom!" Mackenzie leaps off the counter into her mom's arms.

"What's going on here?" she asks.

"We made you dinner," Mackenzie tells her.

Her gaze locks on mine and her brows furrow. "Did you now?"

Macey knows damn well I can't cook for shit.

I fight the urge not to reach for her and pull her into my arms and kiss her out in the open.

Instead, we sit around the kitchen table and eat the best spaghetti and meatballs we've ever had despite the use of jarred sauce—Macey's words, not mine.

And I believe her because they were made with so much love.

CHAPTER FORTY-SIX

Macey

"What is happening tonight?" I ask Kevin and Jan as we work tirelessly in the kitchen.

"This is April for ya." Jan laughs.

"It's wild," Kevin adds. "The second the calendar turns over to April, everyone starts coming from all over the place to the city. I think a lot of kids have spring break the first week of April too. This is the kick-off to our busy season basically."

"Jesus," I mutter under my breath.

I pull the ticket from the printer to get started on the next order. It's two orders of surf and turf, our most expensive dish on the menu.

We make this dish a little different than other fine dining restaurants. We drizzle a garlic cream sauce on top and I must say, it's the most delicious sauce I've ever tasted. It's the perfect pairing with the filet too.

"Heard a rumor." Kevin smirks.

"About me?"

He nods. "I don't know if you know, but Frank is opening that other restaurant in a few weeks."

"I briefly overheard him say something before I started but not much."

"I heard you're up for the head chef position there."

The plate I was just holding falls to the counter while I stare at him. He's got to be playing a joke on me. Kevin is kind of known for that.

"This isn't one of my pranks." He laughs as if he can read my mind.

"W-what? Me?"

"Yes, *you*." Kevin rolls his eyes. "I was the one who suggested it to him."

"Are you trying to get rid of me?" I joke.

"Absolutely not." He shakes his head. "But you are head chef potential. I see how hard you've worked here for the last month. You always pick up shifts when we're short. Most days you know more than me. Most days I let you do more than you actually think."

My stomach feels queasy at the thought of becoming the head chef in a restaurant. It's something I've always wanted. But for it to potentially happen has me scared shitless.

Every bit of self-doubt I've ever had comes barreling into my mind. I've never been to culinary school and don't have an education outside of a high school diploma.

Why me?

I stop my thoughts when I think about Oliver, my new best friends, my coworkers…

About my daughter.

Everyone who's believed in me up until this point.

I lift my chin a little higher and offer Kevin a smile because despite spending my entire life made to believe I can't do it, I really can.

"Thank you," I finally say as I clear my throat.

"No thanks needed." Kevin shakes his head.

"You really do deserve it," Jan interjects. "I've really loved having you work the line with us."

I put the two dinner dishes up to be sent to the table and a server grabs them quickly to bring it out. A feeling of pride engulfs every part of me. It happens every time I send a dish out. I don't rush my dishes, but I always make sure it's made to perfection in a timely manner.

For the next half hour, we continue through the busy rush of dinner and laugh about the dumbest things. Jan tells us a joke about how her dog chased a squirrel in her backyard the other day and tried to sneak under the fence to grab it, only for his collar to get caught in the links.

It wasn't the funniest story in the world, but the way she tells them always has you full on laughing.

"Excuse me," a server says as she comes into the kitchen.

"Yeah?" Kevin and I say at the same time.

"A table out there would like to pay compliments to the chef."

"Which table?" Kevin asks.

"Table nine."

"That's all her." Kevin nods his head towards me. "It's the surf and turf you made."

My smile widens.

Someone wants to pay compliments to the chef? To me?

"I'll be right out," I tell her.

"See… Head chef potential." Kevin grins.

I peel off my apron and walk to the sink to wash my hands before stepping out to the dining area. I take a deep breath, the smile never leaving my mouth.

Once I step into the dining room, nervous energy takes over my body. My skin prickles with awareness and all of a sudden I feel like something is off. Most eyes land on me because I'm in a chef uniform and not the all black server uniform, but most quickly turn back to their food.

Except, when I see table nine come into sight, everything around me fades.

That nervous energy I felt coming back full force when I lay eyes on my mother and father sitting at the table.

They couldn't have known where to find me.

I swallow past the dryness in my throat, straighten my back and walk over to them.

"Well if this isn't a sight for sore eyes," my mom says, her fingers nestled under her chin as she scans my body up and down in disgust.

"Mother," I say flatly.

"Is that anyway to greet your mother when you haven't seen her in almost a year?" she says.

"Nine months," I correct.

"Semantics, dear." She laughs coldly. "I knew we would find you at some point and bring you and Mackenzie home with us."

"How did you find me?"

"You know Bill. Our private investigator," she says with a cheeky grin.

My gaze shifts to my father who sits there in silence sipping on a glass of what I assume is a very expensive whiskey.

"Dad," I breathe out. Begging him for some help here.

"Sorry, dear. I think it's time you stop playing these little games here in this rat-infested city and come back home to Montana."

I will not let them win. I will not let them win.

"I'm sorry, I can't." I shake my head.

"Don't tell me you can't because of this stupid little temporary job," my mom scoffs. "Besides, I asked to pay compliments to the chef, not the dishwasher."

Her words pour out of her like venom. I don't know how I put up with her as long as I did. I already knew leaving was for the best, but this entire interaction just goes to show that it truly was the best thing that's ever happened to me.

I push down the thoughts that start to creep up about what life would look like if I did stay.

Mackenzie would be miserable.

I would have never met Oliver.

I wouldn't be here.

"Excuse me," my mother calls the server over before I can speak. "I asked to speak with the chef, not the dishwasher."

The server's eyes widen as she looks up at me, fear taking over her features.

"It's okay, you don't have to answer her." I place a hand on her shoulder before looking back at my mom, forcing a flat smile to my face. "You *are* looking at the chef, *mother*."

"It's cute you think you could make it here," she adds.

"It's cute that you think I *couldn't*," I retort. "I'm not coming home. I'm a grown adult and this is where I want to be."

"Watch your tone with your mother," my dad hisses.

"Watch my tone?" I can't help but bark out a laugh. I lean down over the table to bring myself eye level with her. "I'm done with that life."

"What life? The life where we gave you everything you could've ever wanted? The life where we raised your daughter because you had to be a little slut and get knocked up at sixteen?" My mom's mouth twists up as if she's won with that argument.

I lower my voice, bringing myself even closer to her to avoid causing a scene in the restaurant. "The life where you made me feel less than I was. The life where you controlled not only my life, but *my* daughter's. Why can't you seem to understand that? Why can't you leave us be and understand we're the happiest we've ever been?"

Mom scoffs and adds an eye roll for exaggerated measures. "You can't be serious. The concrete jungle is what makes you happy? There's no way Mackenzie wants that life. I'm sure she hates it here. She's probably even regressed in school. That poor girl. She was doing so well in her advanced classes."

"The way she tells me multiple times a day how happy she is, tells me otherwise." I shrug.

My mother sits there in silence, but the look on her face tells me she still thinks she's winning this argument.

"I hate to break it to you, *mother*, but we're doing better than ever. I landed my dream job without your help. I'm standing on my own two feet without your help. I'm raising my daughter the way she deserves to be raised *without* your help. She loves her school and is doing amazing for your information. Listen closely when I tell you that leaving Montana was the best decision I've ever made next to keeping my daughter after you told me to… and I quote… get rid of her."

"You were sixteen years old," she seethes.

"It doesn't matter what mistakes I made or how old I was. What matters is how much she's loved and cared for. It matters how god damn happy she is. It matters that she's *my* child and that's something you will never be able to take away from me, no matter how hard you try."

Her lips part in shock before she closes them tightly.

"I don't know, dear." she says to my dad. "Don't you think they should be coming home? This little game she's playing is ridiculous."

I don't wait for my dad to answer. "Not happening."

Her head whips to look at me. "It is. Everything I've ever done for you—"

"You've mentioned that already," I cut her off.

"You owe me," she hisses through her teeth. "For raising your daughter properly."

"I don't owe you a *goddamn* thing!" My voice grows louder than I expected, and a few tables turn to look at us.

Silences stretches between us.

"What makes you think you're so wise?" my father questions over the brim of his whiskey glass.

My head snaps to his. "I've always been wise. You two were just too busy noticing my faults." I stand tall and straighten out my chef jacket that I earned with hard work. "Now if you'll excuse me, I have to head back to the kitchen and cook for the rest of the guests that are waiting on their meals."

They say nothing else.

Just as I'm about to turn, my mother speaks up, "You've

never been fit to be a mother. I'll make sure she comes home where she belongs."

My steps freeze and I slowly turn back to look at them. Rage taking over every part of my body as my fists clench on the sides of my body. I can't help it when I bring myself nose to nose with her.

"I fucking dare you to try. Not in this life or the next will you ever take her from me."

Before she can say anything back, I turn on my heel. I ask the hostess to remove them from the restaurant before I storm into the kitchen. The moment the doors close behind me, I press my back to it and feel my chest rising and falling rapidly. Anxiety I haven't felt in months comes back full force.

I close my eyes as I sink to the floor and try to regulate my breathing.

One… two… three..

"Macey, are you okay?" Jan runs over to me.

"My"—my breathing picks up—"parents."

"Oh shit," Kevin murmurs under his breath.

They know my entire story, know how I got here and why I left Montana for good. I've told them stories about how vindictive and narcissistic my parents are. So the second those two words leave my lips, they *know* exactly what just happened to me.

Jan cups my face in her hands. Sending a small wave of comfort through me. "Tell me what you need," she says.

One… two… three..

I pull my phone from my apron, handing it over to her because I can't even see straight.

"I need Oliver," I say right before sobs rack my entire body.

CHAPTER FORTY-SEVEN

Oliver

"Feel like doing arts and crafts tonight?" I ask Mackenzie.

She raises a brow at me. "You said you're not crafty."

"Must you remember everything I say?"

She taps the side of her head. "I store it all in here."

I pull out a bin of crayons, markers and craft paper I picked up at the store. I love hanging out with her, and since it's one of my favorite things to do with James, although his coloring is just scribbling all over the page, I wanted to try it with her too.

"Look, I got all these at the store the other day for you."

"You got that for me?" Mackenzie asks.

I look around the room, peeking under the kitchen table sarcastically. "I don't see any other nine year olds in the room."

"I'm not nine… yet." She giggles.

"Close. You act like you already are anyway. Plus, there's only two months left and you'll officially be nine."

"I can't wait," she shrieks.

"Alright, come draw with me." I wave her over to the table.

Mackenzie settles next to me and pulls out the colored pencils and the blank sketch pad. She starts drawing flowers and a scenic image. She's *good* for her age. She really has a better view on art than I have in my pinky toe.

"I need you to draw me something," I ask her.

"Like what?"

"Can you draw me a flower? Your favorite kind."

"Oh, yes! I can totes do that for you," she says before she pulls out three different colors and gets to work on drawing the best flower she can.

My phone buzzes on the counter across from us.

I leap up and grab it, noticing it's Macey.

"Hello?"

"Hi, Oliver?" A voice that isn't Macey's says through my speakers.

My stomach bottoms out and my legs feel weak all of a sudden at the thought that something happened to her.

"Yes," I choke out the word. "This is him."

"Hi, it's Jan. I work with Macey..." She pauses. "We had a situation come up at work."

"What kind of situation?" I ask quickly as I begin pacing back and forth in the kitchen.

"It's better if Macey tells you. Can you please come get her? She's in no condition—"

"I'll be right there," I cut her off and hang up.

"Fuck," I mutter. My eyes land on Mackenzie whose eyes are so wide they might fall out of her eye sockets. "I'm sorry. I didn't mean to curse. I have to get your mom from work."

She stands quickly. "Is she okay?"

"She's... she's fine. I just have to pick her up."

My hands shake as I grip my phone, trying to figure out what to do. I don't know what I'm about to be walking into and I don't think it's the best idea to bring Mackenzie with me to pick her up.

I dial the person who lives closest to me.

"Hello?" she answers on the first ring.

"Emiline. I need you."

"Oliver. What's going on? What do you need?"

"Can I drop Mackenzie off with you? I have to get Macey from work."

There's a pause on the other end of the line and I hear her suck in a sharp breath. My sister cares so deeply for Macey and Mackenzie and I'm sure she's sitting there doing exactly what I'm doing right now—running the worst case scenario through her head.

"Yeah. Yes. Of course," she finally says.

"I'll be there in five." I hang up the phone.

I crouch down to eye level with Mackenzie, swallowing before I speak. "I'm going to drop you off at Emiline's for a little bit. I don't know what's going on but I have to pick your mom up from work."

She starts crying and I assume quickly that I'm not doing a good job at handling this.

"It's okay, baby," I tell her as I pull her into my chest and wrap my arms around her as tight as I can without hurting her. "I'm going to make sure she's okay. I promise."

Mackenzie nods. "I know you will."

We grab our things and are out the door in less than a minute. My leg bounces the entire short drive to Emiline's apartment. Mackenzie and I take the stairs two at a time. Her small legs keep up with mine because she's just as eager for me to get to her mom as I am.

The door swings open before I can even knock and Logan stands where Emiline should be. Mackenzie scoots inside and I stand there glowering at my best friend in my little sister's apartment for a beat too many.

"Oliver," he groans like he's finally been caught.

"You're fucking lucky I'm in a rush. We'll discuss this later," I snap. "Don't lay a finger on my little sister."

Logan throws his hands up in defense before I turn and run back down the same way I came.

My brain runs a mile a minute trying to figure out what

happened and why Logan was at my sister's place. My worry turns to anger, but my brain snaps back to the issue at hand.

Macey. Please be okay. Please be okay, I repeat to myself the entire drive to Mollie's.

I park in the employee lot, not giving a damn if I get a ticket or not.

A small black haired woman greets me at the back door.

"What happened?" I ask her.

"Her parents showed up," she says.

All the air leaves my lungs and I feel dizzy. I've never met her parents and I thank god every day I haven't because my fist would be in their faces. I don't care who they are to her. They made Macey feel broken, and for that, I would love to break their fucking noses.

I rush past her, scanning the kitchen for any sign of my girl.

"In there," the man behind the line says, pointing to a small door off to the side.

I throw the door open and find Macey in a ball in the corner of the supply room. Her body shakes as she cries into her hands. My heart shatters into a million pieces seeing how hurt she is. I can only imagine what those pieces of shit said to her to cause this.

I don't say anything as I scoop her up into my arms.

Macey gasps when she notices it's me. Then she envelopes her arms around my neck before she nuzzles her head into my neck, crying harder than she was before

"Shhh, baby," I whisper. "I'm here. I got you."

"Oliver," she cries out. "My parents showed up."

"I know. I know." I sit her on my lap and she doesn't release her hold on me. I rock back and forth giving her every ounce of comfort she needs right now. I can feel myself breaking with her. It feels like everything she's feeling is being transferred to me and I can't help it when my eyes begin to well with tears.

I don't cry.

Except I do. In this moment with her, I let it out. I can feel her tears soaking through my shirt and it breaks my heart to see her like this.

"Babe," I choke out. "I need you to breathe. Breathe for me."

I feel her inhale a shaky breath before Macey releases it in a long, drawn out exhale. She lifts her head to meet my stare. She's looking at me like I'm not even real, like she didn't expect me to be here.

"You came." Her voice is so low that I would have missed it if she wasn't sitting in my lap.

"You called," I offer her a weak smile. "I mean, your coworker called me, but tomato, tom-ah-toe."

And with that, she laughs.

My girl fucking laughs softly, and it's music to my ears. I don't know what the hell happened or what her parents said to her to cause this, but all I know is she's laughing now.

Nothing in this world will ever compare to that sound.

"Tell me what you need," I tell her.

"I want to go home."

That's all I need to hear before I stand with her in my arms.

As we emerge from the small closet, I look at the man behind the kitchen line and give him a look, a silent order that I'm bringing her with me and wondering which way I should go.

Neither of us have to speak the words, maybe it's just guy code or whatever but he nods toward the back door signaling for us to get out of here that way.

I'm taking my girl home.

CHAPTER FORTY-EIGHT

Oliver

We stopped by Emiline's to pick up Mackenzie on the ride home. I was thankful I didn't see Logan when I opened the door but I didn't hang around to find out long enough if he was hiding anywhere.

When I came back to the car with her, Macey was passed out in the passenger seat with her legs to her chest. I kind of expected that with how worn out she was from crying as hard as she did.

Mackenzie doesn't ask questions thankfully. I'm not so sure I want to be the one to tell her that her grandparents showed up and caused this level of hurt to her mom. It's going to destroy her, and she's been through so much.

Plus, I don't even know what was said. It's best if Macey tells her. However, I fully plan to be there when the discussion takes place. Not because I'm nosey, but because *both* of my girls deserve someone in their corner.

I tuck Mackenzie into bed, giving her a brief forehead kiss. It's something that comes naturally to me now. It's gotten to the point that if I don't say goodnight to her before bed, I sleep like absolute shit.

"Will mom be okay?" she asks me just before I flick her light switch off.

"Your mom is one of the strongest people I know, next to you, Kenzie," I tell her honestly.

Mackenzie nods. "Are you going to make sure she's okay tonight?"

I swallow past the lump that's been stuck in my throat since I got the phone call, and give her a reassuring nod.

"Good." She snuggles herself back into bed, pulling the covers over her head and gripping Bert a little tighter.

It's so cute when she does it because she totally sleeps like me. On her side, with a pillow between her legs and her blanket covering half of her face.

"I'm so happy we have you, Ollie."

"I love you, Kenzie."

She yawns. "I love you too."

I close her door. With my hand still on the knob, I press my back to it and let my head fall back, allowing myself a few deep breaths. Once I feel ready to tackle this, I make my way to Macey in hopes that she hasn't fallen back asleep yet so I can talk to her about what happened tonight.

If she wants to, of course.

The second I round the corner, I find her sitting on the edge of the couch with her elbows resting on her knees and hands on her face. As if she can sense me in the room, she lifts her head and looks over to where I'm rooted.

That doesn't last very long though because my hands itch to touch her.

I walk over and wrap my arms around her, pulling her to my side on the edge of the couch. "What do you need? Are you hungry? Do you want to talk? Ice cream?" I rattle the questions off nervously.

God, I just want to make this go away for her.

"I..." Macey blinks up at me. "You have that really nice and fancy bathtub in your room." It comes out as a statement, not a question. The one and only time she's been in my bathroom fully was when she walked in on me jerking off to fantasies of her.

"Done."

If Macey wants to soak in the tub for hours, then that's what she's going to do.

I clasp her hand in mine and don't let go until we reach my bathroom. I pull out a plush towel from the closet for her and some bubbles I had purchased the week she moved in.

I did it because her bathroom doesn't have a tub and if she ever did want to take a bath to relax, she could in this one. Once I turn the water on and get everything situated, I turn around to find Macey staring at herself in the mirror.

She looks... broken.

I move my body to stand in front of her to block whatever negative thoughts are flowing through her head as she stares at herself.

I reach for the hem of the undershirt Macey had on under her chef's jacket. Our eyes lock with an agreement that this is okay for me to do. I want to be the one to take care of her and give her what she needs.

I pull it over her head and toss it to the ground before I reach behind her to unclasp her bra. I keep my eyes on hers the whole time before I hook my fingers into the waistband of her work pants, pushing them to the ground before I do the same with her panties.

This is the first time I've ever undressed a woman for something other than sex.

It has me feeling more connected to Macey and more in love with her than ever before.

But now is not the time to tell her that.

I gently pick her up and place her in the oversized bathtub. Macey's head falls back and her eyes close. She lets the bubbles flow over her body as she melts into the warmth of the water.

She's the first to break the silence. "I hate how much I let them affect me."

"You're justified in your feelings, Macey."

"I know. Trust me, I do. I think it hurts more because they're the two people who are supposed to love me unconditionally. They were supposed to love me the second they laid eyes on me when I was born and never stop. They're supposed to go through hell and back for me. And I can say this because I'm a mom. I know these feelings and I can't imagine doing that to Mackenzie. It makes me sick just thinking about it."

I let her pour it all out. Whatever she's willing to tell me as I kneel down to the side of the tub, grabbing the washcloth and putting some lavender soap on it to rub her back.

"She told me *"You've never been fit to be a mother. I will make sure she comes home where she belongs."* I can't stop those two sentences from playing on repeat in my head. I was doing so good." Macey swipes a tear that falls to her cheek. "And they just had to come and find me, harass me at my workplace and threaten to take my daughter from me."

"No one is taking her from you," I snap. "Over my dead fucking body is anyone going to take Mackenzie." I grip her chin in my fingers, forcing her to stare at me as anger bubbles to the surface. "Do you understand?"

Macey's lips part in shock at the harshness of my tone.

"Fuck." I stand from the edge of the tub and start pacing the bathroom. I run my hands through my hair a few times and quite frankly, I'm ready to pull it out. "I'm sorry. I didn't mean to talk to you like that. But I need you to know, I'll die before anything happens to you or Mackenzie."

Macey sits up in the bath, her hands resting on the edge and her stare doesn't waver from mine.

"Oliver," she breathes out.

"Babe." I sigh before I kneel next to her again before I brush her hair away from her face. "I hate that this happened to you tonight, but remember what I told you in the bagel shop that morning? I've never met anyone more resilient than you."

"I know," she whispers. "I hate that I still feel trapped by them."

"Freedom from them will come when you realize that only *you* hold the power to overcome every obstacle life throws at you. I mean look at you, you're here in the city. You made a life happen for yourself all on your own. Mackenzie has been a whole new kid since the day I met her. That's because of *you*."

"No," Macey stops me. "It's because of *you*."

I shake my head. "Don't you see, babe? You're the one who decided to get on that flight and start a new life for you two. You're the one who decided to get in the car with a complete stranger who lives off of takeout and Pop-Tarts." She laughs at that. "You're the one who trusted me enough to live in my apartment so that *you* could make it happen. Macey. Baby. That's all you."

"I…" She stops herself as tears stream down her face.

Tell me you feel it too.

"Thank you," Macey settles on. "I-I don't know what we would do without you and I don't think I want to find out."

"You won't ever have to find out if I have anything to do with it."

I lean in and kiss her.

Sealing every single unspoken word with our lips.

CHAPTER FORTY-NINE

Macey

I groan as I roll over in bed but it feels different.

My eyes snap open and I immediately notice that I'm not in my room, I'm in Oliver's. I don't sit up in a panic. Instead I find myself nestling a little tighter into his pillow. I attempt to try and find his scent, but all I smell is whatever lavender body wash and shampoo he used on me last night.

Thoughts of the night before come rushing to the front of my brain, and my stomach stings with the pain of my parents' words again.

Out of everything they've ever said to me, I can't get those two sentences out of my head.

You've never been fit to be a mother. I will make sure she comes home where she belongs.

The old me would have spiraled into the dark place I haven't seen in a while.

The old me would have probably agreed with the dark thoughts and said they were right.

But what they said is so far from the truth and all it took was a verbal smack to reality with Oliver's words last night. I can't think of a single time I've seen him angry. I don't think I want to see it again, but it made me understand so much more about myself.

My throat feels so dry and I can't help but choke as I let out a cough likely due to crying so much last night that I depleted my body of any form of liquid it needs to survive.

Just as I'm about to get out of bed, the door swings open and Oliver stands there with a tall glass of water. *Looking* like a tall glass of water. His sweatpants sit low on his waist and he has no shirt on to cover his insane muscles I want to run my hands over.

Relax, Macey.

"Good morning," Oliver says, his voice deep and sleepy.

"I'm sorry, did I wake you?" I ask.

"No. I was laying on the couch waiting for you to wake up."

My eyebrows narrow as I sit up taller. "You slept on the couch?"

He nods. "I didn't want us both to be in here if Mackenzie woke up early. I didn't want her to think anything."

Right. That.

I'm so done with being in the dark with Oliver. I want to bring us to the light. I want to share this with Mackenzie and see how she feels. I want to see what we could possibly be.

"I want to talk to her today. If that's okay with you."

"She was worried last night about you," Oliver says.

My chest tightens realizing that she probably saw me emotionally drained last night and I didn't tell her that her grandparents showed up. I know I need to tell her that too.

"I'm going to talk to her about it. And"—I pause, assessing his features—"us."

Oliver slowly walks across the room before he takes a seat on the edge of his bed. He places a hand on my thigh over the covers and even that contact feels like everything I need.

"Whenever you're ready. Today, tomorrow, or next year. I'm not going anywhere, Macey." He presses a quick kiss to my lips before he walks back to the living room.

I love him with everything in me.

I'm just plating the last pancake when Mackenzie comes strolling out of the hallway that leads to her room. She's rubbing her sleepy eyes and I can't help but chuckle on the inside because when we first moved here, she was totally a morning bird.

Now, she has completely switched to being a full on night owl.

While I cooked breakfast, Oliver filled me in on leaving her with Emiline before picking her up while I fell asleep in the car. My mind and body were so physically exhausted by the time he picked me up from work that I barely noticed at the time.

"Good morning, babe." I say to Mackenzie.

"Morning, mom. Did you sleep okay in Ollie's room last night?" she asks.

"I, uh—"

"She woke up around three in the morning with a bad dream," Oliver cuts in. "I heard her and tucked her back into bed. She watches too much of that Harry Potter stuff." He laughs.

"I do not," she scoffs.

My chest constricts with pain all over again that I wasn't there for my girl. Oliver's room is too far away in this massive apartment for me to have even heard it. She doesn't have bad dreams often, but when she does it's from whatever show she was watching.

"I'm sorry I wasn't there."

"It's okay. I know you had a bad night."

"About that…" I turn off the stove top and bring the pile of pancakes to the kitchen table.

Oliver poured three glasses of orange juice and helped cook the bacon which already sits in the middle of the table. Mackenzie takes a seat next to me, tucking her small leg under her butt as she sits.

"It definitely wasn't the best night," I finish.

She picks up two pancakes and two pieces of bacon, waiting for me to continue.

"Grandma and Grandpa showed up at my work last night."

Mackenzie stills, snapping her head in my direction.

"And they weren't very nice to me."

"They…" She pauses, something that resembles fear crosses her little features and I notice her shoulders go stiff. "They aren't going to try to get us to go home, are they?"

I shake my head but before I can say anything, Oliver cuts in.

"Over my dead body, Kenzie."

Her gaze lands on him. "So we can stay here? We don't have to leave? They won't make us? What if they try?" She turns to look at me again. "I don't want to, Mom. I really don't want to. Please, can I stay here?"

I swallow. Every muscle in my body is filled with tension and pain. Mackenzie rattles off each question with so much worry in her tone and I hate that for such a small girl, she's so concerned about things like this.

But she's old enough to know what she wants and I've grown enough through my own shit that I know what I want as well.

I reach my hand out to cover hers. "We're not going anywhere."

Mackenzie's shoulders relax as I reassure her but she remains silent.

I can only imagine what goes on in her mind and what damage her past has already caused. I wish more than anything I was smart enough to leave when she was smaller. But everything we've been through has made both of us who we are today.

I *know* I'm stronger. I know *she* will be stronger.

"I wanted to talk to you about that, actually," I continue. Mackenzie raises a small eyebrow in question. "How would you feel if Oliver stayed in our lives?"

She turns to look at him briefly before she looks back at me. "I thought that was the plan."

Oliver and I can't help but laugh.

"I really like him, Mackenzie. As more than just a friend to us."

"You have a crush on him? Like you want to date him?"

I nod in response.

A few heartbeats pass while I hold my breath to wait for a response. Her mouth twists in a radiant smile as she clenches her fists together shaking them as if she's... excited?

"Finally," she screams.

My eyes widen as I look at Oliver. His face matches mine in shock. "What?"

"I knew you guys liked each other. Like *a lot*. I mean, what's not to like?" Mackenzie holds her hand out towards Oliver like she's the co-host on *Wheel of Fortune*. "He's so funny."

"So you're okay if we maybe date each other?" Oliver asks.

"I think you should marry each other!"

I practically spit out my juice, but Oliver doesn't react the same way I did. His eyes burn a hole through me and his infectious smile makes my neck grow hot. There's no way I was even thinking about marriage.

But, I do see a life with him. I see a future with him.

"One day," Oliver responds.

Two simple words that hold so much power. I never imagined I would find someone who would love and accept not just me but my daughter into their life.

It takes a special person to love a single mom. You're not just falling in love with her, you're falling in love with someone she loves more than anything in the world. It's a package deal that someone *chooses* to accept.

They don't force themselves to love the tiny human just because they love the mom. It's something that comes naturally.

Oliver has successfully shut down everything I thought I knew about never being able to find love as a mom.

"I love when wishes come true." She beams as she dives into her pancakes.

"Huh?"

"New Year's Eve, Mom. I wished for someone to make you really happy because I didn't want to see you sad anymore."

The dams open and tears spill from my eyes.

I thought I loved her years ago. I thought I loved her yesterday. But every day I love her more than I ever thought possible.

"I love you, Mackenzie."

"I love you the most," she beams. "And I really love your boyfriend too."

The three of us break out into laughter.

Despite everything that's happened in the last twenty-four hours, I've never felt more free knowing that Mackenzie accepts Oliver into our lives and loves him as much as I know I do.

CHAPTER FIFTY

Oliver

Nothing in the world feels better than having my girl in my arms, snuggled close on my couch watching trashy reality television.

If you told me a year ago that my life would look like this right now, I would have called you a liar and brought myself to the bar with Logan to see what kind of fun we can get ourselves into.

I think back to what dad told me about never settling. There's no way he meant something as strong as what Macey and I have together. I don't believe for one second that this would be settling when it feels meant to be.

I was also naive to believe that being in a relationship was stupid. No matter how happy my brothers looked, I just always felt like it wasn't in the cards for me *because* I was living life without a care in the world.

Now, with Macey and Mackenzie, I feel like the luckiest man in the world because I didn't only get one girl. I got two.

Two girls who have flipped my world upside down in the best way possible.

Macey moves under my arm that's draped over her shoulders, and sits up as she lets out a yawn before she stretches.

"I'm exhausted. I think I'm going to head to bed."

She doesn't wait for a response, but leans in and kisses me before she starts to make her way to her bedroom.

"Where are you going?" I stand up quickly and ask her.

She hikes a thumb over her shoulder. "I'm heading to bed. I'm so tired."

I can't help but grin, because it's cute that she thinks she will ever be sleeping in that room again.

It's my turn to hike a thumb over my shoulder. "This way."

"My stuff is this way."

"That's a problem we can deal with tomorrow," I tell her as I take long strides to close the distance between us. "I want you in my bed with me for the foreseeable future."

"You don't think that's moving too fast, Oliver?"

"We're past the moving too fast thing." I laugh. "Besides, even if it is, I could care less about what's fast and what's slow. I know what I want and it's you in my bed. I need to have my arms around you. I need you to fill my sheets with your scent and I need to wake up every day to that smile I've grown addicted to."

Macey's lips curve as her cheeks turn a light shade of pink.

"There it is," I say before I bring her face to mine. Before she can say anything back, my lips are on hers.

I lift her in my arms, refusing to break our kiss as I carry her to my room.

Our room.

As I lay Macey down gently on the bed and hover over her body, I know this time will be different than the others. This is me showing her how much I love her without having the guts to say the words yet.

This is me showing her how she's claimed every part of me.

"Oliver," she pants as she tears away from my lips, frantically trying to push my sweatpants down my legs.

"Shhh," I murmur against her lips.

Her movements still and I stare into the green eyes that are engraved into the deepest parts of my soul. I don't say anything, I let my eyes tell her what I need to say before I kiss her again.

There's no rushing.

It's just us and the fierce electricity that rushes between us when we're connected.

I sit her up slowly, reaching for the hem of her sleep shirt and pulling it over her head. Her eyes bore into mine, soft and gentle. I reach behind my neck and pull my shirt over my head, and even those few seconds were too long to take my eyes off of her.

Macey stands from the edge of the bed and pushes her shorts to the floor before sitting back down for me.

"You're so beautiful," I whisper, cupping her cheek with my palm. Her head leans into me as if it's a magnet on my skin. "I wish I knew what I did so right in life to deserve you, Macey. I'm going to spend the rest of my life thanking the universe for putting us in the same spot at the same time."

I press her down using the weight of my body until her back is flush with the sheets. Her arms wrap around my neck as if she doesn't want me to go anywhere. I reach my hand between us, my finger touching her soft wet skin between her legs before I reach her most sensitive spot.

The spot I know drives her crazy.

"Oliver," Macey breathes out, arching her back into me.

"I got you, baby," I whisper against her lips as I continue to rub slow circles.

There's no rush and no frenzy between us. I would love nothing more than to have my head between her legs or her mouth on my cock before anything else. But right now, I need to feel connected to her more than ever before.

"I need you." She pulls my face to hers, connecting our lips as I give a little more pressure to her bundle of nerves. Hoping like hell I don't get her off yet because the first time she comes tonight it will be *with* me.

"And I need you like the oxygen I need to survive," I say with the honest truth.

"You have me," she moans from the touch. "You have every part of me, Oliver."

"Fuck," I groan in relief. Hearing those words from her is everything I need. I stand for a second to push my sweatpants to the floor. I fist my cock two times before I line myself up with her entrance. "I know we've done it without one before, but do you want me to get a condom?"

"I don't want anything between us," Macey says quickly.

My head falls back and my cock only swells in my hand that much more.

With one thrust, I'm inside of her, but I don't move. I *can't* move. This feels like too much. The sensation that's taking over every part of my body has chills running down my spine and my brain swirling with every emotion under the sun.

Fear that one day I could lose this.

So much love for the only woman who has the ability to bring me to my knees.

But I also feel safe.

It's such a strange feeling because I've never been scared of anything in my life. But this feeling right here, I feel safe in her arms. I feel safe giving her every last piece of me knowing she's going to protect it.

"This feels…" The words fall off my tongue.

This feels like nothing I've ever experienced before.

Because this is what making love feels like. Something I've never done in my life.

"I know," Macey replies as her hips slowly rock into me from below. "I know."

I never take my eyes off hers as I move in and out of her slowly, savoring every moment of this feeling with her.

"I don't know how, but I'm already close," she moans.

"No," I say breathlessly. "Not yet. I need you to come with me."

My movements quicken as she tightens her hold around my neck, and my name comes off her lips in sweet chants between her ragged breaths.

"Oliver."

"Say my name again," I beg.

"Oliver," Macey moans loudly. "It feels so good."

I groan and my face dives into her neck and I thrust harder and harder into her. Her pulse bounds against my lips. "I love the way you say my name, baby. You feel like heaven."

"I can't hold it in," she pants. "I'm going to come."

I drive into her three more times before both of us explode into one another. I feel her convulse around my cock as she milks me of every last drop I have in me. She screams my name through her orgasm and I claim her lips on mine as I fill her.

I don't stop kissing her until we both come down from our high.

"Jesus." Macey breaks free from the kiss. "That was…"

"That was perfect." I finish for her.

And it was.

I want to tell her I love her right here and right now, but it doesn't feel like the right time. It would feel like I'm saying it because of how strong that just felt.

Macey deserves so much more than that.

And I'm going to make sure she knows that.

CHAPTER FIFTY-ONE

Macey

I'm on my third shift of the week and of course, it's the busiest one.

I think the universe just knows when you're tired. That's when it decides to throw a shit show at your face to really test you.

According to Jan, my parents showed up again two days later. Thankfully I wasn't here. I don't understand why they're sticking around. I also don't get why they are showing up *here* if they want Mackenzie so badly.

Since Jan told me that they showed up again, Oliver has been more careful if he runs to the store or does anything with Mackenzie. He had asked me to show him a picture of them so he wouldn't be blindsided.

It's been a whole week since I saw them and for the first time in my life, I'm so damn proud of myself for not falling back into the hole I always end up in. I let myself have that night to soak in my issues and the next day I got myself back up and stood taller than ever before.

If it wasn't for living in New York and finally being content with life, I'm not sure the outcome would be the same. There was a brief thought this week where I wondered what would have happened if they found me while I was upstate.

Would I be this strong? Would I be back in Montana right now?

I had to brush off those thoughts quickly because it didn't happen and can't happen. There was no use in letting it take over when it wasn't a possibility anymore because I was here.

"Macey," a server calls my name through the window. "I'm so sorry, but they are back."

I groan.

Strangely, I don't feel panic or fear anymore. If she came up and said this yesterday, I might have felt differently. I'm just too exhausted to care right now.

"Thank you," is all I say to her as I get back to preparing whipped mashed potatoes for a table.

The potatoes still haunt me and I definitely triple check them before I serve them. I'm happy to announce I haven't messed it up again since my first night here.

"You good?" Kevin asks from my side.

I nod. "I'm good."

"You know, Jan and I got your back. You need me to kick their asses to the curb, I got you."

"And if you need me to put contact lens solution in their potatoes, I got you," Jan adds.

Every part of my body warms at their threats to the people who jeopardize my happiness.

They're not the first people to say things like this either. After I told the girls what happened, their responses had me simultaneously laughing and also in fear for my parents' life.

PEYTON

You have got to be joking.

AVERY

Do I need to pull out the big guns? I can find out where they are staying and put bed bugs in their hotel room.

EMILINE

That's evil and just reading that makes my skin crawl.

AVERY

They get what they deserve, Em.

PEYTON

The fact that you would even come in contact with them to put them in the room makes my skin itch.

AVERY

Girl, my skin is itchy just typing it. But if it gets them away from Macey, I'll do whatever I need to do.

PEYTON

I was just thinking about calling the hotel and having them kick them out on account of fraudulent charges and then contacting every hotel in the city and banning them. Oh, oh! And then calling the airline and having them accidentally misplace their luggage. But really they burn it.

AVERY

Spoken like a true billionaire's wife.

PEYTON

Shut up.

EMILINE

Or we can just have Logan put a restraining order on him?

AVERY

You would find a way to bring Logan into any conversation.

PEYTON

Agree. But also, that's not a bad idea.

Between the girls, my coworkers, Oliver, his brothers, and of course, my daughter, I have everything I could ever want in life. I'm strong. I'm happy.

I'm finally the person I knew deep down was inside of me all this time.

I pull out my phone to shoot Oliver a quick text when my screen saver stops me in my tracks. It's a picture Oliver sent of me looking out over the city when he first took me to the Top of the Rock.

His words ring in my ear as I stare at it.

'No more rock bottoms, dragonfly. Welcome to the Top of the Rock. This is where you stay for good this time.'

I smile and send the text to Oliver.

They showed up again. But all is good here.

OLIVER

That's my girl. Remember what I've always told you. You're the strongest woman I've ever known, babe.

Also, maybe spit in their food.

I smile at his response before I pocket my phone.

"They can sit there and wait all night if they want." I shrug, finally responding to them and getting back to work. "They will never get what they want from me."

"That's my girl," Jan chants.

"Man, I'm going to miss working with you," Kevin says with the shake of his head.

"I'm not going anywhere. No matter how much they want to push me." I laugh.

"No. I mean when you become the most badass head chef at the new restaurant," Kevin says matter-of-factly.

I stare at him with my mouth wide open. He can't mean what I think he means.

"I need you to explain," I tell him.

"Frank wanted me to be the one to tell you," he starts before his mouth turns into a shit eating grin. "But you're going to be the new head chef at their second location."

His words stop me in my tracks. For a second, I forget that I'm standing behind the kitchen line and making someone's dinner.

What was I just making? Did he just say I am going to be the next head chef?

"I don't think I heard you correctly."

"You heard him just fine, girl." Jan laughs.

"The menu will be mostly the same since it's a sister location, but Frank and Mollie also want it to be unique. They don't want people to choose one or the other. They want people to visit both places for different reasons. They want you to put your own spin on the menu if you choose to," Kevin explains.

"That's…" I can't seem to think of the words I have for this news. "Wow. I love their idea to make it its own place."

Holy. Shit.

This was never a part of the dream when I said I wanted to be a chef in the city. Where I'm standing right now is enough for me. It's not that I'm settling, it's just that this is what has made me so insanely happy. Doing what I love and working beside one of the best chef's I've ever met.

How in the world could I ever be anywhere as good as Kevin?

"I don't know. This is a lot to take in. I don't know if I'm ready for that. Being a head chef? Like you?" I say to Kevin. "There's no way I'm qualified enough for this. I didn't even go to college."

He scoffs. "And you think I did?"

Wait. What?

"I'm convinced all of that is a waste of time. Believe it or not, I started the same way you did. You and I are a lot alike."

"You mean you're a dad who got pregnant young and was

forced to give up your life and put your own dreams aside?" I joke.

"Something like that. Minus *me* being the one to get pregnant, of course," he tosses the joke back at me.

Since my first day working here, I've looked up to Kevin in more ways than one. The way he moves effortlessly around the kitchen and his concentration to make every single dish he sends out absolutely perfect. This place runs as smooth as it does *because* of him.

"I don't understand."

"My wife got pregnant when she was eighteen. Obviously, we weren't married then. I know you were a little younger than that, but both of us were forced to grow up. We both gave up on our dreams to go to college despite having each other. It was just impossible." He shakes his head at the memory. "I got a job as a busboy in the city. I washed dishes for three years and when I wasn't taking care of our son, I was reading books about cooking at all hours of the night to sharpen my knowledge. I kept telling myself that when Scotty got older I'd finally make a life for the three of us."

"We really are a lot alike." I nod. "I did the same thing but took a job as a bartender."

"See? We both had similar ideas to get us into the industry. With the kind of drive you have, you deserve to have a head chef role. You remind me of myself a decade ago."

I can't help but shake my head. "This is so much to take in. I don't know."

"Well, take it in." Jan beams. "You're the next head chef!"

"Oh and not to give you more pressure or anything… but you have to pick a name for the restaurant too." Kevin laughs. "Frank and his wife can't agree on anything, so they are leaving it up to you."

Jesus Christ. What is happening tonight?

Just when I think my dreams have finally come true, life tells me I deserve more.

That's when I make a decision.

I throw my towel down and head right through the kitchen doors to tell my parents exactly that.

CHAPTER FIFTY-TWO
Oliver

After Macey texted me that her parents showed up again at the restaurant, my body has been flooded with anger. I have fought the urge to drive over there and deck her dad in the face for allowing her mother to talk to her that way.

I tried to call Logan to get an idea of what can be done, but of course he didn't pick up his phone. He's probably the worst person to get in touch with lately if you need anything.

Mackenzie went to bed about an hour ago and I've just been pacing the living room with my phone in my hand waiting for *someone* to get in touch with me.

Macey, if she needs me. Her coworker, if she has another breakdown. Logan to call back.

I'm pulling out a tub of ice cream to calm my nerves when my phone buzzes on the counter. I reach for it so fast that the quick movement pulls the bandage I have on my chest, courtesy of my appointment earlier today.

"Fuck. Hello?" I answer.

"Are you alright? You sound like you just stubbed your toe on the corner of the wall. Those will jump out at you, ya know?" Logan jokes.

"You're hysterical," I deadpan.

"Sorry I missed your call. How did today go with your appointment?"

"It was a bitch but that's not why I called. I need your help with something."

"Straight to the point. Shoot."

I breathe out a sigh. "So last week, Macey's parents showed up to her work. They were harassing her and said some terrible things and threatened to take Mackenzie away from her."

"Oh shit," he says almost under his breath.

"Yeah. I can't let that happen. Since then they showed up earlier this week when she wasn't there and then again tonight. She texted me that she's okay but I don't know if she spoke with them or decided to let them be. I can't help but worry. Is there anything we can do to stop this?"

"You can file for a restraining order. Being that they don't live in the city, the best option is to just drive them out of town. They don't have much pull because Macey is a stable mother, doesn't do drugs or drink, provides for her daughter, blah, blah, blah," Logan tells me.

"Okay. Okay," I repeat as I start pacing the kitchen again. My chest is on fire and unsure of how to process this. I don't want to take extreme measures if we don't have to, but I know that I will do anything to protect them and keep them safe.

"Regardless, I wouldn't worry," he reassures me. "Macey is a good fucking mom. You and I both know this. God forbid they try, you know I have your back. I'm sure the girls, Thomas and Marc would too. Neither of you are alone in this. You have us. Family sticks together."

Family sticks together.

I've always been so lucky to have the best siblings a guy can ask for. I got even luckier when Peyton, Avery and Kali came into our lives. Now, I feel like the luckiest son of a bitch to have fallen so madly in love with my Macey and Mackenzie.

With that comes the fear of losing them.

It's something I can't even think about. I don't know her

parents and how vindictive they could be with all of this. If they ever took my girls from me though, I wouldn't survive.

No matter how much anyone was there for me.

I clear my throat to keep my emotions at bay. "Thank you."

The door to the apartment opens and I see Macey walk in with takeout containers in her hands. I'm thankful she did because I haven't been able to eat anything except for this tub of ice cream I was just going to force down.

"Macey just walked in," I tell Logan before I hang up on him.

"Hi." She smiles. And I melt on the spot. Seeing that look on her face makes all the tension I have felt all night long evaporate into thin air.

"Hi," I grin back at her.

"I brought home dinner and a few extra cannoli," she says as she makes her way to the island and starts unpacking the takeout containers.

I walk up behind her, bringing my hands around her waist. My palm is flat to her stomach as I pull her back into my body. I breathe a sigh of relief that she's here in my arms.

My breath tickles her neck and she lets out a giggle in my arms. "I'm happy to see you too," she says.

"I'm just happy you're good," I tell her.

Macey spins around to face me, wrapping both of her arms around my neck while my hands stay circling her waist. Except now they are on the small of her back, holding her into me because I can't let her go. I never want to let her go.

She pulls away to look me in the eyes. "I'm better than ever actually."

My brows narrow at her. "Yeah?"

"I got some interesting news at work. Before you panic," Macey says, gripping my biceps now. "Everything is what it is with my parents. At first I wasn't going to go out there and give them that satisfaction. But apparently, life keeps telling me I deserve more so I stormed out there and had a lengthy conversation with them. They didn't threaten me once and actually listened to me. You should have seen the look on my mother's face." She laughs. "They are leaving, Oliver. For good."

I nod and release the breath I was holding.

"On a better note, Kevin had some news for me." She waits for my reaction but I just stay quiet so she keeps talking. "I'm going to be the head chef at Frank and Mollie's new location."

"You what?" I practically yell but quickly cover my hand to my mouth because I don't want to wake Mackenzie up. "You got a promotion?"

Macey grins so widely I can see the whites of her teeth. "I did."

"Holy shit." I pull her face to me, bringing my lips to hers for a quick kiss. "That is amazing."

She releases me and moves to get the dinner ready for both of us. "I'm so happy, but also so nervous. I have a say in the menu. They want to make it similar but with my own unique spin on it so people will want to visit both," Macey says as she moves around the kitchen. "I never in my wildest dreams thought this would happen. I was happy with my sous-chef position. I really was."

"You deserve it."

"And they want me to pick the name, Oliver!"

Her excitement is so contagious that I can't wipe the grin off my face. No one in the world deserves all the good things in life like she does.

"My girl is a head chef!" I beam.

Macey pauses as if she's never heard me call her my girl before. But I know I have. She's been mine since she came into the city.

Which is why I spent the day sealing it over my chest.

She drops the dish and takes three long steps until she reaches me. Her arms around my neck and she throws her body into mine. I wince at the contact but do my best to try and hide it.

Unfortunately, I didn't do very well.

"Are you okay?" Macey gasps as she takes a step away from me.

"I'm fine." I rub the sensitive spot where the bandage lays.

She reaches for the hem of my shirt, and pulls it off me to assess what is causing me so much pain. Her eyes widen when she sees the white gauze layered with tape over my left chest.

"Oh my god," she says, more worried than ever before. "Who did this to you?"

I bark out a laugh. "You've been reading way too many romance books from Peyton."

"This is not funny. Are you okay? What happened?"

I take a step back and slowly unwrap the tape from the top right corner. It pulls some of my baby chest hairs and I hiss until it's completely off of me, exposing the art work I spent all day getting done.

It was only supposed to take an hour, but I learned that needles are not my friend. I sat in the chair for almost three hours.

Her hands cover her mouth, and she just stares.

Her eyes bore a hole into me and my body heats up.

I don't even know what she's thinking right now.

"You got a tattoo." She sucks in a sharp breath. "But it's not an olive tree."

This girl remembers everything.

I shake my head. "It's not but this means more to me than an olive tree. Looking back, there's no better first tattoo for me than this. Honestly, it might be my last too because I'm quite the little bitch with needles," I joke.

"It's..." Macey's fingertips reach up to my chest. A feather like touch skims across the raised outline. "Stunning. What does it mean?"

"The cherry blossom is for you." The minute the words leave my lips, her eyes snap up to meet mine. Her cheeks flame and her eyes start to glisten with emotion. "I had Mackenzie draw me her favorite flower on a piece of paper. The artist was able to take her exact drawing and put it with the cherry blossom, intertwining them together as one. The compass faded into the background is for me. A reminder that all of my travels have led me home where I belong."

"You got a tattoo for us?"

I reach my hand behind her, cupping the back of her neck with my palm as I bring my other hand up to brush away the tear with the back of my knuckle that escapes from her eye. "I did."

"But why?"

"Don't you see? You're everything to me. I don't care if this seems too fast to ink you on my body for the rest of my life. I never want to let you go."

"You want to keep me? You want to keep us?"

"I do."

And I mean it with everything in me.

The words are on the tip of my tongue, but I have plans for the first time I tell her because I need it to be the most special moment of her life.

I know that's reserved for proposals and shit but Macey is going to be the first woman I've ever said those words to, and I swear with everything inside of me, she's going to be the last too.

CHAPTER FIFTY-THREE

Macey

If I thought the first few days moving to the city were crazy, then this is complete chaos. The last two weeks have been the wildest ride I've ever been on.

Last week, Mackenzie was off for spring break and we were in a constant state of doing things—more sightseeing that we hadn't been able to do, and we also spent a full day outside the city at Peyton's house with everyone for an early Easter dinner.

I felt on top of the world being out in the open with Oliver to everyone we loved. I hated hiding it from Mackenzie, but the fact that she loves him as much as I do has made this so easy.

My parents stayed true to their word and left the city after I told them that enough was enough.

Our last conversation was surprisingly civil. Maybe it was because I threatened them with a restraining order so if they came near the two of us, they would end up locked up.

I hated saying that. They're still my parents at the end of the day, but blood makes you related, it doesn't make you family.

For my own peace, I had to cut the ties with them.

I hope someday they can understand me, support me and treat me like a human. But until then, I'm going to keep doing what I've been doing.

It was the hardest and easiest thing I've ever done.

My newfound strength helped me stand up for myself, which was easy, but my heart breaks for Mackenzie because they are her grandparents—her only grandparents, which is what made it so hard.

To add to the chaos, I've been at the new restaurant all week.

When I first heard about this from Kevin, I did *not* expect them to take action so quickly. Apparently things were already in motion.

The place was purchased and sitting vacant ready to go. It took one week for a team to turn it into the vision I was hoping for. It's the opposite of Mollie's so that people will want to frequent both.

Then, I spent this week getting the kitchen set up, showing the new staff what we're planning on doing with the menu and making sure everything is perfect for tonight.

The opening night of Ollie's.

Frank named the other restaurant after his wife, and gave me the freedom to name this one how I wanted. The atmosphere we were going for is bright and a fun time. Mollie's is an upscale fine dining experience. I took that, and twisted it to make Ollie's a night out people won't forget with upbeat music playing softly in the speakers and bright colors everywhere.

Just like the man who pushed me to be the person I knew I could always become.

I know I would have made it here someday. Oliver was just that nudge, that support system, and that infectious smile I needed to stay on track. Him being there for me led to more than I ever dreamed possible.

I love him with everything in me.

I don't know why I've waited so long to tell him, but now that the night has died down, I fully plan to run home after we clean up, jump into his arms and tell him those three little words, solidifying the fact that this really is the best night of my life.

"This was the best night ever!" my new sous-chef, Victoria, screams.

"It really was," I agree. "I can't believe we didn't have one single mistake. There was no delay in orders and it ran as if we've been doing this for years."

"That's because we have the most badass head chef making magic happen," my line cook, Trisha, adds.

"We're a team. This night was possible because of everyone here. I know for a fact that word is going to get out about how great the service and food was and we're going to end up being slammed."

"I can't even begin to tell you how many spinach and ricotta raviolis I made tonight." Trisha laughs. "I have a feeling that one will be Ollie's signature dish. I think that alone is going to make us busy."

I had a feeling it would be.

I kept the menu the same for the most part, making a few small changes in side dishes, desserts and adding a couple pasta dishes to the menu—spinach and ricotta raviolis being the first one. The dish I tried so hard to make when I first moved here, and Oliver showed up to help me perfect it. It's the signature dish. It's *our* signature dish.

"Bring it on," Victoria cheers.

"Let's get this place cleaned up and head home so we can all celebrate," I say.

"Woop woop." Trisha dances.

We spend the next few minutes cleaning up as best we can but we get a few stray orders. It's small enough that it only takes one person to get it together while the others keep up the cleaning.

Otherwise, we'd be here all night if we waited until the front doors actually locked to start cleaning.

"Macey," the young server calls out from the kitchen doors. "Someone would like a word with the chef."

"Oh, for fucks sake," I groan out in frustration except that doesn't stop the nerves from coming to the surface.

I thought we ended it. I thought they understood. If they are coming back with more things to say, I don't think I can handle it. Nor do I want it ruining the greatest night ever for me.

I fire off a text to Oliver.

I think my parents are here. Someone is requesting a word with the chef again and I don't know if I can handle it if it's them again. I may need you.

OLIVER

Whatever you need. I'm here.

It doesn't matter what happens outside of this kitchen, because no matter what, Oliver has my back. He's always been my rock and there for me when I needed him. This would be no different for him.

I pass the server who just told me someone wanted to talk to me and the guy has a grin on his face.

Okay?

Maybe it's not as bad as I think it's going to be. Or maybe he just doesn't realize I'm about to get my ass handed to me since he's new.

Once I open the doors, I'm forced to stop dead in my tracks when my eyes land on the light, hardwood floor. There's cherry blossom petals scattered everywhere and set up like a trail.

"I think you're supposed to follow them," the server whispers in my ear.

I don't acknowledge him as I take slow tentative steps and follow the trail. My eyes scan the dining room and there's maybe two tables left of people eating dinner and their eyes are all fixed on me.

The petals round the corner and I notice they stop at the double doors in the back. That's the room we have reserved for overflow tables for busy Friday and Saturday nights, or available to rent out for events.

Two other servers scurry past me, each of them opening a door to the room as if I'm the Queen of England or something.

My eyes land on the man who flipped my world upside down standing in the center of the room. Not only is Oliver standing there in *my* restaurant but his hair is perfectly styled off to the side and he's wearing a sharp light gray suit with a light green tie.

There's no way the color of his suit is a coincidence. He has to remember that guys in gray suits are my weakness.

"What"—I pause, scanning the room—"what is this?"

"I told you when you texted me that I was here." He shrugs.

Oh my god. This is not what I thought he meant when he sent that.

"But why?" I ask as I move to stand directly in front of him. Being so close, I'm hit with his cologne, a scent I've never smelt on him before but *my god,* it's intoxicating.

"I wanted to be here for your first night to celebrate your new job." He takes both of my hands in his, bringing them to his lips to press a quick kiss to the tops of knuckles. My body ignites. "And I have a few surprises for you to celebrate."

Oliver jerks his head to the right and standing off to the side are Flora and Samuel. My jaw drops, but I'm also smiling through it. My gaze snaps back and forth between Oliver and them and I am left completely speechless.

"Flora! Samuel! What are you guys doing in the city?" I rush to them and tackle them both in a hug.

"You didn't think we would miss your first night as head chef, did you?" Flora scoffs with a hand on her chest. "When Mackenzie called me to tell me the plan Oliver had, we said yes so fast."

"And dinner was delicious," Samuel adds. "I give the raviolis ten stars."

"You're just saying that because you have to," I joke.

"No. I'm saying that because I mean it." He places a hand on my shoulder. "I've never been prouder of someone in my entire life. Since the day you walked into my bar looking for a job, I knew you would make it big one day."

Tears well in my eyes and I have to blink them back to avoid getting overly emotional.

"Mom," Mackenzie screams. I don't have time to react before her small body is wrapped around me and she's clinging to me like a koala in the trees.

"You're here." I hug her as tight as I can and there's nothing I can do to hold the tears back.

Everything I've ever fought for. Everything I've worked so hard for.

Everything was for her.

"How was your first night? Did you make potatoes? The bread and butter was so tasty and that buttered pasta you made was"—she kisses her two fingers before throwing them in the air —"chef's kiss."

I should have known that dish was for a child. I just didn't know it would be mine.

"Slow down, killer. Everything went great. The night was perfect."

Mackenzie releases her hold on me and I put her to the ground. Some of the most important people in the world are here celebrating my success. How did I get so lucky?

"Is it our turn to come out? I'm dying over here?" Avery's voice sounds from around the corner.

My head snaps to the direction of a little wooden room divider on the side of the room set up to block the door to the kitchen for when we have events. Avery pops her head out of the side, laughing.

"This is insane," I say.

Just as the words leave my mouth, all the girls, Thomas and Marc rush out from behind the wall, bombarding me in the biggest group hug. My chest feels heavy as I absorb all the love in this room right now. Everyone has their arms around me and I spot Oliver from the corner of my eye standing off to the side with his hands in his pockets and he looks happy.

"I can't believe you guys are here."

"We wouldn't miss this big night for anything." Peyton claps.

"Em wishes so bad she could be here but she couldn't get off her shift last minute," Kali says.

"Oh my gosh, that's totally okay. I just can't believe it." I shake my head in disbelief.

Thomas hikes a thumb over his shoulder. "This guy put it all together."

I offer Oliver a smile and bring my gaze back to my new friends. My new *family*, the people who have made this transition from small town to big city way less stressful.

I've found my people.

CHAPTER FIFTY-FOUR

Oliver

Seeing Macey's face light up the way it is right now is exactly why I set this up for her.

At first, I wanted this to be the moment I tell her how I really feel, even though I think she has an idea by now. She's been moved into my room for two weeks and I have no plans of changing that.

But this is a big night for her, and I didn't want to be selfish and keep it to myself. I wanted her best friends and the people who care for her deeply in one room at the end of the night.

Getting Flora and Samuel to come on a Friday was rough when they are a two-person show at the Bar and Grill. But they love Macey like a daughter and wouldn't have missed this.

I can't stop staring at Macey laughing and smiling.

I remember the first time I heard her laugh. I called it a sweet song. That fact still remains true. I could die a happy man if the last thing I hear is her laughter in my ears.

Looking at Macey now is different than the first time. I can't help but admire her drive and how far she's come since that first flight. She reached for the stars, but landed on the moon as the head chef at Ollie's.

I still can't wrap my head around her choosing that name—*my name.*

When she first told me, I felt my jaw hit the floor, and after a few seconds of processing it, I fell even more in love with her. I even tried to talk her out of it thinking I don't deserve to have my name on a restaurant. I don't want the credit for getting her here, because *she* did all the work.

Macey took me up on the offer to come stay with me and since that day, she never stopped learning and working harder than anyone I've ever known.

By the end of that conversation, she'd persuaded me that it was the name she wanted and I was honored that she chose my name.

I'll never stop cheering for her.

I clear my throat, hoping I can just get a minute with her before more celebrations.

"We're going to give you two some privacy." Peyton hugs Macey one more time. "Come on, Kenzie, let's go get some ice cream next door really quick."

"Oh, I'm so in for ice cream," Thomas groans.

"For her and James. Not for you."

"I'll let you share mine, Uncle T." Mackenzie laughs

I can't remember when it was, but she started calling him that one day at their house and it just stuck. We all find it so funny. Thomas doesn't have any nieces or nephews, so it makes him beam with joy when she calls him that.

I love that Mackenzie has aunts and uncles here. She deserves the world.

The room clears out and then it's just Macey and I.

My chest feels tight.

All of a sudden I can't breathe and I feel sweat beading down my back.

It's probably this damn suit.

I hate suits, but I remember so clearly the words Mackenzie said to me about it being her weakness.

"Oliver. You did all of this for me?"

I nod.

"You have no idea how much this means to me." Macey takes my hands in hers closing more of the distance between us.

"I love you, Macey Evans." The words come out on their own accord. I can't stop them. I can't hold them back anymore. "I never knew I wanted to build a life with someone until you came into my life. I want to travel with you. I want to slow dance in a parking lot with you. I want to cook meals with you and enjoy them together as a family. I want to wake up to your smile and go to bed with you in my arms. I'm so far gone for you."

I scan Macey's features and see her glassy eyes staring back at me. "I love you too."

I can feel my eyes tear up and finally release the breath I was holding. For weeks I've been wanting to tell her how I feel but I was so nervous to put my heart out there. Hearing the confirmation that Macey feels the same way I do is a dream come true.

I cup the back of her head, bringing her lips to mine and closing any space that was between us. She grips the lapels on my suit keeping me in place. I love the way my body feels when she's this close.

She's like coming up for air after being held under water.

I pull my lips off of hers. "Can you say it for me again, babe? I need to hear it one more time."

She presses to her toes, lips brushing mine as she says the words into my mouth. "I love you, Oliver Ford."

"I'll never stop wanting to hear that." I smile wildly before kissing her again.

"Then I'll never stop saying it."

"Tell me I can take you home now?"

Her cheeks blush because she knows I need her in my arms and her body wrapped around mine. I can go to bed with a smile on my face just holding her in my arms and be the happiest man on earth.

"Let me finish cleaning up and we can head out." She turns

to leave but stops herself and looks over her shoulder. A smirk forms on her lips. "Oh, and by the way..." She pauses. "It's Genevieve."

I furrow my brows in confusion.

"Macey Genevieve Evans." She winks and retreats to finish cleaning up.

This is the greatest night of my life.

EPILOGUE

Macey

June

"Come on, Mackenzie," I call out into the backyard of Peyton's house. "It's getting late. We're going to cut the cake."

We're celebrating my baby girl's ninth birthday tonight. It's hard to believe she's already nine, honestly. It feels like just yesterday they placed her on my chest. Ten tiny toes. Ten little fingers that wrapped around mine almost instantly, like her small body knew I needed her more than she needed me.

We both have grown up so much over the years.

I'm proud of the little girl she's grown into.

She's more herself than ever.

Mackenzie, James, and three of her friends from school come barreling into the kitchen like bulls in a China shop, ready for cake. I don't know how they have any energy left. They have been bouncing around for five hours now, long after the sun has already set.

Peyton was nice enough to let us host the party here since she has space. She was adamant about Mackenzie getting a bounce house after watching her face light up at James' birthday party.

But this isn't your normal bounce house. She upgraded to a

colossal obstacle course bounce house that takes up a huge spot in their backyard. One end of it has a basketball net to jump and play, then there's a little course leading to a slide that you have to climb up to get down it.

It's perfect for her and she's had the time of her life today.

"What kind of cake is it?" Mackenzie beams.

"You know I got the vanilla with pudding and strawberries in the middle," I assure her.

"Yes!" all the kids shriek in excitement.

"Hmm, fan favorite I see," Oliver says as he comes up behind me. My body heats up with his closeness the way it always does. Something I will never get over. "Did you want any help with that?"

"Yes, yes!" Mackenzie jumps in her seat. "Ollie will cut me the biggest piece there is."

"I take offense to that." I laugh. "But we have to sing first."

I turn my head to the left and Avery nods her head, flicking the lights off and making it just as dark as it is outside, our only light being the flickering of the number nine candle on the cake.

The crowd starts singing. Everyone is smiling and all their eyes on Mackenzie.

How did I get so lucky?

The sentence has been on repeat since Oliver and I made it official. I didn't just fall in love with the greatest man I've ever met, I gained an entire family in the process—people who would drop everything for me and my daughter., who show up when it matters the most.

A lot has happened since the last time I saw my parents.

The same two people sitting off to the side singing happy birthday to their granddaughter with an adoring smile on their faces.

Remember when I told you I had to make the hardest and easiest decision of my life? I had to do it again two weeks ago when I found the courage to reach out to them.

Thanks to the support of Oliver and Peyton, I called them

and invited them to her party. We all agreed since the party would be out here, that it was a neutral ground since it's not actually where Mackenzie and I live with Oliver.

This would have been the first party they missed.

As much as they hurt me, Mackenzie was just a pawn in their game. She was an innocent bystander who ended up being just as hurt as me in the process. At the end of the day, these are her grandparents.

The hurt Mackenzie felt during everything was because she was hurt *for me.*

Before I made the phone call, I had a long conversation with her asking her if she wanted them there. No matter what they did to me, I will never take away her happiness or stop giving her what she wants.

To my surprise, she wanted them here, and in the end, they've behaved all day and haven't cause a scene.

They *know* they are here for her and only her.

The singing stops and I snap out of my haze. I round the island and bring my girl in for a hug as tears well in my eyes. "I love you so much, baby," I whisper into her ear.

"I love you too, Mom. To the moon, stars, and Jupiter."

I give her one more squeeze before I release her.

Oliver, of course, cuts the cake and I can't help but roll my eyes.

After everyone is served, my mother taps me on the shoulder.

"We're going to head out," she says, fiddling with her handbag.

"Thank you for coming." I nod.

"No, thank you for inviting us," she says too quickly. "Can I talk to you for a second on the side?"

I look at Oliver and the minute my eyes land on his, they are already glued to me. Like the protective Golden Retriever he is, he doesn't stray far when he knows I'll need him most. He gives me a small nod as if he's overheard her question.

I look back at them. "Sure."

"Listen," Mom starts when we're out of ear reach from everyone. "I meant what I said just a second ago. Thank you for inviting us. With that being said, I think I owe you a major apology."

My eyes widen in… shock? That's what that is. It has to be.

"Mackenzie is really happy, isn't she?" she asks me.

I swallow to try and fight off the dryness forming in my throat and simply nod.

"I can tell. I wish I could take back everything I've ever said to you. I wish I could take back the pain I've caused you that made you run to here. But I can't. It's something I'm going to have to live with for the rest of my life. For what it's worth, I'm going to be sorry I said any of it for the rest of my life too."

"Th-thank you," I stutter.

"You are a good, *good* mother, Macey." My mom brings a hand to place on my shoulder, keeping her eyes locked on mine to tell me she means what she says. "I wish I had seen how good of a mother you were long before today. Seeing the people you've surrounded her with, the friends she's made, how Oliver looks at both of you like you two hung the moon together. It's everything I ever could have dreamed of for you and her."

I can't hold back the tears anymore. The dam releases and I quickly swipe the tear that escapes. As if Oliver can sense it, he clears his throat to interrupt us.

"Everything okay?" he asks me, not paying any attention to my parents standing there.

"I'm…" I look from him to my mother. "I'm good, babe."

"I was just offering my apologies for how I've treated her all of these years," my mom cuts in. "You're a good man, Oliver. Thank you for taking care of my daughter and granddaughter."

He nods. "I'd do anything for them."

"I can tell." She offers him a soft smile. "I have to head out. We have a red eye to catch. Thank you again for inviting us.

Today was the greatest day of my life just being able to see the joy on my granddaughter's face."

With those words, she turns on her heel and finds my dad in the kitchen and is out the door. I can't believe that just happened.

"That was good, right?" Oliver asks with my face in his hands.

"It was…unexpected."

He presses a kiss to my lips. "Come on, babe. It's getting late and it's time for Mackenzie to open her presents. I want you to be there when you see what I got her."

"Oh god, what did you do?"

He runs his finger and thumb across his lips as if he's zipping them shut.

We both fall into a fit of laughter as we make our way into the living room.

This should be good.

Oliver

I watch intently as Mackenzie opens up her presents from everyone.

My knee bounces where I sit on the armrest of the chair, nervous for how she might react when she sees.

There is a very teeny tiny chance I went way overboard with her. But I wanted her first birthday that I get to celebrate with my girl to be the best one ever.

My nerves spike as she picks up the box with sage green wrapping paper. The last gift in the pile. She opens the card first and reads it out loud.

Dear, Mackenzie.

You're a little difficult to shop for. What do you get a nine year old that you want to give the entire universe to? It's an impossible task if you ask me. After thinking long and hard over what the perfect gift would be, I settled on this.

Before you open it, I need you to know how much I love you, which I hope you already know at this point. You mean the world to me and you coming into my life was the greatest gift anyone could give me. I want you to see the world with me, but through your own lenses.

Happy Birthday, my girl. I love you.

Oliver

Mackenzie swipes a tear from her cheek and before she opens the box, she stands and rushes to me to wrap her small arms around me. A tear of my own mixes with hers on her cheek.

"I love you too, Ollie. So much," she says as she squeezes me tighter.

"Go on, open it," I encourage her.

She tears the paper off like it's Christmas in June. Her eyes go wide with shock when she sees the box.

"You didn't," she shrieks. "This is mine? All mine?"

"It's all yours." I smile at her.

"Mom." She turns her head to Macey and she's standing off to the side with a tissue in hand crying. "Ollie got me my own camera to match his!"

"I see, babe."

"This is the greatest gift anyone has ever given me," Mackenzie says, staring down at the box. But it's not long after that her face falls the slightest bit. "I know it's my birthday, but can I give you something too?"

My eyebrows pinch together in question. I look over at Macey and wonder what's going on. She turns her gaze away from me as if she doesn't want me to see the emotions bubbling inside of her at what she just asked.

"I don't need anything, Mackenzie," I finally say, turning back to her.

Mackenzie doesn't answer and inside finds Thomas on the couch. He pulls out a piece of folded paper from his back pocket with a grin on his face. He looks over to me and gives me a reassuring wink.

What are these two up to right now?

I turn to Peyton to try and assess the situation, but she has her head turned as well, blotting her cheek with a tissue to catch her own tears that have fallen.

Mackenzie stands before me, unfolding the piece of paper my brother just handed her. She pauses every few seconds to swipe the tears from her eyes.

"As much as I love the camera, Ollie. Trust me, I really do." She huffs out a laugh. "But there's something I wanted to ask you."

I nod.

"Will you give me an even greater birthday gift and be my dad?"

Everything around me stills. My heart stops and my chest constricts as the air stays trapped so deep in my lungs I can't breathe. I stare into her perfect green eyes that match her mothers, eyes that have the power over me to do whatever she wants me to do.

"You want me to adopt you?" I choke out.

"Only if you want to." Mackenzie shrugs so casually. "I don't have a dad. And you really love my mom and I think one day you two will get married anyway. I could save this and ask at your wedding whenever that does happen, but I thought that *this* would be the bestest birthday gift I'll ever get in my life."

"I plan to spend the rest of your life with your mom, Kenzie. That means you too."

She blinks a few times, more tears leak from her eyes.

I place two hands on her shoulders, leaning down so I'm more eye level with her. "There's nothing in the world that would make me happier than adopting you, Kenzie. You know I love you so much. More than traveling and way more than orange soda."

She giggles. "Is that a yes?"

"Yes. A million times, yes." I pull her into me wrapping my arms around her head and she returns the embrace wrapping her arms around my waist.

"God dammit," Avery huffs, patting her eyes with a tissue. "That was the most perfect thing I've ever witnessed in my life.

"Was everyone behind this?" I say as I scan the room.

"No," Avery snaps. "This was just as much a surprise to me as it was to you."

"Only Uncle T and Mom knew," Mackenzie says. "Aunt

Peyton too."

I press a kiss to her forehead before I stand and make my way to the absolute love of my life, the woman who changed everything for me. The woman who turned my world upside down for the better. Letting love I never knew existed come in and stay.

I bring Macey's face to mine and kiss her with everything I have in me.

I don't take a single kiss for granted with her.

Her kiss will always be the oxygen I need to survive.

"This is what you want?" I whisper against her lips.

"Only if you do," she breathes back without pulling away from me.

"It's the greatest gift anyone could ever give me."

"And you're the best thing that's ever happened to me. To us."

Phones chime in the distance but I don't pull myself out of my bubble with Macey because it's where I want to spend eternity living.

"Guys." Peyton's voice sounds pained.

Our heads snap in her direction. Peyton looks white as a ghost with her phone in her hand, looking at it as if she just got devastating news. Her lips are parted in shock and they move as if she's trying to find the words for us.

"Baby?" Thomas says as he reaches for her. Leveling his gaze with hers. "What is it? Is everything okay?"

The tension in the room is palpable. No one moves.

We all stare at Peyton waiting for an answer.

"It's... it's..." She looks up at him, blinking several times before she finally speaks. "It's Logan."

Want a spicy bonus scene from Oliver and Macey?
Click here to download.

Mackenzie's French Toast

Enjoy her famous french toast from the book.
Prep time: 5 min.   Cook time: 5 min.

Ingredients

- 1 egg
- 1 tsp vanilla extract
- 1 tsp ground cinnamon
- 1/4 cup milk
- 4 slices of your favorite bread (Mackenzie loves potato bread)

Directions

1. Whisk egg, vanilla extract, ground cinnamon and milk in a shallow bowl
2. Dip bread into the mixture. Flip the bread to coat both sides.
3. Heat a non-stick skillet or a griddle at medium heat and cook bread slices until brown on both sides.

** Serve with your favorite fruit topping, powdered sugar, cinnamon sugar and/or syrup.

** Recipe is from Jenn McMahon's kitchen.

ACKNOWLEDGMENTS

Before I acknowledge specific people for the process of writing this book, I need to thank my readers. The whole mass of you. **please hold. I'm getting a little weepy typing this up** I hope you realize the impact you've had on my life from book one until the release of this book. Nothing would be possible without you, your support and your love for these fictional characters. Every message you send me, every social media post you tag me in, and every reviews you leave means more to me than you could possibly know. You are the reason I want to keep writing. So THANK YOU.

My husband – the second dedication alone tells everyone what you mean to me. But in case it wasn't clear, I love you. You fell in love with a single mom who had a two-year-old years ago and welcomed the both of us into your life and family for the keeping. You're the best bonus dad to him and I couldn't be luckier to have a real life 'Oliver' to do life with.

Mel – There's not much to say that hasn't been said in our multiple phone calls a day to each other, but really I just want to say thank you for letting me ruin this entire book before you even read it by talking through scenes with me. HAHA.

Salma – you took on the biggest hot mess you've probably

ever had and didn't even bat an eye. Thank you for taking such great care of Oliver, Macey and Mackenzie, and for every ounce of tough love you've given me.

Kelsey – you have the wildest schedule and took on this book during the holidays, and for that I'll forever be thankful for you. I don't know what I did to deserve your friendship and support, but I will never take it for granted.

My alpha readers (Jessy, Rachel, Tabitha, Cat) and my beta readers (Jackie, Sam, Shima, LB, Kristen) – You my friends… I have no words. You helped fine tune so many parts of this book only making it that much better. Please don't ever leave me.

Last but not least – Brit Benson – my unofficial mentor, friend, author mom, and all-around support. Thank you for taking me under your wing and helping me with all the background stuff that comes with being an author. It's more than I ever thought it would be and you're always there when I have questions and need support. I'll never be able to repay you for all you've done. And because of that I will let you call me Mc-Ma-Hone-e anytime you want. HAHA.

ABOUT THE AUTHOR

Jenn McMahon resides along the shore in New Jersey with her husband, Daniel, two children, Zachary and Owen, and two dogs, Cooper and Piper. She has spent the last couple of years engrossed in romance books, to now writing her own and sharing them with the world. When Jenn is not writing, she can be found reading, watching reruns of her favorite TV shows (Scandal, Grey's Anatomy and Friends – just to name a few), or petting her dog. She also loves taking trips to the beach with the kids, Atlantic City date nights with her husband, and thunderstorms.

SCAN HERE TO SIGN UP FOR MY NEWSLETTER

SCAN TO JOIN MY FACEBOOK READERS GROUP

Printed in Great Britain
by Amazon

40683867R00233